W9-CCR-979

FRACTURE

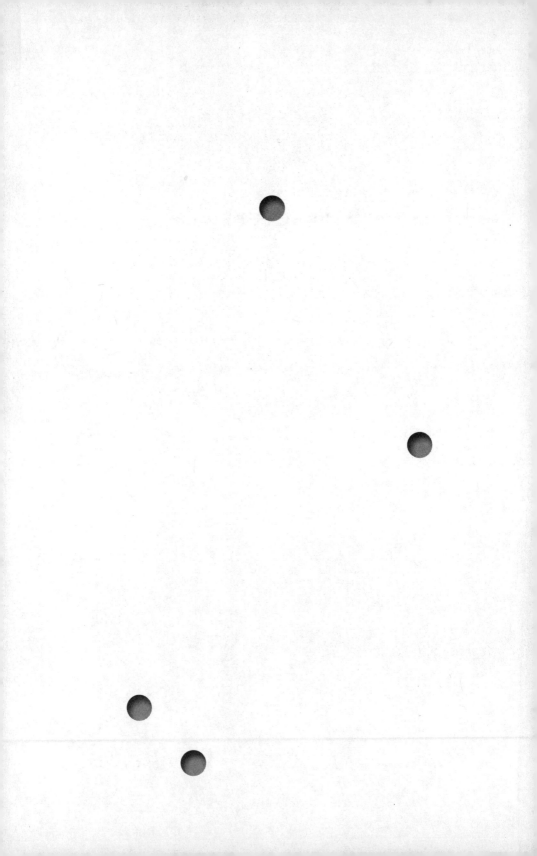

FRACTURE

ANDRÉS NEUMAN

Translated from the Spanish by
NICK CAISTOR and LORENZA GARCIA

Farrar, Straus and Giroux
NEW YORK

Farrar, Straus and Giroux
120 Broadway, New York 10271

Library of Congress Cataloging-in-Publication Data
Names: Neuman, Andrés, 1977– author. | Caistor, Nick, translator. | Garcia, Lorenza,
    translator.
Title: Fracture / Andrés Neuman ; translated from the Spanish by Nick Caistor and
    Lorenza Garcia.
Other titles: Fractura. English
Description: First American edition. | New York : Farrar, Straus and Giroux, 2020. |
    "Originally published in Spanish in 2018 by Alfaguara, Spain, as *Fractura*"
    —Title page verso.
Identifiers: LCCN 2019056426 | ISBN 9780374158231 (hardcover)
Classification: LCC PQ6664.E478 F7313 2020 | DDC 863/.64—dc23
LC record available at https://lccn.loc.gov/2019056426

Our books may be purchased in bulk for promotional, educational, or business
use. Please contact your local bookseller or the Macmillan Corporate and
Premium Sales Department at 1-800-221-7945, extension 5442, or by e-mail at
MacmillanSpecialMarkets@macmillan.com.

www.fsgbooks.com
www.twitter.com/fsgbooks • www.facebook.com/fsgbooks

10   9   8   7   6   5   4   3   2   1

This work has been published with a subsidy from the Ministry of Culture and
Sport of Spain.

To Erika, for the daily novel

If something exists somewhere, it will exist everywhere.

—CZESŁAW MIŁOSZ

Love came . . . after the kill.

—ANNE SEXTON

I wonder if there is
any operation
that removes memories.

—SHINOE SHŌDA

. . . and if my body is still the soft part of the mountain
I'll know
I am not yet the mountain.

—JOSÉ WATANABE

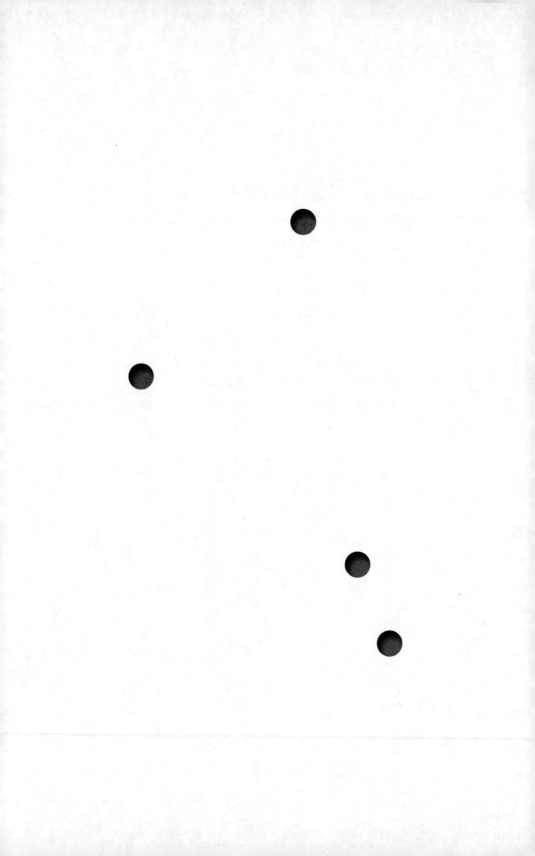

CONTENTS

1

MEMORY
PLATES

THE AFTERNOON APPEARS CALM, and yet time is waiting to pounce. Mr. Watanabe rummages in his pockets as though missing items might respond to insistence. Due to what is becoming a habitual carelessness, he has left his transit pass and glasses at home: he can clearly visualize them next to each other on the table, mocking him. He walks irritably toward the machines. While he is carrying out the transaction, he observes a group of young tourists reacting with bewilderment at the tangle of stations. They are making calculations. The numbers emerge from their mouths, rise, and disperse. Clearing his throat, he glances back at the screen. Vaguely hostile, the youngsters look at him. Mr. Watanabe listens to them deliberating in their own language, a melodic, emphatic one that he knows well. He considers the possibility of helping them, as he has so many visitors overwhelmed by the Tokyo subway. But it's almost a quarter to three, he has a sore back and wants to go home. And, to be honest, he doesn't sympathize with these young people. He wonders if he's simply become unaccustomed to the shouting and the gesticulations he once found so liberating. Half listening to their foreign syntax, he pays for his ticket then walks away. He notices the Friday smell, a cocktail of weariness and anticipation. As the escalator descends, he contemplates those platforms that will gradually be filling up. He's glad he didn't take a taxi. At this time of day there is still room in the trains. He's aware that soon the last passengers to arrive will be pushing against the backs of those who arrived ahead of them, and that the attentive subway officials will step forward to cram them in. Until the doors interrupt the flow, like someone clipping the sea. To push one another, Watanabe reflects, is an unusually sincere way of communicating. At that very instant, the escalator steps start to vibrate. The vibration intensifies to a tremor, and the tremor gives way to unmistakable juddering. Mr. Watanabe is engulfed by a feeling that none of what is going on is actually happening to him. His vision blurs. Then he feels the floor cease to be a floor.

The young tourists study the subway map, its multicolored pipework. They are confused by the overlapping trains, the crossword of public and private lines. They try to calculate how many yen each of them will need. At the next machine, an old man clears his throat. The youngest boy among the tourists suggests that the old man could help them instead of staring so much at the girls. Another adds that if he goes on staring like that he could at least pay for their tickets. One of the girls retorts that this boy seems even dumber than usual today. Which, she points out, raising a finger, is saying something. The tourists insert a cascade of coins, while the old Japanese man disappears. Another girl reveals her preference for the coins with a hole in the middle. The youngest boy compares it to the piercing he himself carries on a certain part of his anatomy. Her friend's hand slaps the back of his head: his hair becomes an asterisk. Their shouts and laughter startle people around them. The tourists become aware of a collective murmur, a strange precision prevailing among the crowd. They try, without much success, to control themselves as they run toward the escalators. They're astonished that no one bumps into one another, at the way everybody respects the regulations. The more experienced of the group opines that in his country this could be achieved only by threats. What threatens the Japanese? When they feel the first vibrations, the youngsters blame the flexibility of the architecture. Not at all like the stations in their own country. The tremors grow more pronounced. With a mixture of panic and surprise, the tourists can't decide whether the other passengers are silent because they're so calm, or because they're counting how long the tremors last. One of the young women remembers what happened a year ago in her own city, when she counted up to a hundred. And as she feels the ground shake, she begins to experience an increasing sense of déjà vu, as if each jolt were taking place a little deeper inside her head, infusing memories.

Shoes alternate at different levels, improvising musical scores. Feet are Friday's metronome. As the escalators transport them, the passengers contemplate the platforms that will soon be filling up. Some vaguely notice Mr. Watanabe. One of them studies his clothes, which seem bizarre or somehow out of place. The inertia of the descent takes over, the hum is a mantra. All of a sudden, the hum changes frequency. The looks pull away from their vanishing points. The escalators respond like leaden streamers. Farther below, the temporal dimension splits into two: the trains don't move, and the passengers start to run. Even the staff appear anxious. They know that anything up to twenty seconds is a tremor, and more than twenty is something serious. Trying to calm himself, one of the guards calls for calm. A language teacher thinks she is witnessing a terrifying tautology: an earthquake is like a train passing close to your feet, yet her train had already arrived. Behind her, the same man who was struck by Watanabe's clothes is overcome by a sense of incredulous fragility. There's nothing to hold on to. He reneges on all his certainties. Directly above his head, on the other side of the vaulted roof, a young cyclist tilts over and falls to the asphalt, still pedaling.

The nerves of the pipes run along the roof. The leaks rehearse their future appearance, form layers of time on the architecture. Weight is distributed evenly on the escalator: some passengers go up, others come down. The forces are aligned. Energies cooperate. When the escalator starts to vibrate, and the vibration intensifies to a tremor, and the tremor gives way to unmistakable juddering, each shape fragments into a jumble of lines. Every object is in hiatus. Doubt prowls the platforms. The underground expresses itself in the underground. Like dice changing their numbers, the walls calculate the throw. A black spot amid innumerable spots, Mr. Watanabe raises one of his shoes.

The objects on the ground play their own game. They move one square and wait their turn. The air currents create eddies, microscopic disturbances. A scrap of paper, an unsuccessful origami, is dragged along. That ice cream melting on the platform used to be round. A lighter offers itself to passing bits of fluff. Next to the machines, two earbuds hanker after their ears. They fell out of Mr. Watanabe's pockets as he went over irritably to purchase his ticket. When the floor ceases to be a floor, the earbuds snake among the footsteps: a stampede in stereo. The lighter bounces, summons its flame. The blob of ice cream lengthens its trail. The scrap of paper relaxes, unfurling a text that no one reads.

The subway's even light pours over things. Each neon bulb emits its dose of anesthesia. The entire space floats in an electric liquid. Shadows drift amid whistles that guide them like buoys. All at once, Watanabe's vision blurs. Reality becomes an intermittence, the vibrating blink of an eye splintered into myriad eyes. Then the noise remains. Only the noise. A broken music, captured possibly by the earbuds. Every spoon tapping in unison against its cup. A nutcracker the size of the country. The subterranean protest. And, in the background, the ancestral sound of strings twanging, like a boat caught in a storm.

An earthquake fractures the present, shatters perspective, shifts memory plates.

AS SOON AS WATANABE STICKS HIS HEAD OUT, a torrent of feet engulfs him. He takes a deep breath before emerging. He still has the feeling that the world is swaying slightly, that every object emits the memory of its instability.

Fortunately, everything outside appears more or less in its place. He hadn't been at all sure of this. The force of the jolts made him fear the worst.

It's cold for March: the hunched shoulders act as a thermometer. On some corners the traffic is at a standstill; at others it is overflowing. Sirens wail in all directions. Lines are snaking around the few vehicles still running. Anyone would think that, in a matter of minutes, the population had multiplied.

The entire city has reverted to an earlier state, before the new road system existed. Its arteries are narrowing. Its circulation has collapsed. After many years—more than he dare count—Mr. Watanabe feels once more that, rather than protecting him, the crowd is crushing him.

He tries to calm down and assess the situation. Despite his fatigue, he decides to make his own way home. His neighborhood isn't all that far away. If he keeps up a brisk pace, he should reach Shinjuku before sunset.

People are occupying the space in a new, or rather a very old, way: with the visceral sense of those who can rely only on their bodies. Pedestrians walk down the middle of the avenues, a tiny displacement that to Watanabe seems radical.

These encounters and passing collaborations have an air of shipwreck and rescue. A sudden solidarity disputes distances.

Under normal circumstances, he reflects, isolation offsets overpopulation. And yet that afternoon, several strangers ask how he is, he asks others, and they in turn ask others. Fear is a twisted form of love.

There is still no phone coverage, or at least he can't make any calls on his device. The emergency has prompted Wi-Fi providers to clear their networks. He sees many people walking and checking their phones: he can read the news on their faces. Envious of their ability to navigate the virtual world at the same time as the public thoroughfares, Mr. Watanabe tries instead to listen to the radio. He pats his pockets. And discovers he has lost his earbuds.

As if the movement of the earth's plates had disrupted the clocks, the lights in Tokyo are dimming early. The contrast is so startling, he thinks, that each place ought to have one name in daylight and another in darkness. Many stores have closed. People are stocking up on food and batteries. The bigger the city, the greater its dread of the dark.

Mr. Watanabe remembers when, in his youth, they abolished height restrictions on buildings. To own the air became more important than to own the ground. People protested, demanding their right to the sun. And so the Sunlight Act was passed, thanks to which buildings started to be erected at an angle.

The city's obsession, its nervous system, is prevention. Containment. Isolation. Ditches. Firebreaks. Anti-seismic constructions. An entire urban plan based on future disasters. The result is a dense weight of trust on a surface of fear. With this in mind, Watanabe stops off at a supermarket. He enters with a very specific objective.

When he locates the toilet paper shelf, he discovers there isn't any. He notices that the people gathering the last rolls are more or less his age. On his way out, he sees that stocks of a second product have been exhausted. Diapers. Senescence and infancy are united by the bathroom.

The advertisements on the facades of buildings have vanished. Today, for the first time since his return, the streets are naked.

It no longer resembles Tokyo. As he raises his eyes, only the sky is shining.

Observing people's necks craned in surprise, Mr. Watanabe realizes how seldom he looks upward. The city center, he reasons, is designed to protect us from the heavens. And yet, the instinct to orient oneself by means of them has resurfaced: a hole has appeared through which they can be seen. The glow diminishes drop by drop, an ocean seeping out through a grating.

Suddenly, the murmurs change in tone. The rumor spreads through the crowd like a current along a cable. Watanabe tries to speed up. Bad news is something he prefers to assimilate on his own.

Behind him, growing ever louder, ever closer, he hears the word *tsunami*.

BEFORE FIVE IN THE AFTERNOON, Watanabe arrives at the entrance to a skyscraper in Shinjuku. On the day of its inauguration, it was vaunted as the tallest in Tokyo. From a distance, it looked like a pencil standing out among a bunch of erasers. Another one soon superseded it. We're addicted to records, he thinks. Or we're simply addicts.

As he enters the building, his sense of relief evaporates. What if, due to some electrical fault, he is forced to take the stairs? Would his lungs and knees withstand it? What would it be like to sleep in the foyer, to camp out beneath his own home?

Once he sees that the elevators are working, Mr. Watanabe allows himself a lengthy sigh. But, before he presses the button, fresh doubts assail him. What if there's a power outage while he's going up? On days such as this, is anyone from the emergency services available? How does the alarm work? Why has he never bothered to learn about these things?

The elevator deposits him peacefully on the twenty-eighth floor. He jumps out. The carpeted corridor is redolent of a muted garden.

Watanabe inserts the key, opens the door to the apartment, walks through the tiny hallway, inserts the key, opens the door, and enters his apartment. This isn't a repetition. Or rather it is, of the apartment itself: when he bought it, among the other alterations, he had a thick additional wall built. Now he lives in a house within a house. He is bunkered within himself. If something terrible happened, part of the skyscraper could get damaged, or the twenty-eighth floor, even the outer wall. But perhaps not the inner dwelling. His home. The survivor's.

Clashing with the rest of the decor, an old black-and-white-striped rug covers the floor like a pedestrian crossing. To compensate for his reclusiveness, Mr. Watanabe likes to imagine he is crossing the street when he enters his abode.

He takes off his shoes before going into the living room, quite spacious by Tokyo standards. Although at this point in his life he can afford it, he hasn't forgotten that when he lived with his aunt and uncle, he couldn't cross his bedroom with his backpack on. Narrow spaces have never bothered him. His claustrophobia is vertical. That's why what he most appreciates is the ceiling, approximately three and a half meters high, one surpassing the norm. Watanabe feels that this meter hovering above his head is the space where his ideas and memories float.

From the very moment he steps into the living room, he senses that something isn't right. As an obsessive, he knows that each space possesses a secret equilibrium, which any imbalance can disturb. Some of the furniture has moved slightly, a confirmation that this earthquake was more powerful than usual. Watanabe advances like a detective investigating the crime committed in his own room.

He instantly notices the disarray among his collection of banjos. Some have slipped off their stands and are lying on the floor. A few strings have come away from their bridges. The necks are pointing every which way, hinting at multiple culprits. The sound boxes sing infinitesimally of their fall.

Mr. Watanabe contemplates this catalog of toppled instruments. He stoops to examine them, then puts them back in place. None appears to have suffered irreparable damage. But then, he corrects himself, to what extent is damage reparable? Wouldn't it be worth doing something different? Why hide the imperfections in his banjos, why not incorporate them into their restoration? All broken objects, he reflects, have something in common. A crack joins them to their past.

One by one, he caresses the instruments that have survived the toppling. He is convinced that things which have been on the verge of breaking for whatever reason—slipping, falling, smashing, colliding with one another—enter a second life. An amphibious state that makes them meaningful, impossible to touch in the same way as before.

This explains perhaps his growing admiration for the ancient art of kintsugi. When a piece of pottery breaks, the kintsugi craftspeople place powdered gold into each crack to emphasize the spot where the break occurred. Exposed rather than concealed, these fractures and their repair occupy a central place in the history of the object. By accentuating this memory, it is ennobled. Something that has survived damage can be considered more valuable, more beautiful.

Inspecting his library, Watanabe discovers that a few volumes on the uppermost shelves have been dislodged. Is there a pattern to these literary movements? Might they make up a kind of seismic anthology? Might certain authors be more predisposed to being displaced? He pauses to cross-check whether these books correspond in some way to his preferences. The result surprises him.

At the far end of the room, a small detail causes him to shudder. He sees that the doors of the butsudan are ajar. And a couple of objects that evoke his parents and sisters have toppled over on the tiny shrine. He dares not stand them upright immediately, as if to do so would be to contradict their will.

Mr. Watanabe heads for the kitchen. He pours out a glass of wine to calm himself, or at least enrich his lack of calm. When he opens the cupboard, he sees that the cleaning products and cans of food have rolled over and are intermingled. He suspects there's a hidden meaning to this disarray but can't think what it is.

He returns to the living room, the glass reddening his hand. He drains it quickly and slumps onto the sofa. He rubs his ankles with difficulty. Then he switches on the television and goes online to immerse himself in the news.

Just at that moment, on the table, he spots his transit pass, intact, hateful: the glimmer of an earlier city where nothing had happened. His missing glasses have slid to the edge. The sun has started to do likewise.

Between his second and third glass, Watanabe learns of the damage caused in the northeast of the country. Particularly in the Tōhoku region, where the army is carrying out rescue operations. If soldiers are involved, he deduces, the casualties must be greater than those reported in the news. This is his fourth glass. His unease spills over the map of the present.

He is astonished to discover the magnitude of the earthquake he has just witnessed: the biggest in the country's history. Bigger even than the Great Kantō Earthquake, which has always served as the legendary extreme. Today a record has been broken that nobody wanted to break.

Mr. Watanabe reads the long list of places affected, and does so extremely slowly, as if by spelling out their names he could restore them. Sumatra, Valdivia, Alaska. Esmeraldas, Arica, Kamchatka. Lisbon. Mexico City. Japan, Japan, Japan.

Every major earthquake with its epicenter in the sea is invariably followed by something worse. He knows they have been called *seaquakes*, *maremotos*, *raz de marées*, depending on where they struck. Until there were two hundred thousand deaths, and a million evacuees on the Indonesian coast. That was the tsunami, terrifyingly global.

He searches for news in the U.S. media. An alert has just been issued in Hawaii, and a warning on the West Coast. Earthquakes are part of history. Or is history a slice of seismology? Watanabe imagines an underground tremor gradually expanding until it shakes the entire planet.

On the screens of his devices, their reflections distorted on the surface of the empty wine bottle, he sees skyscrapers swaying, their tips almost touching.

He sees cracks in the highways, chewing asphalt like a set of teeth.

He sees turmoil in stores, aisles turned upside down, merchandise falling.

He sees spinning houses, walls losing the perpendicular, rattling lights, a rebellion of shapes, their owners beneath tables.

He sees the absurd strength of the tsunami, its sweep of filthy water, planes floating at Sendai airport, cars washed away like boats, the naturalness of liquid drowning civilization's warren.

Apparently, a dozen or so nuclear power plants have been shut down. And conflicting reports are coming in about the Daiichi plant in the prefecture of Fukushima. Watanabe learns that at the time the earthquake struck, three of its reactors were in operation. As soon as it was detected, they automatically shut down. When they did so, they stopped generating the electricity for the reactor's cooling system, which works with boiling water. Under normal circumstances, the external grid would have been activated, but this was damaged by the earthquake. The emergency power generators kicked in. But instantly stopped when the tsunami hit. Simple. Or not.

Watanabe realizes that the information is mimicking the shock waves from the tsunami: estimates of the damage are growing by the minute. To judge by their commentaries, many people regard the official figures with the same mistrust as they did the ceiling during the earthquake.

Soon afterward, a state of emergency is declared in reactors one and two at the Fukushima nuclear plant. People are being evacuated in a limited area around the facility: three kilometers. This distance brings back dreadful memories for Mr. Watanabe. However, the government announces there have been no radiation leaks.

For some reason, his cell phone still has no signal. In his inbox he discovers an email from Carmen, who is writing from Madrid. They haven't been in touch for a while: that's what disasters are for. Carmen has seen the news and is concerned. She wants to know if he's okay, if he needs anything. She tells him she has found a Facebook group called *Spaniards in Japan who have experienced the earthquake*. She ends by saying: I can't believe this is happening on March 11.

Watanabe sends a brief reply. He thanks her for her concern and confirms that he is safe and sound. Then he sends a second message, adding that he is delighted to be back in touch, and inquires after her grandchildren. He immediately starts composing a third message, making it clear that of course they had never really lost touch, but that it means a great deal to him to be able to communicate on a day like this, when the people we are closest to, et cetera. He rereads what he has written, deletes it, and closes his email.

How remote foreign disasters seemed in the past. And yet now, thanks to these screens whose technology he knows inside out, we cannot help but witness them. He wonders whether this has enhanced or diminished his sensitivity. Being a permanent spectator creates a filter, a shock absorber. But it also forces him to endlessly witness ubiquitous suffering.

Watanabe switches on his sound system, which is connected to speakers as tall as a man. A man of his modest stature, at any rate. He chooses one of his favorite recordings. A growling trumpet, meditative piano, smoky double bass. He turns the volume down to the lowest setting. He closes his eyes to cut off the optical torrent. Immerses himself in one of the most pleasurable activities he knows: listening to music without the sound. Re-creating it in his mind. This isn't something that Mr. Watanabe does with just any recording. He is always incredibly meticulous when he chooses what he's not going to listen to.

The only thing he does hear is the telephone. The landline clamoring from his bedroom. Annoyed at the inconvenience of the call and yet aware of its possible urgency, he struggles up from the sofa. He feels a sharp twinge in his lower back. He runs, more or less. Pants. Picks up. Answers.

The voice isn't one Watanabe expected, or recognizes. To his surprise, the caller is an Argentinian journalist who says good morning to him and then good evening. Who apologizes. Who has been up all night working. Who hurriedly explains himself. Who says his name is Quintero or Gancedo. No: Pinedo. And who tries to ingratiate himself by mispronouncing a greeting in Japanese.

This last gesture irritates Watanabe. He considers it condescending, a sort of rhetorical souvenir. To make things worse, the journalist offers to speak in English, even though Mr. Watanabe has a perfect grasp of Spanish.

In any event, he has neither the energy nor the patience. Pinedo stutters slightly, which makes him confusing to listen to. Watanabe gathers that he, he would very much like to, to interview him about the, about the earthquake and the tsunami, yes? because he's planning a catastrophic investigation, or an investigation into who knows what catastrophes, for who knows where.

He finds it strange that this fellow has tracked down his home phone number. He's infuriated that the man intends to ply him for information. And, above all, why the hell interview *him*? Wouldn't he do better with a politician, someone from the embassy, or a fellow journalist?

Watanabe brusquely interrupts Pinedo's stammering. Addressing him in a Spanish that indignantly stresses unexpected syllables, he suggests the man search elsewhere for his sensationalist material.

Taken aback, Pinedo explains that, that this isn't, this isn't at all what it's about, because, honestly, on the contrary, what he's writing about, is, in fact is.

Watanabe responds by saying he isn't interested in making any statements. He hangs up and pulls out the cable to disconnect the telephone.

After the call, he finds it impossible to regain his composure. He walks up and down the old striped rug. He debates whether to return to the news, eat something, or go to bed. As so often when he doesn't know what to do, he freshens up his flowers.

He removes the fallen leaves. Crumples the petals between his fingertips. Replenishes the water in the slender receptacle, which wasn't upset by the shocks. Arranges the flowers, so that they overhang as far as possible. Adjusts the willow fronds. He positions them more for the shadows they cast than anything else. He observes the secret hydrography they trace. Once he is satisfied with the result, he discovers fretfully that one of the stems doesn't reach the water.

A few last temperas stain the glass of the picture window. Reflections splash. Night drenches the skyscrapers. Human shapes move across, are framed, then vanish. Mr. Watanabe wonders if they can see him, if anyone is watching him.

All at once, a banjo string snaps, emitting a shrill note that continues to reverberate.

Watanabe decides to take an *ofuro*. That's what he needs. To scrub his nakedness and envelop it in heat. First exposure, then refuge. A bath that softens him and slowly dissolves him.

He disappears into the rectangle. He tries to allow his skin to absorb the water's compassion, the steam's abandon. He fixes his gaze on the ceiling. He remains motionless, listening to the silent gurgle baths make.

As soon as he gets out, he eats an apple and takes a sleeping pill.

IT IS ALREADY MORNING and Mr. Watanabe's body is tossing and turning in his bed. His pale, flaccid limbs twitch like a puppet with its strings snarled.

He hasn't slept on a tatami for more than fifty years. After he retired and moved back to Tokyo, he forced himself to readjust to the hardness of futons. He soon had to admit that lying down like that, he felt embalmed. All those years on Western beds changed his idea of sleep. After all, when we dream we carry with us all the places where we have slept.

Watanabe uses earplugs in bed, a habit he acquired when his work obliged him to spend a hundred nights a year in hotels. During that period, he discovered that a hundred nights is a lot longer than three and a half months. That they form an independent unit of time, an interval that casts doubt on the notion of home. As he always used to say, when the minibar at the hotel becomes more familiar than your kitchen cupboards, there's no going back.

That's why he has kept up his practice of safeguarding his sleep with the slightly rounded foam plugs that penetrate his ear canals until they create the comforting sensation of a vacuum. Watanabe thinks that to sleep without them would foster the belief that he is at home, whereas using them is to accept that he always dreams somewhere else.

It is already morning and his body tosses and turns, flees. Until a nightmare expels him from beneath the sheets. One of those nightmares that has the feel of a premonition.

Watanabe gropes around on the bedside table. As startled as he, his cell phone has just regained its signal. Instantly a deluge of texts, voice mails, and missed calls is unleashed. The device leaps about, convulsing.

Among the calls he finds several from Mariela in Buenos Aires. Also a message, imploring him to pick up the phone if he's there. He sends her a few reassuring lines and promises to call her soon.

A sudden convention of crickets: the mobile network seems to have been restored throughout the city.

He sits up and turns on the television in the bedroom. It's made by the same manufacturer as all the other devices in his apartment. The thickness of the screen is next to nothing, as if the weight of its images has stretched it out.

There are updates about the Fukushima nuclear power station and by now they are truly alarming. The radius of evacuations has tripled, extending to ten kilometers. The authorities have admitted that there are a few small leaks. They have ordered the valves in the reactors to be opened, to lower the temperature and reduce the pressure inside. For a second, Mr. Watanabe misconstrues this sentence, *the pressure inside*, and reads it as directed at him.

On the one hand, the government is appealing to people to remain calm and trust in their security measures. On the other, it announces that the prime minister will be taking an inspection tour of the plant at Fukushima, where, according to the Nuclear Safety Agency, radiation has reached abnormal levels.

Watanabe realizes he isn't going to get back to sleep. He switches on the lights and the room is inundated with a white glare. He leans his back against the cold wall. He checks the *Yomiuri* and the *Asahi* newspapers on his phone and continues in every language he is able to read.

He soon discovers that many of the media outlets are translating one another, mistakes included. In some newspapers there are reports of several explosions. Others speculate that the accident could have international repercussions and that the evacuation zone extends to twenty kilometers, twice what it was only a few hours earlier.

Amazed, he reads that the previous day's earthquake may have moved the whole country by a couple of meters, and shifted the earth's axis by ten or fifteen centimeters. Nothing occurs in only one place, he reflects, everything occurs everywhere. He wonders whether the meddling journalist who called him at home knew more than him.

Unable to stop searching, he trawls YouTube for homemade videos of the explosion at the nuclear plant. Filmed at a distance, by unsteady hands, out of focus.

He sees the shape of the smoke. That shape. The bulging mushroom. That mushroom. The head of the cloud swelling, swelling in his head too. Growing like a tumor.

And it is these images, perhaps more than the previous news bulletins, that galvanize his muscles. With surprising agility, Watanabe leaps off his bed.

He walks along the swath of light on the floor. Through the picture window he observes with bewilderment that, although it will soon be spring, it is snowing as dawn breaks. The flakes have an air of retrospective insistence.

Mr. Watanabe recalls the winters he spent in Paris, where he loved to marvel at the buildings beneath the snow. Facing the hyperbole of the Tokyo skyscrapers, he thinks about the collapse of beauty and how easily it can be destroyed. All artistic, technical, monumental achievements, everything that is meant to last, in the end proves absurdly fragile. He remembers his fascination and anguish as he walked for the first time along the Parisian boulevards, which he couldn't help but imagine bombed out, in ruins, nonexistent. He wandered around its neighborhoods in a kind of trance, visualizing them as they might have been had history shifted by a few centimeters.

These visions were to haunt him for the rest of his life, increasing his awareness of the drastic magnitude of each thing, the simultaneous possibilities of it resisting or imploding. This, he senses, is what could be called emotion.

2

VIOLET
AND THE
CARPETS

I REMEMBER IT WAS SNOWING when I met him. I don't remember the date or the exact address, but I haven't forgotten the snow. Memory is so trite: it retains only the details that make for a good story.

I remember the party. I don't remember the host. I remember their parents were spending the weekend out of town. I don't remember where. I remember the sofa we all fought over. I don't remember the rest of the house. I remember it was late. I don't remember how much I'd had to drink. I remember that the food quickly disappeared. I don't remember what he was wearing. I remember being annoyed when I discovered a red wine stain on my new blouse. I don't remember if I managed to get it out. I remember we looked at each other several times. I don't remember who spoke first. I remember he had withdrawn to a corner and smiled the whole time. I don't remember if I thought that was a contradiction. I remember his straight black hair. I don't remember how I wore mine. I remember he was the only foreigner. I don't remember who invited him to the party. I remember that at that point in my youth foreign men always seemed more interesting to me. I don't remember how long this naïveté lasted.

Yoshie had come to study in Paris. He said he loved languages, although he spoke approximately one and a half. He had an almost desperate desire to travel, to visit the most far-flung places possible. Just as I did, I guess. Now that I think about it, our idea of traveling resembled an escape plan. He gave the impression that he was testing out his identity, like someone constantly trying on clothes to see if they fit. When he arrived in the city he had a romanticized idea of the Sorbonne, as does everyone who hasn't studied there.

To be fair, the atmosphere was starting to become interesting. A lot of us had earnest fantasies of change. That's to say, '68 was still a few years off. Those were very different times, it seemed that everything was about to happen. *Libération* didn't even exist! What we read, as a kind of alternative bible, was *L'Humanité*. My friends and I felt so important, so sure of ourselves as we repeated those pro-Soviet slogans.

The point is that I met Yoshie at a student party. Parties nowadays just seem like parties, I never know how to explain this to my grandchildren. In those days, having fun was something of an act of defiance toward authority. A political response. I suspect this was partly a moral justification, because we wanted to make our simple desire to enjoy ourselves seem more worthy. Or maybe we could only do it like that, because we were so repressed we needed lofty excuses for doing what every young person wants to do. But it was also partly a generational truth. Pleasure didn't come easily, we had to earn it. I think of that whenever I see my granddaughter, Colette, who is so clued in about all the pleasures in life, and yet somehow so conservative. Honestly, I understand less and less what direction we're headed in.

Someone introduced us, I've forgotten who, and we struck up a conversation. We talked and we didn't talk. We told each other very little and thought we'd understood a lot. That night, I don't know why, I felt particularly awkward. It wasn't just how much I'd drunk. It was a different, rather pleasant giddiness.

To begin with, at least, there was nothing remarkable about our conversation. There was, how can I put it, an acceptance that was wordless. Or rather, beneath the words, which in his case were peppered with small, amusing grammatical mistakes. It was as if we had too much to say to each other, and yet there was no need to say anything. He gave the impression of being a shy young man. This of course hopelessly attracted me. Because I, as a rule so haughty with men, had to flirt a lot more than usual.

We danced for quite a while, he better than I. That's often the case with timid men. They either don't dance at all, and hate to be asked, or they end up outdancing everyone. Yoshie couldn't stop moving. He glided around with amazing agility, dodging people on the floor. Some were stretched out on the rug just to take a breather, others the better to drink in comfort, and still others for neither of those reasons. A little tipsy myself, I think, I asked what he had been drinking to give him so much energy. I remember his reply very clearly: nothing. We must remedy that! I laughed. What an idiot. He laughed a lot. What a sweetie, and what an idiot.

I also remember that Yoshie didn't press up against me at all. He avoided any contact below the waist. He danced with me almost diagonally, forcing me to draw him to me rather than keep him at a distance. I was mystified by this degree of formality. And it was also a challenge. For a moment I was afraid he didn't find me attractive. Or maybe that he didn't find women attractive. But I knew that wasn't the case because of the way he looked at me. I did everything I could to get him to talk. As soon as there was room on the sofa, I quickly sat down, lightly patting the space next to me. He came over obediently. That was my first triumph of the evening.

It turned out he was studying economics. Frankly, that was a turnoff. I told him about my history classes. He explained that he would have loved to study humanities, above all linguistics. Still a little disappointed, I said I was sorry he had given up his vocation for something so dull. Yoshie replied that in fact the two worlds had more in common than they might appear to. That there were many similarities between a country's language and its systems of production. Both had their boom-and-bust cycles. Both safeguarded a heritage, administered their wealth, and negotiated over foreign assets.

This was the first time he had spoken to me for longer than thirty seconds, and although the subject wasn't what you'd call romantic, something about his opinions and the passion with which he defended them captivated me. As if changing the subject had transformed him into a different person. Or as if he could be more himself when discussing more impersonal matters.

Besides (he added, finally looking me straight in the eye as he articulated his entire sentence in the present tense), if I do not study exactly that, exactly here, maybe I never meet you.

As there wasn't so much as a slice of bread left, and both of us were ravenous, I suggested we go out and get something to eat. My parents knew I wouldn't be home before dawn. Whenever I went to a party at somebody's house, they preferred me to simply stay out until I could safely catch the first metro. This precautionary measure worked in my favor.

It had stopped snowing. The street looked beautiful, all blanketed in white. Yes, it was cold. But it was the sort of cold that gives you a feeling of euphoria, makes you want to break into a run. It was a weekend, so there were still a few revelers about. Ah yes, now I remember. We were somewhere in the Marais. That was before the alterations that Malraux brought in, I think. The neighborhood was nothing like it is now, and it had a kind of proletarian charm. Proletarian charm! How I hated expressions like that when I was young.

We walked for a while, until we saw one of those shops that are open all hours. We bought a baguette, some cheese, and the cheapest bottle of wine we could find. I'm sure it wasn't exactly a grand cru. We asked them to open it for us, and then Yoshie jammed the cork back in.

When we met, Yoshie didn't have much money, but he had a lot of imagination about how to spend it. I, too, was in a different situation from the one I'm in now. And my parents, with good reason I suppose, gave me a monthly allowance that covered only my basic transportation costs around Paris. That helped me to appreciate the smallest things with a special intensity. Occasionally, I find myself missing that way of life, then I'm ashamed to feel like that and I tell myself I deserve to lose everything all at once.

Yoshie insisted on paying. As was usual with us girls back then, I was happy to let him do so. I was always struck by the way Yoshie didn't hand over money directly, until I got used to it, or maybe until he stopped doing it. He would never put the note into a shop assistant's hand. He avoided physical contact, and at the same time seemed anxious lest he be considered impolite. You could say he moved in an ambiguous zone between fear and respect. He was the same with me. There was a knot, a desire, and a resistance, which I found exciting, apparently. I'm too old now for such affectation.

Carrying our booty in a plastic bag, we searched for a bench to sit on. We huddled close together. This time we had a good excuse. This must sound odd, but I remember feeling that the cold was keeping us warm. Yoshie broke the baguette in two almost without squeezing it. We ate in silence, grinning at each other with delicious awkwardness. I tried to chew very carefully. Cheese can be tricky. Once I had finished, I checked the state of my teeth in my compact mirror, and reapplied my lipstick. In the end, he drank with me. Sharing that bottle was my second triumph of the evening. When it was my turn to take another swig, I did my best to leave a noticeable smudge of lipstick on the glass.

While we were passing the wine between us, we gazed up at the stars. In fact there were very few, because the sky was still quite overcast. Each time we spotted one, we cheered.

You do see? said Yoshie, testing the limits of grammar. Sky also economizing tonight.

As ever, when I didn't know what to say, I lit a Gauloise to make myself seem interesting. Then he (who still didn't smoke, but who was about to start because of me) took some paper napkins out of his pocket. With lightning speed, he folded and twisted them, producing an origami flower. Then he asked for my box of matches, and burned the edges of the flower with great delicacy, blowing very softly so that the flame wouldn't spread.

When he was satisfied with the flower's appearance, he offered it to me, extending his arm in an exaggerated fashion, as if our bodies were a long way apart. I sat gazing at it. It was a kind of carnation smoldering in the night.

Yoshie spoke his bad French very well. As our relationship deepened, I became addicted to his way of saying my name: *Vio-ré*. Whenever he couldn't pronounce a name, he'd blame it on the katakana. I didn't have the faintest idea what katakana was. But those mispronunciations had an unintended seductive effect on me. They made me listen more closely to him than I had done with anyone else before. He faltered and stammered, concentrating so hard on each sentence that I had the impression I was about to hear a revelation. And although that was rarely the case, I was mesmerized in advance.

When it came to intonation, Yoshie had a different sensibility. Whereas the rest of us focused on vocabulary, he was attuned to other properties of words. He would be shocked for no apparent reason, or would take offense at certain responses that sounded normal to us. He used to say that we French are too emphatic when expressing our opinions, and that our self-assurance intimidated him. It isn't self-assurance, I would tell him. It's petulance.

I regarded these sensitivities—how naïve I was—as a sign of sublime spirituality. Afterward, I got to know him better.

Naturally, we had misunderstandings in reverse. Often I thought I could detect a disparity between what he was saying to me and how he was saying it, as if there were some dubbing issue. He reminded me of an actor reading a text without completely understanding it. Sometimes he would say something sweet to me and it would sound authoritarian. Or he would make an everyday remark in a tone that seemed to me like astonishment. Or he would try to insult someone, and the other person would interpret it as a question.

When he wasn't sure of how to say something, or got fed up with searching for the correct way to say it, he would keep quiet and smile. Those silences won me over. There's nothing less sexy than a man's amorous declarations. His words can (and usually do) leave you dissatisfied. But a silence never disappoints.

If I remember correctly, Yoshie had been in Paris for a year when we met. Possibly two. As soon as he was introduced to someone, he would apologize for his French, which was a lot better than he made out. He boasted that he had learned from French literature, cinema, and music. I must say he had every reason to be proud. It seemed unbelievable he had never studied the language before coming here. That was partly why I fell in love with him.

Every day, every hour, almost whenever he opened his mouth, the poor man was tormented by prepositions. Those spots of language that drive foreigners crazy. He didn't find verb tenses any easier. In the beginning, he would thank people in the past tense. At the tobacconist's, for example, before he left he would say, Thank you very much for having sold me cigarettes. Or if he asked directions from a passerby, Thank you for having been so kind.

He had a fixation with infinitives. For him they were the perfect, the most universal expression of the verb. He was confused by our past and future tenses. He couldn't understand why time had to be divided up so strictly. He saw this, I don't know, as a philosophical fallacy. Apparently in his language the past is indivisible, continuous, with only one form. They don't separate it into imperfect, pluperfect, and all those things that I regarded as natural. And which, all of a sudden when I tried to explain them to him, I, too, found nonsensical.

When we started going out together, I asked him to teach me Japanese.

It didn't work, as two young lovers can't study together without other things distracting them. I gave it a try until the obstacles defeated me. Also my inertia, I guess, because his French improved by leaps and bounds. I'd like to think that those long, passionate love letters we wrote each other helped a bit.

Although his spelling was atrocious (more or less like that of any young French person nowadays), you could say that his ear didn't deceive him. I realized he was continually searching for familiar sounds in a strange alphabet, inventing a kind of frontier phonetics. Over time, I became used to his way of articulating the most common words. When someone pronounced them correctly, to me they sounded predictable and bland.

What I most enjoyed was when our everyday exchanges became unintentionally tender. As I was leaving his attic I would say, I'm going, my love. And, instead of saying goodbye, he would answer, I'm staying, my love. By way of those delightful slipups, I tried to imagine what his own language was like. Rather than speak it myself, I wanted to puzzle it out through him. I gradually discovered that you can learn a language thanks to the mistakes its speakers make in your own. As in love, our mistakes say more about us than our successes.

In contrast to all these difficulties, Yoshie admired the syntactic freedom of the French language. At first he found it chaotic, uncontrollable. Later on, inspiring, revolutionary. He was convinced this somehow influenced French history. The idea never even occurred to me. I remember how surprised he was by the flexibility of our adjectives. He would always put them before the noun, until I pointed out how ridiculously poetic that sounded. What's ridiculous about sounding poetic? he would argue.

The first few months of our relationship were the best, precisely when we were getting to know each other. That's what I always tell my granddaughter, only she won't listen. Why such a hurry to be together all the time, when the most interesting part is not knowing the other person? I found Yoshie's polite gestures seductive. Fool that I was, I attributed them to his appreciation of me. His affable way of saying yes was so pleasing.

It took me a while to understand that, despite his courteousness, a yes didn't have the same meaning for him as it did for me. He would say yes in order not to say no. Then I began to feel terribly insecure, to doubt everything we said to each other. Does he agree or is he just going along with me? Does he really want what he says he wants? And more importantly, does he love me or doesn't he love me? Yes or no?

When the first tensions arose between us, we were terrified. We'd never had the slightest disagreement, so neither of us knew how to react. It even occurred to me that this was the end. My mistake. That was the true beginning. Without masks or fantasies. Him and me. A couple. Two idiots. Love.

I confess that, at the outset, I refused to believe our clashes were real. I preferred to blame them on some linguistic misunderstanding. On an ideal level, I was convinced that if we had shared a mother tongue, we'd have agreed about everything. I responded in a similar way to his lack of sincerity. Every time I caught him telling a lie, I reassured myself by thinking that we had very different notions of yes and no. In France, where we're constantly saying no and contradicting our neighbor, this is instantly noticeable. To communicate with someone, we need to disagree.

Disagree and protest. Yoshie would often say to me that for the French, protesting was a form of happiness. Since to him such an attitude was unthinkable, he would disagree with me by partially concurring. That confused me, or worse still, it allowed me to understand what I wanted to understand. He criticized me for always giving such categorical responses. For being unable to express my refusals more tactfully. This lack of ambiguity offended him, you might say.

As he perfected his use of the language, Yoshie started to regret that what he gained on the one hand he lost on the other. His focus on the conversation, which he was now fully able to comprehend, distracted him from the tone, the gaze, the voice. According to Yoshie, who tended to summarize every problem with an economic metaphor, his accumulation of linguistic capital was impoverishing his acquisition of nonverbal assets. The better he spoke my language, the more disagreements we had. Sometimes, in the midst of one of our arguments, he would say to me sadly, I understand you more if I understand less.

Although he had a tireless curiosity about France, Yoshie spoke obsessively about his own country. He was forever pointing out the differences between the two. I didn't realize I was Japanese, he would joke, until I left Japan. He maintained that what we call culture is invisible to us from within our own environment, that we see it only when somebody else observes us from outside. Like a crane, he said, suddenly lifting off the walls and roof of your house.

Everywhere we went, he couldn't rid himself of the sensation of being a foreigner, even before people treated him as one. When no one was giving him funny looks, he claimed they were. With my family, it took him a long while to get over that. Although I suspect that my father would have been equally if not more mistrustful of any French boyfriend, because he thought he knew all about the wicked intentions of his fellow compatriots.

Yoshie was often shy with strangers. He gave the impression of being overly serious, and would intellectualize every topic of conversation. Afterward he would relax, and could become so chatty he seemed a different person. As if there were two people at odds within him, he veered between profound fears and sudden outbursts of confidence. Just like on the night we first met. He found it hard to make friends. He was easy to like, but very difficult to get close to. Yoshie's big drama wasn't being introduced, saying hello, all those things that I found excruciating. No, it was the second or third encounter with someone. That was when he felt unsure about what to do, how friendly to be, how far to take a conversation.

My girlfriends didn't trust him. Obviously, the more they disapproved, the more determined I was to go on seeing him. My university friends were the type of girls who hate someone to clasp their arm while speaking to them. They all wanted to be Marie-France Pisier, to make men suffer and to appear in a Truffaut movie. I'll never forget the horror on their faces when Yoshie once asked, without meaning to cause offense, how you requested something or other in French if you were a woman. He turned bright pink with embarrassment when he saw their response. In the end, the conversation turned into a discussion about ideology and grammar. Yoshie stayed silent.

He *was* a bit of a chauvinist, all the same. Which is why, eventually, the gestures that had at first struck me as gentlemanly began to get on my nerves. Why didn't I feel attracted to someone in my department, for instance, with a similar upbringing to mine? Maybe I saw it as a challenge to bend him to my will, to change him. Or, worse still, maybe something about his attitudes reassured me.

Only one of my girlfriends, a seasoned traveler, suggested I ignore my classmates' warnings. In the end, alas, we've all settled for falling in love with men we think are a slight improvement on their predecessors. We improved our boyfriends more than we did our lives, an amusing failure, in its own way.

During our first year together, Yoshie continued to write every day to his aunt and uncle in Tokyo. And as soon as he saved enough francs, he would call them. I remember how funny I thought it was seeing him talk to them, bowing at the telephone. It's true that in the beginning I had a lot of preconceptions. I was convinced Japanese people were always cold and aloof. As our relationship evolved, he disproved most of those beliefs. I have to confess that this confused me. If he was so unlike the stereotype of a Japanese person, then in a sense I was at a disadvantage. I knew far less about him than he knew about me, ignorance was on my side, I was the foreigner.

On second thought, maybe that was what I fell in love with. Being able to imagine him according to my needs. Doing that with a guy from my own country would have been much harder work. But above all, what attracted me was the novelty the simplest activities acquired. Eating, sleeping, walking, gesticulating, or saying hello, all those routines I took for granted became fascinating when I was with Yoshie. It was like an infatuation within an infatuation.

Generally speaking, he tolerated quite good-naturedly the clichéd comments about his Asian origins. Only one blunder really bothered him, and on several occasions I saw him respond in a fairly hostile way: being mistaken for Chinese. If that happened, Yoshie was quite capable of giving the person concerned a long lecture. Interestingly, I've seen that same response, if not worse, in the opposite direction. The Chinese aren't amused by the mix-up either.

It was only much later that I discovered a far more serious hang-up. Yoshie didn't like to discuss his memories of the war. Although he'd told me a few things about his family, he left out an essential part of the story. I always thought Yoshie had spent the holidays of 1945 with his aunt and uncle in Tokyo, which is what he told me, and that the rest of his family had died in Nagasaki. What he didn't tell me at the time, and what I was unaware of until well into our relationship, is that he himself was a survivor.

I found out almost by accident, while we were having dinner with friends and talking about the atomic tests France was carrying out in Algeria. When he said it in passing, I was in Hiroshima, I was dumbstruck. The first thing I pictured, feeling like a complete idiot, were the scars on his back and arms. Supposedly acquired when, as a child, he scalded himself with boiling water while his mother was cooking. I had to run to the bathroom to throw up. And I couldn't utter another word through the rest of the dinner. He kept looking at me with a mixture of remorse and coldness. As if to say, If that hurt you, I was hurt a whole lot more.

After the obligatory exclamations and a few well-meaning remarks, our friends tried to pick up the conversation with apparent normality. It was their way of digesting (or not digesting) such a revelation. Or perhaps they simply assumed that I had known all about it.

All I could do was stub out cigarettes and terrify myself in silence. How could he have concealed something like that from me? What kind of man was I sharing my life with, someone who hadn't wanted to tell me the most important thing about his? What did this change? How, and how much, did it change us?

As soon as we were alone we had a huge fight and a magical reconciliation. I cried a lot and then we cried together, which was the best part. In fact, there were two reasons I cried. Because of the horrifying story he was telling me, which he would never repeat. But also because until that moment I hadn't deserved his trust.

Yoshie explained he had absolutely no wish to reduce his identity to that tragedy. If he'd told me about it before, it would have colored our entire relationship. And that he refused to live, and also to love, as a victim in other people's eyes. He'd suffered too much in the past, he said, to sacrifice his future. If he felt healthy, with the necessary strength and desire to live his youth, why should he present himself to everyone as a perpetual cripple, as someone incapable of rebuilding his own life?

It went without saying, he insisted, that he admired the people who had decided to speak or write about their tragedies, leaving a testimony of what had occurred. But, he asked me, didn't I think it unfair to denigrate those who had managed to put the ordeal behind them? All those who had struggled to escape the pain and start anew.

I found his arguments very convincing. I came to the conclusion that they deserved not only the utmost respect, but also my praise. That his refusal to speak about his experiences showed a kind of dignity and fortitude. Who could know better than he, than the victim himself, what the most appropriate response was?

After that night, we scarcely touched on the subject. I decided there were no more secrets. That, knowing what I knew then, there could be no more barriers. I confess that now our silence strikes me as odd. I wonder whether neither of us really got over it. Whether perhaps he didn't dare speak, and I was afraid to ask.

Even so, I remember there were occasional hints. We were taking a stroll through the upper part of Montmartre. The sky was clear. It was summer. He raised his head, and paused. He squeezed my arm very tight. And he told me that shooting stars frightened him. Taken aback, I asked him why. He said they resembled other things that cross the sky before they fall on you.

Around that time, people started talking about the *hibakusha*. It seems many of them were reluctant to speak with the media or to participate in public events. Yoshie considered big speeches the concern of politicians. For him, respecting people's memory was a private affair. Honoring the dead with the silence of the dead.

Politics didn't help people speak either. The bombs and the bombed were scarcely mentioned in Japan. There had been no general condemnation, more like an embarrassed murmur. Indeed, many victims kept quiet, even after they got sick. Unfortunately, Yoshie didn't tell me any of this. I read about it much later. Too late.

To be fair, in France we had our own postwar silence. Despite the obvious differences, I remembered how a lot of people felt awkward speaking about our collaboration with the Nazis. For a long time there was a debate (is there still one?) about the need to remember it, or whether to look toward the future, which nowadays is the official euphemism for forgetting.

The books that most interested me at the *fac* were the ones about the

Vichy regime, which was given the despicable name État Français. I was a child still learning to write when Paris fell. In theory, the armistice with the Nazis was supposed to prevent an even worse agreement. Which suggests, alas, that peace and war are just two stages in the same negotiation. I heard Yoshie say something similar.

The conditions we agreed to, and their consequences, could hardly have been worse. We had to place our police at the service of the gestapo and the SS. To help them suppress (can there be any greater treachery?) the French Resistance. To spread propaganda against foreigners. To cooperate actively in the Holocaust. And to abduct ten thousand Jews in a single day in that Vél d'Hiv roundup, which my children don't remember, and for which the Le Pen family apparently doesn't hold France accountable. In a word: peace.

Comparing this to the Japanese empire, it occurs to me that our regime chose the opposite horror. It humiliated itself to maintain the fiction of the state. Its shell. The seat of government was transferred to Vichy. That doesn't surprise me. A typical French provincial town. Tourism, thermal waters, bijou hotels. *Bon goût.* Europeanness.

Only a few months before the atom bombs, the German village to which the Vichy cabinet had fled was taken by the Americans. And by Free French troops. If there'd been no authority here supporting them until the end, would the Germans have surrendered more quickly? What about the Japanese empire? Would the war have ended a bit sooner? Enough for them not to drop the bombs? Those are questions I never put to Yoshie.

The ending was, let's say, very French. Laval shot. Marshal Pétain condemned to death. De Gaulle commuted his sentence (respect for life, above all, ladies and gentlemen!), and his followers were sanctioned. Among them Schuman, the father of what we like to call the European Union.

As far as I know, Schuman managed to avoid cooperating with either the Nazis or the Resistance. Perhaps that explains why he became justice minister. I remember it well, because I was reading newspapers by then. I hear that Monsieur Schuman's beatification is underway. We can never have too many monuments. And what did we do with the Vél d'Hiv? We knocked it down, naturally.

It was soon after the demolition of the velodrome that we started nuclear weapons testing in Algeria. My friends and I mostly agreed to condemn it. But when the Soviet Union resumed its nuclear experiments it was a different story. A lot of my ex–fellow students chose to defend it. I was sensitized to the subject through Yoshie. Not because of what he said about it, which was virtually nothing, but because of what I knew about him and the secret he had revealed to me.

In my view, it made no difference whether it was capitalists or socialists who made the atom bombs. My friends accused me of being simplistic and not fully committed. You can't casually compare two systems that are incomparable, they protested.

How is it possible that our deepest convictions end up seeming nothing more than a sign of the times, a generational trend? Do we all treat the past frivolously? Or aren't we clear-sighted enough to see our era with the clarity of the following generations?

Many of us university students identified with Castroism. Yoshie didn't seem so convinced. If I remember correctly, his objections had to do with the fact that Cuba's leaders were military men. My friends and I felt this was inevitable considering the situation of the island, and even desirable, because that way the triumphs of the revolution could be better defended from imperialist aggression. My fellow students viewed pacifism as a form of collaboration with the enemy. They didn't see all weapons as equal. And using them to oppress or to liberate wasn't the same thing either. Maybe that's why the men of my generation felt so removed from the flower power of the next decade. To my granddaughter, Colette, the sixties are the best. Then again, who really understands history?

Incidentally, a friend from that group of students ended up as mayor of a small town in Provence. She's also a militant lesbian, which she wasn't in our youth. Well, the militant part, yes. For years the French nuclear missile silos were situated in that region, in Plateau d'Albion. If I'm not mistaken, France still has the most missiles in the world after America and Russia. All to prevent worse wars, of course, our intentions are always altruistic. To broker total disarmament would be naïve. An idea that could come only from women.

When the area ceased to be used as a base, my friend Aude started working with local people to transform it into a solar energy plant. That, to me, is far more patriotic than all the other stuff. They say our nuclear energy industry is bankrupt. That we intervened in Mali to protect our supplies of uranium. And that at this rate we'll be forced to buy electricity from the British, who continue to invest in nuclear power plants.

My friend Aude is no longer mayor, we're too old for that kind of nonsense. But she still campaigns on environmental issues and the rights of the LGBTQ community. She is constantly posting things on Facebook. If Facebook had been around when we were students, I wonder how we would have passed our exams. You end up chatting with complete strangers, from countries you've never been to, which is what happened to me with a friendly young journalist from some newspaper in Argentina. He told me that if he ever comes to Paris, he'd like to interview me in person. The other night I stayed up chatting with him online until two in the morning. My husband thought he was an ex-lover. Good.

Honestly, this habit of calling them LGBTQ sounds like a euphemism to me. But that's how Aude always writes it. Oh, Violet, don't be so vieux jeu, she tells me. Well, if I was such a fuddy-duddy, I wouldn't like all those photos she posts.

As for sex, well, that's another matter. I remember very clearly what it was like with my first boyfriend, Olivier. Such a handsome young man. Sometimes I think more about him than I do my own husband.

I lost my virginity to Olivier, possibly a little sooner than I should have. It's one thing to start sleeping with someone, and quite another to learn to enjoy your own pleasure. I had no real urge to have sex. It was simply that his desire to make love was stronger than my desire not to. Realizing this was far more important to me than the act itself. It was the first time I sensed that a couple consists of a conciliation of desires. A constant (and occasionally delicious) process in which the strongest desire ends up imposing itself.

I was in love with my boyfriend. And yet, how can I put this, I wasn't in love with his desire for me. My experiences with the handsome Olivier were all very much the same. A swift foreplay routine, during which I tried to appear passionate, without really knowing how. It began with his desire imposing itself on my lack of desire. Followed by a feeling of lethargy, a bit like when you've just woken up, which slowly transformed into vague interest. That interest slowly aroused a wish to feel something special. Then came a semblance of pleasure. The start of something possibly intense, all too soon interrupted by his ecstasy, that premature, and for me inexplicable, ecstasy. Then a slight feeling of annoyance. With, to top it all off, the apparent obligation to display satisfaction and affection. And in the end, less enthusiasm for a next time. It never crossed my mind that we were both to blame for this.

Then I met Yoshie, who wasn't as handsome but who had a certain something. To begin with, when he escorted me home, we would stay in the entrance, unable to part. We'd seek out the darkest corner possible. Whenever we heard the elevator we'd freeze, trying hard not to giggle. Whispering to each other, and doing, well, a few other things. I was beginning to want him to suggest we sleep together and I felt a mixture of desire and wounded pride. Wasn't he supposed to find me attractive?

Yoshie wasn't sure whether to be shocked or delighted at the ease with which people here, in his view, went to bed with someone they liked. Delaying that moment was for him a way of committing to the other person. Although I didn't dare contradict him for fear of seeming loose, the opposite argument occurred to me. That being more impulsive could also be a sign of trust, of giving oneself. I was unsettled by my new boyfriend's restraint, and I confused it with sophistication. I thought he was behaving like an *homme fatal*. Ideal for a young cinephile. Compared with him, the boys from my own country seemed so coarse. It was always obvious what they were after. And that prompted me not to let them have it.

I'm sure that Yoshie was still a virgin, although he never admitted it. In any case, I can see that the waiting made the consummation a tremendous event. As if my true virginity, the second one, the one I now truly wanted to lose, was in his hands. I don't know whether as a strategy or out of sheer panic, Yoshie seemed to ritualize every erotic approach. This allowed me to take my time caressing, to enjoy the sense of progression. In the end, of course, I was the one who took the initiative. I tried to appear as inexperienced as possible, so that he wouldn't feel intimidated. I suspect I wasn't very successful.

I won't describe the first time, when everything to be expected happened. Although I also felt some surprising sensations, which encouraged me to persevere. And I have to admit that it soon started to pay off. We changed gear, became emboldened. In that sense, the way we progressed took me by surprise.

During those early days, we walked the streets guarding a secret. We felt we had crossed an invisible but decisive line. One that separated the confusion of adolescence from that other clear-cut, dangerously tangible world that previously had seemed beyond our reach. We constantly yearned to spend the night together. I would make up all kinds of excuses, tell my parents the most elaborate (and no doubt implausible) lies in order to sleep at Yoshie's loft. By now, I can picture my father guessing my true intentions, and my mother intervening every time I invented some party, or a girlfriend, or a late-night study session so I could sleep over.

Or rather, not sleep. Sexual excitement wasn't the only reason. There was also that strange energy, that stream of insomnia that prevented me from closing my eyes as the night wore on and he lay next to me breathing deeply. I listened closely for every noise coming from his chest, as if it were an engine. My euphoria was so great that it seemed wasteful to go several hours without thinking about us, without being fully aware of his physical proximity.

Yoshie's attic apartment was near Gare du Nord. Tiny. Cheap. Dark. With an impossible staircase. Paradise. I remember one winter night, we had just seen a movie by Agnès Varda. No, Chabrol. About two cousins who live together. One of them is always partying and passes his exams. The other studies all day and flunks out. I think I really liked it, and Yoshie not so much. Later, Chabrol's films became so silly, but his early ones were interesting. Or is it me who changed?

The point is, we were leaving the theater, and Yoshie's friend, who had come from Tokyo to do some sightseeing, was staying at his loft. It was impossible for us to go to my house and shut ourselves away in my bedroom, or even stay up talking in the living room until midnight, not with my parents and my jealous sister there. My father had subjected the last boyfriend I brought home to a kind of cultural and financial interrogation. All through dinner, he insisted he must reread Balzac, whom I doubt Olivier knew except by name. He concluded with his usual joke: When I was young, Balzac provided the answer to all my worries. It's different now. Not just because you young people are incapable of understanding Balzac, but because you have no worries! My boyfriend couldn't get away fast enough, and my mother murmured, He seems like a nice boy. He never came over for dinner again.

And so Yoshie and I decided, if just that once, to pool all the money we had left and allow ourselves the luxury of a night at a hostel. We ended up choosing a really awful place in the Latin Quarter. Which, incredible as it now seems, was an affordable neighborhood in those days. I can still recall—how is that possible?—the battered sign on the door: HÔTEL DE LA PAIX—TOUT CONFORT. The only thing we asked, besides the price, was whether the room had a bathtub. Our big fantasy had always been to take a long bath together, because in Yoshie's *chambre de bonne* there was only a very basic washroom.

We ran up the stairs as fast as we could. We were laughing and gasping for breath when we opened the door. We went in, didn't even look around. We didn't inspect everything, the way you do in hotels nowadays, with a look on your face like someone handing out one- to five-star ratings. As soon as we closed the door, despite the icy draft filtering through the window glass, we threw off our clothes, kissed frantically, and stumbled toward the bathroom. There we discovered, exactly as they'd said, an old bathtub. There was just one problem. No bath plug.

With the same intensity with which I had climbed the stairs, in that exaggerated way one experiences things at twenty, I reacted as though the absence of the plug were a disaster. My disappointment was immense and I felt the whole of winter on my back. Fortunately, Yoshie had an idea that proved to be far sexier than a bit of plastic. He went into the bedroom. He crouched, naked and covered in goose bumps, and inspected my tangled clothes. He did something with them that I couldn't make out properly, and came back to the bathroom carrying my black stockings. He tied a knot in them, then pressed them into the drain until it was plugged. He turned on the hot tap and we embraced, dying of cold and happiness.

Actually, I was the only one who shivered that night. That's something that always amazed me about him, he never seemed cold, not even on the bitterest days in his loft. Winter wasn't his problem. I, on the other hand, was constantly asking him for another blanket. And yet I loved that extreme cold. It taught me how to feel each movement. Forced us to be one another's energy.

Even back then I always dressed warmly. My children tease me, they say I can feel a draft before it arrives. I can't help it if the world has become an air-conditioned madhouse. Can anyone tell me which lowlife gave the order to turn summers into artificial winters? Curiously enough, when summer came, Yoshie never seemed hot either.

Another remarkable thing about Yoshie was his sense of smell. He would sniff people and then classify them according to some random criteria. Sometimes, for example, he would insist that someone smelled of birthdays. Or that some other person reeked of anger. According to him, I gave off a strong aroma of origami paper. I thought he was pulling my leg.

We were so young it makes me want to cry. Because we didn't know what we were. Because we believed all that energy belonged to us. We felt so perfect that we needed to caress each other constantly to make sure that it was true. That our tireless bodies were still there.

It wasn't all sheer delight. That fervor had its drawbacks. The constant state of anxiety, even at moments that called for a pause, restraint. The tendency toward possession. The inability to truly listen to the other before touching them, or sometimes when not touching them. The growing jealousy.

In hindsight, we had a lot of sex that probably wasn't very good. Young men tend to suffer from too much romanticism out of bed and too much athleticism in it. It isn't that I miss either of those things. I'm sure I felt more pleasure in the decades that followed, especially at the start of my marriage. Those were the best years. My husband and I had stability and novelty. The perfect combination. The only thing I miss occasionally is losing control. It isn't so much what I do (or no longer do) with my husband, but with what urgency. We aren't desperate to go to bed together, we simply decide to. We do it both better and worse.

We ended up transforming Yoshie's attic apartment into a kind of miniature cultural center. A secret club with two members. There we discussed every movie we saw and we read the same books—bought, borrowed, or stolen. We drank liter after liter of a cheap brew, which I'll call coffee just to give it a name.

Yoshie tried to wade through his economics textbooks as quickly as possible so that he could share the books I was reading. He devoured the pages at an incredible rate, or maybe he only skimmed through half of them, and was smart enough to predict the other half. I read a lot of Simone de Beauvoir (we all wanted to be like her, but none of us dared). And Françoise Sagan (we also wanted to be like her, but were too poor). Or Nathalie Sarraute (with a respectful yawn). Sometimes, when I grew tired of a book, I would ask him to recite one of the hundreds of Zen poems that, I wonder how, he knew by heart. Most amusing was when he tried, not always successfully, to translate them for me.

But mainly we would shut ourselves away and listen to records. I'm referring to a time when actual records still existed. The ones you could clasp to your chest, blow on, and they'd crackle. The ones that spun around measuring time to the sound of rain. My husband tells me I'm retro chic, and that our grandchildren will recall with the same kind of fetishistic nostalgia their current gadgets, which seem so cold to me.

I can see us lying on our backs, eyes closed, a cigarette smoldering between our fingers, listening to the meanderings of Parker playing Cole Porter. Jazz was his thing. My hero was Brassens. "La mauvaise réputation," "Les amoureux des bancs publics." My anthems. Not that Brassens sang about our lives, but we did our best to live the way he sang. I think Yoshie preferred Brel, even though he didn't understand all the lyrics. Finally, as a result of me playing him my Brassens records all the time, he ended up taking his shower every morning to the jungle roar of *Gare au gori-i-i-ille!*

My parents occasionally invited us to the theater. Since neither he nor I could afford it, we went only if they paid for our tickets. I can still remember the evening we saw Simone Signoret. She was splendid. The play was some awful melodrama. Honestly, this habit of remembering my teenage years more clearly than what happened yesterday worries me.

For some reason that I never figured out, my parents adored Yoshie, especially Mom. She treated him more like her son than my boyfriend. The only thing she disapproved of was the noise he made when he drank soup. Papa's appreciation was more technical. As soon as my father tried to browbeat him with one of his typical monologues about economics, Yoshie dazzled him with a meditation on the differences between Western and Asian capitalism. From then on, Dad was convinced my boyfriend would go far. What he couldn't have imagined was from whom.

Eventually I had my own set of keys to the loft. I spent most weekends there. When I opened the door, I'd find him sitting in the weirdest positions. I always wondered about his bones, his knee and ankle joints. Yoshie did some extreme stretching exercises. They worried me because they looked painful. I can't think properly without flexibility, he would explain.

Despite the lack of space, whenever we had tea we would unfurl a kind of mat that was shorter than a tatami. I began to get used to living without chairs. For Yoshie, they were a nuisance, an obstacle between his body and reality. He had a different relationship to the floor than I did. I realized that I tended to avoid it. As though gravity were ultimately an inconvenience. In contrast, he used it to obtain a sort of peace. The rest of the loft might be desperately in need of a clean, but the floor was always spotless.

Something that made our lives easier was his obsessive hoarding of food. Unlike at the houses of my other male friends, I can't remember a single day when there wasn't plenty to eat at Yoshie's, even if it was expired, or a bit difficult to chew. He would keep all his leftovers and knew how to make a meal out of them. His techniques for storing things seemed like precise feats of engineering. He made frugality a science.

Another of his habits was to rescue and look after old banjos, as if they were abandoned pets. A friend who made instruments gave him a few battered banjos in exchange for a token sum. When there was no space left to hang the banjos on the walls, Yoshie started storing them underneath the bed, in wool-lined cardboard boxes. He would spend hours tuning them. If you don't tune them, they suffer, he told me. Of course, he was the one who suffered. Each time he silently contemplated them, he would imagine a concert of discordant instruments. And he found the idea so unbearable that he felt compelled to start retuning them, peg by peg.

I remember one particular morning, in our bed that dipped in the middle. The creak of the shutters. The sudden light on my face. The sound of old strings. His neck on the pillow next to me. Yoshie singing *bon anniversaire* in a hushed voice in my ear as he penetrated me.

At the end of every month, if we had any money left, we would treat ourselves and go dancing at a boîte. When we felt like going out but didn't have enough money, which was almost always, we amused ourselves another way. We entered a brasserie. We ordered only coffee, and we made a game of imagining the lives of the couples around us.

Rather than spy on them while they were eating, we concentrated on the clues they left behind. The way bottles and glasses were positioned on the table (the center tended to denote stability, the edges risk-taking, and the corners crisis). The arrangement of bread, salt, and condiments. Predominant side, if both people used the same hand when helping themselves. Final position of cutlery. Amount and type of mess left. Distance between the check and the woman's chair. And, last but not least, state of the napkin (tense, folded, carefully smoothed out, casually abandoned, and so on).

We felt that observing other lovers elevated us. It gave us the advantage of loving each other and understanding the way others loved one another. We never suspected they might also be observing us. Sadly, I have lost that gift of impunity. Nowadays, I often get the feeling that young couples are giving me sidelong glances, at best with a hint of pity.

We would also go out to read together. Leaving the house without a book seemed to us unthinkable. We would seek out tables by the window, or if the weather was good, we would sit in a park somewhere. We were capable of spending the entire afternoon without saying a word, we liked not talking and knowing we could do that. But sooner or later, we'd end up watching someone. What we read was people.

After paying his university fees and the rent on his *chambre de bonne*, the fact is Yoshie didn't have much left over. To avoid asking his aunt and uncle in Tokyo for money, some months he would ask me to lend him a few francs. Or rather, he'd ask me to make up a good excuse to borrow some from my father. I was surprised to find he'd often use the money to buy flowers for Mom. The same large bouquets with which he would make a gallant entrance, thus becoming indisputably my family's favorite boyfriend. He had a talent for avoiding conflict, and, after a few such visits, he started to bring my sister flowers as well. She would show her thanks by keeping the occasional secret for us.

As our relationship evolved, I started to divide my time between my parents' house and Yoshie's loft. Every now and then we would fantasize about getting married. We made plans and calculations. We played at the future. He even formally introduced me to his aunt and uncle that year when they came to visit. I'm trying to think of their names. I can't remember them, even though he mentioned them all the time! Too bad. Those two took politeness to a whole new level. They barely spoke, smiled a lot, and always seemed slightly uncomfortable. I don't know why, I'm remembering now that they stayed at the Hôtel Delavigne.

What would my life, our life, have been if we'd made real those dreams of marriage? We weren't in any hurry, and I doubt whether either of us was ready for a serious commitment. After all, we were both still supported by our respective families. I'm referring more to what weddings signify. Do rituals change you somehow? Or is the ritual the result of a change in you? Nowadays, I believe more in the evolution of love than in the staging.

Sometimes, he would treat you with an exquisite, exclusive attention. He made you feel like you were the best thing to have happened to him. Until, all of a sudden, he seemed to grow weary, and distanced himself in subtle ways. Then you longed to be the best once more.

We were mutually infatuated in the beginning, but it occurs to me that later on we felt a growing sense of disappointment, which we never admitted. Maybe that's why in my next relationship I decided to get married so quickly? For fear of failing to live up to what the two of us believed we saw in each other?

I could look back and regret the way I gave myself to the men I loved. My one-sided devotion, the sacrifice of my own ambitions. Or my generosity, to take an obvious example, with a new arrival who chose to take off without me at the first opportunity. And yet, after so many years of married life, how can I not be a little self-critical? I was talking about this the other day with my eldest daughter, Adélaïde. She believes part of the reason I'm so keen to throw myself into other people's projects is to avoid dealing with my own frustrations. She didn't put it quite so tactlessly, of course. Instead she made me sense what she was thinking. Naturally Adélaïde needs to argue this to justify her own situation. After all, she is childless.

No sooner had he obtained his university degree than Yoshie started looking for a job. I had another year to go before I graduated. He had two basic objectives: to stop depending on his aunt and uncle, and to leave the loft, which was as uncomfortable as it was wonderful. I daresay it was with his legitimate wish to move on that the decline of our relationship began to secretly take shape.

I don't remember how or through whom Yoshie ended up offering his services to Me—the internationally renowned Japanese manufacturer of television sets, audiovisual technology, and other things of that sort. This was during Japan's economic rebirth, which so astonished everyone. I mean everyone who could afford to buy stuff. France was beginning to emerge from the postwar years. That's to say, transforming depression into productive euphoria.

Me was looking for people to work in the office it planned to open in Paris. Preferably of Japanese origin, who spoke French fluently, and who understood economics. Obviously, Yoshie was an ideal candidate. Even so, I was a little surprised at how quickly he found work, and with no previous experience. I soon discovered that, unlike their European counterparts, Japanese companies hired people with a clean slate. People who could be molded exactly as their mentors wanted. I'm not sure whether this means they believed more in young people, or simply that the rat race began earlier in Japan.

In any case, Yoshie rose rapidly within the company. He was reliable, disciplined, and worked unbelievably long hours. This affected our relationship, in both good and bad ways. At last we had money, and yet we scarcely had time to spend it. I learned a few more Japanese words, relating to the alienating effects his work had on our relationship. *Zangyōsuru.* Overtime. *Okureru.* Arriving late. And so on.

In just two years, Yoshie went from being a lowly employee in the management department (little more than an intern, in fact) to a member of the manager's inner circle. The manager became fond of him, and made him his personal assistant. According to Yoshie, something like that could never have happened in Japan. His promotion went against some kind of military-style tradition regarding employee hierarchy and advancement. Of all the terms that were constantly on Yoshie's lips, another word I remember is *kakarichō*, because it sounded so funny, although I've forgotten what it means.

The manager. What was that guy's name? I'm sure if I saw a photograph I'd recognize him. A man whose hair was too neat. Who was full of the tiniest gestures that he seemed to repress. We had to dine with him on many occasions. He would make a great fuss when greeting me: *Oh, mademoiselle Créton, ah, mademoiselle!* And then proceed to completely ignore me. To begin with, he would give a start whenever I opened my mouth. He would look at me in astonishment, as if it weren't my turn to speak. And in general he avoided responding to anything I said. Yoshie smiled at his boss while casting sidelong, almost imploring glances at me.

I was so outraged by this situation that on our third or fourth evening with him, I made a point of constantly addressing the manager. I asked him a series of ludicrous questions, until at last I was able to make him respond with a degree of normality. My audaciousness ended up endearing me to him. The manager said as much to Yoshie, by way of congratulating him: *Ah, très intelligente! Fille intelligente!* Which made me think: Why the hell is he so surprised?

Invariably when we dined with him, after the second bottle, the manager would tell us the same cautionary tale, with slight variations. How after the war, the company Me had been founded by a certain Monsieur Matsuoka. *That* name I have no trouble remembering! And how Mr. Matsuoka had started off in a tiny workshop on the third (or was it the fourth?) floor of a shopping center damaged by the bombs. How proud the company was to look back at those humble beginnings, when it was still mending transistor radios and electrical gadgets, now that it had become a multinational with branches in more than thirty different countries, and so on. And how every great business should be capable of steadily expanding in concentric circles, blah, blah, blah.

Truth be told, I never really understood what the intended moral of that story was. That if someone works hard they become a millionaire? That ultimately the Japanese, like the Germans, are invincible? Or that after a war ends, the sensible thing to do is to not look back and to start investing?

Yoshie begged me to be as nice as I could to his boss. He asked me to be patient for our own good. He talked a lot about how much our life would improve, about all the things we could do together once we had saved up enough money. Somehow this made me feel as if the future of our relationship was part of his contract with the company. The manager insisted that at Me all the employees were like one big family. He talked to us about bonding, commitment, the sense of belonging.

I found his discourse an excuse to get employees to work more hours in the name of the family. Yoshie started to take offense at my criticisms. He accused me of not understanding the work ethic of his country. For example, in the unlikely event of a recession, the company would stick to the principle of maintaining its workforce, and would do everything to protect it even under threat of bankruptcy. Rather than dismiss a good employee, he said to me completely in earnest, the manager, or even the CEO, would sooner take his own life.

Other people in his department often joined these work dinners. The manager was the center around which they orbited. Only a few brought their spouses, who were without exception Japanese. In my presence, they all went out of their way to speak French as a mark of courtesy, which at the time I was unable to appreciate. Every so often, I would say a word in their own language, and they would applaud as if this were a great achievement.

Sometimes I felt like the protagonist in *Bonjour tristesse*, attempting to sound grown-up while surrounded by these businessmen whose conversations bored me to tears. I secretly fantasized about behaving like the author of that novel. Wearing any old clothes. Acting crazy. Causing a scandal. Needless to say, I always ended up behaving like a proper young lady. Over time, the people at Me started to grow on me, or at least I came to respect them. It was around that time I realized Yoshie had changed.

He was smoking more and more. Some evenings, he would finish his pack first and then borrow from me. We had picked up each other's bad habits. I don't think this was simply because we had more money, something else was triggered in him, in us. A kind of ambition, I wouldn't necessarily call it materialistic. Is ambition inherently materialistic? Or is materialism merely a concrete expression of a different longing? Our feelings for each other didn't change, but they became filled with little clauses. Now we negotiated, we made decisions that were mutually convenient.

On a couple of occasions, I even got the impression that Yoshie was flirting with my sister, who was paying him more attention than before. I'm not saying she was attracted to his new status. Neither my sister nor Yoshie was that shallow. It had more to do with, how can I explain it? His attitude. Now he was more voracious, wanting everything, and maybe that made him more attractive to a certain type of woman. With all due respect to my sister, this was precisely what worried me. I didn't like the women who appeared to like my boyfriend.

Outside of his normal working hours, Yoshie started to attend business meetings at cafés on weekends. At first, I would go with him. I'd sit at another table and read until the meeting was over. I noticed something he would do every time. He'd order two glasses of strong liquor, pay for them, and leave his own untouched. If the conversation became drawn out, he would order another round and repeat the same procedure. The other person ended up getting tipsy, while he remained perfectly sober. As soon as that person left, he'd ask the waiter to take away his own drink and bring him a *noisette*, which he downed in one gulp, as if it were medicine, before the next prospective client arrived. I soon stopped accompanying him and would either go to the cinema or wait for him at a restaurant.

After he joined Me, we began to talk about moving in together. We both wanted to and yet didn't want to. It seemed like the natural decision, and yet we feared upsetting the balance we'd established. We spent part of the week together. We rehearsed being what people call a serious couple. And we also continued to spend some days apart, which helped us make sure we wanted to be together.

Then of course there was the question of money. Although by then he was earning a good salary, I wanted to contribute to our finances. I thought that my future family should be founded on shared responsibilities, which included earnings. If there's one thing I regret after all these years of marriage, it's that I ended up yielding on that point. Did I do it for myself, for my husband, or for my children? I don't even know anymore.

I started private tutoring and worked as a substitute teacher at a few high schools. The plan was to save up for a year or two, and then to look for our nest. Our dream was always a big old house with high ceilings, which we would gradually renovate to our taste. A house that resembled our relationship. During that time, I never actually moved in with him, or he never really insisted that I did.

While we continued to make plans for our future home, he could finally afford to leave his loft. He moved into a small but pleasant apartment on Rue des Cordelières, in the thirteenth arrondissement. There we spent what I believe were our last truly happy moments. In the entrance hall was a black-and-white-striped rug that stretched halfway across the room, a housewarming present from me. I remember that it cost a small fortune, because, according to the antiques dealer, it had belonged to some Japanese imperial family. I fell in love with it. The day I brought it over, I held it up and exclaimed: *Tadaima!* Yoshie smiled, kissed me, and replied, *Okaeri, mes amours!* Those are the kinds of foolish things that remain engraved on your memory. I'm sure he has no recollection of it. He wasn't sentimental in that way.

I remember our Sundays at the Rue Mouffetard market. The street stalls. The brash colors. Those aromas you could almost taste. The smell of fish, like a beach in the wrong place. Cheeses vying with one another. Shiny pieces of fruit. Their different textures. Our hands squeezing them. Our fingers meeting. And in the background, the beloved walls of Saint-Médard church. The same walls where in the old days preachers, pilgrims, and hypnotists supposedly congregated, until the authorities expelled them. And where someone had left a delightful rhyme mocking the prohibition:

In the king's name,
we forbid God
to perform any miracles
on this facade.

Sometimes, while we were having breakfast in Yoshie's apartment, we would imagine my furniture alongside his. We'd visualize all our belongings together, their shapes and edges touching, to see what they would look like. Interestingly, one of the things we disagreed over was the television set. He had installed an enormous Me television opposite the sofa. But I had always told him I would never, under any circumstances, want one in my house. I preferred to spend my time reading or listening to music.

We also disagreed about cats. According to Yoshie, one summer when he was a child, he had fallen asleep with a sick cat in his arms, and he'd had such a strong allergic reaction to it that it recurred whenever he came into contact with one. As I was a passionate cat lover, to me this shortcoming felt no less serious than his reluctance to have children. We never really went into it. I suppose, in my heart, I hoped he would end up changing his mind. We weren't in any hurry. We had time, or so we thought.

I remember our last summer. Coincidentally, it was also the longest vacation we'd spent together.

For the first time since he began working for Me, I'd managed to persuade him to take a whole week off. He usually refused to leave his post. He felt more conscientious if he divided his vacation into small chunks, which meant that we were never able to relax properly. For me this was a triumph. Yoshie taking a break! I was convinced this vacation would be very important for us. My intuition told me we were about to make a commitment, take a decisive step. So much for my stupid intuition.

There was so much sun, it seemed liquid. Summer was brimming over. The light enveloped us. We went by car, a cream-colored Renault Dauphine that Yoshie had just bought thanks to the raise he had received that year. I remember we drove via Montauban, along a road between Bordeaux and Montpellier. In those days there weren't the magnificent highways we have now. It took ages to get anywhere, but that was half the fun. We simply accepted that moving from A to B was a fundamental part of the journey. Knowing that made you more patient, and that patience was enthralling.

We smoked cigarettes out of the window. I think I'd switched from Gauloises to Chesterfields. The smoke came and went like time itself. That's how I remember us that summer. We smoked because we were happy, we were happy because we smoked. The light flowed. The sun set the countryside on fire. We drove with the radio on, though we barely listened to it. We were too caught up in our own murmur.

All of a sudden, the speakers made a different noise. We were invaded by a tumult of sound. We turned up the volume. It was, the radio announced, some young foursome who were causing a stir among music lovers in England and Germany. Yoshie and I had never heard of them. I suppose that goes to show how much life we still had ahead of us. We'd never heard "Love Me Do."

In those days, there was an electricity around us young people that is difficult to explain. Everything had the feel of the first summer in a long time. We'd left behind the post–world war years. We'd signed the Évian

Accords, after slaughtering hundreds of thousands of Algerians. And the independence of our colonies was now a fact. We believed a better world was possible. Even capitalism pretended to care about the middle classes. It was in this climate of disconcerting happiness, of the yearning for postponed pleasures, that my generation moved from jazz to rock and roll.

I clearly recall those days on the coast. The fresh fish we devoured with the hunger the sea gives you. The white wine illuminating Yoshie's smile. His body moving in the sun on the beach at Palavas-les-Flots. His way of running with his arms by his sides.

It was there that I snorkeled for the first time. We loved it so much we bought our own snorkels. One evening, as the sun was going down and people were leaving, we went skinny-dipping. We started to fool around, to fondle each other underwater. And in the end, we couldn't resist the temptation. That was also, how could I forget, the first time I'd done it in water. I saw the whole world in slow motion, just before my life sped up forever. When he ejaculated, I dipped my head below the surface again and saw a medusa of semen float by and then gradually dissolve in the sea.

During that vacation, we looked up at the sky a lot. The universe has always made me dizzy. I find its beauty overwhelming. And yet it reminded Yoshie that nothing mattered very much. Staring into the sky makes me think of distances impossible to reach, and that makes me melancholy. To him, that same vastness suggested that we are part of something far greater than ourselves. I saw my own finiteness. He saw the continuity of everything. I talked to him about urgency and longing. He talked of relief and patience.

At one point during our discussion, I went to fetch the flashlight from the car. I switched it on, and pointed it up at the sky. Showing him how the tiny beam of light vanished only a short distance above us, I cried, You see? We can't get there.

A few months later, there arose the whole matter of the transfer. Me had been stepping up its operations in the United States for a while, and it was doing an increasing amount of business there. It was then that Me made Yoshie an offer, which, according to him, he couldn't refuse. To run the marketing department, or something like that, at the new branch in

New York. When he told me, I wept out of pride for him and fear for us. We argued about the move quite a lot. On the one hand, there was the company, and on the other, my students and my family. He couldn't stay here, and I didn't want to leave.

Our farewell was so dramatic it makes me laugh now. We made all sorts of promises to each other. We planned when we would next meet. We kept saying that this challenge would only strengthen our relationship, bring us closer together than ever. It would be a trial period of one or two years, we told ourselves. If the new job didn't work out, he would come back here. And if things went well, I could move to New York. Look for work over there. Or maybe we would get married: we'd have to see. After the initial shock, the idea began to appeal to me. I even started to study English.

The first few months were filled with passionate letters and endless phone calls. Writing to Yoshie was the high point of my day. Sitting there, alone, I had the impression he was listening and could understand me. His absence turned him into the perfect interlocutor. When I read his words, composed with the grammar we had labored over together, I had a wondrous sensation of happiness mixed with yearning. That frantic method of communication breathed new life into our feelings for each other. Suffering for love, I admit, made me feel special. As if I enjoyed a more intense personal life than my friends. The distance made me start to remember my boyfriend as better than he was. His good qualities grew. His defects diminished. In a manner of speaking, I fell in love with not seeing him.

After his departure, something strange happened to the city. I had difficulty recognizing the places we had walked together so many times. Every neighborhood, every street, every corner (Paris has a plethora of corners) seemed devoid of content. And that content was precisely our shared company, the sum of our gazes. Without Yoshie's foreign perspective, I no longer knew how to look at my own city.

During that time, I started to experience something unknown to me, which I would feel much too frequently after that. A sense of loneliness when I was alone. The sad realization that when I was alone, I wasn't in the company of somebody interesting. Before Yoshie and I met, I'd loved going to the cinema, to cafés, to the park on my own. Once he left, those activities seemed wearisome and rather absurd, like a parody of what we had once been. In my girlfriends' view, I had become a dependent woman and needed to readjust. I suspected they said this out of jealousy, because they'd never experienced a symbiotic relationship like ours.

When we spoke on the telephone, Yoshie assured me he was still here with me. Just as I was always there with him. He insisted that my image accompanied him everywhere in the new city, and whenever he discovered a place, he would show it to me in his mind. He'd look at it for the both of us. He enjoyed collecting all the things that we would soon experience together. And he would ask me, in a hushed voice on the other end of the phone, to do the same. I believed him because I wanted to believe him. Maybe he believed it too. Perhaps we nourished each other's faith.

Finally the time came to organize my long-awaited visit to New York. Our plan was to spend the summer together. Save up all our days off and tour the West Coast by car (Red, it has to be red! I'd begged him excitedly). Imagining us on the California freeways, hair blowing in the wind, made me ecstatically happy. At first, Yoshie participated in all the arrangements with his usual attentiveness. But, as my plans and ideas became more elaborate, he began to leave all the decisions to me. Whenever my husband and I take a trip somewhere together, he accuses me of wanting to control everything. I find that very interesting, considering he could be accused of the exact opposite. Of living in a state of total apathy.

The vacation drew near, and Yoshie's behavior became odd. He would alternate between extreme thoughtfulness and bouts of silence. Sometimes he took ages to reply to my letters. On other occasions, he sounded too effusive, unnaturally eloquent. I myself veered between euphoria and anguish. There were days when I recognized instantly his old affectionate voice, and days when he sounded alien to me, like someone imitating him. I was never sure which of my two boyfriends I was going to find on the telephone.

He explained that his new job required a degree of commitment he hadn't anticipated. That his responsibilities were more onerous than he had imagined. And that he was doing his best to get ahead with his work in order to free up the summer. To free up the summer, he said. As if my arrival were another item in his calendar. He seemed worried that I might be suffering. This condescension was new, and alarming. Occasionally,

I would ask him certain questions, and he seemed to avoid answering them.

Fool that I was, it still took me a while longer to understand (but not forgive) the reason for his ambivalence. I imagine he was afraid to hurt me by telling me the truth. And to keep my hopes alive by saying nothing. I don't know why we seek complicated explanations for obvious problems. Now that my bedroom has witnessed so many secrets, I see that the real problem isn't the lie itself. The terrible thing is the chain of secrets, cover-ups, and omissions that are necessary to sustain the first lie.

Only when my departure date was imminent did Yoshie tell me the truth. I felt I was dying, and at the same time, liberated. I remember that contradiction clearly. He suggested I come to New York anyway, that we end things calmly, face-to-face, and that I allow him to pay for my trip. I angrily refused. It seemed to me the most humiliating flight in the world. I preferred to break off all contact with him. I stopped answering his calls and letters.

For a while, I couldn't say for how long, he made an effort to keep in touch. But this pretense that we were friends seemed to me cowardly. Things hurt less if they're clear. I continued to ignore him until he gave in. I went through the necessary suffering and got on with my life. I never spoke to him again.

To what extent could my story with Yoshie have influenced the speed at which all things happened afterward? I met my husband eight months before we married. We moved in together straightaway, riding a wave of recklessness that we called love. I felt that the pinnacle of happiness was the ability to stop thinking about each step. I didn't want to plan the future anymore. I chose to plunge headlong into it.

Our three children arrived almost one after the other. This may sound strange, but for me, that was the only possible way to be a mother. As a very young girl, I'd had so many reservations, excuses, and mistaken prejudices about it, that there was no other way for me to commit to having a family. I neutralized my doubts through action. I overcame my fears by ceasing to focus on myself. If I'd known how much relief there is in caring for others, to what extent our own lives become clearly defined and ordered thanks to the lives we make ourselves responsible for, I would have had them sooner.

Yoshie had no wish to make a serious commitment. To some extent, that immaturity makes sense to me. How much worse it would've been for him to get to the end and then run away. It's ironic how politically active men of my generation found it hard to commit in other areas. Their personal lives somehow refuted their politics.

To be honest (am I being honest?), sometimes I worry that my daughter Adélaïde's indifference to motherhood isn't just an ideological position, more or less inspired by the education we gave her about her freedoms as a woman, but also a rejection of the type of mother I've been. According to my husband, I have a tendency to be overprotective. He thinks this has had negative effects on our two daughters. The younger one has turned out rather submissive, and the older one is extremely independent. One obeyed me too much. The other is forever contradicting me.

Adélaïde is so busy with her lectures and conferences that we hardly ever see her, except for those perfunctory Sunday visits. We feel more like part of her tutoring roster than her parents. Muriel doesn't seem able to tear herself away from that sleepy town where my son-in-law's parents live. The views are charming, and I don't deny they grow excellent vegetables. Apart from that, what the hell is my daughter doing there? And what can I expect from our son, Jean-Pierre? Since his separation, the poor boy falls in love every year. His main activity seems to be starting relationships and breaking them off. And so his concerns are always elsewhere.

To top it all off, my granddaughter, Colette, just got married. That was the biggest shock. When did we grow so very old? I realize that from now on she will hardly ever come to see us. At least not until she has children of her own.

It hurts to be told that I'm needy. I feel this description simplifies who I am. I've always tried to be there for my children, to be a help, not a hindrance. Have I failed in that? Or is their father mistaken when he judges me? Young girls these days seem slightly overwhelmed by family life. As if they've suddenly noticed the sort of burdens that their grandmothers and mothers had to bear. I try to remind myself that we aren't to blame for this.

When such thoughts torment me, I call Adélaïde and she reassures me. As she rushes about all over the place, she insists I've been a wonderful mother to all three of them. That her decision not to have children is a personal choice and in no way reflects upon us. What's more, the reason she hasn't started a family, among other things, is because she realizes she will never be as good a mother as me. It pains me to hear this. As if I'm being punished for mistakes I don't know about. Whenever I talk to my kids, I end up feeling they know more about me than I do. Precisely the things I most need to know.

As for my husband, well, same old, same old. He is heroically absent, and when he's at home, he wears the expression of someone who has abandoned the troops on the Normandy beachheads. I accepted long ago that he would never retire from his research. We don't get on so badly. I know of worse marriages. After all these years, we agree without the need to speak. We even argue without raising our voices.

He behaves more or less the same toward the children. He is interested from a distance. He doesn't retain details. He asks them about things that happened ages ago. We must put ourselves in his shoes. When someone decides to become responsible for the well-being of the entire human race, a case of flu in the family must seem very trivial.

More than once, he has criticized me for not understanding his professional commitment. Untrue. What I find hard to comprehend is not that he loves his work, but that this love leaves so little room for him to love others. Personally, I would have suffered if I'd been absent when my loved ones needed me. It amazes me how many men accept a situation that will sooner or later turn against them.

My husband says that I think like this because I've never really had a vocation. And because I chose to give up working at a certain point in my life. That theory puzzles me. Looking back, I don't feel I made a choice. But that circumstance, the needs of my family, certain habits in our relationship, ended up pushing us into our respective roles. That our life moved in an inevitable, and for me unfavorable, direction. Am I fooling myself?

One thing I'm sure of is that I never wanted to depend financially on anyone. That happened to us gradually. And I regret it now. When I was younger, I used to wonder if I should have secured a steady job before we had Adélaïde. If I should have made more of an effort to carry on teaching after I had Muriel, and especially after Jean-Pierre. I try not to dwell on these things now. The problem is, I have a lot more time to think about them than I used to.

I'd rather not know how long it's been since I last saw Yoshie. Tallying the years terrifies me. That reminds me of Gide, who said nothing threatens our happiness so much as the memory of our happiness. I'm not sure that's true. Sometimes we old people are happy only when remembering. Which is why we end up sweeping the most unpleasant memories under the rug. In the end, only one thing is for certain. That the present, this age I am now, is the only time in my life I won't get to look back on from afar. I'll never see what my life is like now.

I remember everything, and everything seems so distant. Not just Yoshie, but the way I was back then. My life without my family. It's as if your children construct your future and they also monopolize it. They throw up a barrier between you and the life you had before them. Or rather, everything that existed before them belongs to an imaginary time. That's why I haven't thought about Yoshie in so many years. And yet lately, with all that's happened in Japan, I think of practically nothing else.

It's not that I miss him all of a sudden. I don't miss my youth either. If anything, I miss the circumstances of my life back then, or rather the lack of them. All that I could have been when I was still nobody. If I could travel back to those days, I would just stay perfectly still, filled with wonder, contemplating the brutal vastness of the future. That's the closest thing to happiness I can imagine.

If he's been in my thoughts lately, why don't I try to get in touch? It's hard to explain. I fear not being part of his memories. I wouldn't even know what to say to him, or how. Because there is no language of the past.

Or is there?

3

THE SIZE
OF THE
ISLAND

YOSHIE WATANABE GREW UP IN NAGASAKI, the city of his childhood and his forgetting. They had moved there because his father, Tsutomu, worked as a marine engineer for a zaibatsu armaments manufacturer. Not that the move to Nagasaki entailed any drastic change for the family. After all, they remained in the same region, and only a prefecture away from his native Kokura, at the time a town that produced munitions.

While it was true that Tsutomu worked too hard (for which even his brother in Tokyo used to criticize him), the family was comfortable. But the war complicated the situation: longer hours, less money, a worse diet.

Mr. Watanabe remembers how rice and sweet potatoes became staples throughout the war. When he asked why they couldn't eat something different, his mother replied that sweet potatoes possessed magical properties that made children invincible. Nowadays, he can't help feeling a vague anxiety whenever he tastes one of these root vegetables.

From time to time, on a weekend, fish would appear at their table, colorful and juicy. And, on rare occasions, a few morsels of meat—treats in the rice, cleverly rationed by his mother, Shinoe. Not very often (because of the scarcity and the expense) nor too infrequently (so as to keep the children's expectations alive). Shinoe succeeded in turning these privations into a game.

Their mother had instilled in them a rule they didn't dare disobey: never throw anything away even if it was broken or old. It's a crime, she would tell them, this thing might come in handy. His father laughed at her obsession with holding on to every object. It would take Watanabe years, at least until he lived on his own, to understand what his mother had meant. If we don't know how to put something to use, then we are the useless ones.

The family of five lived north of the city, in a traditional house with wood and tiles, close to the School of Medicine. The bells of Urakami Cathedral would declare that Yoshie must finish eating his breakfast and leave for school with his two little sisters, Nagae and Sadako. Their father (who had brought them up in an unorthodox Buddhist faith based on little Zen poems) told them they may just as well have the God of the Catholics ringing in their ears, since you never knew what gods you might need. He and his sisters would get to school a few minutes before eight thirty. Punctuality, insisted Tsutomu, means arriving early. If you arrive on time, you are already late.

Yoshie mostly got on well with his schoolmates. He was charming enough to attract them and shy enough to avoid their resentment. He was a good student without having to try too hard, which allowed his grades to go more or less unnoticed. His sole enemy was Yukio Yamamoto, a tirelessly competitive child with strident hairstyles, always ready to suck up to the teachers or bully his classmates. The only good thing about him that Mr. Watanabe can think of is that he taught him how to hate. Which, in his estimation, was a lesson well learned.

The other lesson he learned was about his hands. He preferred his left, which felt more agile and precise. It drew animals that his right hand couldn't. Until his teachers made him see that to write with the wrong hand was a form of treachery.

During his first year at school, a soldier came to show them a map of Asia. The Japanese empire was shaded in red and included several regions of China. The soldier, Watanabe recalls, told them about Chinamen who ate their children, Chinese girls who beat their mothers and Chinese boys who spat at their fathers, Chinese teachers who mistreated their students. However, most of them have no wish to live in this savage way, the soldier explained. They envy our glorious nation, he said. That is why we are fighting over there. To free them from their misery, so that they can live like us.

Throughout the following school year, the principal himself would enter the classroom to inform the students about the patriotic army's exploits. Battles in which they were heavily outnumbered, or which even appeared lost, would end happily in a victory. The war was always about to be won. And the enemy on the verge of surrendering to the emperor. This was an image that thrilled Yoshie: thousands and thousands of American soldiers lined up on their knees.

During the lunch recess, he and his sisters would gobble up the rice balls and boiled sweet potatoes Shinoe had cooked for them. Which made their schoolmates jealous, especially after Yukio Yamamoto made it his business to tell everyone what was on the Watanabes' menu. Spurred on by hunger, the children would chant before the break: *We were born thanks to His Imperial Majesty and for His Imperial Majesty we shall die. If His Imperial Majesty gives us a single grain of rice, we shall not waste it.* Still in her first year, Nagae sometimes cried because she missed their mother. And Sadako would sing in her ear.

In his gym class, Yoshie pretended to perform pull-ups. He would hang by his arms, unable to lift himself above the metal bar. As soon as the teacher turned his back, he and his friends would play imaginary Ping-Pong. The first to reach ten points had the right to pull anyone's hair. Yukio countered by getting hold of a real ball and began to organize matches during recess, which soon put an end to Yoshie's invisible games. Meanwhile, on the playground, his sisters made straw dolls. The dolls were the enemy and the girls would stab them with bits of bamboo.

If anything excited Yoshie, it was going on excursions. The more distant the place, the more interesting he imagined it would be. He was frequently disappointed. Mr. Watanabe can recall maybe two unforgettable excursions in his childhood. The first, with the whole family, was to the city of Shimabara. The forty kilometers from Nagasaki seemed an immensity to him that day. He was most impressed by the volcano.

According to his father, Mount Unzen had last erupted a hundred and fifty years before, and had caused the biggest volcanic disaster in history. However, now it was at peace. Yoshie peered at Mount Unzen in the distance with a mixture of fascination and incredulity.

If a volcano can't explode anymore, he asked his parents, what use is it? Volcanoes are of no use, his father replied. Yoshie still didn't understand how something so big could be useless. But why is it still there? he insisted. His mother explained to him that mountains spit fire when they are alive and stop when they die. This new piece of information only perplexed Yoshie further. So mountains are alive?

The second excursion was very different. On Sunday, August 5, 1945, he accompanied his father on a brief trip to the city of Hiroshima, in the neighboring Chūgoku region. The aim was to obtain new parts for the

Nagasaki shipyard. To Yoshie, who had frequently begged to go with him, this was proof of how grown-up he was: Dad and me, working together! It also gave him the perfect excuse, at least for a couple of days, to get out of doing the homework he'd been given during the holidays.

In response to Shinoe's repeated objections (she considered it dangerous to visit a city that was a naval base and a rallying point for the imperial army), Tsutomu reminded her that Hiroshima had never been bombed. Which meant it couldn't be one of the enemy's prime targets, he explained to his wife. In fact, he added, it was less dangerous than Nagasaki, where they had mounted attacks on ports and factories in the southwest. Not to mention the thirteen students bombed the previous week at the university. So she needn't get alarmed over a simple train journey.

When Shinoe got down on her knees (a gesture that was to remain Mr. Watanabe's clearest image of his mother) and implored her husband not to go, or at least to reconsider his decision to take the boy with him, Tsutomu simply insisted: We can't stop living just because there's a war.

AT A QUARTER PAST EIGHT THE FOLLOWING MORNING, when the B-29 *Enola Gay*, named in honor of the pilot's mother (exactly what kind of feelings did he harbor toward his creator?), dropped its uranium bomb Little Boy at the beginning of the working day, Yoshie was walking with his father some three kilometers from the center of the blast.

They had just crossed Kanko Bridge. People were doing their best to go about their business as usual. Shops had opened, though they had few goods to sell. His father moved with the urgency of Mondays. Or perhaps, seen from the point of view of Mr. Watanabe's memory, with a degree of anxiety. Yoshie had difficulty keeping up with him. Two steps of his equaled one of Tsutomu's. What was worse, his shoe was chafing him.

Not long before, the air raid sirens had sounded again. No one paid them much attention. Almost every day, enemy planes flew over, dropping pamphlets, which he was forbidden to read. In those days, such things didn't prevent people from doing what they had to. They simply took precautions (water, fire extinguishers, first aid kits) and carried on. In fact, the sirens had already sounded twice the night before. His father had continued to undress (flesh folds on his tummy, armpit hair), and Yoshie had helped him into his yukata. Then they had both fallen asleep. Tsutomu's snoring had protected them. With that racket, nothing and no one would've dared come near.

Suddenly, Yoshie could hear engines in the distance. He looked up, cupping his hand to shade his eyes. It was an aircraft. Just one aircraft. It didn't make much noise. It didn't even frighten him. Nothing like those squadrons that terrified him so much. Nor did Tsutomu show signs of fear. But Yoshie felt, or perhaps Watanabe now thinks he did, his father squeeze his hand.

Yoshie saw it fly by for a few seconds. Like a model airplane. A four-propellered one. With a sheen of silver. He loved it.

His shoe was hurting his foot more and more. Yoshie stopped in his tracks. Tsutomu ordered him to keep walking. Yoshie wriggled free of his father's hand. Ran to lean against a wall, and bent over to adjust his shoe. That wall painted yellow. His father was waiting for him up ahead, at the corner, a look of impatience on his face. He called his name. He ordered him to hurry up.

The aircraft let something drop. A trace in a sky with no clouds. No more than a trace in the sky.

The flash filled the horizon. X-ray light. The skeleton. The blindness.

Swept off his feet by a wave of heat, Yoshie flew through the air. The blast spread and seemed to have no end.

Afterward, an emptying. Darkness in broad daylight. The negative of the sky.

When Yoshie opened his eyes and saw the blackness, he thought he was dead. That this was death. But around him things started to clear, and soon he recognized his father's body a few yards away, his head beneath an uprooted tree, and then he knew that he was still alive.

He coughed. He spat. Felt his limbs. He could see only a few cuts on his hands and arms. The skin on his back was burning. His muscles ached, as if he'd been straining them for hours.

His disbelief stunned him more than the hit. The wall. That yellow wall. His shoe, his father, his disobedience.

Then he saw the mushroom and a glow ascending.

He tried to shift the tree trunk off his father. For some reason, Watanabe reflects, possibly because of the comics he used to read, he was sincerely astonished to find he couldn't do it. He tried to rouse his father. He called out his name several times. He couldn't bring himself to look at his face.

Soon enough, he realized that there would be no reply. No reaction. Zero movement. He lay down next to his father, and for a while copied his stillness, hoping this gesture might unite them.

Only then did he become aware of the screams all around him, the fire, the crackling, the crunching, the collapsing. There was more. Much more. All of a sudden his focus widened.

Deafened by so many things shattering, Yoshie wandered in search of assistance. He wanted help moving the tree. The buildings weren't there anymore. Only a few were left, in positions he had never seen before. There was a hole, Watanabe remembers, where the city had been. A map erased. Hiroshima was now a scar the size of Hiroshima.

Yoshie scanned the horizon. He could see, mysteriously in place, the dome of the Prefectural Industrial Promotion Hall. The same one his father had proudly pointed out to him the previous afternoon. Still a long way from becoming a symbol.

Everything made of wood was blazing. Every house burning in its own way. A wind of a hearth, or of an open oven, began to blow. As a precaution, or perhaps instinctively, Yoshie skirted around the most devastated area. He couldn't have known it, but it was also the one most exposed to radiation.

On his search for the help that nobody could give him, he saw charcoal shadows. Shadows on walls. He saw burnt objects that he didn't even know could burn. Nothing had kept its color; the mushroom had drained it away. Debris and bodies were intermingled. Everything was in pieces. A type of jigsaw puzzle that, Watanabe can see now, was never meant to be assembled. He saw the same expression on every face he passed. The same corpse, over and over.

He had no saliva, and he couldn't find his tongue. He heard the babble of a spring. He walked toward some children more or less his age, their heads surrounding a pipe from which flowed a stream of water. The sound was music. When Yoshie tried to approach, the other children barred his way with pushes, scratches, kicks. Their tongues lapped ceaselessly. One boy raised his head and glanced sidelong at him. His lids were so swollen that he couldn't open his eyes.

Yoshie discovered that few of the faces left looked like faces. He touched his own brow, his nose, his chin. Everything appeared to be in place. The only pain he felt was from the cuts on his arms. And the stinging on his back. Many people ran past him. Hair like firewood. Cheeks like balloons. Eyes like slits. They dived headfirst into the river. Others stopped short, plunging instead into the water tanks. He still remembers feeling revulsion rather than compassion for them. Not so much sympathy as disgust.

He considered returning to the tree to watch over his father's body. He glanced about. Realized he couldn't even see where he'd set off from. With each step, he could hear Tsutomu's voice among the other voices.

His scream among all the screams. When he tried to follow the sound, it faded until it vanished. Everywhere, he came across people crying for help, arms flailing amid the wreckage. Yoshie didn't stop to help anyone. He simply passed by, in a trance, walking along the river.

Something glistening on the ground caught his eye. A pot shone in the August sun. The sun roasting itself inside there. Slowly, Yoshie peered into the pot and saw that his face was still his face. Among the debris, he also discovered a pocket watch, with arrow-shaped hands. He stooped to pick it up. The glass front hadn't a scratch on it, but the mechanism had stopped. He tried to wind it up. Stare as he might, the hands indicated the same time. A quarter past eight. A quarter past eight. He has kept it since. He hasn't tried to fix it.

In the distance, Yoshie saw a black rain begin to fall, as though painted drop by drop. Mr. Watanabe can barely admit his fascination with that rain back then, not knowing what it meant. Can it possibly retain any beauty in his memory? Does it deserve to be remembered as he saw it?

The air began to cool. A rainbow enveloped the remains of the city, its ends tying them up like a garbage bag. When Yoshie lowered his gaze again, he saw a horse in flames galloping by.

On the banks of the Ōta, Yoshie at last found refuge in a school. The ruins of the building were being turned into a first aid post. A hospital without beds or doctors, where people came to lie on the ground. Or, in the more serious cases, on a desk. Yoshie felt reassured by it being a school. It was the only place with which he could identify. The students' drawings still hung on one wall. His little sister Nagae could draw better than that, he thought.

A woman offered him water. Without alarm, she said, There's blood in your eye. Although it didn't hurt, Yoshie ran to rinse it in the river. The blood washed away easily. It wasn't his. Bodies drifted slowly past him.

He'd entered the first aid post to seek help for his father. He soon saw that no one was in a condition to provide it. Mr. Watanabe has never been able to convey what he saw in that place. Not for a lack of words, but rather of meaning.

More than the suppurations, which he avoided looking at, what

shocked Yoshie most were the women's backs. Many bore the marks of
the clothes they had been wearing at the time of the blast. Dark-colored
clothes, he learned, had been imprinted on their skin, while lighter colors
absorbed less energy and therefore left fewer traces. And so he discovered
that, as well as the yellow wall he'd leaned against by chance, dressing in
white had protected him.

The tangles of clothing and skin repulsed him more than the wounds
themselves. He noticed many men who looked like they had bowl cuts, because they were wearing hats when the bomb exploded. Skin had become a
focal point of horror. It felt, they cried, as if they were tearing it off.

Few doctors were left. Many seemed in a similar state as the patients
they were treating. Spots that had hot running water and strips of cloth,
two luxuries in short supply, were turned into makeshift operating rooms.
The wounded got worse after being treated. They caught infections that
festered in the summer heat. Reduced to chemistry, they died uttering the
word *water*. Yoshie couldn't understand why the worst affected were left to
die instead of being tended to first.

Piles upon piles of them were cremated beside Sakae Bridge, Kyo
Bridge, Hijiyama Bridge, at the rate of matches. The stench of those bonfires would disturb his sense of smell forever.

Contrary to what one might think, Watanabe recalls, many people in
the refuge were concerned with details of seemingly no importance. Finding some geta among the debris, or at least a pair of socks, was enough to
bring solace. Any trifle could take on, for a moment, the significance of
a lifesaver. And also talking to someone. Telling them. Making sure that
this had really happened. Each person recounted, over and over, the same
minute. Like the watch that Yoshie had found.

A clerk was thrown against a filing cabinet, which acted as a barricade.

A teenager ignored his mother's protests, as he did every morning, and
stayed locked in the bathroom, which became a bunker.

An old woman managed to cover her head with the pan she was going
to use to cook vegetables.

A police officer stepping out of his house had time, as the flash spread,
to roll under the stairs.

Two boys, who were sweeping the fire walls at their school, collapsed
on top of one another and were able to help each other out of the rubble.

A woman was hanging out her family's laundry and the walls surrounding her flat roof protected her. She was still clasping a T-shirt.

A civil servant managed to get out of the carriage of the streetcar he was on, only to discover a line of corpses digging their nails into the shoulder of the person in front of them.

A music teacher was saved by her piano while she waited for a student who never turned up. Some of her neighbors had accused her of high treason when they heard her playing.

One man said nothing and just walked around and around in circles, not listening to anyone.

Everyone talked about the whistling. The whistling before it happened. A subtlety heralding the destruction. Some people's eardrums had been pierced and even then, they could hear it.

At the time, each person believed that their house, their office, their factory, their school was the only one that had been bombed. After the explosion, they explained, they couldn't understand why no one came to help them. How could they be so completely ignored? Maybe that's how tragedies work, reflects Watanabe. We make them ours to the point that we are incapable of believing there are others. The fact that there are is both a comfort and an affront.

When the survivors managed to dig themselves out and look around them, there was no name for what they saw. Where were the craters? What was all this nothingness? There was no framework. Only a fear of everything and an understanding of nothing. This they said without words, even as they continued to search for them.

Yoshie saw a young girl curled up taking notes. She was perhaps the only person in the refuge who had found a corner where she could observe her own suffering. Watanabe remembers her well because that night she got him a blanket to sleep on. And because she was called Sadako, like one of his sisters.

Rumors began to spread like the fires outside. Some spoke of fifty thousand or a hundred thousand dead, possibly more. Figures Yoshie was incapable of imagining with any accuracy. And which years later, when he was a numbers expert, he still found impossible to comprehend.

And yet none of this was mentioned in the war communiqué that day. They were forced to resist until the end of something they didn't know.

In the shelter, the same questions were passed back and forth. What type of weapon had attacked them? What had they done to deserve such punishment? Nothing, they repeated to themselves, nothing whatsoever. They had simply obeyed their parents. Who had obeyed the authorities. Who had obeyed the emperor. Who had obeyed what was written in the stars.

What was most needed were water and shade. A human chain was formed to fill receptacles from the Ōta. Yoshie went over and was immediately handed a bucket, which was too heavy for him. Someone took it from him and the chain continued.

Jostling at the river's edge, the flames had the shape of waves. A tsunami of fire.

Many people gazed toward where a grove of trees had always stood. The earth was a naked body. The pines now looked like folded umbrellas.

The burn victims needed shade. They piled up wood and other debris, which promptly collapsed. No cloud softened the rays. What constituted good weather? The sun beat down. The sun.

As the *Enola Gay* retreated from the skies above Hiroshima, the co-pilot, Captain Lewis, whispered: My God, what have we done?

The pilot, Colonel Tibbets, replied: We did what we had to do.

An entire nation occupied one seat or the other.

A DAY AND A HALF LATER, Yoshie was included among a list of passengers who were to travel by train to Nagasaki the next morning. Because of where it was located in the city, the train station hadn't suffered too much damage, and a few locomotives were once again up and running. Residents, pregnant women, and children had priority. All he could think of was returning to his mother and sisters. He checked the time constantly. It seemed as though his stopped watch had infected all the other clocks.

Mr. Watanabe has a clear recollection of that night. Agitation and fear kept him from closing his eyes. The absence of light amplified the noises in the darkness. The echo of the prayers for the dead, *namu amida butsu, namu amida butsu,* alternated with cries of *water, water.* Bones spluttered and crackled along the riverside. And beyond, a blade of silence. He couldn't hear the insects that so fascinated him. A summer without insects couldn't be summer. Yoshie tried to calm himself by repeating the syllables for mother, *haha, haha,* and by imagining his room.

In the early hours, there was a smell of roasted sardines. He sat up with a start, and headed toward the river. Then he saw they were burning bodies. He returned to his floor tile in the refuge and curled up under his blanket. A man sleeping beside him opened his eyes very wide. It seemed to Yoshie that the night was pouring into them. The worst part, murmured the man, is that there's no waking up.

As streaks of light began to appear, Yoshie's yawns became more frequent. Soon, once the sun was up, he would go to the station. He had to wait only a little. Hold out a bit, a few more minutes, no time at all. His head tilted forward. His eyelids drooped. He thought of asking the man next to him to help him stay awake. Daylight was arriving. The images were fading.

When he opened his eyes, it took him a moment to understand what he was doing there, what had happened to the world he woke up to. He sat up with a jolt. His joints cracked. Sleeping outside wasn't what he'd imagined.

Many of the others were already on their feet. Yoshie asked what time it was and started to run toward the train station, on the far side of the river.

The first bridge was damaged. Tree trunks had been used to block access to it. The shape of the railings, a shadow in negative, was imprinted in white on the ground. To avoid a detour to the next bridge, Yoshie considered swimming. But he scarcely knew how. And the idea of floating among corpses terrified him.

He walked on, until he came upon some boys inching their way across two girders, which spanned the river in a V-shape. Once they reached the end of one girder, they had to swim only a short way to the other. He followed them cautiously. The boys jeered at his slowness. They yelled that he would drown and the current would sweep him away.

His trousers dripping water, Yoshie ran as fast as his legs would carry him. He hurried across Enko Bridge, a stone's throw from the train station. He recognized it. He saw it growing. It was already before him. He reached the entrance. He pushed his way through and arrived on the platform gasping for breath. Only to discover that his train had just departed, leaving him in Hiroshima.

With no other plan, Yoshie returned to the first aid post. Inside the building there were no more supplies, not even space to lie down. The man next to him mussed up his bangs in greeting and didn't question him.

Some army vehicles came to take away many of the wounded to the island of Ninoshima. He was surprised to see them resist.

More trucks soon arrived. Together with a group of children and mothers with babies, they moved Yoshie to a reception center in Eba, in the south of the city. A soldier assured them that from there, attempts would be made to locate their relatives. The girl who had gotten him the blanket, Sadako, smiled at him in the distance.

On the way to Eba, he met two students from the school where he had taken refuge. One was very ill. He couldn't swallow anything without immediately throwing up. And yet he continued to clutch the lunch box his mother had prepared for him, before she'd gone out to help with safety and maintenance tasks. Noticing he hadn't touched its contents, his classmate asked for permission to eat his lunch if he died. The boy told him he would think about it.

Another boy told Yoshie that, unlike those of some of his friends, his parents had decided not to evacuate him from the city. They considered it his duty to continue his studies as soon as the vacation ended. That life should carry on as normal. Yoshie remembered his father had said exactly the same thing.

The next morning, many of the passengers from the train he'd missed were to die in Nagasaki, together with his mother, his sisters, and tens of thousands of others. The B-29 *Bockscar*, piloted by Major Sweeney, dropped a plutonium bomb near the Mitsubishi arms factory. This second bomb, named Fat Man, supposedly in honor of Winston Churchill, produced a fireball that burned like the sun. A sun shattered into pieces. Fat Man. Is there a connection, wonders Watanabe, between humanizing a bomb and dehumanizing a people?

His family wouldn't have the good fortune of being saved by the terrain. On one side of the hill, survival. On the other, the void. The explosion occurred in the Urakami valley, on a tennis court next to the School of Medicine, exactly half a kilometer from the cathedral whose bells Yoshie used to hear every morning.

The reception center was surrounded by a field with pools of water, debris, bits of machinery, and backs of people floating up to the surface. Flies swarmed back and forth. Like Yoshie, they distrusted that water. It was a color he'd never seen before. A mixture of oil, earth, and blood.

The flies played a leading role in those days. They buzzed with the insistence of a premonition. They were attracted only to certain patches of skin on the wounded. For all that the doctors succeeded in treating the burns, their patients' insides were liquefying. Human anatomy was no longer as they'd studied. The bomb had stripped them of knowledge.

Although it surprises him now, Mr. Watanabe can't forget how accustomed he grew to the suffering of others. His childhood games had taught him that a word repeated many times ends up losing its meaning. The repetition of pain seemed to obey the same rule. What was the meaning of *nausea, blood, agony*? Bodies seemingly without harm would collapse all of a sudden. They were heaped up, doused with fuel, and burned.

One afternoon, Yoshie saw a nurse help her colleague who was in labor.

At that moment, he discovered where children came from, and that his parents had lied to him. The following morning, the midwife was dead. Bringing forth life and losing it were one and the same job. The summer sky insisted on parading its blueness, adding to the refugees' frustration. As if, in the midst of calamity, they were waiting for the heavens to offer an opinion.

Watanabe recalls the density of people's rage in the south of Hiroshima. A kind of crust that adhered to and united them, a solidarity in reverse, that resulted less in sympathy toward victims than in a hatred of the enemy.

Some mothers' milk dried up. Babies were passed from breast to breast, suckling a few drops from each mother. The children now belonged to all mothers. Or no one belonged to anyone anymore. Of the many curses he heard uttered in that place, one in particular still echoes in his head. It came from a mother clutching the remains of her child in her arms. Without swearing or raising her voice, she said: I wish this upon them. Exactly this.

They had to wait another week—during which there was an attempted uprising and the Ministry of War declared its intention to fight to the death—until the government finally announced its surrender. A word that, in any event, Emperor Hirohito abstained from pronouncing during his radio speech. The first one to unveil his voice to the world. And the last one, if Watanabe is not mistaken, that an emperor would address to the nation until the Fukushima disaster.

Their flag had been transformed into a halo of blood on a background of bones. Empires fall, mountains endure.

But even so, Watanabe thinks, the Allies knew Japan was close to surrender. Negotiations of the terms of their defeat had been ongoing for several months. Their navy and air force had barely been functioning. Their cities were under attack every day. Food was scarce and transport networks were starting to collapse. The Pacific islands had been taken. The Third Reich had already surrendered. What doubt could there have been?

Possibly around March, he concedes, during the bombing of Tokyo, his country had still been an enemy to fear. Even in June, up until the Battle of Okinawa, there may have been some reservations. But, by the summer, absolutely none. Not in August. Not on the sixth. Nor on the ninth. Saving the world, warning the world. What was the difference?

Prior to their defeat, the Nazis were suspected of experimenting with nuclear energy. Both sides were fighting from their laboratories as well. Of course, Watanabe reasons, this was a justification for building the bomb. Not for dropping it. Maybe that was why those scientists who contributed to its invention, including Einstein, started a campaign against its use. Their advice was ignored: it was no longer necessary. The Allies had declared that peace and harmony reigned once more. Any further questions were obliterated, just as the two cities had been. The terror was over. A new terror had begun.

In early September, after a search through the debris and the bodies that he would prefer not to remember, Yoshie learned that none of his family in Nagasaki had survived. Occasionally, he still wonders whether they felt any pain or if they evaporated on the spot. If they tried to flee or called out a name.

His aunt and uncle on his father's side, Ineko and Shiro, who had lived for years in Tokyo, managed to locate him. They took him in. That was how he went to live in the capital, which was gradually starting to rebuild itself. Rubble and tunnels surrounded his new home.

His aunt Ineko would often remind him how, after he arrived in Tokyo, for many weeks Yoshie slept, ate loads of *yōkan*, and remained plunged in an impenetrable silence. When he started to speak again, he didn't say a single word about his time in Hiroshima. Nor did his aunt and uncle think it good for him to be reminded of that. Forgetting was a daily medicine.

Almost directly opposite their house stood a former police station, now filled with members of the occupying forces. At the entrance fluttered the star-spangled banner, to which his aunt and uncle seemed averse, but which Yoshie, in spite of everything, found luminous, brimming with sky. It was around then that he first tasted ice cream: those multicolored balls that vanished into the Americans' unintelligible mouths. He had difficulty persuading Shiro to buy him one. His uncle maintained that losing the war was no excuse to imitate the enemy's customs. That's when Mr. Watanabe developed a quirk that has stayed with him to this day: choosing desserts according to their color.

This was also the first time he had slept in a strange house. Could wander around a different bedroom, kitchen, and bathroom. Explore shelves and open drawers. This was a discovery that had immeasurable consequences.

Whenever the opportunity arose, Yoshie would try to gain entry to the house of a neighbor or classmate. Nothing excited his curiosity, his embarrassment, and his pleasure more than snooping around inside. Becoming familiar with other houses—which he always found more interesting than his own—showed him that it was possible to live in a different way. With new furnishings, spaces, rules. On the eve of his tenth birthday, without ever having reached the boundaries of his island, Yoshie had become an emigrant.

He was amazed to discover that, contrary to what he'd imagined, not all the cities at war had had their own atom bomb. Uncle Shiro revealed this information with visible unease, before adding that certain topics weren't suitable for children. He was even more astonished when, at school, he learned that only two cities in the world had experienced it. Yoshie couldn't help but feel absurdly proud that he knew both of them. Nobody else in his class could say the same. He was unaware that between five and ten thousand *hibakusha* lived in Tokyo.

As though they had been trained, recalls Watanabe, his fellow classmates rarely inquired about it. His teachers, especially at first, treated him with a concern he found most agreeable. They didn't even scold him for spending hours in a trance, detached from his surroundings, drawing in his notebook, doodling eyes, and more eyes. An almond with a black spiral inside.

The only subjects that caught his attention were math and language arts, two excellent ways to use thinking as an escape. He also quite liked history, although it was taught very differently than in Nagasaki. The textbooks were filled with pretty illustrations. One contained a list of all the adversities their great nation had suffered, a list Yoshie was quick to memorize: "Fires, earthquakes, tsunamis, viruses, wars, riots, and others." That last category was the most terrifying.

When his teachers—seldom and fleetingly—did mention the war, they would allude to the bombs as if they were natural disasters. They spoke of them only as dates, framing the current era of reconstruction and peace. Nobody had dropped the bombs. They'd simply fallen.

On one occasion, the students were asked in what natural form they would choose to be reborn. They excitedly cried out the names of different animals. When Yoshie's turn came, as his aunt Ineko would remind him for the rest of her life, he said he'd like to be turned into sand. And not just any old sand, he specified: the kind at the bottom of the ocean, so that no one could tread on him.

IT'S A MONTH AFTER the earthquake and the tsunami. The disaster at the Fukushima nuclear plant has monopolized the country's news, debate, and imagination. The International Atomic Energy Agency has raised the incident to the highest possible categorization on its scale: the same as Chernobyl a quarter of a century ago. It's spring.

Every day, Mr. Watanabe is outraged by the conflation of the two catastrophes, the seismic and the atomic. An earthquake is unavoidable, he argues in his discussions, a natural phenomenon. But a nuclear power plant, like a bomb, is man-made. There's no comparison between the devastation they cause.

Even the notion of a *natural* disaster strikes him as increasingly suspicious. Earthquakes and tsunamis occur spontaneously, that is incontrovertible. But before they happen, precautionary measures are planned. Financed. Developed. And the response to them depends on training, and especially on the authorities. All of these factors are controllable, can reduce or increase the amount of damage. That's why, in the strange arithmetic of catastrophes, a magnitude 7 earthquake in Haiti can be greater than a magnitude 9 in Japan. Watanabe thinks that should be the real news.

Throughout this long month, news reports about the nuclear plant in Fukushima have created a ladder of alarm, denials, and omissions. He has been scaling it rung by rung. Now he looks down with the dizziness of a climber who makes the mistake of wanting to gauge how far he's climbed.

The weekend after the earthquake, more than two hundred thousand people were evacuated from the immediate area surrounding the nuclear power plant. The explosion in the first reactor left four people injured, and a fresh explosion in the third reactor wounded another eleven. The electricity company assured everyone that the temperature was stabilizing and that the emergency was over. That same day, Watanabe recalls, another explosion, in the second reactor, split part of the containment vessel. The Nuclear Safety Agency had no choice but to admit that there was a probable radiation leak.

At the moment of the announcement it was raining in Tokyo. He was listening to the radio with his eyes fixed on the picture window: the raindrops grew, collided, fused. They usurped the image and distorted the world. With the latest news the rain became something to be feared. The changeable winds were a portent like in ancient times. As the level of background radiation increased for a few hours, a silent panic (this national characteristic, reflects Watanabe) gripped the city. His neighbors hurried home. In elevators, they exchanged looks the way astronauts might just before liftoff.

The following day, the authorities requested that people within a thirty-kilometer radius of the power plant refrain from opening their doors and windows. Everything was being divided into *uchi* and *soto*, inside and outside. That same day, a fire started in the fourth reactor. The U.S. Army was brought in to help douse the flames.

Meanwhile, radiation leaks were confirmed after a fire in a fuel depot. Watanabe read that the director of nuclear security in France had declared the containment system no longer hermetically sealed, and that in his estimation, the accident had reached nearly peak severity. We should listen to the French, Watanabe says, sighing. They've carried out more nuclear tests than any other European country.

Columns of smoke were seen next to the third reactor. Due to the radiation, only helicopters could get near enough to drop water. The European Union's commissioner for energy described the situation as *literally* apocalyptic. This adverb alarmed Mr. Watanabe more than any other piece of information.

The director of the International Atomic Energy Agency, who, of all things, was Japanese, accused the commissioner of being alarmist. The use of face masks became widespread. Like a lung, the streets of Tokyo filled and emptied. People went to work, but few ventured out in the evenings, as if leisure were more radioactive than productivity.

The next day, thermometers plummeted due to a sudden cold spell that reflected the collective temperature. The government imposed restrictions on energy consumption, after announcing that demand for electricity now exceeded capacity. Transport services were reduced, hotels filled with workers unable to return home. As the manager used to say during Watanabe's apprenticeship in Paris, someone always makes business out of a lack of business. The city lost its color once more to avert a massive power cut. Flashlights, batteries, and candles filled pockets and conversations.

On that night of anomalous silence, Watanabe discovered that his fear of the dark was greater than his fear of acid rain. As if he might never emerge from darkness. The impossibility of switching on the heat took him back to his Parisian winters, when cold was part of the shared language.

A week after the earthquake, a hundred Tokyo firefighters traveled to spray water cannons on the nuclear power plant. In particular the third reactor, which contained plutonium, the lethal element in the Nagasaki bomb.

When traces of radiation were found in some food in the prefectures of Ibaraki and Fukushima, a ban was imposed on the sale of produce from that area. Even so, the government assured people that the contamination posed no immediate risk to the consumer. Mr. Watanabe's eyes narrowed when he read the word *immediate*.

People rushed to devour kelp, which is rich in iodine and prevents the absorption of radioactive elements. The stomach has its own obscure memory: something similar had happened with miso in Hiroshima. For the first time since the postwar years, rice and bread were becoming scarce. Customers in supermarkets avoided buying spinach and milk, which were as suspect as a government spokesperson.

The following day, the government announced it was shutting down the Fukushima nuclear power plant. As if there had been any doubt, Watanabe thinks with astonishment. Gas stations ran out of gas. Suddenly petroleum, hitherto considered expensive and polluting, became welcome and essential. As his boss in Paris had said, et cetera.

When traces of radiation were discovered at a water treatment plant in Tokyo, the municipal authorities ordered that children stop drinking tap water. Bottled water became a basic necessity that was sometimes impossible to find. Things previously taken for granted now took on a sinister aspect. We have no control over our basic needs, he thinks. They've taken it away from us while we were at work or watching television. Of course, he's in no position to complain about the latter.

That same evening, he followed on a public channel (on the ultra-slimline Me television in his bedroom) the kamikaze exploits of the fire-fighters. These were the first images ever shown of the emergency services: out-of-focus helmets, hi-vis outfits, garbled loudspeakers, nocturnal sirens, gas masks. They are heroes, reflects Watanabe, and that's the problem. When a nation broadcasts its heroism, no citizen is safe.

The next day, two firefighters were hospitalized after being exposed to excessive levels of radiation. Heroes don't protect, they merely predict. They act like seismographs.

By now, traces of contamination had been found in the water supply of six prefectures. He used his remaining bottles to make liters of green tea.

The following day, the Japan Meteorological Agency announced that the cherry trees had come into bloom.

When the disaster first struck, the majority of Watanabe's acquaintances refused to believe there was any real danger of the power plant exploding. He believed it right away. Assuming the worst gives him a morbid sense of relief. Some people prefer to envisage the lesser evil, and to modify their expectations as the facts grow bleaker. Such a strategy plunges him into a state of anguish. It makes him feel like a deer in the sinking sun, moving along the shadow line.

When news of the possible radiation leaks at Fukushima first spread, his friends blamed it on foreign propaganda. Specifically, on the nuclear rivalry of the French. After all, many of the countries showing solidarity are the very ones that ban Japanese imports and try aggressively to capture Japan's position in the market. His friends refused to believe the nonsense published in Western media. Japan didn't function that poorly. Their technology couldn't possibly fail like it did in other countries. Truth be told, Watanabe shares this belief. In his view, Japanese industry is intrinsically superior.

But, since it's been proven that inadequate seawalls allowed water to penetrate the power plant, flooding the instruments and causing a chain of malfunctions, disillusion has been rising like a tide. It seems there were also some fatal design errors at play. Those involved in both the plant's internal administration and its external supervision are being accused of neglect. According to revelations made in the past few weeks, not only had the highest waves flooded the reactors, but smaller ones had knocked out the emergency generators as well. The latter were, inexplicably, located in a basement.

Watanabe continues to read, his brain also feeling flooded. The waves were equal in height to those of the 1896 tsunami. Which means they've had over a hundred years to defend themselves against another disaster like this. Their failure to do so has resulted in many deaths. In a final act of trust, victims fled back to the same shelters that had saved them on previous occasions, or ran to shield themselves in vain behind the faulty seawalls.

These findings have given rise to a general sense of defenselessness, as if he and his compatriots were also running blindly about in a desperate attempt to escape being engulfed by a cascade of truth.

All along the coast, ancient stone markers warned of the heights reached by tsunamis. In the tiny village of Aneyoshi, for example, one inscription still reads: DO NOT BUILD YOUR HOUSE BEYOND THIS POINT. This time, Watanabe learns, the waves stopped a few meters short of the warning. These markers have gone unheeded. When their villages expanded after the war, most of them spread down the mountain toward the shoreline.

AFTER HE HAD RETIRED AND SETTLED BACK IN TOKYO, Mr. Watanabe realized that the culture shock of returning to his country was greater than that of leaving. He found that he didn't understand some of the expressions used by his youngest compatriots. And that to them, he sounded hopelessly old-fashioned.

Once, in response to a question about a downtown address, a young man, wearing his cap backward and mistaking him for someone who wasn't fluent in the language, replied to him in English.

Nice cap, Watanabe had growled back in Japanese, exaggerating his Tokyo accent as he walked away.

For the first few months, he noticed that in certain situations, he was prone to act like a Latino. Spanish speakers had frequently remarked upon his reserve, but now in the eyes of his own countrymen and women, he appeared to suffer from an incurable garrulousness. If he missed his stop on a bus or train, he would jump up and rush toward the doors, while the other passengers looked at him as if he were a madman. He would shout on his cell phone, much to the annoyance of his quiet neighbors.

As other languages had entered his life, Watanabe became aware of the extent to which his mother tongue limited the possibility of improvisation, of meandering through a sentence in search of its point. The flexibility of Spanish, in particular the long-windedness of its Argentinian variant, was a structural impossibility in Japanese. Once he'd vanquished his doubts and insecurities, he'd learned over the years to enjoy that slipperiness. Which, he is sure, even altered the way he walked. He suspects now that his gait gives him away as much as his intonation.

The first thing he did after setting up his desk was place the mouse on the left side of the keyboard.

———

In spite of the cost and the advice of his friends, he decided to move to the hectic neighborhood of Shinjuku. Among other reasons, because of its convenient proximity to public transportation. The only thing he feels increasingly miserly about is time. In Watanabe's opinion, wasting time requires more effort than making the most of it: the supply is infinite.

Contrary to the numerous objections he has heard, he continues to believe that living in the center of a city, aside from being extremely practical, is the best way to live nowhere. Its equidistance turns it into a multiple frontier. The center seems to him less a fixed point than a revolving axis, where currents converge for an instant, only to scatter in all directions. During his wanderings, Watanabe has come to understand that the Western image of the urban nucleus differs from his own. Instead of something full, to him it represents a dynamic void.

Not far from where he lives, the train station unfurls with hundreds of departures that lead to as many other worlds. Mr. Watanabe remembers it being rebuilt when he was a child. He's aware that virtually none of the passengers who use it today have seen the station in that former state. When he compares those ruins with its present vitality, it seems to him he can see his entire country: it has been raised at the expense of forgetting its foundations, like a skyscraper floating in air. Shinjuku Station is inhabited by *nojuku, mendigos*, or beggars, depending on the language of the person averting their gaze.

Although Watanabe seldom writes letters, he finds the proximity of the post office reassuring. Watanabe feels that every individual is a potential castaway. The greater the access to help, the happier isolation can be. The only things that bother him are the adjacent districts of Chiyoda and Minato, where several rival companies still have their headquarters. He occasionally walks past them, pausing to observe the comings and goings of employees, suppliers, executives, public officials. Not knowing who they are makes him feel a mixture of relief and bitterness. In his mind, the senior employees always look older than him.

But above all else, he has chosen this neighborhood because of the number of foreigners. Here, the movements of every possible race and nationality overlap, like a whirlpool drawn by hand. At this stage of his own disorientation, Watanabe would be incapable of living in a zone that is too homogenous. His previous cities have accustomed him to melting pots.

They make him feel he is in several places at once. It could be said that nothing in Japan is less Japanese than Tokyo. Perhaps this is a sublime form of being a capital city.

His friends claim the area has been invaded: hotels and tourists are popping up all over the place. This invasion doesn't upset Watanabe. Were it not for the nervous astonishment of the new visitors, he would scarcely notice his surroundings.

The neighborhood also offers a variety of nighttime entertainment, some of it respectable. Its lights and sounds are as tireless as its consumers. Filled with video games and slot machines, the area itself seems to him like a video game, one that accepts all kinds of currency. During the day executives work here, produce, act like responsible citizens. And at night they spend recklessly, invest in vice, sponsor exploitation.

Mr. Watanabe avoids certain places, for cardiovascular reasons rather than on moral grounds. He dines at a small *izakaya*, where he orders a plate of sashimi with vegetables and sesame dressing. Or, if he is allowing himself a treat, tempura squid and fried bread. He has lost weight since his return. After decades of gastronomic adjustments, he is glad to be reunited with this landscape of paper lanterns and cloudy fish tanks. He has missed wiping his hands with an *oshibori* before his first mouthful. We Japanese, Watanabe often says, have always been good at washing our hands.

An increasing number of working women enter, often unaccompanied, and seat themselves near him. He is intrigued to see them so absorbed in their own affairs, confident of their own space, so different from the young women in his day. He exchanges fleeting smiles with them (his somewhat intimidated, theirs a shade granddaughterly), and they begin to chew over their respective lives.

Unless there is a major disruption (of which the earthquake has doubtless been the most grueling), he spends a couple of hours in the Somewhere Jazz Bar, one of a cluster of establishments crowding the Golden Gai district. Almost impossible to find amid the profusion of signs, it is hidden in one of the few alleyways that still remind him of the postwar city he used to walk through, before the roads were widened everywhere.

After dinner, Mr. Watanabe is accustomed to having one or two—let's say three—drinks at the Somewhere. (If he goes there during the day, he is careful to order tea first: in his opinion, to get drunk before nightfall is the height of bad taste.) Its cramped quarters, with seating for only half a dozen customers, plus the few stoics who stand at the bar, make for a perfect cocktail of intimacy and mistrust. If the venue is full, he waits as long as necessary. He doesn't want just a bar. He wants his bar.

One of his fellow patrons is Ryu Murakami: the author of novels he would like to read; the director of a laconic sadomasochistic film, in which Watanabe vaguely remembers a series of dildos, anxieties, and mirrors; and the TV host of a program about the economy, which he occasionally watches.

Murakami is from Sasebo, in the prefecture of Nagasaki, less than a hundred kilometers from the town where Watanabe was born. That small town was destroyed during the war and was on the list of targets for the atom bomb. The victorious military forces occupied it, and as far as Watanabe knows, it is still a U.S. base. Both men have briefly exchanged their memories of the Kyūshū region, long before the new bullet trains, and their respective apprenticeships in America. Never in too much depth, of course; neither likes to poke his nose into someone else's drink.

Murakami has told him that, although he is currently living in Yokohama, he spends several nights a week at a hotel in Tokyo, where he keeps a secret office and writes. Murakami seems like a man striving to prove his uniqueness, as if he were fed up with being mistaken for the other Murakami. More than once, Watanabe has seen him sign a book by his namesake, perhaps to avoid the tedious explanation he has been repeating half his life.

Among the regulars at the Somewhere Jazz Bar is also a young German translator who speaks with a disconcerting accent in remarkably fluent Japanese, and whom Watanabe usually finds taking notes or discussing politics. The translator always turns up in an old-fashioned hat that looks like a costume. A few strands of hair escape from it, which Watanabe—especially after his second drink—is convinced belong to a wig. The young German is the owner of a small black-haired dog with triangular ears, which waits for him obediently by the door.

Barmen who cater to so few customers become not so much passing conversationalists as established confidants: what they serve up is their ear. The barman on the late-afternoon shift at the Somewhere (whom Watanabe has gotten to know better, perhaps because the tempo in the afternoons is slower and more meditative) insists on being called John, despite being born in a small town to the south of Nagoya. Watanabe hasn't asked his real name, for which John seems grateful.

As he serves a drink, John will spin the glass on the counter. Sometimes he does it with an astral slowness. At other times with Olympian verve, as if his gesture were being awarded an official score. For Mr. Watanabe, it is a ritual warning before starting to drink: anyone entering a bar knows that verticality is an art. If a customer happens to halt the spinning glass, fearing a possible spillage that has never occurred, John takes offense in a silent, irreversible manner.

On his right, when his hands aren't darting hither and thither as in a game of Ping-Pong, he keeps a board on which he plays himself at shogi. Dividing his attention between serving some customers and chatting with others, John keeps an eye on his most dreaded opponent's moves. At nightfall, when he finishes his shift, he changes his shirt, leans on the other side of the bar to drink a Scotch, and won't allow anyone to interrupt him.

At the far end of the Somewhere are a couple of triangular boards. They slide apart and lead to a cellar where merchandise is stored. Every so often, John disappears into that opening. Watanabe imagines a catacomb concealing unmentionable stories. And yet he suspects that were he able to descend and satisfy his curiosity, he'd be seriously disappointed.

WHEN HE REFLECTS ON his ties with Hiroshima and Nagasaki, Mr. Watanabe feels as if he has died twice and been born three times. Depending on the day, he feels like the most fortunate or unfortunate man in the world. Generally speaking, he dislikes being told he has been lucky. *Fukushima* means precisely that, "good luck island." And at Fukushima, there has been something more than just bad luck.

Luck itself is relative and depends on where you are. He always believed that yellow brought good fortune. The color of the sun, of gold, of the wall that protected him from the atomic blast. Until he discovered that many other countries consider it an ill omen. The color of disease, of treachery, and of sensationalism.

Theories about destiny also strike him as superstitious, as though suspended from some religious angle. If he were forced to say what he did believe, he might choose contradiction. He doubts there is a greater truth. In hindsight, his entire life has been a plan and an accident. A path and its detours. A gift with its burdens.

His twin survivals (the first in spite of being there, the second because he wasn't) somehow cause him guilt and shame. Because he did nothing remarkable in order to be spared, or for those who weren't. It's similar to what he felt on his last day at school: instead of being proud at having reached the finish line, he thought of how his sisters had hardly been able to start, and he felt like a usurper.

When the war ended, he forced himself to construct his life (literally construct it: living seemed to him an arduous chore) as normally as possible. To keep on breathing, walking, talking, touching things. And yet he realized that the texture, the volume, the weight of all things had changed. It was an alteration of the world's consistency.

Mr. Watanabe recalls how as a child, after both *genbaku* were dropped, he secretly suspected he was immortal. If no one among the living was an expert at dying, why did everybody seem so sure that they would die? And what if he were an exception, a mistake, an oversight of nature? During that time, he even questioned that poem by master Hakuin which, of the many his father had taught him, had become one of his favorites:

> *O young folk—*
> *if you fear death,*
> *die now!*
> *For if you die once,*
> *you'll never need to die again.*

As a child, he had interpreted these lines as bellicose: brave youths should on no account fear death. As a teenager, he read it as more ironic. With defiant humor, the old master was urging his disciples to abandon their youthful impatience. Once Watanabe reached adulthood, however, he was convinced the poem alluded to death in a figurative sense: all young people should explore and live their lives while being conscious of their own finiteness. In other words, those verses were saying that there's no coming back from the awareness of mortality.

For a long time, Watanabe expected he would fall seriously ill, or suffer aftereffects similar to those others had experienced. When he realized this didn't seem to be happening, his sense of unreality grew. He is amazed now to have reached old age, as if he hasn't quite managed to refute that immortal child. He has become the perplexed spectator of his body's durability. After all, the oldest man in the world is a survivor of Auschwitz. Perhaps that man, thinks Watanabe, has lost his ability to die.

Deep down, he doesn't see himself as a genuine *hibakusha*. He feels something different than they do, more tangentially painful. And yet, he wonders, do victims always see themselves as victims? Is self-identifying as a victim a spontaneous response or an awkward process?

If for him the true *hibakusha* are the people who became fatally ill, then he is not one of them, for in his case the damage is mostly invisible. Perhaps that's why he never added his name to the register of victims. Or demanded compensation from the state, which, financially speaking, he could afford to refuse. A little more money, he argued, wouldn't give him back his family, and in a sense it would have placed a monetary value on them. The deaths of his loved ones were unique. They didn't deserve to be jumbled up with others in an administrative procedure, to be swamped by the numbers on an endless list. At least this had always been his reasoning. And so he preferred to keep moving. To forget the unforgettable.

Now, toward the end of his life, he wonders if all of his travels weren't the quest for a shifting goal. Like a sprinter pushing the finish line with the tips of his toes.

As he went through high school, he was overwhelmed by a feeling of claustrophobia. He needed to get away, although he wasn't exactly sure from what, and even less where to. Mr. Watanabe remembers clearly the first time he felt the need to travel abroad. He was on his way to school on the train. The carriage moved silently through the city, which had reached the final stages of its reconstruction. New buildings resistant to earthquakes, fires, and other disasters rose from their preceding ashes. Once again, Tokyo was reborn. As though, emulating the interiors of its dwellings, the entire country was movable. Detachable matter.

In his opinion, the successful restoration of Tokyo betrayed, in a sense, the spirit of kintsugi: it was done without leaving any trace of the bombings. However vast the destruction of the capital city, which encompassed forty percent of its surface, the damages were limited in space, and above all in time. Tokyoites understood what had happened to them. And therefore, at least in theory, they were able to leave it behind.

Yoshie was on his way to school on the train. The carriage moved silently through the city. The passengers were busy pretending to be asleep so as not to open their eyes, not opening their eyes so as not to look, not looking so as not to bother anyone. All at once, among the many heads facing the floor oblivious to the truncated shapes filing past the windows, Yoshie saw a raised head observing the landscape. It belonged to the only foreigner in the carriage. His gaze was fixed on the rows of half-finished buildings. Yoshie focused on that gaze, and through it reclaimed his own. He sensed what he wanted to do in the future: to learn to look out of the window like that.

The second time Watanabe remembers feeling the need to go abroad was when communist troops from North Korea, armed by the Soviets and the Chinese, crossed the dreaded thirty-eighth parallel, and the U.S. forces, which had remained on Japanese soil, responded by mobilizing in South Korea.

There was no way he could forget the climate of fear leading up to that moment. Just as now, news came in the form of public leaks, seeping through the roofs of every dwelling. No one was safe. There was no more *uchi* and *soto*. The Cold War escalated, and the Soviets boasted that they had built their first bomb.

As the year crawled toward Christmas, President Truman—in a press conference that Yoshie's aunt and uncle managed to tune in to on a neighbor's radio—threatened to use atomic weapons in Korea. When the broadcast had finished, their hosts turned off the radio, smiled at their guests, and silently went about preparing seaweed salad and hot miso soup.

That same night, Aunt Ineko lost her voice: her own way of emitting and omitting her opinion. Even Uncle Shiro, a man known for his self-control, went through a period of anxiety. Overnight, or so Watanabe remembers it, things that had never before worried his uncle made him fearful. If Yoshie went out on his own. If he didn't say exactly where he was going. If he didn't tell them his friends' names. If he came home after dark.

Yoshie attributed his uncle's anxiety to his own development: ceasing to be a child is the cruelest thing you can do to a guardian. As he grew up, he began to connect it to Uncle Shiro's aging. After all, everything seems more fragile when we ourselves become fragile. Now, however, Mr. Watanabe believes it was another aftereffect of the war. Uncle Shiro was terrified that this new one might reach Tokyo. And, above all, that his teenage nephew could end up being conscripted. The invisible scars definitely last much longer. No one can cure something that officially doesn't seem to exist.

As the battlefront extended across the Korean peninsula, on his way to school Yoshie would watch the nervous proliferation of buildings, the compulsion to construct in every corner of the city, as if urbanism were anticipating its own destruction.

He has wondered countless times which is more bloodthirsty, the swiftness of the automatic or the persistence of the manual. When he first started thinking about this, thousands of U.S. troops had already died in Korea, almost always in a grueling way. Freezing to death, hand-to-hand combat, bayonets in the night. The Chinese soldiers didn't have radio transmitters and would terrify the enemy by attacking as they slept to the blare of bugles. Traditional or technological. Patient or fast. Northern or southern. Communist or capitalist. Attackers and attacked. All afraid, all dead.

Toward the end of high school, Yoshie learned of the suicide of Tamiki Hara, who on the day of the bomb had returned to Hiroshima to scatter his wife's ashes. Hara, one of the few authors able to foil the censorship of the American General Headquarters, had written: "Inside me there is always a sound of something exploding." Six years after surviving the explosion, he'd thrown himself onto the train tracks near his house in Tokyo.

A couple of years later, Yoshie started college and underlined the following passage from one of Hara's books: "I envy people capable of instantly taking charge of their lives. And yet those who appear before me are the ones gazing despondently at the tracks. Broken people who, although they writhe and struggle, have already been tossed into a pit from which they will never escape. Perhaps my shadow wishes to vanish soon?" Mr. Watanabe often wonders whether that August, on the banks of the Ōta, he might have walked right by Hara without recognizing him.

Yoshie secretly hoped that when he started college, being in a more like-minded, stimulating environment would help him overcome his unease. But all it did was fill him with theories and opinions. At Waseda University, he did a year of French, his favorite and idealized language, but he failed to find the remedy for the suffocation dogging him. The clamor of his hormones didn't help, either. Apart from his frequent visits to the bathroom, his only relief existed in the labyrinth of a foreign grammar, in the garden of its phonetics, in the treasure of a different vocabulary.

Halfway through that first year at university, the U.S. Army carried out its biggest-ever nuclear test, on Bikini Atoll, causing a subterranean blast a thousand times more powerful (a thousand, Watanabe repeats to himself) than the Hiroshima bomb. Dawn had just broken, and according to people on the neighboring islands, it resembled the rising of a second sun. The bomb was named Bravo, as if it were a curtain call. It was March, once again March. Thanks to some of his better-informed classmates, Yoshie learned that since the end of the war, the superpowers had tested at least twenty devices in that area. This discovery astonished him almost as much as not having known about it.

Just before he finished his first year of French, taking advantage of his good grades, Yoshie informed his aunt and uncle that he intended to continue his studies in Paris, the city of his dreams, about which he knew absolutely nothing. At first, his aunt and uncle were firmly opposed to the idea: There wasn't enough money and no good reason for him to do such a thing. They had too many hopes pinned on him to risk it all on a whim.

Faced with Yoshie's entreaties (which included kneeling solemnly in imitation of his mother; a bout of depression that was somewhat premeditated; and an attempted hunger strike), Ineko adopted the role of mediator. Once Shiro had recovered from the blow, he agreed to pay for his nephew's studies in Paris, on the strict condition that he would pursue a degree not in language and literature, but in a serious subject that promised a future. His uncle spoke a great deal about the future. And so Mr. Watanabe chose, or rather was forced to choose, economics.

By the end of that summer, Yoshie was already wandering around Paris, contemplating the boulevards with delight and the cost of lodgings with horror. During that time of initial confusion, he would have found it hard to believe that on those very streets, he would meet the first love of his nomadic life.

Nearly ten years later, one overcast morning while perusing *L'Humanité* in a café on Rue Pascal, he came across a headline that startled him. The paper fell, covering both cups. Violet's eyes peered at him over her book, like two notes on a staff. She asked him if everything was okay. He smiled and stared into the distance.

According to the article, a young reporter called Ōe had traveled to Hiroshima to cover the international conference against nuclear weapons. The event had almost been canceled due to political differences. While the disagreements between local and national advisers, socialist and communist delegates, Chinese and Soviet representatives grew increasingly heated, people gathered for the Peace March. Another on-the-spot reporter described the situation as a war between pacifists. Weary of speeches and meetings, Ōe instead decided to collect testimonies from the forgotten victims of August 6, 1945. He was no longer interested in the official events of the conference. All that mattered to him were those people's stories.

Watanabe had been born in the same year as Ōe, in a neighboring region, just one prefecture away. They were both from towns close to Hiroshima, brought up under a militaristic nationalism, but had opposite approaches to dealing with the past.

His near neighbor wrote about the lessons the world could learn from the nuclear tragedy. About respect for the victims. The dignity of the survivors. Ōe promoted these ideas with the best of intentions. The problem was that Yoshie himself felt very far from embodying those supposed lessons. He had no sense of being ennobled by everything he'd experienced or lost. All he retained, with brutal clarity, was the fear, the harm, the anger, the shame.

Soon after that article appeared, Me offered him a transfer and a promotion. In spite of his increasingly formal commitment to Violet, whom he pictured as his future wife, he accepted without hesitation. They would find a solution together. No distance could defeat them. He cleared out his apartment and moved straight to New York.

FOR SOME TIME NOW, Mr. Watanabe's sex life might be described as passive, although he prefers to think of himself as an enthusiastic voyeur. Contrary to what he believed in his youth, this seems to him less a renunciation than a refinement: where energy is lacking, there is more subtlety to finding pleasure. The ability *not* to do, he senses, is the greatest attribute of potency.

As his vigor declines (without, he is surprised to note, his desire waning in equal measure), Watanabe has discovered that masturbation is a mental exercise. A reflex more closely associated with fixations than with the showiness of orgasm. This is why he now masturbates visually, without having to touch himself.

His sexuality has survived its extinction. Every spectator enjoys apocalypse, providing it takes place far away. Distance enables people to become excited about things that would be difficult to look at up close. In that respect, Watanabe decides, the citizen and the pornographer concur.

As he learned when he started studying Spanish, *eschatology* and *scatology* can be united by the very same word. Physiology and finality. The innermost depths of the body, and what lies beyond death. Perhaps that is why old people understand sex better than anyone: they are aware of their own finiteness.

The true voyeur believes that their act is as radical as any other, that daring isn't about taking part, but about watching to the end. We are profoundly fascinated by what in some sense we fear. That explains our obsession with sex and why we so seldom engage in it. We are—he concludes as he opens his favorite porn site—degenerates by omission.

Mr. Watanabe is intrigued by the increasing numbers of *sōshoku danshi*, or herbivores, who renounce sex and embrace playful celibacy. Timid, delicate men who refuse to compete in the physical arena. As if the financial bubble and the business of virility were bursting simultaneously.

According to the statistics he has read, as many as fifty percent of single

Japanese people under thirty-five are virgins, and the percentage keeps rising. At this rate, based on the predicted number of births and deaths, researchers are fairly accurately able to pinpoint Japan's extinction. Which should take place on August 16, 3766. On the 1,821st anniversary, Watanabe calculates, of their surrender to the Allies.

As physical contact decreases, the number of sex products continues to grow; a sort of platonic libido. The natural corollary of this type of consumerism, he deduces, would be its self-annihilation. A capitalism without customers.

His former colleagues remain at the opposite end of the market. Many of them continue to exhibit a tireless enthusiasm for prostitutes. More than offending his principles, this has never succeeded in arousing him. The transaction removes uncertainty, which is the very thing that drives his desire. In fact, close to his house is the Kabukichō district, where nightclubs and love hotels abound. More than a few of his acquaintances go there to ease, as he understands it, what men of his generation call loneliness.

Working with loneliness, taking the absence of the other for granted, is more attractive to him than avoiding it. Among the selection of toys on offer these days, packages containing used underwear most draw his attention. Many include a photograph of their previous owner, of the body they once encircled. You can also buy shoes that have obviously already been worn. In some cases they are more expensive than a new pair. The object's past life is revered, as in kintsugi.

Since he has become old—since others started to label him as such—he feels a profound sense of disquiet when he goes out in spring, as he does now, and observes the young people. Not on account of the painful chasm between them and himself. But because he suspects that many of their blossoming bodies will fade without ever being sufficiently caressed. By the time they understand, it will be too late, they'll be over on his side. The side that watches with melancholic envy as the next young bodies go by.

In the books and films he comes across, Mr. Watanabe rarely identifies with the urges of the characters his age, who seem desperate for a final coitus. His body has reacted to old age differently. Even if he no longer feels the old impulse, his curiosity is still alive. It remains alert in his body, searching constantly for something undefined.

In contrast to some of his fetishist friends, erotic films exasperate him.

Their omissions strike him as not only supremely inept—each shot being the victim of a laughable insistence on concealment—but also deeply mistaken. The notion of seeing *everything* is unachievable. Whatever is revealed, it will leave us with the sensation that we could have seen something else. In this sense, erotic cinema is sustained by the fallacy that merely showing copulation signifies the end of concealment.

As the years go by, Mr. Watanabe believes he has found a kind of purity in porn, which releases him from the tyranny of self-contemplation, and which allows him to abandon himself to a lascivious otherness, to a desire that is devoid of a leading ego. The ritual begins with choosing *how* he will arouse himself, the superior pleasure of organizing his pleasure.

Naturally, not just anything will satisfy him. He has never much liked Japan's porn industry. Having experienced different pornographic tastes in foreign countries, he has become aware of the limitations of the national tradition. In it, fantasy seems to advance in only one direction: stalking, assault, domination, submission, outraged moans, and, in general, a sad sense of awkwardness. As for the censorship of genitals, he admits that he is changing his mind about it. What he once considered absurd prudishness now seems to him an ingenious way of renewing mystery.

After the indie enthusiasm of the genre's early days, Watanabe lost interest in X-rated films, unmoved by silicone implants and glass vibrators. As the texture of the images changed, so did his idea of flesh. The unabashed folds of the seventies. The celebration of color in the eighties. The pretentious flashiness of the nineties. The insipid productivity of the twenty-first century.

Growing disillusioned with the industry, he developed the habit of watching the films without sound. This turned everything into a parody: the provocative looks, the lovers' gestures, the to-and-fro of their bodies. Without voices, the images lacked substance. That was how he discovered that pornography is a musical genre.

In his view, the remote control didn't help with the education of the audience either. The possibility of fast-forwarding the image impoverished desire. Skipping parts of the experience precluded those transitions that encouraged everything else. The pause button introduced another aberration, as each instant ceased to be ephemeral. He concedes, nevertheless, that the rewind button is sublime. Its sole function is to reproduce the obsessions of our memory.

The plots in X-rated movies have never convinced him. The idiotic scripts are apt to nullify their own aim, leaving both those who wanted a story and those who didn't equally dissatisfied. Sex scenes without context frustrate him even more. For him, without a character there's no identity, and without an identity there's no desire.

With the advent of internet porn, amateur home videos—where there is no pretense of a story and people's real identities are the starting point—fulfilled many of his requirements. But only when he discovered home webcams, with their radical slowness and uncertainty, did Mr. Watanabe reach the peak of voyeurism.

During the past few weeks, the ground under people's feet has been shakier than ever. Each tiny echo of the March earthquake has turned fear into a question of one's politics: being afraid is now a matter of whether you trust the state. Outside in the street, Watanabe notices people exchanging suspicious looks. Are you trusting or doubtful? Patriotic or not?

As far as he can remember, this is the second time Japan has had to question its own identity, the version of the country which it tells to itself. In some of the places where he has lived, in the Spanish-speaking world in particular, people live in a state of permanent suspicion and frantic self-flagellation. This impulse, which he initially considered a weakness, now strikes him as a strength.

Mr. Watanabe keeps himself informed, or confused, by reading half the world's press. He is watching an information battle unfold. It's nebulous at first, and then he starts to see it more clearly. He thinks he has identified a Franco-German alliance with alarmist tendencies. The forecasts from these countries are usually bleaker, which makes them a useful alternative source. A large part of their diplomatic corps has shut down its embassies, canceled flights, or moved to the west of Tokyo.

He also detects an Anglo-Hispanic alliance, which has attempted to preserve some measure of normalcy and is more circumspect in its news coverage. That, or these countries are just more accepting of the government's versions. Although in theory their embassies are still active, a number of diplomats have left as a precaution. Among the most illustrious contradictions is the advice given to his citizens by the president of the

United States, the country that is providing the biggest disaster relief effort: to remain at least eighty kilometers from the nuclear power plant.

There are also journalistic factions within each of these alliances. Alongside coverage that seeks to be impartial, it isn't hard to find articles lobbying for multinational energy companies: optimistic assessments of the damage, refutations of reports run by independent sources, debunking antinuclear arguments with the help of biased government data. For the time being, while the shock is still fresh in people's minds, it's possible that the former will hold out; in the long run, the latter will prevail. Within a few years, Watanabe predicts, vast investments will be made to publicize the reconstruction of what has been destroyed.

Social media, another kind of universal wave that Watanabe insists on ignoring, has inflated the extremes. It's able to knock down any official secret, as well as spread false alarms. The most diverse tweets have begun to appear in newspapers, ranging from bold denunciations to apocalyptic ravings. The newspapers must have their reasons, he imagines, although he doesn't even quite understand how Twitter works.

Instead of *gaijin*, Watanabe has heard some of his neighbors refer to foreigners as *flyjin*, considering how swiftly they've flown away. Every immigrant who flees Japan is deserting a land that has never assimilated them. It goes without saying that foreigners will always be deemed outsiders here, regardless of how long they have lived in the country. Watanabe thinks that this is both a limitation and an advantage. Ultimately, there is no greater hospitality than when a country, instead of forcing you to fit in, allows you to remain a foreigner.

He can't understand why the word *gaijin*—literally "outside person"— has replaced in common parlance the somewhat rhetorical but more precise *gaikokujin*: "person from a foreign country." The second doesn't prevent someone from joining the *inside* of a different country. Yet again, a binary culture dividing reality into inside and outside. Mr. Watanabe wonders where people who occupy both spaces, or neither, would fit into these categories. Where *he* would fit. He wonders what to call an island within an island.

Of course, one could also use the faintly comical term *gaijin-san*. Mr. Foreigner. It wouldn't bother him in the slightest to be called that.

———

Since Fukushima, another tsunami has been unleashed: that of global fear. And another explosion: that of money fleeing.

The German chancellor, Watanabe learns as he sips his first drink at the Somewhere, has ordered the deferral of a law extending the life of the oldest power plants. A Swiss minister is to block plans to construct further ones. Spanish ecologists are demanding that the power station in the Garonne be closed. Its reactor, identical to those at Fukushima, went into service the same year and was manufactured by the same company. The Chilean government has been forced to justify an agreement with the United States for the training of nuclear power plant personnel. For its part, Washington has decided to carry out safety checks on all its nuclear installations.

All measures taken in response to the accident—and to stabilize the Japanese economy—have won the backing of the International Monetary Fund. Given his career as a business executive, Mr. Watanabe is aware of where decisions are made and what the priorities are. He isn't surprised that the expert responsible for the decontamination of Chernobyl has criticized the International Atomic Energy Agency's lack of independence.

What does surprise him is that, according to the Chernobyl expert, the third reactor at Fukushima uses a dangerous mixture of uranium oxide and plutonium. Sixty-four kilos of uranium in Hiroshima, Watanabe recites mechanically. Six of plutonium in Nagasaki.

And in spite of these precedents, he thinks as John spins his second drink, successive governments have continued to foster the nuclear energy industry. They have blessed it with laws, budgets, communiqués, portrayed it as essential to the country's growth. Doing so serves a network of different interests, but it is also, reflects Watanabe, a defense mechanism. A refusal to remember. As if, by ignoring what happened in the past, its consequences would be less damaging.

He sucks the tiny bit of ice holding out at the bottom of his glass. He polishes it with the tip of his tongue, a shiver is tattooed on the roof of his mouth. John is watching him out of the corner of his eye, checking to see if he needs to be topped off.

As he contemplates the alcohol pouring into his third glass, he thinks once more about the links between energy and politics. It doesn't take too much imagination, or alcohol, to imagine what companies donate funds for public works, for instance. Not that Japan's antinuclear principles have prevented the presence of U.S. atomic weapons on sovereign territory, either. Diplomacy, he thinks, smiling, is the art of saying yes to no.

Having himself done good business in many of them, Watanabe is sure that no world power is going to renounce nuclear energy. Not until the operating life of power stations has been maximized, and renovating them is more costly than shutting them down. That will be the moment for a supposedly environmental change of heart.

In fact, this economic expediency is debatable. A single accident in one plant is enough to destroy not only many lives, but also the balance sheets. Rebuilding Fukushima is going to cost a fortune. The full figure will probably change in a planned, incremental way. In concentric circles.

Naïveté being one of the few vices he prefers not to indulge in, Watanabe is aware of what rejecting nuclear energy would entail. Japan would have difficulty surviving among the elite economies, unless it increased its consumption of oil and coal to stay competitive. Which in turn would increase its greenhouse gas emissions, leading to further problems with the global protocol.

That leaves only three possible options, Watanabe concludes. A gentle decline, which might herald the genuine end of the island's imperial fantasies. A drastic change in immigration policy, opening the country to young working people, resulting in a cultural revolution. Or massive investment in renewable energies, which would transform the country's major industries. Would they be able to build a green identity after Fukushima, the way Hiroshima and Nagasaki reinvented themselves following their disasters?

Beyond all these calculations lies the problem of democracy. No government in the world allows its people to make decisions about their own energy resources, and they don't even tell them the truth about how they are managed. Nuclear energy, inspiration strikes him as he drains his fourth glass of the evening, is an anachronism: it belongs to the era of big secrets.

And yet, he promptly contradicts himself, the problem does involve the citizens. Would we really be willing to use less energy? If he's not mistaken, in a national survey a couple of years ago, over eighty percent of the national population were in favor of nuclear energy. Since the accident, the *Asahi* has published another survey in which nearly sixty percent continue to show their support. Maybe we prefer to carry on as usual, and to blame the authorities in the event of a tragedy?

Mr. Watanabe rises to his feet. He feels slightly dizzy. He pays for his drinks and leaves the Somewhere.

MR. WATANABE'S SOCIAL LIFE is increasingly restricted. A dinner or two each month with his healthy friends, whose numbers are dwindling with awful regularity. Meetings with former executives at Me. Sporadic calls to Madrid and Buenos Aires, and very occasionally to New York. A hint of a smile when passing a familiar face in the street. Since his return to Tokyo, he's preferred his recent friendships. It feels liberating to not have shared a long history.

Aside from this, he maintains cordial relations with his neighbors, in particular with Mr. and Mrs. Furuya. The Furuyas are both a charming and a bewildered couple. They are at that delicate age when their children's departure still overshadows the home, and feel neither young enough to invent a new life nor old enough to act as such. Mrs. Furuya is forever walking their little dog, which shows signs of understanding her verbal commands, while Mr. Furuya forces himself to go running in the park beyond the train station. When Watanabe bumps into them in the elevator, it occurs to him that, though they are young enough to be his children, he'd have liked to have parents like them.

He also exchanges pleasantries with two young foreign women who share a studio on one of the lower floors. Watanabe isn't sure if they are friends, colleagues, or lovers, or an enviable mixture of all three. They are employed at some job that demands an insatiable consumption of pencils. They don't speak any language he recognizes. One of the women is tall and athletic, with a cheerfulness that seems to originate from her abdominals. The other is short and a tad more pensive, with a sedentary figure. During the last national holiday, they both came up to give him a cake that looked Central European or possibly Scandinavian. He tried to give them a banjo, which they politely refused.

Disinclined to reproduce and having been unable for most of his life to look after a pet due to his constant travels, Watanabe has developed a certain fondness for plants. It is his humble way of bestowing life. He communicates with his plants in a uniquely sincere, precultural language. They say to one another: water, air, sun, wind, spring. No more, no less. If he is honest, this is already far more than he'd reveal to his neighbors.

From what he can see, pets have assumed an overwhelming emotional importance to their owners. They have become substitutes for (not to mention optimized versions of) personal relationships. This explains why in the aftermath of the earthquake, special task forces were organized to search for people's lost pets. He has always been a little skeptical of domestic animals, because they put their owners on the perpetual verge of loss. It's possible that he belongs to an anthropological minority: human beings who, in spite of everything, prefer other human beings.

On this morning of sunshine and uncertainties, Mr. Watanabe has gone for a walk to Yoyogi Park. During his childhood, the U.S. Army officers were garrisoned there, which perhaps explains why visiting the park gives him a rare feeling of pleasure, as if he were reclaiming the place. At a brisk pace, it takes him approximately forty-five minutes to get there: just what the doctor recommends. Since he stopped practicing aikido, this is his only form of exercise. If he begins to tire, he will return on the Yamanote train and change to the Ōedo line.

On the way, he passes several people clutching their pets with tenderness and unease. In recent years, he has watched with interest the animal business, which he imagines is more profitable than that of technology. Renting pets is a growing industry. Since his return to Tokyo, this custom seems to him increasingly natural. The city has become a place littered with obstacles to and dangers in raising animals: a jungle in reverse.

Urban planning plays a part in this new demand, he suspects. Even when landlords allow pets, there is barely room to move in the minuscule apartments. No less important is the emotional aspect. With rentals, customers get the balm of physical contact without any of the responsibility. Money is paid for the fleeting pleasure of unconditional love.

Close to Yoyogi Park, which Watanabe is now about to enter, is a shop that rents out animals by the hour. The customers, a majority of them men in late middle age, can sit and caress more than twenty different breeds, or take them on excursions through the park. A half-hour seated play session with a quadruped costs approximately one thousand yen. Wandering freely outside for an hour costs four times that. As he trails his fingertips over the tree trunks, Watanabe works out how many yen it would take to fill the solitary hours of the average adult.

As soon as he leaves the park, he pauses in front of the stores displaying picnic candy, which almost no one has been buying this spring. The Takashimaya department store is still posting information about the cherry blossoms on its billboards, in Japanese, English, and Chinese. But this time the light is heavier, it possesses a different density.

Watanabe considers himself athermic. As usual, he scarcely notices the faint seasonal breeze on his skin. He doesn't know if this is some kind of aftereffect of the radiation, and he has no wish to find out. He accepts it as his own way of being, or not being, in the world. That's why he has learned to heighten his other senses. Today, the chirping in the branches, the brightly colored flowers, speak to him of April.

The ringing of the phone in his bedroom startles him. Partly because hardly anyone calls his landline these days, and partly because it sounds odd. He's always had the impression that, depending on from where and why they are contacting him, the phone rings in a different way. As if the device could register distance, urgency, and purpose: a seismograph of voices.

It seems the journalist from Buenos Aires, this Pinedo guy, refuses to give up. Argentinians don't know when to surrender, reflects Watanabe, a dangerous trait that reminds him of the Japanese.

Pinedo says good morning and good afternoon, apologizes for calling again, and then persists with his objective. Still stammering slightly, but less nervous than last time, he repeats how much he would like to, to interview him briefly, at least, because in fact, he's looking into the entire situation, that's to say, this recent disaster would be only the starting point, and well, and besides they have a close friend in common, whom he's sure he.

Watanabe interrupts at this point. He doesn't care about the friends they have in common, he replies. Not only is this intrusive, declares Watanabe, he considers it useless to talk about this now, weeks later, when the aftermath of the earthquake is no longer fresh.

Pinedo points out that he, that he isn't interested in the earthquake or the tsunami, what interests him is the, the nuclear power plant, and. Like everyone else, retorts Watanabe, like everyone else. Pinedo tries to defend himself and qualifies that this is very different, isn't it? an in-depth approach, the topic is much more, it's much more focused on collective memory, let's say, this isn't about current affairs, he is examining the way, the way different countries respond to disasters and, and to genocide, when circumstances don't.

Mr. Watanabe cuts in again. He is more agitated than he thought he would be. He tells Pinedo he has nothing to say about it. He wishes him luck with his work. And says goodbye abruptly.

His quickened pulse resembles the beeping sound when someone hangs up.

As night falls, he browses several Latin American newspapers. Reading about his country in a different language always gives him a feeling of awkward lucidity. Everything sounds much more remote and simple.

In the area surrounding Fukushima, Watanabe reads, there are dead bodies still lying on the ground. Many refugees, who are continuing to flock to shelters, are angry at the authorities for burying their loved ones without permission, when their religion demands they be cremated. Since March 11, the tally of victims has reached more than ten thousand dead and nearly twenty thousand missing.

This latest revelation causes Watanabe to leap from the sofa. He crosses the old striped rug. Goes to his closet. Rearranges hangers and drawers. Doing this helps him organize his thoughts, order them according to size. He flicks through his clothes swiftly. As swiftly as he'd decided, all those years ago, to leave Paris and move to the worst, to the best place possible.

4

LORRIE
AND THE
SCARS

I REMAINED DOGGEDLY YOUNG for half of my life. And the next day, I realized I was growing old. I think he showed up right around then. Maybe that's why everything happened so fast. We were both starting to appreciate what time does to you if you wait too long.

Outlandish as it may seem, we met at a funeral at Green-Wood Cemetery. There was the scent of rain, but it wasn't raining. The deceased, if I remember correctly, worked at the Japanese embassy's press office. I assume we both knew him professionally. I was listening attentively to people giving their condolences. I focused on each speaker as though I were about to interview them. From those who spoke emphatically, as if they were afraid to appear vulnerable, to those who broke down without shame, who in my view were the wisest.

I felt out of context, or maybe the complete opposite. After all, in a cemetery you are never more *in* context. So I wandered off to take a breather. I started to think of all the stuff you usually think about when you see a coffin. Work nonsense, a friend's birthday, buying a new pair of shoes, the upcoming election, making an appointment with the hairdresser, your niece's dress. Anything that takes you away from there. I was jittery the way you get at funerals. That urge to flee and change your life, just when you feel you've understood something.

That's when I bumped into Yoshie. We looked at each other and smiled. I'm not sure if we started walking together then, or if we had already been strolling side by side. We moved away from the mourners, supposedly to smoke a cigarette. And I don't quite know how, but almost without exchanging a word, we started to fool around.

When we pulled apart to head back to the ceremony, he asked me my name. He repeated it several times, Lorrie, Lorrie (or rather, *Lohie, Lohie*), trying to hear it properly or to savor it.

If I'm being honest, it wasn't that I was especially attracted to him, more like my body was telling me what to do. I never admitted this to Yoshie, but in that moment, I suspect that I'd have done the same with almost any decent-looking guy who showed an interest in me. I imagine it was a sort of involuntary response. A physical protest at my surroundings. As a matter of fact, this had happened to me before. I don't mean letting the first man who came along grope me. I just mean feeling horny when I was at a cemetery.

He'd been living in New York a few years. With the odd exception, he spoke decent English. I find that speaking any language other than your own is admirable. Yoshie was prone to exhibiting his linguistic efforts as those of us who aren't bilingual tend to do. He was still able to marvel at everything he heard. In the middle of a conversation, for no apparent reason, he could look astonished or happy, and you knew it wasn't because of what you were saying, but because he'd become suddenly aware of the language he was communicating in.

He had trouble tolerating irony, and thanks to his difficulties, I realized that in English, we overuse it. We really do use it for everything, be it diplomacy, euphemism, or an insult. He attributed this to America being a modern empire, an expert on negotiation. I replied that Henry James was the one to blame.

Yoshie struggled with phrasal verbs, which he would mix up in the funniest ways. He would confuse *switch on* with *turn on*, *run out* with *run over*, and so forth. These misunderstandings didn't so much get in the way of our communication as feed my imagination. For example, according to him we lived in *New Oak*. I loved the idea of us being forest dwellers. Other good ones were the way he pronounced *peace* as *piss* or *Coke* as *cock*. Slipups like these were liable to turn any innocent topic into a risqué conversation.

I remember one evening we were at a movie theater on the Upper West Side, the Thalia. No, the New Yorker. With the sloping floor and the legendary murals, it was as quaintly pretentious as we were. He asked the vendor for *soft porn* instead of *pop corn*. The girl looked at us, bemused. But he kept insisting we were both desperate for soft porn. I'm sorry, sir, stammered the girl, we don't sell anything like that. Of course you do! Yoshie replied angrily. Why do you think all these people came here?

But what confused him most was intonation. In a musical sense, he never stopped sounding foreign. I found that sexy. He maintained that in English we count and even narrate in an interrogative tone. As if to make sure the other person is still listening. Yoshie attributed this to a combination of pedantry and insecurity specific to the English-speaking world. He had theories about everything. Especially things he knew nothing about.

He wasn't entirely off base about the insecurity, though. I had this face, few curves, and more than a few misgivings about my body. I could go a whole day without eating and then scarf down half a dozen Milky Ways. As soon as I'd finished chewing them, I'd go brush my teeth. I did it quickly and guiltily, hurting my gums. Like I wanted to erase not only any traces of food, but also the memory of having eaten. I was skinnier than I am now. I liked to take up very little space when I spoke. I was under the impression that being skinny and being smart were related.

I'm afraid that when we first met, I was still way too scared of getting old. Obsessed with staying young, just as I was ceasing to be that. It's a trap we women fall into the minute we let down our guard, however much we think we're feminists. I laugh now when I remember what I used to consider old.

We've become both more understanding and more hypocritical on the subject of age. There's no such thing as an old woman nowadays. No one would dare call us that in public. We're all young seniors or happily mature, about to conquer our freedom. Go fuck yourself, honey. We're old. Period. And proud of it. Well, not entirely. I'd love to be, I don't know, not twenty or anything. That'd be awful. Or even thirty. But fortysomething or fifty? Definitely. If someone gave me the option, I wouldn't choose to start over, I'd just ask for a second adulthood. God, I'd enjoy it so much better this time around.

Of all the extensive and pathetic comments men permit themselves to make about women's bodies, one I particularly despise is how good we look *for our age*. Not just because no one says this to a man, or even because, at this point, it's the only flattery I get. But because it doesn't make any sense. Do only women of my generation have an *age*? Don't young women also have a very specific one that determines what we think about their appearance? Aren't they better or worse for *their* age? Or are they a fucking absolute, until suddenly, they get old like us?

My idea of old age is different. I just don't want to depend on anyone to buy food or go to the bathroom. As long as I'm still able to do those things, personally I couldn't give a shit how old I am. Beyond that, I don't know. If things get unpleasant, one has other options. I prefer not to think about that too much. In the meantime, I have my adorable nieces and nephews who visit and make a fuss over me. I try not to let them see how excited I am when they come. Otherwise, they wouldn't enjoy coming here so much. They have enough on their plate with poor Ralph.

My brother, Ralph, and I grew up in Washington Heights, like most of the Solomon family. My parents were liberal about everything unimportant, conservative about the important things, and Jewish very much in their own way. I dreamed of going to Hunter College, like my radical friends who didn't want to stay virgins. I also had the occasional fantasy about studying physics at Swarthmore.

Unfortunately, my parents listened to Grandpa Usher, who had been the shammes at a synagogue before I was born. Invariably, he ended each conversation on the matter by removing his pipe from his cavernous mouth and declaring: When you're ready to have a serious conversation, my dear, we'll pick up where we left off. And so they got me a scholarship to a liberal arts program at Barnard College instead. Which cost more than Hunter or Swarthmore and forbade skirts more than two inches above our salacious knees.

After a whole semester of chaste behavior, during which I was permitted to attend a few classes at Columbia, I refused to follow my family's plan for me. Thanks to a couple of good dramatic scenes, including threats of suicide I had no intention of carrying out, I finally got my way. And that's how I ended up studying journalism at NYU, which had just gone completely coed. Those years were incredibly formative, as it were, with regard to my extracurricular education.

After graduating, I spent some time at Stinson Beach and Topanga Canyon, California. There I read about Buddhism and did some other things I'd rather not get into. I soon tired of this and went back to New

York, where I applied for every job available. I worked for a variety of publications, the most sophisticated of which was a weekly food-industry magazine. My task was to appraise canned products. The following year I landed my first contract with a tabloid, which, out of professional pride, I will permit myself not to name.

As much as I despised that rag, it enabled me to earn a living and gain my freedom at last. Working there was my real training. I learned to pursue a story, whatever it might be. To make it sound more urgent, important, and controversial than it actually was. To write with one eye on the facts and the other on the readers. To produce open-ended, structurally flexible copy, in case anything changed at the last minute (and it always did). It was a lesson in raw journalism.

What most intrigued me was how willing the victims of those dramas, or their relatives, seemed to be interviewed. I never quite figured out why. Did we pressure them too much? Did they need some sort of therapy? Had they spent their whole lives feeling like no one cared about them? Or were they simply more shameless than I'd imagined?

I joined the *Liberty Chronicle* sometime after that. I had to work my way up the ladder, starting as the girl who made coffee, then replacement typist, then proofreader, accidentally. With a bit of luck and patience, I finally joined the culture beat. It was my second choice after politics—the *Chronicle*'s forte, and probably the only reason people bought our newspaper. I instantly loved the job. It seemed to me ideal, a way to write without writing. To take part in a life of culture without the absurd pretense of being a *creator*.

That paper spoke of a different world from the one we live in today. As ever, dissidents were in the minority. But here's the difference, it was a minority that truly believed in the possibility of challenging the system. It believed that, however fucked-up things were, they could change. My nieces and nephews accuse me of being a pessimist. They insist that rebellion still happens, just not on the streets. When I ask *their* kids where the young radicals are nowadays, all they talk about is social media.

How the hell can they expect so much from the tech industry? Don't they realize it's in the hands of Big Business? Of course, they reply, the same way newspapers like yours were owned by large publishing companies.

The newsroom at the *Chronicle* was like a political convention with typewriters. There were Democrats, Socialists, Anarchists, Social Democrats, loyal and not-so-loyal Communists, moderate liberals, pro-Soviet and anti-Soviet Marxists, Black Panther sympathizers (*my* doing!), as well as the odd Maoist. And among all those men who confused revolution with testosterone, an increasing number of women. Two or three were connected to militant feminist groups. To be honest, I was never that radical. I was just happy if my male colleagues didn't comment on my legs during meetings.

In its early days, before I joined the newspaper, people like the economist Paul Sweezy used to contribute. The eternal candidate Norman Thomas. Upton Sinclair, James Baldwin, and other authors. The son of Ring Lardner, who was one of the office's heroes. Activists like Ella Winter, Paul Robeson, and Bayard Rustin. Even the then-promising novelist Norman Mailer, who, against all evidence, was also young once.

For my part, I did everything I could to meet my favorite authors in person. I got to interview Susan Sontag, who showed more interest in my hair than in my novice questions. Robin Morgan, one of the few autographs I've ever asked for. Kurt Vonnegut, who made it a condition that we talk in bare feet. And Mary McCarthy, who cooked me a meal and ended up getting me drunk.

I remember we managed to publish two long interviews with Lennon (in particular about issues like the arrest of John Sinclair) and Bowie (about sex, drugs, and sex). Sadly, I didn't get either of those assignments, even though I begged my boss. They were given to some guy who'd worked longer on the beat. That, and he had a big swinging dick.

The *Chronicle* was valued for its coverage of international affairs and for our caustic reporting on the cultural scene. The idea was to bring to the mass media the brazen style of *The East Village Other*. Or, to a lesser extent, *Rat*, which I read with a mixture of admiration and frustration at what was so obviously porn for straight men. That is, until a bunch of female workers mutinied and took the office by storm.

In national news, our focus was on the civil rights movement. We stood out because we went for what nowadays is called independent journalism. Which just means that we had more ideas than money. In addition to

Vietnam (which, at the time, was the subtext of virtually everything we said, wrote, or thought), we opposed nuclear testing, much to Yoshie's pleasant surprise.

We also appeared to side with various anticolonial movements in Asia and Africa, though I'm not sure how deep our understanding was. We had a few veteran correspondents out there, who accepted less pay because no one else would publish their lengthy articles.

As I was promoted within the paper, I witnessed the rise of the student movements, which I would have loved to have been part of during my time in college. These activists were attempting to construct a political space outside of the two-party system and the style of the old left. They believed more in taking to the streets than in institutions. I covered some of the cultural events they organized. My bosses thought this was important. They saw it as a way of converting the new generations into future readers of our paper.

That made me feel vaguely guilty, as if somehow I was taking advantage of them. Well, I probably was. And I should add that none of these scruples prevented me from continuing to do so.

When the next generation of female journalists came along, I noticed they no longer believed in peaceful feminism, or in the meritocracy. They were basically fed up with all that, as well as with those nice guys (our lovers, boyfriends, brothers) who claimed to support women's lib while continuing to objectify us.

Supposedly my job was to show these women the ropes, but in fact, I was the one learning from them. The paper soon started to publish occasional articles about the harassment of women in the workplace. We were proud when they caused quite the stir. Which was interesting, because at the *Chronicle* we'd had cases similar to the ones we were denouncing.

By then I had my independence and a chaotic lifestyle, which aroused a rather twisted interest in some men. They seemed to want to bring order into my life. When they discovered that I actually liked my chaos, they fled. My relationships were usually short-lived. That is, until I met Yoshie. I was surprised that I got along so well with a businessman, he wasn't really my type. Maybe that's why it worked. I had to reexamine the idea I had of myself. People like me (meaning those who have no money) were a great relief to him. He said we were the only ones who didn't try to talk business with him.

I've always been aware of an obvious truth, the one behind the lie. The myth that love has anything to do with fate. Couples are the product of chance. The man with whom you end up raising a family, buying a house, and celebrating your birthday isn't someone you choose after a careful casting session. Most of the time he's simply the guy who happens to be around, or who shows up when you're thirtysomething and want some emotional stability.

A lot of women in my generation were convinced of the need to be unfaithful from time to time. That this was a perfectly reasonable way of being sure that we'd truly chosen our partner. That we weren't just staying with them out of fear or repression, but because we really wanted to. If that *was* the case, then so much the better for us. And if not, it was high time we realized it. That was our way of thinking. I'm sure we had fun. And sadly, some of us ended up alone.

Generally speaking, Yoshie was fairly well adapted to Western ways. After all, he'd lived in Europe. He'd had a relationship with a girl there, at an age when nothing was really serious and everything seemed way too important. A girl, so he said, who never wanted to come visit him after he'd left France.

Every so often, he'd have these authoritarian outbursts that drove me nuts. If he tried to go samurai on me, I'd cut him off midsentence and walk out. For some reason, he found this fascinating. He didn't quite believe I could do such a thing to him, and felt the need to have it repeated, just to make sure. I was flattered by his persistence. He must've been considerably attracted to me not to be put off by my behavior.

Around that time, I objected to marriage and the contract of ownership it entails. I thought women were more enslaved by the institution of family than by capitalism. Personally, I was always against procreation. I've had enough with my nieces and nephews (and their kids after that) to satisfy my meager maternal instincts. Being a working woman was complicated enough, I didn't even want to think about how it would feel to be a working mother. My girlfriends who had kids insisted I was wrong. That your children actually set you free. From yourself, your ego, your phantoms. My phantoms *are* my children, I'd tell them. I've been nurturing them my whole life.

Yoshie and I agreed on that point. His experiences seemed to have shown him the recklessness (and also the terror) of continuing to populate the planet. As if he'd come to believe that every family, in one way or another, was close to extinction. All the same, I'd sometimes imagine myself with children. More precisely, with daughters. But I suspect this was just another form of narcissism. Those imaginary daughters were more or less myself as a child.

I didn't want to have a baby, and Yoshie didn't want to get me pregnant. This gave me a kind of sexual freedom. A freedom that in turn left me feeling guilty. It's hard not to feel guilty about the things you don't want. The tyranny of procreation reared its head on all sides. In my family. At work. In my social circle. In the media. In biological theory. In art. And, of course, in my head. That's why, after I reached a certain age, being happy without kids started to feel like a silent act of rebellion. I don't know, or I can't remember, to what extent Yoshie shared these beliefs, but in any case, we seemed pretty aligned.

For example, we were both weary of couples who could talk only about their offspring. Of course, there are practical reasons for that. But often it was also a pretext for them to subject us to other forms of despotism. Moral pressure. Implying that we were missing out on something. Interestingly, this harassment never occurs the other way around. People without kids never try to impose their viewpoint on others, or to make themselves the example.

Before hooking up with Yoshie, I tended to separate love and sex. I thought that mixing them might prove fatal. This was an ideological position, a defense mechanism, or possibly both. I got the impression that some men (alas, the ones who were more fun in bed) derived some twisted pleasure from my emotional unavailability. They found rejection exciting. As if space alone enabled them to feel uninhibited, to go further. I think I'm right in saying that they found it easier to sleep with us without the burden of emotions or responsibilities, to immerse themselves without thinking. Or maybe some of them got their kicks from wounded pride, from the sexual rage they felt at not being so terribly special to us.

I'd had my share of flings, and at least where men were concerned, I preferred to get straight to the point. With the girls I was sometimes attracted to, the pace was different. Not that they were prudes or anything (they were usually more imaginative in bed), but with them, it was possible to mix affection and desire without getting hurt too badly. But I soon learned that with men, the important thing wasn't really the sex itself so much as the possibility of it. You didn't have to actually sleep with them to keep them interested. You just had to act like you might.

I still have a clear memory of our first date, which was at my place. It was a few days after our bizarre encounter at the funeral. We'd already met for coffee (coffee and a tea, actually) to make sure that neither of us was as crazy as our behavior at the cemetery might've suggested. We both seemed nervous. When you meet someone for the first time, the lack of expectations lowers inhibitions and allows you to act recklessly. After all, you can't spoil an image you don't yet have.

But this time, we sat on the couch not knowing what to say to each other, or how to initiate something that had previously required no preamble whatsoever. Yoshie stared at the ceiling and smiled at me out of the corner of his eye.

As usual, I turned to music for help. I made sure not to choose anything too sensual, which would only have made us feel more awkward. The last thing we needed was a voice from the record player egging us on, like: Go ahead, young 'uns, go on and touch each other. In the end, I put on a record by Phil Ochs, my idol at the time. His ironic, combative voice gave me the courage to laugh at how scared I was.

I guess some people might consider poor Ochs's lyrics totally dated. Okay, how about this one? "I love Puerto Ricans and Negroes / as long as they don't move next door . . ." Or this one? "Yes, it must have been another land / That couldn't happen in the U.S.A. . . ." As for this last song, I prefer not to wonder whether he's referring to our future. "Back to the good old days / God save the king!"

Despite everything, I still believe some things could never happen here. *He* could never win, I'm sure of that. We'd never allow it. We'd never choose a wall in this land of immigrants, or a guy who believes that climate change was invented by the Chinese, who surrounds himself with deniers, and is in the pay of energy lobbyists. A guy who claims you can learn all you need to know about missiles in an hour and a half, and who just can't wait to have access to the nuclear button.

Anyway, while the music played, I went to get us some drinks. When I came back to the sofa, I found Yoshie with his shirt off. He looked very serious. And then I saw his scars.

Like most of my friends, I have more than a few operations under my belt. An appendectomy. A stent. That valve in my lung, after which my doctors insisted I lay off the cigarettes. Cervical cancer. Two abortions, neither of them with Yoshie. (He was convinced he was sterile, that his sperm had somehow been jinxed.) And that tumor in my breast, which changed how I perceive things, including pleasure. It no doubt affected my relationship with Yoshie.

That happened a couple of years before we met. I had to have an operation for mastitis. I'm aware that this is a common condition among women who breastfeed, but I'd gotten it without having kids. I can't help seeing the irony in that. They put me on antibiotics, which didn't work, and that's how I developed a big lump. I went to see my gynecologist. I didn't want to worry anyone, or create drama for no reason. Actually, I had a date with a very good-looking journalist later that evening. I decided to keep it, not knowing what was going to happen. I felt that to cancel it would be to assume the worst.

No sooner had the gynecologist examined me than she asked if there was anyone waiting for me outside. She made an urgent call to a colleague at a clinic and advised me to have a relative take me there. No way, I told her. I belong to one of those families that overreact to any sort of health scare by getting sicker than the patient. So I took a cab to the clinic instead. From there I made a brief call to my mother, as I did every day, without saying a word about the situation. I pretended to read while I waited. They performed a biopsy and it was painful. Then I left. I changed clothes, took another cab, stopped at a pharmacy to buy the drugs they'd prescribed. And then I went out to dinner with the good-looking journalist, who was not allowed to touch my left boob.

I spent the next week with my mind elsewhere as people were talking to me. Besides the terror, there was also bewilderment. I felt I was the victim, not of a health scare, but of a serious misunderstanding, and that I was living someone else's life.

When they told me that it was only an infected mastitis with an abscess, and could be remedied with an easy operation, my relief was so overwhelming that I felt liberated from my own body. Now my body was more closely related to survival than to beauty. Or to the beauty of survival. The doctors warned me that my breast would suffer some damage from the operation. I replied that I earned my living with my brain, and then I signed the consent form.

They made three small incisions in the lower part of my left breast. As soon as it healed, I went to see a plastic surgeon. The solution he offered was to scrape out the entire breast and replace it with silicone. To add insult to injury, he recommended I have both my breasts done if I wanted them to be symmetrical. I wasn't interested. Not if it meant removing healthy tissue to insert a block of garbage.

At first, the scars were quite obvious. Now they're only really noticeable when I'm lying down. There's a void, a void filled with meaning. No one has ever seemed to mind this asymmetry, but I realize I'm no oil painting. I guess my charms have aged better than my two tits. One and three-quarters tits, to be exact. Or maybe they liked my freakishness. Why not? Let's call it my lefty charm.

The largest scar, at the base of my breast, has become the most important part of my body. Like that old Cohen song: "There is a crack in everything / That's how the light gets in." The other day I read an article about Marilyn Monroe's last photo shoot. The biggest diva of them all, and apparently even *she* had a scar on her belly from a gallbladder operation. So, even Marilyn had a gallbladder! The scar isn't visible in those nude photos (which just goes to show, nude photos are never truly nude), and yet that was what distinguished her. Not her ass. Or her boobs, which were nothing special. But that incision. Her insignia.

That first evening together, when I came back to the sofa carrying our drinks, I found Yoshie with his shirt off and he showed me his scars. A fine mesh covering his forearms and back. They looked like inner branches, as if he were carrying a tree. Then I showed him mine. He touched them. Kissed them. Blessed them. We felt light, a little ugly, and very beautiful.

Later, in bed, when our breathing had calmed again, we examined the blemishes on our bodies. We gave each other a tour of all the parts of our bodies we were normally embarrassed about, and we recognized one another.

Yoshie looked shorter lying down than standing up. His upper and lower body weren't quite in proportion. He had a different kind of harmony.

Another memory I have from that night is Yoshie learning to pronounce the word *thigh*, which he would confuse with *tight*. I joked that if he insisted on calling a thigh tight, then mine wasn't a good example. He practiced the word, pressing his forefinger into my thigh. According to him, from that moment on he'd imagine my legs whenever he said it.

Our eyelids growing heavy, and our legs entwined, I had the feeling that the mattress was expanding. As if it were breathing along with us.

I never understood how, despite being a smoker like me, he had such a keen sense of smell. Yoshie smelled between the lines. He could deduce bodies from their clothes, fruits from their peels. I wonder if this was related to our shared obsession with supermarkets, especially at night. He was crazy about these stores and their contradictions of delicious and horrible smells, of filth and cleanliness.

My palate was less discerning but I found that combination of sordidness, desire, and capitalism to be deeply erotic. To see all of the things you could take home with you, devour, and introduce into your body. I've always suspected that in supermarkets, it's not the products you're paying for, but that orgy of possibilities, that lustful illusion of freedom. If it weren't for that seductive fantasy, consumerism would be easy to resist.

We never did it in a supermarket. Our bashfulness got the better of us in the end. Instead, I had to be content with a few quick gropes between the aisles. I would clench my thighs until we got home, trying to hold on to that wonderful frisson. Some of it always got lost along the way. In the end, we couldn't avoid feeling a little disappointed. That's the second rule of consumerism.

Yoshie was intrigued by my habit of painting my nails after I masturbated. For me, both things are part of the same impulse. Touching oneself is the opposite of being dirty. It cleans you, reboots you. Pleasuring yourself gives you a shine.

Timid with strangers? Overly serious? Not at all. If anything, Yoshie was rather extroverted, which for some reason surprised me. Probably be-cause of the stupid stereotypes we have about the Japanese. I can see how someone might misinterpret his initial silences. The truth was that he used this restraint to his advantage, winning the sympathy of people who were eventually amazed to discover his sociable side.

Part of his charm was that ability to make each of us believe that we'd managed to get close to someone so hopelessly shy, which also allowed him to get along with people he had little in common with. Including my brother, Ralph, who developed an inexplicable affection for him, consid-ering how radically different they were. He had disliked all my previous boyfriends, which wasn't so strange. I always dated guys who were the antithesis of my family.

Yoshie wasn't reticent, he just had a delayed reaction. He always had a lot to say about things, though rarely while they were happening. He wasn't being cautious, he was simply terrified of being wrong. He'd sooner keep quiet than make a mistake. Before he spoke, he wanted to be sure that his opinions would outshine yours. That way he wouldn't waste time on un-necessary debates. This made him a skilled businessman. Meanwhile, as a journalist, heated debates were an occupational hazard for me.

He would alternate between lengthy periods of calm and sudden out-bursts of rage. In that respect, we complemented each other. My moodiness was tempered by his typical serenity. On the other hand, when he did let off steam from time to time, he could do so without much opposition from me. My day was invariably punctuated with so many petty disputes that by the time I got home, I didn't have the energy for any major arguments.

Best of all were his roars of laughter whenever we made up. There was something primitively sexual about his exuberance after a fight. I've always thought that the way we laugh reveals who we really are. We can put on a face, adopt a tone, control our gestures. But it's very difficult to laugh insincerely. I've known laughs that are nervous like their owners. Tight-lipped laughs that conceal more than they show. Or shrill laughs desperate for attention. Some are strangely long-winded and don't want to end, as if masking pain, while others grow gradually louder as they gain confidence. Some are a single burst that cleaves the air before snapping shut like a knife. Others sound rough, because they've been through a lot. None of these describe his laugh.

With other people, he hardly ever mentioned his native country. He had spent practically half his life abroad. I think it was a subject that was awkward for him to talk about with anyone other than his closest friends, he was fixated on the idea of assimilating as much as possible. He would often downplay the differences between our two cultures, and preferred to point out what they had in common. I saw this as a gesture of devotion, now I'm not so sure. There was always a part of him that he refused to share, something that ran much deeper. The one thing he consistently talked about was his aunt and uncle, whom he truly worshipped.

I knew he was a victim of the bomb practically from the get-go. He blurted it out that first night, when he showed me his scars. I was shocked. I couldn't help feeling guilty, and grateful that he was telling me. His secret brought us closer together. Naïvely, I believed that if he was willing to tell me about something so big, then he was unlikely to hide the small things. I was so young, I didn't yet understand that sometimes, revealing a difficult truth gives you more of a license to lie.

Yoshie couldn't bear people pitying him. Whenever he got to know someone better, he would reveal his secret so calmly. He'd let them pose the usual questions and answer succinctly. And then he'd never raise the subject again. That way he could avoid their lamentations or having to give further explanations.

I admit I found it weird that an atom bomb survivor would choose to live in the United States. And that he could be so fascinated by our way of life and our music, particularly jazz. That was one thing we didn't agree on. I preferred hard rock and protest songs.

Another thing that surprised me about Yoshie was that he loved the Mets, whom I'd rooted for all my life. Of course, back then I had no idea that the Japanese adore baseball. And I would never have imagined that hamburger in Japanese is a *hanbāgā*, or that they call beer *bīru*. These were the things I learned right away. What took me longer to work out was that he saw assimilation as a kind of personal challenge. I think he thought that if he integrated successfully into the world of his former enemy, then maybe he could vanquish the ghost and leave it behind forever.

Maybe there was another reason for Yoshie's behavior, one that wasn't so benign. Japanese companies were determined to overtake America and Germany, especially in the tech industry. Maybe outstripping Western brands was a question of postwar pride. I read the other day that Japanese companies are investing more than ever in American businesses. A famous life insurance company, for example, and a pharmaceutical company specializing in nervous system disorders. It occurs to me that both are related to war.

Around the time that Yoshie and I started going steady, aspects of Japanese culture were becoming consumer items here. All of a sudden, Japanese products were equated with perfection and elegance. You know, the idea that any radio manufactured in Osaka would sound superior to some junk from Detroit. We were in the midst of the so-called Japanese economic miracle, which the finance section in newspapers talked about incessantly. I remember the articles were full of praise, but also a sense of alarm. Our former enemy and present-day ally was becoming a fierce competitor. Experts seemed to be hinting that there was something suspicious about this growth, and that we must do something to stop them.

I doubt Yoshie could've risen so quickly through the ranks at his company at any other time. People who are lucky (and especially those who are unlucky) depend on hard work and chance as much as they do on politics. He was doing great at his job, and was extremely proud about his position at the company. He was marketing director of Me's main office in Lower Manhattan.

The name of his company obviously caught my attention, how could I forget *Me*? The word means "eye" in Japanese. Yoshie explained to me that the founder, with great commercial foresight, had taken advantage of that fact, ensuring that we foreign consumers would remember the brand while learning a simple word in his language. I don't know if this also occurred to Me's founder or if it was a coincidence, but it's interesting that *eye* has the same sound as *I*. As though, just there, English had an intimation of Japanese.

Yoshie was like a working machine. His own most efficient slave driver. He and his colleagues were a reminder of what capitalism could be. But I believe they had a totally different mind-set from that of American employees. Compared with the way things worked at my newspaper, for example, the Me employees stayed behind the scenes. Individual initiative seemed less important than teamwork.

I found this philosophy very wise, if a little nerve-racking. It meant that nothing you did was entirely on you. It also meant you could never change anything alone. On the contrary, he replied, it's the opposite that's nerve-racking. Trying to change everything on your own. Believing that you should. Believing that you can. There's no worse delusion.

At first, I couldn't help but feel flattered by what I thought was Yoshie's deference. It was such a relief after all the pushy guys I'd dated, who were always trying to impose their will on me. It took me a while to realize that he just had difficulty saying no, and that this didn't always mean he agreed with me. How the hell can a society function when insistence is considered poor taste, while failure is forbidden? That seemed to me an appalling combination. The amalgam of a Japanese problem and an American one.

From the impression I got from the employees at Me, the Japanese had been taught to fight their foes to the death, only to show them respect, loyalty, and even admiration the moment they were declared friends. Yoshie introduced me to many of his compatriots, and I noticed they would do anything to change the subject so as to avoid mentioning the atom bomb to an American. He saw this as a token of goodwill. Apparently we could annihilate one another, but we couldn't regret it together.

As far as I can recall, there was only one time that I'd succeeded in getting one of his colleagues to mention the subject in my presence. It was his old friend Kamamoto, or Yomamoto, or something like that. Seeing an opportunity, I ventured to suggest that, considering what had happened, it was inevitable that his people should feel some bitterness toward Americans. Yoshie's friend just kept shaking his head and smiling at me.

It is the wish of all good people in my country, Yomamoto or Kamamoto said very solemnly, especially those of us who have endured the worst, that we be alone in experiencing this. What we desire, dear madam, Kamamoto or Yomamoto went on, is for the disaster to be a lesson to the world, so that it may never happen again. (He referred to it as *the disaster*, which struck me as too vague for something as definite as the bombs.) It is our duty to serve as an example. That is why I consider friendship much more valuable than bitterness.

Yoshie stared at him in silence while he spoke.

No American school could have done a better job, I thought.

———————

Even among liberals, Yoshie avoided criticizing our country. And he didn't argue for pacifism when we socialized with my colleagues from the newspaper. Whenever we started to discuss international affairs, he'd look at me helplessly out of the corner of his eye, and then I'd feel the urge to hold him tight and take him to bed with me.

But if ever anyone (including my beloved brother, Ralph) tried to defend the heroics of World War II, that was a different story. The slightest attempt to justify the bombings by invoking the attack on Pearl Harbor, the Potsdam Declaration, or the doctrine of necessary evil would turn Yoshie sober.

He didn't bother criticizing the monstrosity of nuclear annihilation, or to point out the difference between military and civilian victims. Didn't argue that the bombs could have targeted only local infrastructure, or been dropped at a time when there were fewer civilians around. He didn't cite the Geneva or Hague Conventions. He didn't even mention his family, who were at the root of all his silences.

He was simply content to remind us that, after decades of peace, our country still had many army bases in Japan. That, like the French, we continued to carry out all kinds of nuclear tests. And that those things didn't stem from emergency circumstances, but from the same age-old political interests, which existed before and long after the war.

Incidentally, some of my colleagues had no idea that American bases in Okinawa took up one-fifth of the main island. That its inhabitants were forced to live alongside the army of their former enemy and, worse still, its nuclear arsenal. It made me wonder what the hell our newspaper was even writing about.

After meeting Yoshie, I admit I also had a lot of reading up to do. There were so many things we never spoke about here. I was amazed to discover that we still had jurisdiction over several Japanese airfields, even in Tokyo. It took us about thirty years to hand some of them back. If I'm not mistaken, Yokota is still an American base to this day.

Facts like these, which I didn't know or otherwise had long forgotten, made me realize that censorship didn't occur only in Japan. In subtler, more veiled ways, perhaps, it also happened here. No one had told us the truth about what we did when we won the war. Or, of course, about the consequences of the bombs. Military secrecy has always been far, far more important to us than democracy.

Given that we're supposed to embody the great democratic ideal, we can never admit our very own authoritarianisms. Oh, not here. The quest for freedom, prosperity, and security (or at least one of the three) drives each and every one of our actions. And if things get really ugly, we resort to political assassination. Yoshie found this astonishing. He told me that he knew of no other Western power that had assassinated so many of its presidents. I don't recall the exact stats. I think I prefer not to know them.

I remember the tenth anniversary of the Tsar Bomba, at a time when I was growing increasingly committed to Yoshie. We published a special report about it that day in the *Chronicle*. It's been long forgotten by now, but it was the most powerful explosion in the world. Three thousand times more powerful than the Hiroshima bomb. It's a number so big that it sounds like a typo you make at the end of a long day, when your fingers are going too fast and you add an extra zero. But I know it's correct because it was one of our headlines: THREE THOUSAND TIMES HIROSHIMA.

The Cold War was at its peak, and the Soviets had been looking for a dramatic way to demonstrate their might. They'd wanted to respond to the missiles we'd developed and to our tests in the Pacific. To me this seemed to prove that the nuclear deterrence theory was a failure, a lie, or both. The only effect it had was to intensify the urge for self-preservation of the enemy, which in turn triggered our own. We call this vicious cycle military defense.

The blast radius from the Tsar was big enough, I don't know, to wipe several American cities off the map in seconds. The shock wave caused a tremor that registered on every seismograph on the planet. Yes, I know it didn't kill anyone on that occasion, because it was just an experiment on an island in the Arctic. But knowing that didn't allay my fears. It upset me to imagine all the pain it could have caused anywhere else.

I wonder what kind of grief unborn tragedies deserve. The ones you know *could* have occurred. I feel that to answer this would be a political achievement.

———

Once he got comfortable with Yoshie, Ralph, who as well as being conservative is tremendously knowledgeable—yes, he's *that* type of conservative—began to criticize Japanese imperialism. We Americans love to expose foreign acts of barbarism. I'd even go as far as to say we get a kick out of it, possibly because it gives us an excuse to go on committing our own.

My brother would invite us to lunch, for instance, and between mouthfuls would speak of the tortures in Nanjing. Of the suffering the Japanese had inflicted in China and Korea. Including (and he looked at me as he said this, because he knew just how much these things freaked me out) the Korean sex slaves exploited by the soldiers. Apparently, there were about a hundred thousand of them. They called them comfort women. I admit that I'd never heard of them then and I wondered how the hell my brother had.

Whenever I tried to talk to him about our military occupation of Japan, Ralph would mention the annexation of Korea. He reminded me that Japanese troops had appropriated its land, subjugated the farmers, and seized their crops. The inhabitants were prohibited from using their own language and were even forced to take Japanese names. Laws were changed to enable Japan to import huge numbers of Koreans, who were used as forced labor in its armaments and coal industry. What would you say, my brother asked me, if we were doing things like that in Vietnam?

During one of these diatribes, Ralph even confessed to Yoshie how at the climax of World War II (that was the word my brother normally used, *climax*), everybody at his school had repeated the words sung by our Chinese allies against the Japanese invaders:

> *Arise! All who refuse to be slaves!*
> *Let our flesh and blood become our new Great Wall!*
> *As the nation faces its greatest peril,*
> *All forcefully expend their last cries.*
> *Arise! Arise! Arise!*
> *Our millions beat as one.*
> *Brave the enemy's fire, march on!*
> *Brave the enemy's fire, march on!*
> *Braving the enemy's fire!*
> *March on! March on! On!*

Having heard the song frequently at home when I was a child, I knew the lyrics by heart. Preppy girls would also chant it while raising money for charity in the city center. That same song would later be adopted by Chinese communists as their national anthem. How much more ironic can you get?

My brother seemed oddly enamored of those World War II years. Of course, he was too young to be drafted, and, in any case, he would never have passed the physical because he'd wrecked one of his knees playing football. For a long time, I attributed this nostalgia to his political beliefs. Now I have a different theory. Those war years coincided with his coming-of-age. He was growing up fast. Starting to feel like a man. The world might get blown to pieces, but for him life was just beginning.

Ralph had the nerve to say, in front of Yoshie, that the Japanese government was equally if not more responsible than ours for the bombs. It had ignored the Allies' ultimatum. August 3 had been the deadline, my brother insisted, and the emperor had had an extra three days to surrender if the lives of his people mattered so much to him.

From the get-go, Yoshie merely agreed. Ralph was astonished that he refused to counter. Then, in a whisper, Yoshie added that America's reasons for dropping those bombs hadn't been to protect Japan's neighbors in Asia, and even less to promote democracy in the region. After all, it had also killed many of the Koreans held hostage there.

Wait a minute, wait a minute, my brother interrupted. Okay, so a few innocent Koreans died. How can you demand compassion from the enemy when . . . ?

And no massacre should be justified by a previous one, Yoshie went on coolly. Otherwise we'd be fighting the same war forever.

The way I saw it, the bombs didn't signal the end of World War II so much as the start of World War III. Which is why I often pointed out that since then, the world in general, and our country in particular, was less safe.

Ralph argued that although the atomic bomb had been an extreme solution, objectively speaking it had saved many more lives (both American and Japanese) that would have been lost had the war continued.

This line of reasoning drove me nuts. To compare real dead bodies with theoretical ones seems to me an obscene exercise. And above all, I don't believe this problem should be reduced to a statistic, which is what we always do whenever anything gets too complicated. What about the ethics? The fact that the extermination was premeditated? Our leaders knew beforehand that a significant part of the population would die. Those people weren't collateral damage, or unavoidable casualties of war, or anything. I saw a qualitative difference there.

But my brother argued that there was essentially no difference between dying from a bomb, from a bullet wound, or from being run over by a tank. According to him, if every life was of equal value, then a death was just a death. It didn't matter by what means. I remember him saying this to us one night, while my nieces and nephews were asleep.

Yoshie chimed in to say that perhaps it didn't matter to the person who died. Or at least to those who died instantaneously, because many others suffered protracted deaths or illnesses. It did matter hugely, however, to the families mourning their dead. And to society, which, whether consciously or unconsciously, grieved with them.

I suspect that when my brother attempted to justify the nuclear genocide, it came from a place of fear. If he acknowledged the enormity of what our country had done, we'd be in a position where we'd have to fear some kind of reprisal.

Ralph rejected the word *genocide*. And he admonished me for using it to refer to something that wasn't the Shoah. He argued rather ingeniously that if anything, a nuclear attack was an *omnicide*. Okay, I protested, that's even worse. Killing everyone, indiscriminately?

He replied in that tone of his, halfway between successful lawyer and eldest son: You're wrong, my dear, quite wrong. It's still preferable, despite everything. Or would you have preferred us to select our victims according to race, religion, or class? We would never have done a thing like that. Look, I'm not saying that the A-bomb isn't every bit as brutal as you say. But at least it responds to a radically democratic notion of war. It establishes no distinction or privilege among victims. Doesn't it make you sick that civilian casualties, as newspapers like yours like to call them, are in fact always the poor? And here I thought you were a leftist, Sister.

Arguing with Ralph is no easy feat. Like Grandpa Usher, he has authority running in his veins. My mother used to say that, as a child, my brother didn't beat up on his friends because he wasn't able to reason, but *in order to* get them to argue with him. He would literally punch them to make them listen to his opinions. And if they still disagreed with him, he would apologize for hitting them.

Like the rest of my family, he truly hated it when people compared any other massacre to what the Nazis did, even as metaphor, and I understand why. If everything can be compared to Auschwitz, he'd say angrily, then it serves only to normalize Auschwitz.

According to Ralph, my boyfriend and I championed a reductive pacifism. My brother maintained that Japan's current stance was too self-serving. It opposed war and nuclear weapons, yet accepted our military protection. Japanese diplomacy was taking advantage of our alliance with its ambivalence. Yoshie argued that it wasn't ambivalence, but impotence.

Despite not seeing eye to eye, Ralph and Yoshie never really lost their tempers with each other. They were content to engage in a different kind of male ritual—neither of them budged an inch. The curious thing is that when Yoshie wasn't there, my brother took his side against my family.

When we were alone at home, Yoshie would let down his guard. Occasionally he would speak of his fear during the bombardment, which he said felt physically similar to the panic you feel during an earthquake. The insignificance of your body. The permanent threat of it happening again. The sensation that clings to your senses. Like when your ears go on hearing an alarm even after it has stopped, he said.

Ever since I was young, I'd considered waking up early to the sound of an alarm clock a divine punishment, the ultimate misfortune, the end of all happiness. At least for a few minutes. But as soon as I'd had a shower and a cup of coffee (well, two), I'd realize it wasn't so bad.

Yoshie got up early because he had to, and also, I suspect, by choice. Whereas the working hours of a journalist are as unpredictable as the news. That's to say, they happen at any and all times. Your day is no longer divided into hours. Your week is no longer divided into days. Your time becomes an open-ended pursuit, a fever that subsides only once you've caught your prey. For many years, I adored that rhythm governed by chaos. If anyone had told me back then what my routine would become—breakfast at dawn, running errands in the mornings, and tending to my beloved plants—I'd have called them a bigger liar than Nixon.

I loved that in my job, I never knew what to expect. Having to be alert in the newsroom, on the street, at home. Observing people without being seen. Cab chases or running like crazy to catch up with someone. Getting a call from the newspaper and having to pack in a hurry. Editing a sentence just before it goes to print. Going out for a late dinner and getting drunk after finishing a difficult job. Transcribing interviews into the early hours. Continually juggling a succession of deadlines. The thrill of feeling that I wouldn't make it and then finally making it. Adrenaline as a form of love.

Journalism is bipolar, and so are those of us who practice it. We veer daily between euphoria and despair. Between sudden disappointment and our next discovery. Many people are like that, but we have a professional excuse. We're addicted to the scoop. Deadline junkies. I imagine this affects the way we relate to others. If a person didn't strike me as unusual or exceptional, complicated even, I found it impossible to feel attracted to them. Did others find me as surprising, as special? What a cruel question.

I documented every interesting thing I saw or heard, jotted it all down, because you never know. That was how I avoided depression. I didn't always know why I was taking notes, but the act of doing it reassured and inspired me. In the end, I found it impossible to read a book, watch a film, or talk to someone without imagining that sooner or later I'd be writing an article about it. Or an obituary. In the end, it was all useful. A lot of the facts I mention now were in my notes from back then.

I can't say exactly when I grew tired of that life. I know that if I could travel back to the time before I met Yoshie, I'd be a journalist again. But if I were a young person today, I'd look for a different occupation. That's what I told that Argentinian guy who interviewed me. News doesn't really matter these days. Actually, nothing really matters. There are a billion other things waiting for you to click on them. How can you write seriously when you can no longer take reality seriously?

Even if I had the same vocation as in those early years, I have no idea what I would do in this jungle of giant corporations and investment funds, how I would earn my living in a gig economy of instant layoffs. Nowadays, what counts isn't who reads you but who finances you. Your investors are your public. People no longer want to pay for quality information. They're prepared to spend a fortune on the devices they use to read, but not a cent on what they're reading. A newspaper's income doesn't come from its readership. One day they'll invent media that doesn't even require an audience.

And what about those new toys? Outside demands and pressures have grown as much as or even more than technology. On any objective ledger, exploitation has increased. I know, I sound like an old woman. The world has never been a very nice place. So where the hell did I get all my youthful optimism back then?

I wonder whether these concerns seem ridiculous to my great-nieces and great-nephews. They seem so savvy about today's world, they fit into it with such ease. In fact, the youngest has dreams of becoming a journalist, bless her.

It's a despicable, beautiful profession. If you don't do it right, it will stick out like any of those mediocre works of art we had to write about. After all, watching art is an art.

Early on in my career, I remember that writing in the imperative was de rigueur. If you didn't use it at least half a dozen times in one article to rouse your readers, you were at serious risk of failing to connect with the middle class.

Second, you had to create a sense of intrigue by starting off with a question. This was practically obligatory if you were writing about a chamber music ensemble, a French sociologist, a philosopher of language, or any of those things that scare people off.

Third, you had to try to pull off the most outrageous comparisons. For example: "The Andy Warhol of medievalism." "The Joe Frazier of peace." "The Virginia Woolf of movie starlets." "A masterful combination of Fellini, Engels, and Mickey Mouse," or "An explosive encounter between Proust, Eva Perón, and Kareem Abdul-Jabbar."

But most important, you had to analyze the classics through the aesthetic of camp and glam. What would Haydn in black leather have sounded like? What would have become of Tolstoy if he'd had a penchant for sequined boys? Could graffiti improve the Sistine Chapel? All of a sudden, these questions became transcendental. There came a point when post-Marxism, semiotics, and structural anthropology were acceptable only if they were being used to introduce a punk rock band.

In the small world of underground criticism, the use of such unfashionable concepts as *content, conclusion,* or (even worse) *message* was strictly prohibited. We saw them as distortions that tainted the aesthetic experience. They could ruin your reputation over the course of a weekend.

Naturally, all this had a sexual connotation. We expected to enjoy art without preconceptions, the same way we wanted to fuck without having to worry too much. We were sick and tired of keeping our distance. We demanded skin. We wanted to touch. To conquer our senses as we fought for control over our own bodies.

Yes, it was time to assault the pantheons of high culture with our base instincts. What we never imagined was that the latter would replace the former. As an old friend who wrote for the *Chronicle* said to me, this amazing wave led many theorists to abandon their prejudices, but an equal number of dilettantes to cling to theirs.

The visceral was trendy again, and it seems to be enjoying a comeback. Cultural journalism became a celebration of pain. If a novel didn't churn your guts, you hadn't really read it. If a record didn't make you go deaf, you hadn't heard it. If you didn't feel actors were flaying themselves alive onstage, you were unworthy of the theater. I started to think that art schools would be replaced by nursing courses.

I wonder whether this was somehow related to how tortured we were by the war in Vietnam and the agony of Watergate. If you think about it, Nixon's resignation sparked a rhetorical healing process. Public opinion was focused on national reconciliation and first aid. Our new president spoke a lot, you know, about patching up wounds. Politics, the media, and psychology came together in the illusion of an instant cure.

Nobody had done anything wrong. Or if they had, it was for the common good. No one was actually guilty. Or rather, they were both the guilty party *and* the victim. Justice was less important than forgiveness. So you went to your shrink, who told you to go easy on yourself. In other words, if you dug too deep, everyone might end up being implicated, starting with you. It was in your interest to cooperate a little.

In all fairness, Mr. Ford had made history. He became vice president and president without getting a single vote. During his brief mandate, he also had time to pardon his boss without trial. My brother thought this was the least we could do for someone who had sacrificed his job for the good of the nation.

Rather than making a living as a journalist, I was just scraping by. I realize that would be a luxury nowadays. The fact is that, for a few years, I could barely pay the rent on a one-room apartment with about half a kitchen and not quite a bathroom. Nor could I afford regular visits to the therapist, the way my mother had all her life. She was convinced that her shrink was as crucial to her survival as her butcher.

Yoshie was horrified by therapists. He believed they couldn't help you, or that their help made you feel worse. I explained that they teach you to think about your problems. Even more than we already do? he protested. I accused him of having a resistance to therapy. Resistance is good, he retorted.

At some point in our relationship, which to my surprise was becoming increasingly serious, Yoshie and I decided to move in together. I'd say it was a big step for us both, I mean as individuals. He'd never officially lived with anyone before, or so he said. And I'd promised myself a very long time ago that I'd never do it again.

In California, I'd been in an abusive relationship with a controlling boyfriend when I was too young to understand what that meant. At twenty, living with him was a forgivable mistake to have made. But at thirtysomething, no way. My biggest fear was that Yoshie wouldn't respect my space, that he wouldn't accept my chaotic habits, the erratic hours I kept, the trips I made for the paper. I was in love, yet pretty much convinced things wouldn't work out.

When we met, I was living in an area of Queens where a lot of Manhattan cabdrivers refused to go at night. Those motherfuckers would tell you, I don't do Queens, ma'am. I really loved that borough, with its mishmash of identities, and I detested how some people reacted when you told them where you lived. New York has always been divided into three areas. The *Wow*, the *How nice*, and the *I see*.

Yoshie was keen for us to move to Manhattan, and had difficulty accepting my only condition. That we live in a place where we could afford to split the rent, a place that would be mine as much as his. The thought of depending on his money to pay for my own apartment horrified me. He had classic fantasies about the city center. The wide avenues of Midtown. The fatuousness of the Upper East Side. At the time, Me was expanding. It had just launched those old color TVs with the Cromesonic system. His successes made me happy, but that was his budget to spend, not mine.

Before making a final decision, we considered the West Side. If I remember correctly, we looked at several options there. Either we didn't fall in love with any of them or they were too small for his damn banjo collection. More and more Latinos were moving into the area. When I asked for advice, my contacts told me it was going downhill. And from what great white heights? I'm afraid they weren't able to say.

We ended up renting a fairly spacious apartment in central Harlem, which was the most I could afford. We were steps away from the Apollo Theater and Spanish Harlem and not that far, it turned out, from my family's neighborhood, where I wouldn't have gone back to live in a million years, by the way.

He was more enamored of the apartment than of the area. He couldn't have imagined that in the future other yuppies would live there. Ironically, the whole of Harlem is becoming hip nowadays, meaning expensive. Meaning on its way to becoming mummified. It's the same old process. They start to build, plant a few trees, prices go up, and they kick out the locals. Afro-fusion restaurants, hell yeah. But barbecues and kids playing in the streets? Hell no. Property speculation is a toxic stain chasing out cities, which have to flee to survive.

Yoshie seemed traumatized by the prospect of moving to a different neighborhood. He'd barely set foot outside of downtown and the environs of Central Park. I don't think he'd heard of the Harlem Renaissance, the New Negro, or any of the other black cultural movements. I suspect he even thought Harlem and the Bronx were the same place. As far as he was concerned, Manhattan ended on Ninety-Sixth Street. He took some convincing. I explained that if he really wanted to assimilate, he had to experience all four corners of the city. I wonder whether there wasn't a bit of racial prejudice going on there as well. I don't suppose he would ever have admitted it.

Near where we lived, African American girls, some of them minors, hung around in bars and on street corners, pacing slowly up and down, as though aging with each step. I would see them soliciting white guys who came uptown. Watching them brought to mind Claude McKay's poems, which still packed a punch back then.

> *Through the long night until the silver break*
> *Of day the little gray feet know no rest;*
> *Through the lone night until the last snow-flake*
> *Has dropped from heaven upon the earth's white breast,*
> *The dusky, half-clad girls of tired feet*
> *Are trudging, thinly shod, from street to street.*

Those white sons of bitches treated Harlem like their private hunting ground. And they were the ones who most claimed they loved the place.

As for me, I guess I hoped to behave like the writer Jean Toomer, who, thanks to his mixed heritage, was considered both black and white, or neither, depending on who was looking at him. But coming from a nice, typical Jewish family, I'm afraid my aspirations were slightly self-righteous.

When we first moved there, it was difficult for me not to feel awkward when striking up conversations with strangers. Like an idiot, I exaggerated my friendliness, as if, instead of just mutual respect, they needed to be treated with kid gloves. I was trying to convey notions of equality that can't be shown in a single moment, only applied over time.

I soon realized that my inadvertent condescension made them uneasy. Apparently, they didn't give a damn if I was a liberal, signed petitions, or thought of myself more or less as a supporter of civil rights. All they wanted from me was to be left alone. I found that frustrating. Only when I relaxed and learned to be a bit rude with everyone, including Latinos and African Americans, did I start to feel that I fit in with the locals.

One evening, Yoshie and I were out walking after having dinner downtown and seeing a Cassavetes movie. I don't remember which one. We had just started living together. It was summer. We were happy and reasonably tipsy, so rather than take the subway or a cab, we decided to walk home. Getting back to our new neighborhood took longer than we'd imagined, or maybe it was a weekday, because the avenue was deserted. Around 115th

Street or so, with my typical nocturnal high spirits, I suggested a nightcap. Yoshie was ready for bed, but he agreed with that generosity that exists solely in couples who are still honeymooning.

The movie, it's coming back to me now, was about two people who are exact opposites, poles apart, and unexpectedly end up falling in love. Cassavetes used a technique based on muscle memory. The basic idea is that actors repeat the same gestures and actions over and over, until they become not as much a role as part of their own behavior and identity. I wonder whether this could work in reverse. Whether we could omit something over and over, until the event in question is erased from our memories.

Anyhow, we stopped for a drink at a nightclub near our apartment. The live music was over, and the place was almost empty. We were the only customers whose skin was a different color. No one said anything to us. No one messed with us. But Yoshie admitted that he was struck by the looks people gave us, the way their bodies stiffened as soon as we came into their field of vision, the conversations dropping off as we walked into the room. When the barman served us our drinks, the counter between us suddenly seemed a lot wider than before.

Yoshie was worried about drawing our neighbors' attention. He felt hyperconscious of his appearance, the way he dressed, his accent, the food he bought. He was afraid he'd have to start all over again with his efforts to assimilate, that he was back at square one.

Sure, for a couple of months people gave us funny looks. I was a white woman who thought she was liberated, among other middle-class beliefs. And Yoshie was a double intruder. Not only a guy from some distant land, but also a yuppie carrying a briefcase. Gradually, they got used to seeing him around and stopped looking askance at him. They began to chat with him in stores. Greeted him in the street. Exchanged banter with him. And before long, he was on a first-name basis with every shopkeeper on the block.

Whenever we went out, he'd end up introducing me to someone. He'd adopt AAVE to put people at ease. Yoshie became an even bigger fan of the neighborhood than I was. He acted like moving there had been his idea.

He was crazy about Harlem's music. Not just what was playing in the clubs we went to on weekends, many of which no longer exist. He maintained that the neighborhood had its own subterranean rhythm, a special beat beneath its streets. As a matter of fact, we were out walking when he came up with that famous TV commercial for Me. You know, the one with the multicolored balls bouncing up Fifth Avenue until they reach Harlem. There, they change into scoops of ice cream in all different flavors, sampled by laughing children. Then the camera pans out to show families of different races and classes having dinner, and watching the commercial on a Me TV set.

Critics praised the ad for its inclusive message and its interracial imagery, for using the metaphor of technology as an egalitarian utopia, or whatever. I was bemused. Those were my values, not his. If I remember correctly, sales of Me televisions in the States doubled that year. Yoshie used to tell me that advertising is a self-fulfilling prophecy. For a product to sell, you have to say that it's selling.

Once we'd resolved the issue of the apartment, we organized ourselves with relative ease. I guess like any couple built on mutual respect, we argued only about trivial stuff.

I can recall a serious disagreement over how to decorate the apartment. I like things in pairs or sets. Yoshie visualized everything in singles. Odd numbers didn't bother him. He loved subtlety, I preferred clarity. He liked things to be movable, multipurpose. I was partial to stationary objects. I don't want to know what that all said about us.

One of his foibles was to drag that dreadful old black-and-white rug with him everywhere. He insisted on spreading it out in the center of the living room. I gave in. I had won the battle of the neighborhood, so I let him have his way about stuff like that.

His obsession with banjos had turned him into an *otaku*, a word he taught me himself. His instruments started to invade every wall in the apartment. I half-jokingly accused him of trying to conquer my territory with my own country's weapon. He had a substantial collection, which I imagine was valuable. He declared proudly that he'd stolen the French ones from a music store in Paris, when he was a penniless youth. I envied him those adventures. Who wouldn't want to live in Paris? The French, my love, the French, he'd reply. We often said we'd go there together. We never did.

I think it was around that time that we discovered the banjo player

Charlie Tagawa, who became one of Yoshie's idols. They were both Japanese immigrants and had studied economics. Zenzo, his first name is Zenzo! he objected to the guy's stage name. What wrong with that? He said that if he ever went on a business trip to California, he'd try to meet him in person and ask him.

Despite learning to enjoy each other's music, the only group we truly felt the same about was the Beatles. Well, not entirely. We both agreed that *Abbey Road* was superior to *Sgt. Pepper.* But John was my favorite. I particularly admired him in his later years, when he was politicized and a feminist and had the guts to break with the entertainment industry. Who refused to become a slave to his teenage persona. Who, rather than settle for a young groupie, had married an older artist who wasn't exactly a beauty. Who had shown us that we're not the same at twenty as we are at thirty. And the cherry on top was that he was living in my city.

Yoshie preferred George, because he was the foreigner in the group. The one who reminded the other three that the East existed as well. In any case, he thought that taking a rock star as your role model was stupid. He argued that messianism was adolescent, too, which is why he defended Paul. That all he demanded from a musician was good music. That Lennon's violins were cheesier than McCartney's, and that of the two solo albums that had just come out, *Band on the Run* was far superior to *Mind Games.* As for Ringo, well, we both loved the guy.

Living together improved not only Yoshie's English, which he spoke with obsessive precision, but also the idea we had of each other. We lost some of that blind trust that unites strangers and we gained a sort of reciprocity. Everything between us became verbal, more argumentative, less intuitive. We were able to communicate more easily than ever, with a new expansiveness, in the same way that we were able to disagree with greater understanding and openness.

After we moved in together, he began to express viewpoints and objections, and he even complained in ways I hadn't anticipated. Maybe it was just the normal frictions of sharing the same space. And yet I sensed that the reason was mostly linguistic. He had moved in with me, and also with my language. It was no longer a mere work tool, he now knew how to sleep, yawn, and brush his teeth in English.

He now understood puns and was keen to invent some of his own. You could say that he fell in love with my language all over again. This made up for the vague affront I felt at him being able to manage without me. I still have the blackboard he gave me. I placed the easel next to my desk and we would write messages to each other. More than about practical matters, they were a kind of intimate code or collaborative thinking. One of us would scrawl a random sentence. The other would rewrite it the next time they walked past. And it would gradually evolve, until it became the summary of something we couldn't quite figure out.

When we decided to move in together, we knew that both of us would frequently have to go away, in my case to cover events in other cities, or to interview people or research an article. And in Yoshie's, to visit other Me branches or to attend creative training sessions or meet with investors, shareholders, or whatever they were (I've never been able to distinguish all that well between people who earn a lot more money than me). At first I was worried that these trips might make living together a problem, but they ended up bringing more relief than conflict.

Those brief interludes were like a sort of ventilation system. They kept us fresh, ready to rediscover the joy of meeting up again. They were a reminder of how lucky we were to be sharing our time and space. And that there's no closeness without distance. On the other hand, we were constantly being forced to re-adapt. The person coming home doesn't usually have the same expectations as the one doing the welcoming. This impeded the flow that comes only with daily interaction. At times, our relationship behaved like a skittish animal, retreating with each period of absence.

If ever being together wasn't enough, a little pot never hurt. Smoking in silence brought us closer again, filled us with ideas and questions that drifted about in the smoke. In those days I was more likely to take uppers, which in my profession were as common as typewriters. They gave you the necessary reflexes to make you feel quicker than the news itself. Of course, the illusion lasted only a couple of hours, but by then you already had yourself half an article. Occasionally, Yoshie would take hallucinogens, the ideal counterweight to his world of figures, sales accounts, and other deceptively tangible realities.

I have to confess that our conflicting schedules made me slightly anxious at night. To me his sleepiness was somehow a form of abandonment. I felt he was deserting me when I was at my peak, elated after finishing an article. At the end of my working day, the night was still young. For Yoshie, on the other hand, night was the end of everything. During weekends and vacations our conjugal jet lag was less pronounced. But not by much, because Yoshie's body was a punctual mechanism. He was wedded to his schedule. That's what I thought. In fact, neither of us was willing to break with our own routines. Maybe that's why we didn't hurt each other too much.

Once, after he returned from a trip, I noticed Yoshie behaving particularly strangely. He wasn't distracted in his usual way, fretting over some problem at work. Instead he seemed to have come back with different facial expressions, a different voice, different gestures. Like an actor who overplays naturalness, some stereotypical idea of it. After eating our dinner in silence, I opened a second bottle of wine and asked him what was the matter. Then, almost immediately, he told me he'd had a fling.

As I filled both our glasses, what I most wanted to know was whether it had meant anything to him, whether he had special feelings for this person. He assured me he didn't. It was simply a release, the culmination of several difficult weeks of bad reports and failed business deals. While I finished my wine, I asked him if this might continue, if we were talking about a more serious liaison. He swore that it wasn't like that at all, that he scarcely knew the woman and had slept with her only once, or only during that trip (he stupidly specified, as if the exact number of intercourses was of any great interest to me).

I rose very slowly from the table. Then hurled my glass onto the floor. Kicked my chair. And asked him why in hell he had told me. If you're going to do these things, I screamed at him, you've got to be more grown-up about it. You own up to them only when they're serious, and when they aren't, you keep them to yourself without dragging the other person down. It's a different kind of generosity, I said.

I meant what I said. Particularly since I'd had the odd fling myself, and had never allowed it to affect our love for each other.

Then I asked him to clear the table and sweep the floor. And I went to take a shower.

Yoshie seemed reluctant to go on marches. When I first met him, he'd smile skeptically whenever I told him I was attending one. Not that he was against the causes we were supporting. He just disagreed that taking to the streets and stopping traffic was in any way useful. Or perhaps he simply mistrusted any initiative by an angry crowd. I'd like to believe that Harlem and I helped to change his mind a bit.

Along with some colleagues from the paper, I would often go to civil rights rallies. It wasn't only about defending the dignity of African American citizens. Actually (did we realize this at the time?), it was about the dignity of the entire nation. By disrespecting black people we were disrespecting ourselves and misunderstanding our own country.

I had similar thoughts, and still do, about the feminist struggle. I'm not talking simply about achieving complete equality for women, but about ceasing to maim ourselves as a society. About damn well realizing, once and for all, that *them* is part of *us*.

How could I forget the graceful anger of James Baldwin? A guy who was capable of writing with equal perceptiveness about blacks and whites. Women and men. Gays, straights, bisexuals. There aren't many like him. He came on the scene at a time when an African American author talking about gay whites was still somehow shocking (and when no straight white person had the slightest interest in finding out if gay black people even existed). We hadn't forgotten the banners in Arkansas: RACE MIXING IS COMMUNISM. How easy it is to feel ashamed of them now. I wonder if we're able to recognize their present-day equivalents.

The other major issue, of course, was Vietnam. The peaceful Dr. King, swayed by all those young people of the Black Power movement with whom he never really saw eye to eye, became increasingly passionate, until he came out against the war and was shot to death. The same way they stopped Ali from being able to box, because he was a tough guy who refused to fire a gun. I think that's when a lot of white women started to broaden our focus: when we got the relationship between racism, militarism, and patriarchy.

I'd have given my right arm to interview Angela Davis. Before they threw her in jail, Governor Reagan (yes, *that* Reagan) had ordered them to expel her from the university. A black female activist, she was doubly discriminated against. Triply, if you counted her lesbianism. I'm afraid that included her own comrades.

The most exciting thing about Watergate was that it democratized the political debate. Virtually everybody, regardless of color, creed, or class, seemed to have an opinion. The coverage was so extensive that there was no longer an elite of experts, only millions of viewers. I think that the problem with Vietnam (as with most of our wars) was the opposite one. We had a minority determined to know what was going on, most of whom were activists. The rest of the population knew relatively little and preferred not to know too much.

Until they saw the press photograph of the little girl and the napalm, as far as a lot of people were concerned, kids in Vietnam didn't die. All that violence was happening light years away from our bedrooms. But that scream, running straight at us, was the embodiment of our nightmares. The girl's back was in flames, but we can't see it in the photo. We can't see the past. Only an excruciating present that demands explanations. This ellipsis in the photograph, which leaps from eye to memory, was pure journalism. Some people weren't sure if it should be published, not because of the violence but because of the girl's nudity. Where civilian massacres are concerned, we mustn't descend into obscenity, you know.

In the end, the girl survived. Her name is Kim, and now she's a Canadian citizen. Closer and closer to us.

Yoshie loved TV sets, but he hardly ever watched television. He believed less in the contents than in the box encasing them. I wonder whether something similar wasn't true of Nixon, who seemed much less interested in telling his people the truth than in being seen by them. He forgot that the appetite for narrative is never sated, that we spectators need plot development and a satisfying ending.

Even Yoshie was unable to resist a political thriller in real time. While we were watching the live hearings (needless to say, on a brand-new Me color set), he told me that he thought the United States was trying to wipe away the blood of Vietnam with the Watergate papers. The napalm, the Agent Orange, and the cluster bombs, all with a bunch of illegal tapes. His remarks struck me as unusual.

I realized that very week, one of Nixon's lawyers referred to Senator Inouye as "that little Jap." Besides being on the Watergate commission, Senator Inouye was the most prominent U.S. politician of Japanese origin and a war hero who had lost an arm fighting the Nazis.

The lawyer finally apologized and, in a further show of diplomacy, added that he wouldn't have been offended if someone had called him "a little American." For some reason, he appeared to believe that the senator was less American than he was. I can picture Mr. Inouye's right arm, abandoned on some battlefield, slowly giving him the finger.

Before I was with Yoshie, I admit to having signed a petition against paying taxes in protest against the war (along with several friends who now make six figures). I'm afraid that our agenda didn't include what might happen in Saigon after the troops left.

We Beat fans were on the lookout for a copy, stolen if necessary, of the anti-war poems anthologized by Diane di Prima's publishing house. That woman gave the impression that she was leading several lives, all of them exhausting. Also Lenore Kandel's banned booklet that a court in San Francisco had declared blasphemous and obscene. Naturally, this boosted sales once it came back into circulation. How can one forget that Buddha on the cover copulating with an enviably supple female? As a thank-you for the success it had gained due to the ban, the author donated some of the proceeds to the police. Whenever we bumped into an officer, my girlfriends and I would recite a poem for him. We felt like a cross between Gandhi and Patti Smith.

The universities were in turmoil, or maybe it's just that the students had come to their senses all at once. There was even a student uprising at the university where Ralph lectured (although his politics majors boasted that they were apolitical). I don't recall exactly what happened. I know that they rebelled against the authorities and took over the dean's office to demand changes to the system. Actually, the boys occupied the deanery for male students, and the girls the deanery for female students. I guess every revolution has its red lines.

Yoshie used to tell me that I couldn't start the day without my dose of anger. And he added, jokingly or not, that our sex life depended on it. That I felt hornier after ranting about politics.

He was more moderate in his personal, and of course his economic, politics. He thought that all strident declarations inevitably strayed into the ridiculous. I learned to wait a little before expressing my opinions. And he, to the extent that his temperament allowed, became slightly more radical.

I seem to remember persuading him to accompany me on one or two anti-war demonstrations, as well as a few antinuclear protests. Yoshie said that every place he had lived had either been subjected to, perpetrated, or feared such an explosion. That it was all a matter of concentric circles.

One day I asked him if we could do an interview for the paper. He told me he'd rather swim back to his native village.

A while before, groups of women in different cities had gone out demonstrating. They were mothers of families, with no clear political allegiance, who called themselves Women Strike for Peace. Those are the first female protests I can remember. They'd discovered that breast milk had been contaminated by radiation in Nevada. I wonder how many women in Nevada thought about the women of Nagasaki. Maybe a lot, maybe just a few. Dozens of nuclear tests were carried out aboveground in that state. Troops were stationed there, a few miles from the explosion. They say you could see the atomic clouds from Las Vegas.

Three Mile Island hadn't even happened yet. If you add up the people affected by that catastrophe and those living in the vicinity of power plants, uranium mines, and nuclear test sites, as well as the officials participating in all those maneuvers, you realize that upward of a million Americans have been exposed to atomic radiation.

How relationships fall apart is a mystery. We don't know when it happens or why. All we know is that it takes us by surprise, like one of those natural disasters made worse by human intervention. In my and Yoshie's case, I couldn't say exactly what happened. We lived together peacefully. We were more attuned to each other than ever. When we were together, we gave off an unsettling appearance of happiness.

Everything had become predictable. Our gestures, our responses, our Sundays. Our arguments and reconciliations, our positions in bed. The novelty was over. Peace was killing us. Then it hit me. I didn't know how to live, let alone love, without adrenaline.

You spend years creating rituals with someone, and then one day you realize that you don't like that person anymore. You're just in love with the ritual. And yet you feel incapable of separating, so you spend the rest of your life cultivating the perfect ritual with the wrong person.

In all fairness, the situation at work didn't help, or it confirmed what I was already feeling. The *Chronicle*'s circulation was dwindling, it was in debt, and then came the first round of layoffs. The atmosphere at the office became hostile. We no longer went out for beers together, we didn't even go on marches. We would work late. Everyone wanted to prove that they were making more sacrifices than the person next to them.

We veterans had our backs against the wall for a while, watching as they canned our colleagues, and kept assuring ourselves that it couldn't happen to us. After each layoff we feigned indignation and heaved a sigh of relief. It was like a fucking Brecht poem. The newcomers at the bottom of the pay scale survived. So did a few seniors whose dismissal (like mine) would've been too costly. I felt lucky and wretched. In other words, salaried.

Everywhere there were budget cuts, downsizings, zero-hour contracts. Although the situation at Me was never as drastic, it, too, suffered the effects of the recession and the oil crisis. Behind the calm that Yoshie maintained (which could set my teeth on edge), he seemed more anxious than usual. Sometimes he would come home after dinner and find I wasn't there.

The evening of Nixon's resignation, I threw a party with a few friends. Yoshie was away, and he caught an earlier flight back. We invited the guests to our apartment. Fed them everything we had in the kitchen. We debated, got drunk, got high, danced, and then collapsed, exhausted. When we got up late the next day (was it a weekend?) I could see with alarming clarity, despite my headache, or maybe through that pain, what had been wrong for a while. I had the feeling, I don't know, of a rude awakening, like when you're dreaming and suddenly someone pulls up the blinds.

We held out one more summer. But that morning, I knew it was over. We'd been waiting so eagerly for the start of a new era, and we were barely able to celebrate it. I wonder to what extent political hopes fill the gaps in our lives. Whether a shared rejection does more to bond us than any of our virtues.

I was the one who took the initiative. I conveyed my doubts and disappointments to Yoshie. At first he seemed surprised. He interpreted my attitude as an attack, and he denied the seriousness of our problems. During that last year, it seemed he'd been living with someone much happier than me.

After that, we had some bruising arguments. He fluctuated between bitterness and exaggerated indifference. I tried to not lose my cool. Assuming he was telling the truth, this was the first time anyone had dumped him. His male pride had lost its virginity and gained something hard to define, which you get only when someone dumps you.

I think I'd grown bored of our life together, or I'd started to check out other people, or possibly both. I suspect the same went for him, even if he hadn't the courage to admit it. I was particularly attracted to a young intern I'd been flirting with at the newsroom. I laughed a lot more with him than I did with my boyfriend, and for me, that has always been *the* sign.

Yoshie couldn't understand my unwillingness to fight for our relationship. He spoke to me about strength, endurance, perseverance. I tried to explain to him that for me a couple wasn't like a battle that you refused to lose. When it stopped working, moving on was the least bloody outcome for both parties.

Little by little, he accepted the situation, or at least he stopped resisting the inevitable. I came back one day from covering an event in Philly, only to discover that, without a word of warning, he'd moved out his stuff. I mean *all of it*. Our apartment had been left precisely half-empty and spotlessly clean. As if nobody had ever lived there with me. What struck me most were the walls stripped of banjos, the tiny perforations. And the bare space in the center of the floor, right where the rug used to be. He had left his keys on my side of the bed.

I soon found out that Yoshie was living in a loft in Tribeca or SoHo, I'm not quite sure which. I moved into my present apartment in Brooklyn, near the Gowanus Canal. I found it thanks to that young intern, with whom not much happened in the end.

During that period, I broke my personal record for eating chocolate bars. And for the first time in my adult life I heard my mother ask me if I had gained weight. Ralph seemed sad that we had split up, I even thought I saw his eyes grow moist when I told him. He embraced me warmly, and told me I could stay at his house for as long as I wanted. You never know how my brother's going to react.

Fed up with losing money, one of the owners of the *Chronicle* decided to cash in his shares. A few of the section heads got together and bought him out. This changed the internal dynamic of the paper. There was more opinion, less news. That was our new style and it was less costly. The editorial line became more radical. We gave more space to militant movements, and yet it became increasingly difficult to disagree with the editors. A few colleagues proudly declared that we weren't journalists but activists. Sales continued falling at the same rate as our spirits.

It was around that time that Phil Ochs took his own life. According to him, he had died a long time ago. Later it was revealed that the FBI kept a five-hundred-page file on his activities. It still considered him a dangerous individual even after his death.

Just like the country, I began a new life. I met up again with Richard. I think we had always liked each other, but when he was available I was with someone else and vice versa. We had unfinished business. Despite claiming to be a liberated woman, I hadn't yet learned how to live alone. I avoided the grieving process by eagerly moving on to the next challenge. Which part of me identified with Yoshie in this?

In the meantime, Carter seemed better at winning people over than at making decisions. He might be the only guy who did a better job governing after he left office. In spite of everything, there was some good news. The Egypt-Israel peace treaty and the agreement with the Soviets to restrict nuclear warheads. I felt sad for not being able to celebrate that with Yoshie.

After a prudent silence, we met up again. We both avoided asking questions about the other's love life. It was all very civilized. In other words, we were terrified of being hurt.

Every New Year, Ralph would send him a card with drawings by my nieces and nephews. I invited him to one of my birthday parties, which I'm afraid was unforgettable. In the summer of '77, during that damned heat wave.

My guests had just arrived when the power went out. It was the blackest of nights, both indoors and out. Richard lit every candle we had, and announced that the entire apartment was my birthday cake. There were fires, looting, chaos. They arrested so many people that they didn't know where to put them all. Nor do I understand how they managed to identify them in the dark. My guests had to sleep on the floor. Yoshie and I agreed that this proved we shouldn't meet too often.

I heard from him until he moved to Latin America. After that we lost touch. That wasn't all I lost. All of a sudden, everyone seemed young except me. I had always been young, I *had* to go on being so. Even my drugs (which by then I rarely took) started to sound antiquated. Crack was all they talked about in the media.

The paper's editorial line became more moderate. We criticized Reagan, but sounded only cautiously Democrat. Sales rallied a little, then took another nosedive. We started to get paid late.

Before the end, the editors made a last-ditch attempt by aligning with the new green parties. I was asked to start writing about art and the environment. I actually enjoyed it. Our readership less so. In the end, the *Chronicle* filed for bankruptcy and closed for good. Almost everything in my memory has closed down.

Fortunately, I had racked up a lot of years in the profession. I had made my name, as they say, so I managed to get by. I continued to freelance for various publications, some better than others, including some magazines that reminded me of the ones I'd cut my teeth on. Then I realized I had aged more than my métier.

We haven't heard from each other since. To be honest, I'm not even sure what became of him. I saw his name mentioned somewhere a couple of times, that's all. It amazes me how seemingly important people are in your life, and the ease with which they cease to be.

I still live alone, in the same small apartment in one of the less pricey areas of Brooklyn. I don't have a lot of expenses or a lot of savings. I think I can feel proud of that. It's all that remains of our revolutions.

Sometimes I find it hard to believe just how much these streets have changed. I can still remember what they were like when I was young. Transvestites, criminals, cheap dives. Those were crazy times. Worse times, I suppose. A long way from these indie stores with their tattoo artists and their artisanal beers in the backyard.

There's a toxic canal close to where I live. I'm not quite sure why, but dirty water makes me think about the past, more so than clean water. That ugly canal, lined with workshops and warehouses, once had its glory days. Now it's just pollution and expectation, a mixture of waste and opportunity. As soon as you cross a bridge, you're back in the present.

I know there are voices in the depths of those waters. Voices of all the people who navigated them, poisoned them, gazed into them. Stagnant voices. One day they'll need stirring. Everything I see speaks to me of what I can no longer see. My city is an echo.

That's why I was surprised to remember Yoshie like this. I had rarely thought of him until that Argentinian journalist contacted me and sent me all those questions. Some were way too personal. Even so, I told him *nearly* everything I knew. Let's call it professional solidarity.

Except this time it wasn't just his face that came to me. A face that no longer exists. Suddenly, I could hear his voice, too, seeping back to me like a gas. It was just for an instant, in the kitchen, as I read the news about that bonsai.

Apparently, at the National Arboretum in Washington, D.C., there is a four-hundred-year-old white pine bonsai. A master gardener from Japan gave it to us for our bicentennial, around the time Yoshie and I split up. Not much was heard about it until a few months before 9/11. In the spring of that year, two Japanese brothers went to the arboretum to see their grandfather's bonsai.

The family owned a nursery in Hiroshima, barely two miles from ground zero. The tree was strong enough to survive the bomb. Strong and fortunate. As the story goes, it had been planted behind a thick wall, which protected it from the shock wave. I've seen in the papers the photos they took of it after the explosion. There it is amid the rubble, intact, the little pine.

If the fact that they presented us with such a tree is incredible, equally incredible is that it has already doubled its life expectancy, and spent a tenth of its history transplanted in Washington. For the tree to have lived this long, many people must have cared for it. I don't know what that means exactly. But hell.

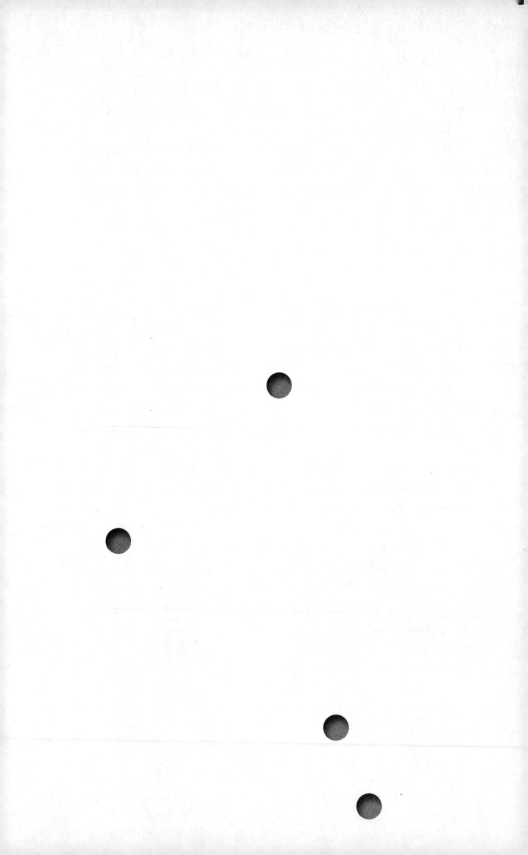

5

EYE
INWARD

ON THE AFTERNOON HE LANDED in New York for the first time in his life, Mr. Watanabe recalls that he made his way to his hotel in the Financial District with a company representative, who eyed him warily, as one scrutinizes a superior of the same age.

During the journey from the airport—which at the time, unimaginably, everyone still called Idlewild rather than Kennedy—he at last made out the silhouette of that city which for him had been only a collection of myths, photographs, and preconceptions. This collection of prepossessed images made him feel that the city somehow already belonged to his past, even before he'd seen it. Contrary to what he'd imagined, the real New York made him feel as though he were dreaming; it seemed more fictional than what he'd seen in any movie.

As he took in the East River through the car window, mesmerized, his host murmured, in an unmistakably southern Japanese accent: Yes, it's awful, but you get used to it.

His arrival at the hotel, the name of which he has forgotten, was far from glorious. Due to some mix-up with the reservation, they weren't expecting him until the next day. And as the hotel was fully booked—*terribly sorry, sincerest apologies*, and so on—they wouldn't be able to offer him a room that night. Flushed with embarrassment, the representative from Me fell over himself to apologize to the branch's new marketing director. Perhaps, Watanabe thinks, the man was also secretly pleased.

After finding another hotel nearby and taking leave of his vexatious host with the excuse that he felt tired (which was actually true), he decided to go for a short walk and have dinner at the first place that caught his eye. Then, in a momentary fit of madness, as he wandered through the SoHo neighborhood, Watanabe stopped at all the hotels he came across, and reserved a room in each of them. At every reception desk, in his as-yet-faltering English, he gave alternative versions of his arrival, adopting a different identity and profession. Each time, he finished by assuring the receptionist that he would return straightaway with his luggage to make the payment and complete the other formalities.

In doing so—as he remembers with a smile—he felt he was a number of different travelers in the same city, numerous guests on the same night, always a new arrival.

Once settled in New York, Watanabe went through a phase of conflicted fascination. Despite his serious misgivings, he couldn't help feeling a frisson of admiration when faced with the emblems of this nation that had devastated his own. He walked around gazing up at the sky. He felt that he expanded in the wide avenues. He took up jogging on Sundays in Central Park. He grew dizzy at the top of the Empire State Building. He dined at every jazz club recommended to him. And he crossed the Brooklyn Bridge in the evenings, feeling that it was injecting the night into Manhattan island.

Yet, as if it were a final inner bastion, he refused to visit the Statue of Liberty.

Watanabe had hoped that working in the country that had bombed his people would have a liberating effect. He saw himself as a child, petrified of the monsters in his room until suddenly, he looks below the bed and wriggles underneath. New York was a city as young and expectant as he was, full of strangers who made him feel at home. In the circles he started to move in, he was always meeting people who claimed they were horrified by the memory of the bombs, and who considered it their duty to take their own country to task. This was so typical—he reflects now—quaint, even, of American liberals.

These individuals, often introduced to him by Lorrie, treated him with an obsequiousness that at first he found comforting, and then, as time went on, humiliating. In their eyes he was, forcibly, a victim. A perpetual casualty of war, whose status was only emphasized by reassuring pats on the back from those who did not share the same burden. And who, thanks to their solidarity with victims like himself, were subtly exonerated.

Mr. Watanabe realized that most of his acquaintances, including those with the best intentions, needed to identify good and evil as mutually exclusive. Rather than a debate, they wanted a painkiller. They seemed content once they had clearly determined the heroes and villains, victims and executioners, regardless of who was what to whom (the Nazis, the fascists, the Japanese, the communists, the traitors, the American bombers).

As he began to adjust to his new environment, his anger became tinged with confusion. He rejected the version of the story his American friends had learned about the *genbaku*, yet he couldn't help but understand; the Japanese hadn't received an impartial education, either. Lorrie's conservative brother, who would eventually earn his respect, had taught him more about the country's sensibilities than those liberal journalists whom she so proudly introduced to him.

The idea that seemed to predominate in the media, schools, and families of the country that had welcomed him so warmly was a kind of self-justification, elevated to the point of military conviction: the attacks had been terrible but necessary. In addition to ending the worst of wars, the bombs had dissolved forever the possibility of such a conflict ever being repeated. This was what they told themselves, and this was what the majority of people there sincerely believed. Which is why living among his former enemies, Watanabe reflects, taught him that memory is more than just the effort to not forget. One should also remember the *way* in which one remembers.

Possibly the biggest shock he had in New York was bumping into Yukio Yamamoto, his former classmate and rival from his school in Nagasaki. Over lunch on the Lower East Side with executives and investors from the Japanese community, Mr. Watanabe was forced to take in too many things at once: that Yukio had survived; that he also worked in the audiovisual technology business; that he had grown into an athletic thirtysomething guy with slicked-back hair and stylish glasses; that he had recently moved to New York City and was working for one of Me's competitors. Sometimes, he thinks, our lives seem contrived by a satirical scriptwriter.

After the two men exchanged bows and insincere words of affection, Watanabe felt the old enmity resurface, disturbingly intact. And so he discovered that hatred—possibly more than love—is born with the will to survive. It would be interesting, he reflects now, completely distracted from the record he is playing, to examine to what extent that influences the cycles of war. Yukio Yamamoto appeared to be more or less informed about his life, and behaved in a suspiciously casual manner. Whereas he was unable to disguise his own facial tics or the tremor in his voice.

Obliged for professional reasons to attend the same events and receptions, both men began to develop an unhealthy watchfulness, yet they expressed their mutual aversion in very different ways. As he had at school, Yukio Yamamoto was apt to mock him and underestimate his virtues. Mr. Watanabe preferred to humiliate him by being overly polite. He trusted that while in the short term Yamamoto's attacks might harm his image in the eyes of some of their colleagues, such a crude strategy would end up working against his rival. Watanabe admits that this wasn't at all the attitude of a pacifist. He earnestly, desperately hoped that his good manners would slowly destroy his enemy.

As he was to discover during professional social gatherings, Yukio Yamamoto seemed to have built part of his personal success on his status as a *hibakusha*, using it to his advantage with supreme skill, appealing to the guilty conscience of the Yankees as a way of doing business. Watanabe cannot now recall a single occasion (including a couple of cocktail parties he went to with Lorrie) when Yukio didn't make some oblique reference to his experiences during the war. Only to then declare, once he had the attention and admiration of those present, that he preferred not to talk about it out of respect for the peace between both countries.

If he himself hadn't resorted to such subterfuges, Watanabe wonders, abruptly switching off the music, was it out of so-called good taste? Or because he was afraid of being stigmatized? Out of consideration for those victims who hadn't been fortunate enough to rebuild their lives? Or possibly because, by remaining silent, he prevented the damaged memories from creeping into his new reality?

During that period, he began to develop an increasingly complicated relationship with the figure of his father. Tsutomu had been the victim of a massacre, but he'd also been employed by a company that produced the armaments for the war that had killed him. Many years later, because of something his aunt Ineko had let slip, he discovered that his father had had friends among the officers of the imperial army. His father's collusion with those who made life-or-death decisions had been greater than Mr. Watanabe had first believed. He swore to himself that this family secret would die with him.

The mixture of veneration and reproach he feels toward his father reminds him, notwithstanding the obvious differences, of the legacy of the writer Masuji Ibuse. Before producing one of the most important books ever written about the victims of Hiroshima, the prefecture in which he grew up, Ibuse had worked in the propaganda department at the Ministry of War. In other words, he'd composed pamphlets to encourage people to continue supporting what would lead to their own annihilation. Japan was heading for surrender, but without the intense work of that department, who knows whether it might not have done so earlier. Possibly earlier enough to avoid the bombings. For this reason, he interprets Ibuse's great novel as the reverse and the atonement for those pamphlets. The alternative writing of the war.

Watanabe has always found it difficult to visit Kokura, the town of his birth, spared both atomic bombs only by chance. Toward the end of the war, the U.S. military faced a strategic dilemma. Conventional explosives had successfully razed the enemy's largest cities. This rendered them useless as targets for the culmination of the Manhattan Project, which had to be put into practice to justify the gargantuan amount of money and research poured into it.

Where, then, could they test this new weapon, which reports claimed would revolutionize the history of war? They carried out a detailed study of the few cities left standing. On August 6, several reconnaissance aircraft checked visibility conditions around Hiroshima. According to a record of alternative plans, had the sky been cloudy that morning, the bomb would have been dropped on Watanabe's hometown instead.

Three days later, the arsenal at Kokura was the priority target. However, the second bomber flew into fog, thick cloud cover, and plumes of smoke from neighboring Yawata. After circling the city for as long as its fuel levels allowed, the bomber made a detour and ended up destroying the nearest industrial town, Nagasaki, where the Mitsubishi arms factory was located, killing the remainder of his family.

It was the weather that had dictated the final decision. The mood of the sky. It seems inconceivable, muses Watanabe, that such an elaborately planned destruction should leave this essential decision—*what* to destroy—in the hands of fate. In that sense, or defying any sense, Hiroshima and Nagasaki were not only targets of annihilation, but also of a lethal form of arbitrariness.

Perhaps he, himself, resembles Kokura too closely. He, too, has been both spared and not spared. Caught unawares on the map. Nobody remembers Kokura, because Nagasaki had the misfortune to supplant it. His memory has the shape of a passed-over city.

Mr. Watanabe feels that inside him is a simmering pot of contradictory emotions; he is randomly exposed to its churning contents. How this affects his inability to settle in one place, or to take a firm stand on the issues about which he feels most intensely, remains a mystery to him. Ironically, this lack of definition defines his character.

Men who lack definition are excluded from the epic. Their only battle is with tension: the impossibility of trusting what they know. Maybe the doubters, Watanabe tells himself, are less useful to the state. Absolute certainty usually leads to destruction of one kind or another. And what if his peripatetic behavior were a ruse, so that in the event of disaster at least one of his lives might survive?

IF HE'S BEING HONEST, Watanabe now regrets not having returned to Nagasaki when the horror was still fresh. He fears he has done to the city of his childhood what others did to its victims: averted his gaze as quickly as possible.

Besides his fear of radiation, for a long time Watanabe believed that by staying away from that place, he was protecting his prenuclear memory. The one he'd preserved in a glowing capsule of play, affection, and ignorance. Without the erosion of the future.

The whole world had a habit of reducing Nagasaki to its destruction. He realized that when he told people where he had grown up, it left him trapped. If he mentioned the bomb, he promoted a stifling association. And if he didn't, he was deemed a cynic or pro-American. The city remained shrouded in a "long cape," which was what its place name meant. No one could see it anymore.

Mr. Watanabe belongs—it astonishes him to describe it this way—to the last generation that can still remember the bombs. Very soon there won't be a single person on the face of the earth who was there. When that happens, Hiroshima and Nagasaki will be only broken things that no one saw break. How dreadful, he tells himself. How wonderful.

With the passage of time and the overlapping of collective images, his memories are starting to look like a movie. His own experience of the *genbaku* has become interlaced with other people's imagery and fictions. While there has been an accumulation of books, documentaries, and even manga about Hiroshima, Nagasaki has inspired fewer tributes. It is saddled with its bomb and its relegation in the tragedy. Truly, muses Watanabe, if any city were worthy of love—an intricate love—that city would be Nagasaki.

He regrets having deemed that his experience somehow exempted him from going to these places of pain, and yet he would find it meaningless to visit them now, when the original damage is almost invisible. They have been transformed into museums, and are so universal that they no longer belong to him. As he explains to any tourist who is interested, *Hiroshima* means "large island." Something small that grows bigger. What size is an island, in fact? Can it be separated from the surrounding sea that touches other shores? Aren't all countries joined by water, memory, and money?

However, no amount of distance can help him escape the conflict. Because, why deny it, he reads obsessively about the cities that he eludes. He's aware of the splendid boulevards of Hiroshima and Nagasaki, their confident skyscrapers, impeccable parks, cool cafés, designer stores, their peace monuments, their happy (happy!) children, their gardens filled with white flowers.

They say that Hiroshima has more bars than any other place in Japan. How could anyone have the moral right to judge that fact? If no one had looked to the future there, all they'd have would be a pile of rubble. Watanabe thinks of the doctors at that time. If a good soldier prolongs the war, a good doctor helps undo it.

He sees that Nagasaki has kept its cathedral bell, a mute symbol of the thunderclap. That its mayors write manifestos and mobilize protests against nuclear testing. And that on August 6 each year, Hiroshima Bay is covered with lanterns bearing the names of the dead: the permanent memory is that of the river. Sometimes he has the eerie feeling of having failed to keep a promise he never made.

But what if it wasn't too late for him to honor other places? To set foot on another patch of earth that is being abandoned now?

Mr. Watanabe stands up. He fills his pockets, slams a couple of doors, and goes out to the Somewhere. He needs to consider the idea that has just occurred to him.

As soon as John sees him, he nods in greeting and reaches for a glass to spin. Watanabe raises a hand. Places it on the bar. And he draws close to whisper in John's ear. I'd like to see the cellar, he says to him.

He walks home, trying to make his thoughts and feet work as one.

The city has regained a semblance of order: it's possible once again to walk around believing in the mirage of the world as a safe place. The evening burns reflections.

As he moves along one of the teeming pedestrian streets of Sanchome, he comes across a string quartet. Two boys and two girls who look like students, playing with the utmost delicacy, as if all of Tokyo were listening to them. Or possibly, Watanabe corrects himself, with the freedom of knowing that nobody is listening to them. He slows his pace without realizing, until he's almost stationary.

All of a sudden, an ambulance bursts in at the far end of the street. The siren bounces from side to side like a pinball. A path opens up amid the crowd. The young quartet endeavors to carry on, despite the noise that has started overwhelming their strings. Those strings bowed with increasing conviction and intensity; increasingly in vain.

The siren goes past the music and eclipses it. The musicians' arms trace silent perpendiculars, their fingers climb the masts like sailors in a storm.

The ambulance moves on. Gradually, the notes reemerge. The waves of people close again.

Mr. Watanabe stops walking. He stays where he is, one leg raised as a quaver, listening to them play.

When the movement of the piece and also that of his foot ends, he has made a decision that he has been postponing all his life.

At the entrance to his building, he greets Mr. and Mrs. Furuya, who are taking their little dog out for a walk. Mrs. Furuya is flanked by her two loves, holding the leash with one hand and her husband with the other. For some reason, Mr. Watanabe envies the dog.

He inserts the key, opens the door, crosses the hallway, opens the second door, and rushes in. At the far end of the living room, stretched out on the sofa, silence awaits him.

Barefoot and resolute, Mr. Watanabe steps onto the striped rug, like someone jaywalking.

He brews himself some tea. Although it won't help calm his anxiety, it will at least confine it to a definite space: his anxiety floats there in that cup. He drinks it. Absorbs it. Metabolizes it.

Then he goes on the internet, and, his breath quickening, begins to search for flights.

Once he has bought his flight, he resorts to pornography to calm himself a little. Amid the ocean of virtual sex, home webcams have become his island. In them objects of desire are transformed into talking subjects: through a game of inversion, the observed impose their will.

What most excites him about these videos is their mix of communication, porn, and trivia in randomly varying proportions. The impossibility of predicting the erotic exposure—at times swift, at times leisurely, at times absent—brings him back to a state of candor: Will they undress? Will they touch themselves? Will somebody else appear? Will they do anything? On those screens, each and every sign of nudity regains its importance, restoring the incredulous joy of glimpsing a breast, a buttock, a testicle. Home webcams are unadulterated life at the window. They can satisfy or frustrate, delight or pass by the neighbor, provide you with company or leave you to yourself.

In his close study of webcams, Mr. Watanabe has noticed that the majority of younger broadcasters put exhibition before pleasure. They copulate to be looked at, rather than to let themselves be seen copulating. The older broadcasters usually have sex in a nonchalant way, watched by strangers they pretend to forget. The youngsters perform with vehement calculation and constantly change position. They are trying their best, he thinks, to be conventional. The veterans adopt relaxed postures, their moans are unscripted, and they climax naturally. In their disconcerting simplicity, they become transgressors.

For a wide variety of reasons, Watanabe prefers watching English, French, or Spanish-language webcams. He can't think of a more stimulating and interactive way of practicing a tongue. By going back to the same broadcasters, not only has he gotten to know their bodies as if he were sleeping with them, but also their linguistic habits, obsessions, and singularities.

One of his favorites, a college student from California, whose nickname is Kate Mmhh, has strictly forbidden her watchers from calling her a whore. It's one thing, she maintains, to exercise your freedom temporarily and behave like a whore, and quite another to be labeled as one. That's the difference, Kate argues, between playing and people using you. One day, Watanabe asked her what would happen if someone played at calling her a whore, without believing that she actually was one. Kate Mmhh paused for a few seconds and then replied that, in that case, she'd appreciate it if people used quotation marks.

Another of his favorites, a Latin American lady married to a large, hirsute individual who occasionally participates in her broadcasts, says she detests diminutives, and won't allow people to use them to address her. *Bitch* is okay, depending on who and how. But *little bitch*, no way. Go sweeten the pill with someone else.

Watanabe also follows a young Andalusian woman, whose behavior alternates between verbal pedantry and sexual narcissism (assuming they aren't one and the same). Her nickname is Persephone, and she employs adjectives such as *benevolent, refractory,* and *sublime* while undressing herself. When one of the chat users hints that her breasts aren't natural, she accuses him of being a *skeptic* or even *insidious.* She intersperses that sort of vocabulary with declarations like "I need more fingers inside me," or "I'm a virgin around the back." For him these outbursts are the epitome of style: obscenity is possible only alongside modesty, as a contrast power. Persephone has a boyfriend and believes profoundly in faithfulness.

When he likes a webcam, he leaves comments that are slightly quirky, partly due to his grammar. His interventions succeed in making some users pay more attention to the chat than to the images, a minor conquest that stimulates Watanabe's libido. A few find him ridiculous, others play along, and still others accuse him of being a party pooper.

Mr. Watanabe isn't a proponent of excessive promiscuity where webcam porn is concerned. Constantly switching from one to the other doesn't have the same effect on him as revisiting those he feels a greater affinity to: one of the conditions for him becoming aroused is knowing the people who are displaying themselves. Rather than watching a striptease in a club, he has always preferred spying on neighbors undressing.

This year, he has become addicted to a couple who reside in a Czech city and speak English with a Slav sentence structure. Each recognizable gesture, such as the girl's laughter or the boy's faces during their shenanigans on the roof terrace, reinforces his sense of cohabiting with them. Thanks to the multiple camera angles, Watanabe has an idea of the layout of the apartment where his unknown Czechs live. It's the closest thing, he feels, to being in a couple alone.

THE SITUATION AT THE Fukushima nuclear power plant is growing steadily worse. Or maybe, suspects Watanabe, it's just that the information about it is starting to coincide more closely with reality.

According to UN experts, he reads, nuclear lobbyists have ensured that the health authorities disregard the victims of such disasters. An agreement signed between the World Health Organization and the International Atomic Energy Agency fifty years ago, he is astonished to discover, has a great deal of bearing on the matter. Why didn't he know this? Why isn't the whole world talking about it?

The summit meeting on Chernobyl, which has just ended in Kiev in commemoration of its twenty-fifth anniversary, gives little cause for hope. The scientists complain that the organizations responsible for controlling the companies are full of people from the industry. In Fukushima, not exactly for the first time, they have failed in their job of overseeing the management of the power stations.

Mr. Watanabe reflects upon the repetition of tragedies, or on tragedy as repetition. He tries to remember those opening verses in Ōe's book on Hiroshima. For years, he knew them by heart. He digs deep in his memory like a child in an empty cookie jar. In the end he gives up, searches his shelves for the book, and reads:

> Who will be able to understand
> among the generations to come
> that we fell once more into darkness,
> after seeing the light?

He closes the book and reviews his plan. He is flying tomorrow morning to Sendai, the nearest operational airport to Fukushima. And when he arrives he'll hire a car. He still doesn't know where he'll stay, he prefers to improvise. He wants to travel blind. Or rather, by traveling there, he will be opening his eyes at last.

Watanabe rearranges his papers, which are already compulsively neat. Then he packs a sparse suitcase. He places Ōe's book on top of his clothes, as he might a hat.

The last flowers he bought have started to wilt. He has the impression that they took less time than usual to wither, as if spring had made them hurry. One of the flowers seems about to crawl toward the window. Mr. Watanabe observes it without trying to straighten it. Drooping like that, it has a familiar air. Like a deaf creature that nonetheless insists on continuing to listen to the light.

After dinner, Watanabe turns on the television in his living room to watch a documentary about the anniversary of the Chernobyl disaster. With some minutes left before it starts, he idly channel surfs.

All of a sudden, on a British sports channel, there's a jockey speaking in Japanese. The gallop of his mother tongue captures his attention, and he concentrates once more on the flat screen. It is a documentary about an Olympic horse rider called Hiroshi, whose aim is to become the oldest competitor at the London Olympics. When you see him mounted, the announcer declares excitedly, he doesn't look seventy. That's no compliment, protests Mr. Watanabe.

He learns that Hiroshi was born during the bombing of Pearl Harbor. He is a descendant of medieval pirates. Studied economics. Lived in the United States. Worked in the orthopedics industry. After retiring, he returned to his youthful passion: horses. In Europe, Hiroshi saw the dancing horses, his wife explains, and fell in love. He eats only seafood. Hasn't gained a pound in forty years. Every night he does stretching exercises. If you have goals, the rider says, you will always feel young. Watanabe rubs his eyes. The presenter's last comment is: Hiroshi goes like a bomb. He gets up to take an aspirin.

Then he checks the time and hurriedly changes channels. Right on cue he catches the brief introduction to the documentary and the Chernobyl plant. Better known during the Soviet era, the announcer reminds the audience, as the Vladimir Ilyich Lenin Nuclear Power Station. Mr. Watanabe had completely forgotten that fact, which seems as much of a revelation to him as his own forgetfulness.

His face professionally twisted in a mournful expression, the announcer adds a last-minute comment, comparing the case to that of Fukushima, the only ones in history, he points out, to have reached a seven on the nuclear scale. Watanabe is alarmed to hear that the Chernobyl authorities consider Fukushima a sister, and have decided to put up a simple plaque twinning the two towns.

The nuclear installations, begins the voice-over, were located twenty kilometers north of Chernobyl, which derives its name from a local plant, the meaning of which, some linguists claim, is "black pasture." Again, twenty kilometers, Watanabe thinks. The radius that conceals the worst silences. The blackest pastures.

He gets up and pours himself a glass of wine, possibly to counteract the mental clarity the aspirin has given him.

Apart from the emission of a lethal form of energy, the voice-over continues, the accident at Chernobyl can be linked to the atomic bombs by three factors. The first of these is political. The nuclear race between the two great powers began with Hiroshima and Nagasaki, and then the paranoid obsession with military defense systems became official. The second factor is statistical. The number of casualties in one case and of evacuees in the other are remarkably similar. The illnesses discovered over the long term are also comparable.

Watanabe feels the film of alcohol gnawing at his gums.

The third factor is perhaps less well known, says the voice-over. The size of the Chernobyl plant was directly related to the requirements of a defense complex, secret at the time, named Chernobyl-2 or Duga-3. This vast radar, consisting of a low-frequency antenna that measured a hundred and fifty meters tall and half a kilometer long, together with a second high-frequency radar measuring a hundred (Watanabe becomes distracted as he tries to visualize these aerials, which he imagines as giant, hypertrophied insects) and consumed a third of the plant's total energy output.

Following the accident, physicists calculated that there was a ten percent risk that a nuclear explosion on an unimaginable scale would take place within a fortnight. Such an explosion (Watanabe hears without reacting, as if he were watching science fiction) would have been equivalent to forty Hiroshima bombs going off at the same time, and would have rendered Europe uninhabitable.

When, the voice predicts, our species becomes extinct in thousands of years' time (if, Watanabe thinks with a cough, we're being wildly optimistic) the radioactive isotopes from Chernobyl will still be alive in the air (if *alive* is the word! he specifies, raising the glass to his lips). This is why experts agree that we have entered a new geological age, the Anthropocene. An era in which human activity has left its scars, which are clear from the strata of cliffs and caves (you have to be incredibly old, he tells himself, swallowing, to have lived in two geological ages). The residues from nuclear testing are our indelible marks on the entire planet.

However, the voice explains, Chernobyl released very different types of radiation (the wine corroding his gums, enveloping his titanium implants), more harmful at a short distance. The authorities permitted cattle to continue grazing in areas where the wind had scattered the radioactive particles, and potentially contaminated crops were not destroyed.

A good part of the surrounding countryside, the voice insists, will never be inhabited again. The people of Kopachi (while the screen shows aerial views, Watanabe lowers his head to refill his glass) were assured that they could soon return to their homes (the liquid spills out of the glass and several drops redden the table). Their houses were demolished and buried. All that remains of the village today are those bushy knolls, on top of which have been stuck the famous yellow symbols (*amarillo, kiiro, jaune*). Curiously enough, the voice observes with a somewhat inappropriate trace of irony, in the ancient Slavic language, *kopachi* meant "gravedigger."

In the wake of the disaster, the voice concludes, recovering its solemnity, the Chernobyl plant continued to be operational for another fifteen years, approximately. Only the construction of a fifth reactor was halted, and its structure surrounded by cranes currently welcomes visitors. Shortly before it was shut down, a fire broke out in reactor number two. The possibility of replacing it was explored. But by that time, Ukraine was an independent republic, and its young members of Parliament were questioning its energy future.

Mr. Watanabe stretches out his arm, and—as he does frequently when watching porn—mutes the sound. Activists, politicians, and intellectuals file across the screen. He wonders whether, before the republic became independent, there were fewer nuclear objectors or just fewer possibilities of broadcasting them. He drains his glass. He turns up the volume again. His attention to the voice-over alternates with the flow of his own thoughts.

Chernobyl is a realm divided into nuclear provinces, administered according to their levels of toxicity. The currency has long since changed from the ruble to the roentgen, the voice explains, the traditional measurement of radioactivity that (radioactivity is already a tradition). To travel from one province to another, you have to go through passport control. To enter the exclusion zone, which extends over a thirty (twenty, thirty, yes), military authorization is required. The customs posts are equipped with Geiger counters and power showers that can eliminate any (exclusion, military, showers, eliminate: the combination couldn't sound worse).

The nuclear realm of Chernobyl also has its heroes. The firefighters who, on that night, prevented the flames from spreading. All of them accomplished their mission without knowing what was really going on, and without the necessary protection to (if they'd they been told, how many of them would have gone?). None of those strong, healthy young men, the voice recounts, survived more than two weeks. Their remains are stored in sealed and reinforced concrete caskets. Even at some distance from their graves, the radiation levels are so high that no one is allowed to approach to pay their respects. (Few heroes resemble their country so much.)

Although the accident took place on what is now Ukrainian soil, it was Belorussia that received most of the fallout. And, the voice explains, it is still suffering the worst effects. Mental impairment and disabilities, genetic mutations. Cases of cancer have increased seventy (did he hear that figure correctly?). Less than one percent of Russian soil was badly contaminated. In Belorussia, it rose to twenty-three. This is why (the irony is there wasn't a single nuclear power station in Belorussia. The disaster simply crossed the border).

On the day of the accident, raised levels of radiation were recorded in Germany, Austria, Poland, and Romania. Four days after that, in Switzerland and Italy. Two days after that, in France, Belgium, Holland, Great Britain, and Greece. A day later in Israel, Kuwait, and Turkey. Lofted high into the atmosphere, these substances spread across the globe, and were even detected in China, India, the United States, and Japan. Nearness and remoteness therefore lost all meaning for the (and that's why he has always thought that economics cannot be separated from the ecumenical. He doesn't believe this out of a sense of solidarity: it is what he sees as an observer of business throughout the world).

In any event, he wonders, as he considers turning off the television, if it weren't for the bombs and the promotion of nuclear energy, would plants like Chernobyl and Fukushima have existed at all?

One witness recalls: He was swollen all over. His eyes had practically disappeared, recalls another. He kept asking me for water and more water, recalls another; the doctors gave him milk. They didn't tell us what was wrong with him, recalls another. The doctors died as well, recalls another. When they moved their head, recalls another, their hair stuck to the pillow. I haven't been able to sleep properly since, another says. Our reactors were the safest, says another. Bad energy brings death, says another, good energy brings light. I thought the worst was over, another says. What hurts most isn't the past, says another, it's the future. (All so familiar, so remote, so close.) Belarus, the voice-over suddenly announces, is to go ahead with the construction of its first nuclear power plant. The International Atomic Energy Agency supports the initiative. The current director, who is Japanese, will advise the country at each.

The bottle is finished. The documentary isn't. At the center of this imbalance, Mr. Watanabe's body resists getting up.

The documentary is now focusing on the task of submerging the remains of the plant, which linger like a hot coal no one knows how to extinguish. In the months following the catastrophe (and now he has the impression that a different voice is telling the story, or possibly the same voice on a day that is more humid and liable to cause colds, what do announcers think about when they report tragedies? Are they distracted? Do they get involved? Do they distance themselves in self-defense?), to a huge temporary patch, the steel and concrete sarcophagus we can see in this aerial shot.

The sarcophagus, the voice goes on (this other voice), no guarantees. It was designed to last only thirty years. In other words, until 2016. By now, it is covered in cracks. It has been estimated (by whom? How?) defective area already measures more than two hundred square meters, and through it, radioactive aerosols are seeping out. When the north wind blows, uranium, plutonium, and cesium emissions are detected in the south (the wind, even the wind shows that what comes from the north is harmful to the south). Sarcophagus, a breathing corpse.

The ongoing efforts, the voice resumes after a dramatic pause (rising in pitch, he notes, as though coming to life), solution to these flaws, is the work of a prominent French consortium which (or as though the documentary itself was sponsored by a prominent French consortium) largest mobile structure ever made. In the words of its creators, it will be the mother of all domes. Due to its unprecedented complexity, the European Commission, the G-7, and the European Bank for Reconstruction and Development (watch out, here we go!) the unavoidable rise in the cost of this historical feat of engineering. The two rings will be ingeniously assembled until (the official cost overrun, Watanabe checks on his phone, already stands at six hundred and fifteen million euros).

Impossibility of building it on top of the damaged reactor, he listens to the voice again, the dome is being constructed in this adjacent area, which has been decontaminated using the (how can they be so sure? And why aren't they interviewing the construction workers?) of the place. Once the parts are completed, they will slide on rails. The structure, designed to withstand earthquakes, will be large enough to house two Boeing 747s, one next to (paranoid, he searches in vain for a hypothetical connection between the French production company of the documentary, the U.S. company Boeing, and the energy multinationals). Because of its texture, explains one of the engineers, it will look something like the Eiffel Tower.

And this will be the cage, the voice-over says dramatically, that will chain the beast resting beneath the sarcophagus, in the face of (Watanabe imagines he is listening to a story about zombies and vampires: the entertainment industry ends up cannibalizing everything). Tons of uranium melted into the piles of waste, sand, lead, and acid that were dropped from helicopters. The amalgam created this incredible incandescent mass, a highly toxic magma that no civilization had confronted before, not even (the alleged solution, then, is to gain time in order to find a solution) still being examined (not a solution: a cover-up). The new structure is designed to remain hermetically sealed for a hundred years. The air inside will be monitored and kept free of moisture to avoid the corrosion of (to make sure that inside this dome, as it were, the past doesn't exist).

And so our future, the voice declares decisively, will also remain sealed, finally laying to rest the tragedy that terrorized Europe twenty-five (the future sealed, the tragedy laid to rest).

As the credits move up the screen and vanish, Mr. Watanabe is reminded once again of kintsugi. The art of mending cracks without secrecy. Of repairing while exposing the point of fracture.

After the commercials, the announcer appears once more on-screen, and staring into the eyes of the viewers, announces the crucial point of today's special report: a series of aerial images of the exclusion zone, filmed by drones, shown here for the first time. The shot zooms in on the announcer's face. His eyebrows seem to take off.

Suddenly, Pripyat appears, the nearest town to the power plant, which since its evacuation has remained in a phantom state. Mr. Watanabe wonders about the hypnotic effect abandoned spaces have on him. What impossible anticipation they provide him with.

Trying to blink, he recalls a trip he once made with Carmen to an abandoned hospital on the Lido, that citadel for consumptives, which became a temple to the strangest kind of hope. Many people with incurable illnesses traveled there in the belief they would be saved, surrounded by palaces and beauty. To him it had seemed like a very moving place. But she'd found it sinister. Experiencing such contrasting emotions somehow distanced them. Between the two of them, he now realizes, they'd spanned the arc of a single response: the place contained both extremes. As they walked through the stripped offices, Carmen wanted to take with her one of the typewriters. And he begged her not to touch anything.

Empty places, observes Watanabe, are often filled with contradiction. For example, around Pripyat, nature is crowded and it spreads with vengeful force. Cattle graze along its avenues. Horses gallop in wild droves. Wolves, whose tracks abound, have made their lairs in houses. Eagles snatch impossibly large prey. Black storks outnumber white ones. Some of the soldiers who patrol the area allege sightings of bears that have been extinct for more than a century. And everywhere, the zoom shows, are millions of swarming ants, like a relentless calligraphy rewriting everything.

Why life is so insistent, even in the most hostile of environments, continues to be a mystery that produces in Mr. Watanabe a perplexed gratitude. For the local fauna, Chernobyl has been transformed into a paradise. Paradise, he reflects, would be the absence of human beings.

At the time of the explosion, he hears, the average age of the inhabitants was below thirty. They called it the city of the future.

Pripyat is archaeologically pure. There is no need for excavations: the layers of memory are exposed. The building that strikes him most is the post office. Lying amid the moss and weeds are all the undelivered letters. If someone ran over to read them, he imagines, would time begin again?

Watanabe glances at the time. He doesn't feel tired, but he knows he will be tomorrow if he doesn't go to bed straightaway. Just as his finger is touching the red OFF button, he is shocked by the Pripyat fairground. Childhood and graveyard seem to coincide in its attractions. Most disturbing is the way happiness and wretchedness have lost all distinction. A nuclear celebration.

On the screen gleaming bumper cars jostle their own stillness. The empty carrousel, bewildered as a tree with no branches. The yellow Ferris wheel like a broken wheel of fortune.

Beyond its random appearance, Watanabe thinks he can see some coherence, a sick sense of a museum: it is a monument to interruption. This isn't death, but something more insidious, its sudden implantation.

Minutes later, a finger presses a button, the screen goes dark and everything disappears.

As he slips into bed, Mr. Watanabe forgets his earplugs. He is too lazy to sit up and turn on the light, and so he closes his eyes. He falls asleep more easily than he had imagined, thinking about how strange the sounds in his house seem, the breathing objects, the hum of reality.

AFTER NEARLY TWENTY YEARS WORKING IN NEW YORK, where he felt lost, exhilarated, alienated, happy, and alone; and at the end of a fruitful relationship with Lorrie, with whom he learned as much about himself as he did about love, Mr. Watanabe was obliged to move again, this time to the unfamiliar south.

Now that the recession produced by the oil crisis was over, and the foundations were conveniently in place for the rise of neoliberalism, Me had been developing a project to expand its business throughout the continent. This project was summed up in a set of concentric charts that involved the prospect of a tentative promotion for him. From marketing director on the East Coast—an attractive position, but with few possibilities of advancement due to internal competition—to deputy director of the future branch in the Southern Cone. At first, he made no attempt to apply for the position, although something resembling an internal calendar made him think that this was the moment for his next move.

According to the reports he received, surveys charting the market for technology products in Latin America appeared as promising as they did uneven. Below the Tropic of Capricorn, Watanabe learned, there was zero production. That imaginary line separated producers from consumers.

The majority of Latin American factories owned by the competition were based in the industrial cities of Brazil or Mexico, where markets were potentially much larger. From there they exported to the rest of the continent, their path smoothed by the military governments in the region, who had decided to do away with all state interference by means of massive tariff reductions and favorable exchange rates.

In this context, Me's strategy consisted first and foremost of gaining a foothold in Argentina, Chile, and Uruguay, without for the moment exposing itself to any direct confrontation with the leading companies on their territory. The intention was to establish itself as a model in the Southern

Cone before launching a second phase, which was a progressive occupation of northern markets. Because of its convenient amalgam of initiative and vagueness, *Why not?* was one of the first expressions Watanabe had become accustomed to saying in English.

Following his arrival in that strange country, so committed to its own passions, so awash with local codes of behavior and heterogeneous last names, he began to notice that life in Buenos Aires had a few things in common with life in New York. Both possessed a kind of electric quality of permanent vigilance, as if the streets had been designed for a type of creature with peripheral vision. A daily swordfight, where every gesture appeared dramatic, but was in fact unimportant. A ceaseless stimulus that tried to avoid depression by acting on its reflexes. The impression that everything was urgent, impossible, and simultaneous.

Of course, he encountered major differences. Regardless of how honest they were, the residents of the great U.S. cities cited their laws as if quoting the Bible. By contrast, in Buenos Aires the gray areas seemed infinite; you could act against the law, despite the law, according to a parallel law, or even zigzag between contradictory laws. Rather than a guarantee, the system was seen as a threat. Instead of adapting, it was better to mistrust it, question it, fight it.

Whereas Americans tended to leave the state out of their calculations, Argentinians seemed to have a profound need of it, whether as enemy or protector, as a structure to be feared or to militate in. It was customary to explain violence as a repressive system rather than social alienation. The political temperature on the streets of Buenos Aires was without a doubt the polar opposite of New York. He started to suspect that democracy and dictatorship didn't work the way he, as an outsider, had assumed they did, like two regimes that repel each other. They were, if anything, two shorelines riddled with bridges and tunnels.

There were even some similarities, Watanabe felt, to Paris. The city of Buenos Aires was a hodgepodge made up of bits from many parts of the world. You could go from the financial districts, like those of Tokyo or New York, to the most touristy colonial quarters, and from there to its many squalid shantytowns and back to Parisian boulevards. Whereas the French capital was prone to behaving like a museum obsessed with self-preservation, the Argentinian capital did the exact opposite: it eradicated all tradition, it stormed the museum. It was the same as far as pretentious-ness went. Its driving force was the opposite. For some years, Paris had been showing signs of exhaustion, a measure of paralysis that affected any dreams of transformation. Buenos Aires exhibited an extraordinary anxiety to always be otherwise, a compulsion to relaunch itself.

And, at the center of this chaos, Mariela awaited.

If he began studying French out of youthful romanticism and a love of slow movies, if he got to know English through work and the influence of rock music, then Mr. Watanabe didn't learn Spanish: he collided with its words and fell in love with it. He let himself be conquered by its music, he murmured it in his sleep, he misconstrued it with a passion. After a period of extreme effort, when he had overcome his initial impotence, he realized that with this change of language he had once more shed his skin.

Rather than someone who spoke different languages, he felt that he was as many different people as the languages he spoke. In French he tended to be oblique, more fastidious, and a little grouchy. In English he was surprised by his own conviction, the self-assurance with which he made what for him were unusually forceful assertions, his casually dry wit. And what about Spanish, what was he like in Spanish? Perhaps a little vociferous in his opinions. More cheerful. Less concerned with his image. The Spanish language taught him the pleasure of speaking improperly.

Accustomed to living in dictionaries and their minutiae (those symbols that seem to suggest a coded message, those barely recognizable abbreviations, more elaborate than the language they are attempting to explain), he often wonders about the people who write the most redundant entries. In dictionaries for students of English, for example, all those universal terms like *shock, zoo, crack*. Or in the bilingual French–Spanish dictionaries that were so indispensable to him in Buenos Aires, entries such as *avion = avión, frac = frac*. Can there be any greater commitment to a language than to transcribe thousands of words that designate themselves, that peer at their own reflection?

Watanabe muses upon that legion of linguists, perhaps young interns or exploited assistants, devoting their time to compiling definitions they know no one will read. Then it seems to him the saddest, most beautiful job in the world: unknown patriots of foreign languages.

He remembers Mariela, who occasionally copyedited English text-books, telling him that many dictionaries and encyclopedias contained false entries to identify plagiarisms. If another publisher printed any of these made-up concepts, their rival's copying was obvious. This fascinated him. And he asked her, if ever she had the opportunity, to include in some volume an imaginary equivalent to kintsugi. He felt that the absence of that word in other lexes, the nonexistence of the concept itself, was an important omission.

As for his tastes in literature, which have also traveled widely, he considers himself a capricious reader. He seldom proceeds with the thoroughness of some of his friends. As in life, he prefers to jump around. His successive libraries have ramified in an endless diaspora.

Chekhov is one of the few authors to have always accompanied him. In addition to his stories, Watanabe is fascinated by his incessant wanderings. What with his work, his health, and his doubts, Chekhov was never quite sure where to settle. His stories seem narrated from that very lack of definition; the habit of looking in all directions had allowed him to adopt any point of view. Watanabe often repeats an idea of Chekhov's, which at times he has agreed with and at other times not: our interest in new places lies less in our getting to know them than in escaping from a previous somewhere. And what about the languages we speak? he wonders. Do they run away from each other, or try to catch up with one another, to merge into one?

However, most memorable is the story of Chekhov's own death. One night, Watanabe recalls having read, he was delirious with fever in a German hotel. When a doctor succeeded in bringing down his temperature, Chekhov, perfectly aware of his condition, told his colleague: *Ich sterbe*. I'm dying. The doctor ordered a bottle of champagne to be brought up immediately. Chekhov accepted and said: I've not had champagne for a long time. He drained his glass. He lay back. And stopped breathing.

In Watanabe's view there could be no better death.

During the early stages of his emigration, his visits to Tokyo were very intermittent, and their main purpose was to visit his aunt and uncle, whom he missed a great deal. Over the years, his homecomings became more frequent and prolonged. The excitement at meeting childhood friends was equaled by the pleasure of cultivating new relationships. The more past he accumulated, the greater his need to balance the scales with some experiences in the present.

During those homecomings, Watanabe had the opportunity to meet other survivors. Whenever this occurred, his empathy matched his unease. They would recall lost relatives, who became present in the act of telling. The rest of the time, however, they were content to sit facing one another. They would sip tea in silence, gaze over each other's shoulders. Then say goodbye.

Back then, he believed that some things needed no words. Now he's not so sure. He remembers that old Japanese tale. Whoever sees hell and speaks of it, a devil warns, will be dragged down to hell a second time.

One of the things that most affected him about the victims he met was the difficulty they had in telling their stories. Few were able to get beyond platitudes. They couldn't find the words for their memories, were bound by verbal conventions, which in a sense were other manifestations of silence. Some of their testimony was inconsistent, as if they hadn't actually been there. Or as if they'd been there *too much*, and hadn't yet completely emerged.

Many people returning from wars and massacres are quieter than they were before. Their communicable experience seems diminished. Survivors no longer share a common space with their fellow human beings, they have set foot in a land without a tribe. That's why many victims develop a misanthropy that continues to harm them for a long while afterward. He's well aware of this: he has spent all his life starting another life, moving to a different place so that certain emotions cannot catch up with him.

As these meetings continued, he noticed that the extent of people's silence seemed to correspond to their proximity to ground zero. The farther someone had been from the epicenter, the more likely they were to talk about what had happened. This would explain, muses Watanabe, the (very) relative fluency he himself has achieved. The waves of silence, the map of victims, the evacuation zones: always a matter of concentric circles.

The unspeakable nature of suffering, with which he himself has struggled on many occasions, was intensified by the victors and vanquished alike. First came the prohibitions imposed by the occupying forces.

American and Japanese agents were charged with enforcing them at the Civil Censorship Department, where they scrutinized every public utterance. They even went as far as to confiscate from many presses type-faces bearing the ideograms for *atomic bomb* and *radioactivity*. A decade after the slaughter, Hiroshima newspapers were literally incapable of expressing it.

He remembers a second tyranny. Virtually no one seemed willing to disclose the effects of the bombs. Not the people who had dropped them, nor those who had suffered them, and who saw in the bodies of the *hibakusha* the most hideous portrayal of their own defeat. Mr. Watanabe has never forgotten his summers in long sleeves. Even on the hottest days, his aunt and uncle insisted he wear those shirts for grown-ups that were so uncomfortable to play in. Children like you must always dress elegantly, his aunt Ineko explained, petting him as she helped him into his clothes.

Survivors with noticeable scars were also discriminated against by their fellow countrymen. Facial disfigurements kept them from making new friends, forming relationships, finding employment. They inspired shame rather than compassion. This, he reflects, was the other bombing. Day after day. Wars that are lost, Mariela used to say of the Malvinas, have no heroes.

Watanabe knew one or two women whose fiancés had stood by them, but who had been rejected by their in-laws. Within the survivors' own families, many relatives had behaved similarly. A fear of spawning some sort of monster—a monster whose features mirrored each and everyone's worst nightmares—was the main anxiety of those young women. One of them once confessed to him: I've been harboring a bomb inside me for thirty years. I can feel it in my stomach, about to explode, like a baby unable to be born.

Her words horrified Watanabe, who had secretly feared passing on to a child of his not just a deformity resulting from the radiation, but also some of the postwar suffering. This fear increased during his time in Paris, where he succumbed to reading several authors who had studied the ways such trauma is transmitted. Bequeathing a massacre, he learned, is a terrible thing. Bequeathing the cover-up of a massacre is worse.

By the time the victors lifted their restrictions, few among the vanquished were interested in hearing the survivors' stories. It took the authorities twelve years to provide them with specialized medical care and other state subsidies. For many this came too late.

For decades, the Ministry of Health, in accordance with other international organizations, resisted admitting any link between cancer and radiation. He believes that deep down this reluctance implied an acknowledgment of shared responsibility. Something prevented the state from portraying itself solely as a victim of the enemy. Especially after the enemy had become its ally and a sponsor of the country's reconstruction.

He first heard about this change of policy toward the survivors—Watanabe remembers as if it were yesterday, as if it were always yesterday—when he was reviewing for his final exams in Paris, underlining textbooks on accountancy and staying up through the night. This was his excuse for not making an immediate decision. As he also considered himself in perfect health, he refrained from taking the initial steps to register on the official census of victims. He told himself that he had time and could do so at a later date.

To what extent would he have felt acknowledged, he wonders now, or permanently stigmatized? Would the cracks have been closed, or would they open again?

What gets you drunk, thinks Watanabe, sighing and opening another bottle, is asking yourself questions.

When I realized what had happened to us, another survivor once told him, I began not to care about anything. At first, do you remember, there's a sort of gratitude. All you can think about is whether you'll soon be joining the dead. But as time goes on, you become accustomed to surviving. It was then—the man went on, and Mr. Watanabe has the impression of rescuing that voice from the well of his ears—that the fits of rage started. I think my friends began to feel awkward in my company, like those drunks no one wants to invite to parties. And so I shut myself away. Incidentally, come to think of it, this is the first time this year I've made two cups of tea, you know?

When he met a *hibakusha* who had been severely scarred, Watanabe would mention only the loss of his family in Nagasaki, and would conceal his own experiences in Hiroshima. He was ashamed to have emerged from there almost unscathed. He felt that placing himself on an equal footing with the others was unjust. He wasn't like them. He didn't want to be.

He was surprised at the many cases of blindness. Maybe, after glimpsing hell, it was impossible to see anything else. Others developed a specific type of cataract, very noticeable close-up. That gigantic flash of light seemed to have stuck to their retinas and, with time, risen to the surface.

This was the case of one of his aunt and uncle's neighbors, an extremely thin lady called Kioko, who had lost the sight in one eye at Nagasaki. As a child, Yoshie had been frightened of her and did his best to avoid her gaze. As he grew older, he became interested in the old lady's life. During her final years, Watanabe would make a habit of stopping by her house to visit, and bringing her candy that she never touched.

One afternoon, he at last plucked up the courage to ask her about her right eye. Kioko seemed oddly pleased. She maintained that it wasn't lost. Now, she explained, it simply looked inward.

With his accumulation of comings and goings, transfers and moves, Mr. Watanabe developed an emotional ubiquity. Each of his emotions was, partially at least, always somewhere else; he had started to feel in harmony.

This rootlessness wasn't confined to space. Intimacy with his loved ones became problematic. He no longer knew how to be with anyone undividedly. No sooner had he attained an instant of fulfillment than half of him was already envisaging his next move, going over travel arrangements, planning tasks in distant places. Nor did making those journeys alleviate his restlessness: his other half, no less sincerely, longed for the refuge of home and to lounge about in pajamas on Sundays.

As people have pointed out, Watanabe constantly gives the impression of being unintentionally absent, concerned about some matter that isn't what's at hand. He has tried all his life to suppress this tendency. Which might, according to Mariela's theories, be derived from the traumatic hiatus in his childhood. But for this to be true, he used to protest, first of all he would need to know what a hiatus is.

Not deterred by his skepticism, Mariela insisted on the disruptive nature of tragedies, which she maintained were characterized by the impossibility of giving them one's full attention, of looking straight at them. That's exactly how trauma works, do you see? she exclaimed, with her distinctive syntactic zeal. He recalls with sudden tenderness his Argentinian partner's declarations, which he would often start off by rejecting, and which later on, when he was alone, would end up getting the better of him.

They had several arguments of that sort the summer they visited London. Because he had bought their tickets from Buenos Aires and insisted on paying for all their meals, Mariela had covered their accommodation costs. She ended up choosing a cheap hotel in Bloomsbury, an area where touristic interest and her personal memories coincided. The room they shared was engagingly awful. The carpet seemed to contain its own ecosystem. The shower had two temperatures: cold and freezing. And there was a ridiculous charge of two pounds for using the hair dryer. He would later learn that three stars in France or Britain are equivalent to one and a half in the Spanish hotel trade.

He liked to take a morning stroll in the small park in Tavistock Square. He would usually pause for a while near the cherry tree planted in honor of the victims of Hiroshima. Not exactly facing it, but not far away. They would sit on a bench, look at that tree, and he would force himself to think about something else. Or rather, he would focus solely on that, on the tree and its parts, the stubborn trunk, the digression of the branches, the transparency of the leaves: he resisted the symbol. When he got up from the bench, emptied of conclusions, somehow he felt lighter. Prior to himself.

The following summer, or shortly thereafter, Watanabe isn't sure, during the period of catastrophic hyperinflation in Argentina, his company suggested a transfer to one of the countries in southern Europe, where it was pursuing a different strategy following the sudden growth of the European Economic Community. He considered the choice of Milan, the most active and profitable branch. Someone else took the post. Then Me mentioned Portugal and Spain, both recent signatories, which had started receiving massive funds to encourage investment.

Weary of change, and with the intention of avoiding yet one more language, Mr. Watanabe opted for Madrid. He was delighted by their preference for fish over the beef of Buenos Aires. And the warm climate was a relief after all those winters in Paris and New York. The Madrid streets occasionally reminded him of Buenos Aires. Although instead of charcoal, beef, and confectionery, they reeked of fried oil and cured meat. The rhythms of the city were similar, the music different. Its confident energy provided him with a kind of respite. Accustomed to immobile conversations at café tables, he was surprised by the Spaniards' habit of standing in bars, as if they were just about to leave but always stayed for one last drink. He ended up finding this ritual curiously in tune with his own way of inhabiting cities.

To begin with, he was constantly startled by the Spanish brusqueness. For months, he couldn't rid himself of the impression of having vexed his fellow human beings. However, gradually he discovered that this same extravagant energy flowed through every strand of daily life, including humor, pleasure, and friendship. Madrid was where he completed his final years of service for his company. Where he would begin his retirement—that bittersweet privilege he still doesn't feel completely accustomed to. And where, most important of all, he was to meet Carmen. An autumnal romance that brought fresh warmth. And the main reason why, year upon year, he delayed his return to Tokyo.

THE PLANE IS DUE to take off in a little over an hour and he'll arrive quite early in Sendai, a place he has never been before. Connecting flights to Tokyo have recently resumed, and are being temporarily stepped up to alleviate the emergency in the northeast of the country. Cheaper flights were available from Narita, but they arrived later and he prefers to get going as soon as possible. He has always found it nerve-racking to travel only hours before it grows dark.

As he crosses the squares of the central hall at Haneda, feeling like a pawn on a board with ill-defined edges, Mr. Watanabe reflects that he knows some foreign airports better than the ones in his own country. As if domestic tourism were something of a contradiction, and long-distance flights made more sense for aircraft. It occurs to him now that this notion, which he actively cultivated as a youth, has eventually created a paradox: nearby destinations have become exotic.

When the war ended, the Japanese government lost control over the airport he is now walking through. Only the birds could fly wherever they pleased. Although, he reflects again, don't birds also obey the dictates of a higher power? It was more than ten years before flights returned to normal. International flights were moved to Narita. As people began to travel more, the facilities at Haneda were expanded, until the international terminal there reopened and a conflict of interest arose between the two airports. Now the companies that operate them compete, not always cordially, for ascendancy over the clouds. Where there is sky, there are storms, as his father used to say.

The soles of his shoes glide past the shops, which cover an increasingly wide area. They no longer build airports that house shops, Watanabe says to himself, rather shopping malls that house airplanes. That morning the airport is only semi-operational: there are more concerns than passengers. Over and above the warnings and evacuations, fear is still palpable. Panic has two speeds, he reflects. One is running, flight. The other—staying put, immobility—is worse for trade.

Watanabe finds the departure screens, locates the gate, retains the flight number almost unintentionally. He is so used to planes that occasionally he forgets that they fly, the same way he finds it strange sometimes that trains don't take off from the tracks. Although the train would take him about the same length of time, he has chosen to fly. To make a radical break with his point of departure.

In his experience, each form of transport alters him as a passenger. Flights inoculate him with distance, a break in his perspective that inclines him toward small revelations. Trains immerse him in a state of gradual contemplation. His emotions in a railway carriage don't usually change all at once: the flow of the landscape sets a process in motion. Buses transmit a sort of earthly determination. The straining engine, the difficulty of the terrain, the patience of the driver reaffirm him in his plans.

After many migrations, Watanabe no longer feels that airports are neutral places, devoid of identity. Quite the opposite. He senses in them an overwhelming compactness; they contain too many superimposed places. The state, the customs, the law, the police, fear, business, farewells, greetings: everything is concentrated in the same space, filled to bursting. He places his luggage on the moving walkway. He sighs with relief. Then, behind him, he sees a young man pushing past everyone like a skier slaloming between poles.

It occurs to him that, if they could, many passengers would prefer to cut out the waiting. They'd choose to disintegrate and reappear instantly somewhere else. And yet, precisely because everything is much faster, the places of delay seem vital to him. Whenever he is about to travel, his sedentary hemisphere clings to stillness, while his nomadic hemisphere anticipates movement. The collision of these two forces gives him a feeling of being lost that makes it impossible for him to know where he wants to be. Perhaps the secret mission of airports and stations is to resolve that doubt.

The nervous youth passes him without the slightest consideration, banging into him with his backpack, and continues on his way toward the realm of confusion. Mr. Watanabe feels piqued when he sees that the boy hasn't even turned around to apologize. Farther along, a young girl in sports gear lets him go ahead of her at the security check. He can't help feeling offended again, this time for different reasons. He smiles, accepts, and regrets it.

With the passage of the years, his perceptions of space as well as time have changed. Entering an airport gives him a feeling of vulnerability he never experienced before. Increasingly, traveling seems to depend on passengers' ability to react. Therein, Watanabe observes, lies the subtle but constant aggression it exercises over people his age. An elderly person is a soft target. A target of what? Of nothing. Of everything.

At the security check, it's easier to see how the different rhythms aren't purely physical. Compared with that purposeless hurrying, that banging into things they pass, that precious energy young people squander, is the cautious slowness of the elderly. At its heart is a weariness that isn't exactly bodily. A weariness resembling a conclusion. Our bodies have understood, he reflects, that however fast we run we cannot escape. It's a sort of awareness that's been communicated to our muscles.

Of course, there is also the envy, the emotion he experiences when he contemplates the determination of the most youthful passengers. At the opposite end of life, he is nonetheless in the same line as they are. Rather than fellow travelers, to him they seem like beings he has come to bid farewell to.

As he walks through the scanner arch, Mr. Watanabe involuntarily closes his eyes. Metal detectors still make him nervous. Exposed, disarmed, faced with a weapon that knows everything about him.

The plane seat receives his weight with a creak like a hinge, as though by sitting there he has opened a door. Watanabe sighs, adjusts the safety belt, and undoes the top button of his trousers.

Flights to the Northeast still haven't gone back to normal, and there are quite a few empty seats. He turns to glance down the aisle and discovers a strange harmony in the half-full plane. Head, space, head, space. One of the few exceptions is the row behind him, where two brothers are playing on a tablet, cheek to cheek, creating a bicephalous child. Their mother, motionless, grazes the porthole with her nose.

From what he can deduce according to the things they say and do, the other passengers seem to be traveling for family or work reasons. He is probably the only person heading for the prefecture of Miyagi out of choice. And yet, he has as many if not more reasons than any of them.

When the surrounding landscape grows hazy and the wheels leave the tarmac and the noise of the turbines grows louder and the aisle tilts as if everything were toppling backward, the children burst into shrieks of laughter, excited and scared by that invisible force pressing them back into their seats. Their mother asks them to be quiet. They fall silent for an instant then start up again. Infected by their amazement, Mr. Watanabe imagines birds applauding.

Then it occurs to him that this would be a perfect moment to have an accident. There, listening to laughter and imagining birds.

Soon afterward, he falls asleep.

The flight attendant wakes him, pointing at his safety belt. The plane is beginning its descent. Why is his safety belt undone? Could he have loosened it, to be more comfortable, while he was asleep? He turns toward the row behind. The boys look at him and giggle.

The wheels touch down, bounce, start to roll. The brothers clap their hands. The pilot's voice welcomes them to Sendai airport. As soon as the plane comes to a halt, the passengers around him stand up. They are not unaware they'll have to wait a few more minutes, and yet, there they are, huddled awkwardly, sniffing at their imminent exit.

Is this what we are? he wonders, also rising to his feet. A horde of impatient creatures waiting for the signal to stampede? Even though we all know where we'll end up, we do everything we can to hasten our arrival.

The line advances. Feet move in the direction of the light at the far end. Bodies pile up. And Mr. Watanabe sticks his head outside.

The morning is clean and sharp. The shadows appear cut out with scissors, he notes, still under the influence of the two brothers. As he descends the steps from the aircraft, he recalls Gitoku's little poem:

> *A clear sky.*
> *There from whence I came*
> *I now return.*

As soon as he reaches the terminal, he stops to check his phone. The backlog of message alerts increasingly irritates him. Where the hell is the comfort of having it all there, immediately available, when every commitment and appointment has become equally instantaneous? This proliferation of notifications and updates not only forces him to live at a pace he never chose, it also disrupts the mental order of his priorities, conferring upon the most recent things an importance they don't actually have.

With a sigh, powerless to resist the contradiction, Mr. Watanabe quickly checks his new messages.

He finds a lengthy email from this Pinedo fellow. Pinedo again! Who seems incapable of taking no for an answer. He slides his finger down the text, imagining he is placing it on the journalist's lips, imploring him to be silent.

This time, the language flows and is to some extent graceful, Watanabe admits, as he skims Pinedo's detailed explanations. A friend in common, Mariela, gave him his contact details. Some time ago she told him about the et cetera, et cetera, he apologizes wholeheartedly for not having explained this to him before, but it wasn't easy given the brusqueness of their previous exchanges, during which he regrets not having been able to convey the true et cetera behind his article, so he finally decided to choose this method of communication, which while less personal allows more time for reflection et cetera, in the hope that he isn't bothering him too much by sending him, with all due et cetera, a brief list of questions, which if he would be kind enough to et cetera, the different ways of forgetting, et cetera, against this habit of dividing by country the tragedies that et cetera, collective memory of people affected by et cetera, et cetera.

By now this is a question of honor: no means no, even for a Japanese who once lived in Argentina. So, exasperated, Mr. Watanabe deletes the message even before he has finished reading it.

He resumes pushing his little red suitcase, which now seems to offer some resistance, as if its load had grown heavier. Then he stops in his tracks. He takes out his phone again. He buys something, pays for it, and types in the details of an addressee: Ariel Kerlin. Avenida Independencia three three et cetera, Ciudad Autónoma de Buenos Aires, et cetera.

6

MARIELA
AND THE
INTERPRETATIONS

MISS HIM, NO. Think about him often, yes. They're different things. I find the mambo of nostalgia a tad dangerous, as if you had nothing to do in the time left to you. On the other hand, you can think a lot about someone you no longer miss. That's the case with Yoshie. He went on with his life, I went on with mine. But when our paths crossed, both changed direction.

That's more or less what I told Jorge. Jorge Pinedo, the journalist. Huh, and writer. That's what he says, what he wants, as far as I can see. When I told him about my story with Yoshie, he went kind of crazy. He kept asking me about everything I remembered. He wouldn't stop badgering me until one day I gave him Yoshie's details. Never his cell phone number, but in a moment of weakness I sent him his landline. And can you believe it? He picked up the phone and called him in the middle of the night, right after the earthquake. Well, the middle of the night here.

Jorge likes working at night. He's a night owl, like nearly all journalists. Journalists who haven't got children, that is. Like that gringa who went out with Yoshie. He thought it was very funny or something special that she'd stay up late. Tell her to raise a kid and then we'll talk. You think yours truly didn't study nights too? Nowadays, I start translating early, no sooner than I get up and have breakfast. I have the impression that words are freshest in the morning, and as the day goes on they grow weary and grubby.

At first, it was great sharing all that with someone so young, so keen to listen to me. I hadn't sifted through those experiences in a long while. There were some memories, which, until I told him about them, I didn't even know I had. After that we got a bit obsessed with it, I think. Whenever we met, he'd jot down every word I said. Even the most intimate bits. We couldn't even have a quiet coffee together. Do you mind if I record this? Jorge would ask. Well, all right, I used to say, but no names, right? Obviously not, he replied, don't worry.

We went on like that until I got tired of it. I started coming up with excuses to avoid meeting, although we're still friends. In fact, he's my friend Elsa's son. He could be my own son. Maybe that was the problem.

I met Yoshie at a boring conference on economics, investment opportunities, and I don't know what the hell else. It was being held at the congress center in a downtown hotel, which I don't think exists anymore, or is something else, over on Paraguay and Libertad. Or was it Talcahuano? Anyway, I'd just come back from abroad and had a lot of interpreting work. It paid better than translating books, and obviously a lot better than my seminars at the University of Buenos Aires. Let's just say that you have to choose, here. You're either a lecturer or you can actually afford to go to the supermarket.

I remember that day they wanted consecutive interpreting. In theory, consecutive gives you time to think about what you're going to say, but it sends me into a blind panic. I feel exposed. Everyone is looking at you, waiting for your translation, and they grow impatient over nothing. Mistakes are conspicuous and can be compared with the original. You're like the faint echo of another person. By contrast, simultaneous sends you into a sort of trance. You become a voice chasing another voice. An invisible being that speaks and listens at the same time. Most people think simultaneous is harder, but I prefer it. It's like the difference between summarizing the plot and recounting the story in your own words.

Yoshie was taking part as assistant director of the Argentinian branch of his company, which was promoting new videocassette players that recorded at three different speeds. Just before his presentation, when we were introduced, I said I wished that I could translate at three different speeds, depending on whom I was translating. I thought the idea was quite funny. He didn't laugh at all: either he didn't agree or he didn't get the joke. I repeated what I'd said in English, just in case. And he smiled faintly, as if he was being polite. I thought: This guy's an idiot. The organizers came to usher him away. He bowed slightly and said, With you, I'd always choose slowly. Only then did I notice that, though the guy was quite a few years older than me, he wasn't bad looking.

It appears that Mitsubishi, Honda, Sony, and other Japanese companies had never had their regional headquarters here in Argentina. The norm was to establish themselves in Brazil, and sell us their products from there—taking advantage of the fact that the dictatorship had fucked up our national industries, Yoshie explained. That year, his company had started sponsoring a football club, I don't remember which. One of the big ones, my son, Ari, would kill me if he could hear me. The fact is that Me was becoming well known in the country. I guess that's why Yoshie had been invited.

He couldn't speak Spanish fluently, and it seems he chose to give his presentation in English because he didn't trust his embassy staff's Spanish. Even less so the Argentinian interpreters' Japanese, however nikkei they were. The Nichia Gakuin bilingual school had only just been set up, so my colleagues then didn't have the skill level they have nowadays. He complained that his Western translators used far too many glosses, scattering them all over the place to fill in the gaps they left along the way. All of which prevented them from keeping the flow of speech. In other words, from accepting what is untranslatable to concentrate on what is translatable.

To top it all off, they had offered me the job practically at the last minute. I wasn't sure whether to agree: it was a weekend and I'd promised Ari I would take him to the movies. But the organizers thought I was playing hard to get and so they offered me almost twice the normal rate, and then I couldn't refuse. I called my ex and we negotiated. Since we got back from London, Emilio and I had made a pact. If one of us had the chance to earn good money, the other would step up, because it was in our son's interests. So my meeting Yoshie really was purely accidental. Well, not accidental. More precisely it came down to cash, like everything else in this world.

Translating English into Spanish for a Japanese guy who considers himself a polyglot is pretty close to my worst nightmare. I wouldn't recommend it to any colleague with a fragile disposition. Generally speaking, there's nothing more difficult than interpreting for someone who thinks they know the target language. They get suspicious about simple things, confuse decisions for slipups, try to correct you and make the problem twice as bad. Yoshie was particularly stubborn that morning. He didn't raise any direct objections to my translations, that wasn't his style. The opposite of Argentinian men, he was more lethal silent than when he spoke. And yet each time I took the microphone, he glanced at me out of the corner of his eye and pulled a face.

I felt so nervous it took me a while to realize that, with the utmost discretion, Yoshie was checking out my legs under the table. When a guy does that, you have two choices. If you don't fancy him (which is usually the case), you take offense and make that instantly clear to him. And if you are attracted to him, you can't help but feel flattered, so you let him keep looking for a bit before you react. To calm myself and regain control of the translation, I tried a variation of the last option. I raised my thigh and crossed my legs firmly. Then I pushed back from the table so he could see me better, given that he was so interested. He responded by letting out an embarrassed little cough, averting his eyes, and gazing up at the ceiling. It was then I knew I would ask him for a coffee as soon as we had finished.

The sun was still high when we stepped out into the street. I remember thinking: How funny, leaving a hotel together even before our first date. It was a kind of premonitory joke.

We exchanged polite trivialities in English as we headed toward Santa Fe. There I suggested we catch a bus to take a walk in the Botanical Garden. Or better still, in a slightly ridiculous gesture of intercultural courtesy, to the Japanese Gardens. Yoshie smiled at me and said, I here. That was his way of saying that he preferred new places. Buses here scare me, he added. Buses go very fast. A man who tells you this, I thought, has to be gentle.

We walked a few blocks and turned onto Callao. I paused to look in the window of the Clásica y Moderna bookshop, which was teeming with books by authors who had been banned or had just returned from exile. We went in to buy some book or other, I wish I could remember what it was. The idea was to head to Avenida Corrientes, which in those days was practically a must. We ended up stopping off at a little café before we got there.

As ever, I downed several espressos. He drank tea terribly slowly. I was struck by the fact that he avoided coffee. In Buenos Aires that's tantamount to a diplomatic incident. Unlike the English, we can barely differentiate between proper tea and an herbal infusion. I tried to explain to him that here coffee is an act of speech. A way to strike up a conversation with a stranger. Like drinking maté but not as intimate, you could say.

Yoshie told me that, compared to tea, he found coffee less interesting. It didn't encourage reflection. He had drunk it in Paris because, well, that was Paris. But coffee didn't actually make conversing any easier for him, as he drank it so quickly, and it left a strange taste in his mouth.

When he said that, I got up and went to brush my teeth and freshen my lipstick. By the time I got back to the table, he had paid and was staring at me.

As Ari had gone to sleep over at his father's place, we continued talking, and all the rest, well into the night.

Yoshie was a little hesitant about sharing the metal straw we use for drinking maté. It just so happens that we didn't need to drink maté to feel at ease. Before I knew it, we were sleeping together practically every weekend. I immediately got into the habit of calling him Yo, the perfect nickname for a narcissist who worked at a company called Me. He laughed, but was slightly annoyed. How can I be a narcissist if I work all day long? he asked. Darling, I replied, do you have any idea what narcissism is? Anyway, I also loved the way his name had two personas, *Yo-She*. Yo and his other self. His inner female.

For the first few months, we spoke in English. He felt more comfortable with that, and it was the language in which we had first met. I think both of us imagined we might stop fancying the other if we switched languages. Although I was used to translating, my partners had all been Spanish speakers. I soon noticed that my reflexes were different in English. Like when you want to say one word and another comes out, or you're following a map, take a wrong turn, and suddenly find yourself in a more interesting place.

Yoshie on the other hand did know what it was like to date bilingually. He knew what it meant to live with the impossibility of explaining your feelings precisely. Gradually, we started to communicate in Spanish. Because of the way he constructed his sentences, I always got the feeling he was translating himself. I don't think he was quite ready to have an identity in my language. He preferred to think in the one where he felt more at ease, and to subtitle his thoughts as best he could.

Smartphones would have really come in handy! Or not, who knows. We might have found ourselves trapped in some sort of metadiscourse, looking up word after word, utterly incapable of moving the conversation along. I remember he always laughed when we said *chin-chin*. He told me what it meant in Japanese. And to this day, whenever I clink glasses with someone, I can't help thinking of a nice dick.

Regardless of the language we used, I realized we had different understandings of the same expressions. This even applied to basic vocabulary so that, almost unwittingly, the relationship gradually gave rise to a whole code of ambiguities. It aroused my desire to interpret him. Every gap in his speech became a turn-on.

Ultimately, translation requires an element of attraction. You desire their voice. You recognize yourself in a stranger. And both are transformed. Doesn't loving someone also include making their words your own? You struggle to understand, and you misinterpret. The other person's meaning bumps up against the limits of your experience. For things to work with someone, you have to accept that you won't be able to get them perfectly. That, even with the best of intentions, you're going to manipulate them.

In the same way that we translators leave our mark in the mistakes we make, Yoshie and I revealed ourselves in our misunderstandings. It happened whenever we argued. We each lost the thread of the other and retreated into our own frame of reference.

We used to compare the three languages he'd learned. He had genuine respect for English. There's no doubt it was the one he was most fluent in. He spoke it fast, with mechanical precision, and a kind of gringo accent that I found amusing. French was still close to his heart, perhaps because it was the language with which he first set off on his travels. His first foreign identity. Yoshie spent two hours a day studying Spanish. I wouldn't say he ended up speaking it incredibly well, but proficiently enough, yes. He had great difficulty writing it, but his reading skills were quite good. I would occasionally lend him novels by Argentinian authors. Mysteriously, they looked newer when he returned them.

He used to tell me that Western grammar had upset his concept of time and of things. If I understood correctly, Japanese nouns are invariable, with no indication of gender or number. Which means that for a Japanese speaker things don't change according to circumstance. They are what they are. They may combine with other things, but they retain the same form. Isn't that well on its way to being a political statement? Yoshie had problems with definite and indefinite articles. Sometimes he got them mixed up, other times he would simply leave them out. Can you give me glass of wine? he would say. His glass of wine sounded to me like a concept, an absolute category. A more lasting pleasure.

Another habit of his that has become fixed in my mind was the way he stressed words. He would emphasize each syllable with a sort of diplomacy, as if to avoid favoring one inflection over another. This gave his speech a slightly disjointed tone. Each of his sentences resembled an inventory or a scale, and I wasn't quite sure where it would end. So I listened, waiting for the next sound.

His habit of never quite saying yes or no both intrigued and, in some ways, excited me. He gave the impression (and this motivated me to persuade him) that his desires were made of a very fine, reversible material. Like a woman's stocking. Yo derived pleasure from those interconnecting vessels between wanting and not wanting something, between accepting and refusing. My acquaintances found him a little exasperating. Where I saw insinuation, they read indecision.

He tried to explain to me the tricky little word *hai*. It's roughly equivalent to our *ajá*, like giving a nod of assent. Japanese speakers need to tack something else on to it, so that you know for sure that they are saying yes. To provide added emphasis. For example: Yes, I agree with you. Or: Yes, I promise I will do such and such. In Yoshie's opinion this was clearer than our version, when we simply say yes or no, and then only afterwards start to think about it.

He was always getting *usted* and *vos* mixed up. It was completely beyond him why *ustedes* is the plural of *usted*, whereas *vosotros* isn't the plural of *vos*. Go live in Spain! I would say to him as a joke. And guess what, he ended up in Madrid. If I understood him correctly, when you speak to someone in Japanese you have to employ several virtually untranslatable forms of address. Besides being casual or polite, you can also place the other person higher, lower, who knows what else. I imagine that having so many different ways of addressing someone creates a complex interlocutor. Others within the other.

However, what confounded him most were the verb tenses. From what I can remember, Japanese has a past and a nonpast. Two poles separated by an abyss! I see this as an example of how grammar conditions the memory of its speakers. The very concept of a nonpast blew me away. An entire country could fall down that hole.

———

Yoshie first lived on Avenida del Libertador, in one of those apartments that seem to float above the city and have no wish to be part of it. He quickly grew tired of living there, and wanted to find a neighborhood with more of a past. This isn't Paris, I mocked him. At last, he found a large, refurbished mansion in San Telmo. Near the old market, on Calle Perú. Funnily enough, only a couple of blocks from the Nikkei Federation, which didn't exist at the time.

The house was delightful, with those hardwood doors, high ceilings, and corridors that are typical of the neighborhood. He rented it from the descendant of Japanese immigrants. A guy from Burzaco who had made a fortune in the textile industry. No, wait a minute, that was someone else. He came from Escobar, from a family of flower growers or something. I remember clearly the guy's surname, Fukuyo, because I made crude jokes about it. Yoshie couldn't understand why we found oriental names so hilarious. He said we never laughed at English or French ones.

He told me that in the countries where he had lived before, he hadn't really become involved with the Japanese community. He was afraid that if he did, he would find it more difficult to assimilate. And he didn't see the sense in traveling halfway across the world just to live as if you hadn't moved an inch. What he never foresaw was the number of Japanese tourists who came to visit San Telmo. And so it was here, in this distant land, that Yo ended up reconnecting with his people. He started to sponsor various cultural projects. That was how I got to know several translators. He couldn't believe how well he got on with the Argentinian nikkei. Maybe because, deep down, they all felt much more Japanese than they'd imagined. Or because none of them were a hundred percent Japanese.

He also did good business with them, of course. He managed to get I don't know how many subsidies out of the Japanese government. And, obviously, the nikkei community became huge fans of Me. Yo was amazed not to find any left-handed people. He was always hoping someone would sign a document with their left hand. In the end, I got on well with the nikkei. I can still remember several of them. The Nakandakaris, the Muratos, the Iwasakis. Lovely people. I found a video of some youngsters on YouTube recently who I thought might be their children. Or grandchildren!

If you ask me, he idealized New York too much. Especially when comparing it with Buenos Aires, which kind of got up my nose. We have good things here too. What can I say? In my book, skyscrapers are just phallic symbols. And to make things worse, he could never praise New York without mentioning that journalist chick, Laura, or Laurie, or whatever her name was. If she was so amazing, why did he leave her?

He was obsessed with collapsing borders. Imaginary ones, I mean. He wanted somehow to unite his cities, his languages, his scattered memories. He saw a connection in everything, a possible proximity between things that in theory were very far apart. He jumped from one reference to another like a kind of computer translator. And at times the results sounded as crazy as one of them. I think the poor guy needed to be in several places at once. He had the fantasy of intermingling, something that can lead you to solitude as much as exile.

People always referred to him as a Chink. Well-intentioned or not, here that's what we call anyone whose eyes aren't round. It made me feel really ashamed and mad at my friends. It didn't exactly amuse him either, but he took it with a pinch of salt. Once or twice he told me that basically he deserved it. That every country should have the experience of being mistaken for its ancestral enemy.

Yo loved how familiar and touchy-feely we Argentinians are. But he also found it unnerving. If everyone can talk to you about anything and instantly become your friend, he said, how do you know who your real friends are? Until he trusted someone, he was usually quite reserved. He spoke very slowly and in a soft voice but he would have sudden moments of cheekiness, like the day we met. I'm sure that both things were related. After all, aren't there some urges that only shy people have?

Our contrasting views about the sanctity of rules created a hint of friction. I'd already run into this problem when dealing with English people, but it was even worse with him. For Yoshie there was no such thing as an exception to the norm, or at least there shouldn't be. That's why he never thought about how to react to unexpected events, only how to avoid them at all costs (and in this, I have to admit, he was largely successful). For me, the unexpected is part of the plan, the exception is the rule.

Imagine what a headache it was for us to plan a weekend away. We would end up staying at home, or going to a restaurant where every option was at least printed in black-and-white, in perfect order. But even then the poor guy was hounded by exceptions, because I'd always ask if they could leave something off a dish or change an ingredient in a salad.

When he first moved to Buenos Aires, Yoshie would turn up so early for things that everyone thought he'd got the time wrong. For him, to arrive on time was to arrive late. With his economic reasoning, he wasn't wrong. If you come to a meeting at the agreed hour, by the time you start work it's always later than intended. That kind of time management only ever brought him frustration. He would spend whole days waiting, feeling offended, abandoned, God knows what else. He was accustomed to working in France and the States, where time is money. They don't realize it's the only thing we can all afford to spend.

What most intrigued me was that no matter how early you arrived at a rendezvous with him—and believe me, I went out of my way to surprise him—Yoshie was always there first. I don't understand how he did it, with all the barricaded streets, the strikes, and the shambles we have here every day. Maybe he arranged various meetings in the same place. Several times I thought I saw someone leave his table as I came in. I'm the kind of person who thinks that excessively punctual people are hiding something. Sorry to sound skeptical, but I find any model behavior suspicious.

Yo's punctilious habits reminded me of the psychos you see in movies. You know, those characters who seem so perfect, but then turn out to be monsters? In his case, though, this didn't scare me, I was attracted to it. That's often been my experience with tranquil men. I think they must have an energy that's unleashed only in intimacy. I always preferred to sleep with the calm ones, because they know how to change gear. How can someone accelerate if they're always living on the edge, at full throttle?

At his place he was capable of waking up hours before me, preparing breakfast and starting work without making a sound. I imagined he had to have very special hands to do all that. And even if that wasn't really the case, the mere idea led me to feel it was true. That's the way I am. I get into bed with my conjectures, and then take pleasure through auto-suggestion.

I think that after a certain age, which is more or less the age I was when I started seeing Yoshie, sex becomes only relatively important. Or rather, it becomes extremely important, but for reasons that are no longer sexual, if that makes sense. You tend to put more value on everything that happens in the name of desire, what you talk about afterwards, what you remember, or imagine beforehand. Those things would be impossible without sex, and yet they aren't themselves sex.

As a young woman, you get used to screwing in a way that prioritizes the other person, in order to not disappoint them, to satisfy their expectations. That's why you sometimes go over the top in bed: it has nothing to do with deception, that's just a stupid male chauvinist idea. It's more a question of replacing your own lack of enjoyment with the other person's approval. If everyone else thinks you do it okay, then you do it okay. As no one has ever taught you that you're important, at least you can be important *to* someone.

Later on, you learn, or unlearn, to really shag, and to give yourself pleasure. To make pleasure happen when you're with someone else. Since you don't really know how to achieve it, you're constantly pursuing that goal. And then, as the years go by, you learn to do it for the other person once more. Only this time, the pleasure you give serves as a lever for your own. Sex is no longer about a goal, or the goal now is to become close to someone. Even if only for a little while.

And time again continues to pass, and you desire differently. Maybe you don't want to get so close now. What you want is to get away, to get far away from everything, and from yourself. Your life, your struggles, your obsessions, because you're starting to know yourself too well. That's usually when people take up fetishes, I think, when you don't so much try the things you like as the things you thought you didn't like.

With Yoshie, well, I occasionally had the feeling that I was getting far away from myself. It wasn't a high-wire act. He, how can I put it, didn't hold me back. It was more like he helped me get away. He realized that he wasn't the goal. As you grow older, pleasure becomes a bit of a fugitive. Life's hard knocks start to accumulate and it is more like solace, a kind of reward for enduring.

Yoshie had this ruse that worked really well. We'd be walking down the street and suddenly he'd ask me what I would do if I knew I was going to die that day. He did that several times when we were strolling past Recoleta Cemetery. Then we'd rush into a rooms-by-the-hour hotel on Calle Azcuénaga. (Maybe it's still there, I don't know. Sadly, I haven't been there in a while.) I remember one night, in that hotel, right after I came. I saw my body reflected in the ceiling, and I said to him, I don't know whether I had an orgasm or a premonition. I saw him turn in the mirror. Where did I read that? he wanted to know. Whenever I tried to say something profound to him, he gave me the same reply.

He'd insist that when I was naked I smelled of sand. What type of sand? I'd tease him. Dry or wet? From the Atlantic or the Pacific? Neither wet nor dry, he'd answer.

At first, Emilio saw Yoshie as an intruder who was invading his space. He was jealous, not because of me so much as because of Ari. He hated the idea of another man playing with his kid. I understood how he felt, of course. But I also had the impression he was using our child to stir up other stuff.

I thought the most sensible thing was to keep my ex as far away as possible from my new partner, but that didn't work. Not seeing Yoshie only made him more apprehensive. In the end, I decided that the best solution was to do the exact opposite. I forced Emilio and Yoshie to meet. We had lunch together a few times. And, after two or three uncomfortable afternoons, Emilio started to treat him with a friendliness that I suspected was strategic. I wasn't sure how to react. I was prepared for the war of jealousies, the duel between proud males, the battle of the phalluses. But not for the two of them to laugh, talk behind my back, and ply me with questions about each other.

All of a sudden, I felt uneasy seeing Ari play with these two men I had slept with. Emilio and Yoshie eyed each other, I don't know, with that look of gratitude men get in the supposed absence of rivalry. Of mutual admiration at having decided not to come to blows. Or am I being unfair? When a guy relaxes and stops competing for a second, he must feel such relief, such love for everything!

Yoshie took to Ari like a house on fire, and that surprised me, because I had him pegged as a bachelor who hated kids. To my son, it seemed like a huge exploit for someone to come from so far away. Whenever we ate a meal together, Ari would ask him to say something in Japanese. Yoshie used the opportunity to teach us how to say, Enjoy your meal. *Itadakimasu.*

And afterwards, *Gochisousama*. I loved that one, The food was delicious. And loads more that I've forgotten.

I think he would have made a wonderful uncle. The way he got along with Ari was astonishing, as were the clear boundaries he set. For example, he would spend a Saturday with him. He would look after him, attend to his needs, give him affection. And when on Sunday he went back home, he would forget about my son until the next time. You could say he preferred being a guest star to being a father figure.

Ari and I were still living in the Palermo neighborhood, in the tiny flat Emilio and I had bought. The move from London was so strange. The dictatorship was coming to an end, and we'd decided to come back here for the elections. So we cashed in the few pounds we had managed to save. We grabbed our scant possessions, and without giving it too much thought, the three of us boarded a plane. We met up with our friends (at least with those who were still here). We were really pleased to vote. Ever the loyal Peronist, Emilio voted for Luder. And when Alfonsín won, we split up. Instead of starting a new life, all the baggage we'd been dragging around came crashing down on us.

It was a pleasantly luminous two-bedroom flat with wooden floors on the junction of Calle Mansilla and Aráoz. Back then, Palermo hadn't yet become Soho or Hollywood or anything of the sort. It was an authentic neighborhood. If you know where to go, parts of it are still like that. The people who've lived there all their lives (meaning those who weren't bought out) feel very strongly about this. That was when the fractures started to appear, sometimes on the same street. You can see the scars on nearly every building. The people who arrived before and after the money.

In fact, there are so many clichés about Palermo that you can't see the real thing anymore. What you see is the image that's projected of the neighborhood. Most people seem to go there simply to reinforce these projections. There's the posh Palermo (boutiques, chefs). The intellectual Palermo (bookshops, cafés). The nocturnal Palermo (bars, cabs). The traditional Palermo (family ironmongers, homemade pasta). The alternative Palermo (charity shops, organic tea). The conservative Palermo (patisseries and Macri). The tourist Palermo, obviously (chargrills and Malbec). And so on. All of these visions are as real as they are biased. I think that, despite everything, this lack of a true essence is one of the best qualities of the neighborhood.

The point is, Yoshie got used to coming to Palermo more and more frequently and he became a constant for Ari. This made me both happy and anxious. Relationships being the way they are, I realized I was exposing my son to another potential loss.

When he started to sleep over at my place on the weekends when it wasn't Ari's turn to stay with his father, I would ask him not to smoke in the apartment. And remember that back then, being anti-smoking was really something. If you didn't smoke, you were considered a bore by the assholes who were choking you. But with that military discipline he occasionally demonstrated, Yoshie instantly obeyed, and started to smoke less at his own place too. He told me that way, he would feel fewer cravings when he was at my apartment.

The poor guy had so many allergies and phobias. He dealt with them in his own way. I suspect that deep down they helped him prove that he could overcome them if he had to. For example, the cat problem. Before he entered the apartment, I had to shut it in the kitchen and give the place a thorough hoovering. There couldn't be a single hair left on the sofa, the sheets needed changing, a whole rigmarole. But my son felt sad that he could never play with both of them together. That he had to choose between Yoshie and his cat, Walsh.

Until one day, Yoshie went and swallowed the most powerful antihistamine he could find at the pharmacy, then got down on the floor with Ari and the cat. You can't buy the kind of happiness I felt when I saw them rolling around together, screaming like crazy. It's worth an entire relationship. Afterwards, he seemed to be breathing strangely, and I got scared. I imagined having to call an ambulance. How are you feeling, Yo? I asked. Surprised, he replied, nose streaming, eyes bloodshot.

Walsh, who was a bit mistrustful, didn't care very much for Yoshie. I think he sensed that he touched him only begrudgingly. Walsh allowed him to do so, maybe because he sensed that it was a triumph. Even so, he would arch his back and instead of closing his eyes, would gaze at Yoshie while he was stroking him.

Emilio is nuts about football, and every Sunday his ear would be glued to the radio. Even in London, he managed to organize a group of Boca fans.

He tried to explain the tactics to me. He made a sincere effort to share his enthusiasm with me, the way we did with everything else. I showed him how to revise translations. And Emilio had even succeeded in getting us to read the penal code together. Football on the other hand never grabbed my attention, I grew instantly bored. When I met Yoshie, I could see that football didn't interest him either. That was another reason we got along. Being in the minority together is another kind of homeland, I think.

To him, kicking around a ball that hardly bounces for ninety minutes, trying to get it through a hole disproportionate to its size, had to seem like a stupid activity. As a boy he played Ping-Pong, and in New York I think he became a fan of American football, or basketball, or something. But Ari is like his dad, a loyal Boca fan. And so Yoshie ended up sitting down to watch their games with my son. That and anime. Not that he understood much of what went on in the matches, though he enjoyed applauding the goals with Ari. Whenever they scored, Walsh would flee the room.

What interested him wasn't when the teams scored a goal, as much as the absurd possibility that nobody scored any. He found it intriguing that such a long match could end tied at zero, in an empty score. He saw it as a Buddhist joke. I must say, I never imagined for a moment that football could lend itself to any kind of philosophical comparison. I think Yoshie saw nil–nil as an objective. Instead of rooting for a team like the rest of us (I support either my son's team or the poorest country or the one with the cutest players), he celebrated draws. He explained to us that the Japanese tradition cannot accept defeat and that the only honorable solution for both teams is a draw. This infuriated Ari, So do you or don't you want Boca to win?

Close to where we lived, on the corner of Calle Perú and Avenida San Juan, were some miniature football pitches, known as Nikkei. Maybe they still exist. Some weekends we'd take Ari there to play with his friends. For years, my son rejected English. I fretted over the problem. If Emilio or I made even the silliest remark to him in English, he would reply in Spanish. He had blocked out everything to do with our exile in London, which is where he'd learned to speak. And yet with Yoshie things were different. We discovered this by chance one afternoon, while watching him play on one of those mini pitches.

At some point during the match, Yo let slip a typically Yankee shout of encouragement. Then Ari, perhaps without thinking, yelled back in English. I nearly fainted from shock. I asked Yoshie if he could keep talking to him like that from time to time. To my astonishment, Ari went along with it. As if he were being invited to play a simple language game, without the burden of family obligation. Isn't that what translation does? It allows you to discover part of your identity, thanks to some foreign pretext.

At the end of the dictatorship, when we told him we were going home, Ari had wanted to take his English radio with him. A small yellow plastic transistor, which he would fall asleep listening to every night. We told him that we could buy him another in Buenos Aires, but he insisted on bringing it with him, and so we packed it in our hand luggage. Emilio and I were on edge throughout the journey. I remember we had an argument at the airport. We weren't sure what had messed up our son's life more, leaving or returning home.

Ari was totally relaxed during the flight. It was his first long-haul, and he kept pointing out the window and asking questions about Argentina. He even fell asleep for a few hours, something neither his dad nor I was capable of doing. No sooner had we landed at Ezeiza than poor Ari turned on his radio and discovered he couldn't find any of his favorite stations. Then he burst into tears and cried all day. He was about five years old. I'll never forget that.

At first, Ari was inclined to blame me for the separation. Not that he ever said anything to me, but his attitude towards me was always accusatory. He'd be grumpy and tiresome from Monday to Friday, and then when his dad came to pick him up, he was all over him. I felt awful. It was like the only love he got was on the weekends.

I imagine this had to do with the way his father and I divided space, not only time. Emilio had been forced to live somewhere else, and Ari somehow interpreted this as me having kicked him out. Mom stayed in her domain, slept in the same bed (and with another man), while poor Dad had been banished. The only one on my side was Walsh, who would wind himself between my legs whenever Emilio came by.

My greatest fear was that Ari would never forgive me. That I would be judged by my grown-up son, having not done enough to be pardoned. I don't even think about it now. A mother's fears are largely preemptive, they arise before the event itself. I'm not sure whether my guilt vanished naturally, or if I fought against it by trying to be the best mother I could be.

As Ari grew older, he started to be more critical of his father, and the role he fulfilled, or didn't always fulfill. Although my son denies it, he also felt jealous of his siblings. Emilio treated all his children the same, which in theory is a good thing. Only sometimes he forgot that Ari was the one who saw his father leave, and so maybe needed a little more attention, I don't know.

After giving it a lot of thought, Ari decided to make use of the new legislation. He changed his surname and adopted mine. Now, instead of Molinari, he is officially called Kerlin. I felt proud, why deny it. Emilio was hurt. From the start we had agreed to bring him up as a goy. No communion, no bar mitzvah, nothing. He could choose when he got older what he wanted to be. And the fact is he had no interest in these things. But lately, I don't know, he's got a bee in his bonnet about Judaism, or a grudge against his father. If you'll forgive the tautology.

I always tell people about my father, who, because he wasn't born here, never learned to pronounce my name properly. He had a slight problem with the *r* in Mariela. And even today, my name sounds ugly to me. Whenever someone says it, underneath I can hear my father mispronounce it. Although he spoke perfect Spanish, there were words he had difficulty with all his life. Sometimes I think that's what made me decide to study another language. To get away from the one that hampered my father.

In all fairness, a possessive mother is no walk in the park either. My sisters and I know what it means to endure the love of a *yiddishe mame*. When we told my in-laws we weren't going to circumcise or baptize Ari, they were understanding. They came from a more diverse background that included Italian Catholics, agnostics, and atheists. Or maybe they were relieved not to have such a Jewish grandson, who knows. It annoyed Emilio that I thought that. He accused my family of being addicted to conspiracies. Welcome to my people, *mio caro*! My sister backed us a hundred percent. Dad protested less than I'd expected. According to him, he'd feared this from the start, as he did with all bad things. Mom, on the other hand, true to herself, screamed to high heaven. She's probably still screaming up there now, poor thing.

Instead of enjoying their freedom after their children leave home, some mothers are left feeling empty. They can't stop grieving. They're lonely, unloved, abandoned, that whole Oedipal tango. As soon as I notice such feelings toward Ari, I try to suppress them. Yoshie maintained that a lot of parents operate with an emotional economy, with its ledger of sacrifices and unpaid debts. And they act like emotional creditors, because they expect their kids to return their investment. I found the idea unpleasant but interesting. He grew up with a gap, and had to build a defense around it.

As far as I know, he never wanted kids, or he was afraid of wanting them. I think he felt shriveled up by his nuclear experience, as if reproduction were the prelude to genocide. He thought of himself as the last of his race: his identity was strongly associated with extinction. In my view, he still couldn't cut that tie.

As a mother I knew he was missing out on the most beautiful, the biggest thing in life, even though part of me understood that kind of dilemma. I remember when I had my son, I not only felt that I was perpetuating myself, prolonging my life through him. I also had the sensation, how can I put this, that he was emphasizing my own mortality. I didn't doubt that he would outlive me, and that I wouldn't get to experience all his different ages. To begin with, this shocked and even depressed me. We chose Ariel as his name because it was included in mine, Mariela. And Ari for short was the ending of his father's surname, Molinari. My son says we took advantage of his name.

In the end, I don't know, your baby is born and fortunately he is healthy, and so beautiful. Well, not really. Aren't newborns quite ugly? They grow to be beautiful. And this complete human being is supposedly yours, you created them yourself, and that's almost incomprehensible. Emilio became committed as never before, he fought to earn his place. So much life all of a sudden, when all he had done was impregnate me. It made him feel slightly insecure. Or, as Yoshie would say, indebted.

I think this happens to other men, especially with their first child. As women our initial experience is different. You may end up being a terrible mother, but from the very beginning, you feel you have earned maternity with your body. That you worked hard for this child. I sometimes wonder how our marriage might have been affected by that. Because at the time you can't deal with it, you have enough on your plate looking after the baby and trying to snatch a couple hours of sleep.

When Yoshie and I got to know each other better, and as often happens with people I love, we started to exchange stories about our childhood. He spoke of his sisters. Of his school in Nagasaki. And the spirals he used to draw in the shape of eyes. He still occasionally sketched them, almost unconsciously, on paper napkins. I told him that when I was a little girl, I would draw a tree with wings. Looking at it made me anxious, because if you have roots you can't fly. When I showed my father those drawings, he would stroke my head and say, Very pretty, my girl, very pretty.

I remember how the death of Yoshie's aunt affected him: she was the only close relative he had left. We were at his house in San Telmo when he received the news. Someone called him from Tokyo. A neighbor, I think. He answered in that funny singsong voice he had when he spoke Spanish. Then he instantly switched language, tone, and volume. The conversation can't have lasted more than a minute. He barely said a word. He listened to what the other person was saying, repeating the same monosyllable. When he hung up, he looked awful. That's it, he said, now I'm only one left. I think this loss closed something in him. Or rather, reopened it.

Yo told me in passing a small detail that stayed with me, because somehow I felt it was important. He was a breech baby. He was born with his back to the world. His mother had remarked on it several times, he didn't want to leave her, he didn't want to come out and see the world. He had his reasons, that's what I told him.

His parents had died too young, but at least they were old enough for him to attach an identity to them. As for his sisters, what most tormented him—as I interpreted it—wasn't having lost them. It was that he had never gotten to know them. He missed all the experiences they hadn't had.

I think that he most struggled with the memory of his father. In that story, he wasn't just a victim. Yoshie was plagued by the fact that his family's comfortable status had depended on his father's job in the armaments industry. This put him at odds with the patriarchy, even though he never used that word, of course.

Mostly, he blamed himself for not trying to resuscitate his father when he saw him sprawled on the ground. Not touching him more, not dirtying himself with his father's corpse. Yoshie wasn't one for this sort of thinking. In fact, he recoiled from it. Yet he spoke of his father's smell, his build, his hands, his hair. Too physical a memory for a man to whom he'd never been so close.

Once I suggested we go to La Plata to celebrate the Day of the Dead with the Japanese community. I said maybe we could pay tribute to his family and, clumsy me, honor their memory together. Yoshie gazed at me with a mixture of gratitude and bemusement. He said that his family had no tomb, that he didn't need to go anywhere to commune with them. That he did so every day at home.

It's true he'd made a—what was it called?—a, oh, it escapes me. Like a little shrine, next to the dining room table. With photographs of his parents and sisters, and his aunt and uncle. He would give them fresh fruit, and sometimes rice or tea. I was going to say he left it out for them, but no. He *gave* it to them. As if they, too, needed to receive it. That seemed to me like a very sensible way of communicating with the dead. Somehow the food made them corporeal again, they were well-fed ghosts. I wish we would do the same here. We have no lack of dead people without bodies.

As the years went by, he got to know our customs quite well, and I learned something of his. I don't know which one of us was more surprised.

His descriptions of my country made me laugh. I felt that I was in front of one of those fairground mirrors, on the one hand you look disfigured, and on the other, you know that it's showing your defects more clearly. In his view, the average Argentinian sees themselves as a leader, and is convinced that collectively, Argentina will always be a disaster. So they choose instead a ferocious individualism, which is at once part of their charm and also their problem. He may not have used those exact words, but anyway, that's what I learned about us through the eyes of a Japanese person.

Naturally, he had his own issues. I found it hard to understand how a country brought up with religions that worship nature could invest so heavily in nuclear energy, especially after what had happened. In nature, he argued, there are species that, when faced with an emergency, decide to self-destruct. It's their instinct to distinguish themselves from other species. Like lemmings, Yoshie said.

Well, actually, lemmings don't commit suicide. I explained that to him one day. It's a myth, Yo, that's not how they die. And the way I see it, deep down, countries are never that different from one another. That's something I've learned from translating. No matter how many differences and limitations you come across, in the end what endures is what's translatable. What we succeed in doing with the things we understand.

And yet the myth is seductive, isn't it? If a Japanese person commits suicide, we look no further. They're Japanese, after all. And we don't bother to ask questions. Instead of introducing us to a culture, stereotypes prevent us from getting to know it. Just as Yoshie started out believing that Gardel made all Argentinians dissolve into tears, I discovered that he couldn't stand Mishima. He found his militaristic nationalism very unappealing.

I've always been fascinated by Mishima's death by seppuku. Until I met Yo, I thought he had committed hara-kiri. So many different ways of doing yourself in! According to Yoshie, Mishima wasn't really following the samurai code when he killed himself. Rather, he'd found a convenient pretext to glorify his self-destructive urge, and to pass it off as an act of patriotism. Yoshie considered that tragic end, when he failed to complete the ritual, to be the most profoundly Japanese thing about his life. But there's a huge difference, I think, between self-immolation and sacrifice. Hara-kiri requires the total responsibility of the victim. And during World War II, an entire population was sacrificed, of two cities in particular, without being given any say over its fate. It was, so to speak, a suicide perpetrated on the body of another. The authorities over here are familiar with this practice. Go and ask the boys who fought in the Malvinas.

I was very shocked by the stories about Okinawa. When they lost that last battle, the army convinced civilians that the enemy would torture them and massacre their families if they didn't take their own lives. They say that many people got their friends to kill them. Others lay in a circle around the grenades they had been given. Whole families committed suicide together. The father was usually the one who removed the pin.

For the few who didn't kill themselves, falling into enemy hands proved less deadly than obeying their own army. That must have felt very odd. The survivors ended up strangely grateful to the invaders for having spared them. A Japanese-style Stockholm syndrome.

Yoshie once told me a story about Hiroshima. He'd told me several already, but this one was special, because he wasn't sure if he had seen it with his own eyes, heard about it there, or read it in a book. It seems that after the bomb, in the midst of the destruction, a regiment had received the order to commit suicide on the spot. Out of the entire regiment, only one young soldier disobeyed the command. The narrator of the story.

We spoke quite a lot about that. He even confessed to me that, over the past few years, he had the impression of having more and more memories of the bomb. He never seemed to find raising the subject difficult. He would bring it up himself, if it was pertinent. The day he asked my permission to talk to Ari about it, I knew that our love was serious.

He used to say that we visualize our personal memories in three speeds, like the videocassette players made by Me. There are memories that come to mind over and over again, obsessively, in slow motion. Then those that seem to skip constantly, as though missing some important scenes. And those that always go by too fast, that we'd like to slow down but don't know how. If there's any truth in this, it occurs to me that the first and second speeds would be the speeds of trauma. The third would be more like pleasure.

Following a similar logic, it seems to me that one could distinguish three types of collective memory. The re-recorded one, you might call it, where the official account is recorded over memories to conceal them. Memory on pause, which is frozen at a key moment. And fast-forwarded memory, where part of the story is deliberately omitted. I mentioned this to Jorge recently. Can I write that down? he asked again.

Apparently, societies that have gone through wars have higher rates of senile dementia. That sounds reasonable to me. As we age our memory starts to engage with the distant past, and that's precisely when our ghosts can come back to haunt us. In that case, madness and forgetting seem like natural reactions, don't they? Maybe that's why I'm trying to recount everything I remember about my life. In order to tell my son, who doesn't share those memories. And to tell myself, in case I've started to forget.

Yet I like to think that memory fulfills a creative function as well. Not just because it invents what it can't recall, or didn't fully comprehend. To me, a good memory asks itself: What can I do with what was done to me? Who do my memories turn me into, how do they reinvent me? I think I learned that when I was in exile in England. And here, with Yoshie.

Of course, there are always plenty of people who say you should forget to some extent, that there are things you're better off not remembering. The problem is that this condemns you to an endless contradiction, because a trauma that isn't spoken about can't truly be forgotten. It literally can't rest. Like those ideas you don't write down, which keep you from sleeping or thinking about something else. That's what my therapist always said to me, may she rest in peace. What hasn't been inscribed cannot be prescribed.

I once asked my therapist, who was a big shot, how she would apply that same principle to a genocide. According to her, for the first generation of every genocide, the experience defies description. There are no words for it. For the following generation, it becomes unmentionable. Inconvenient. And for the one after that, it is already unthinkable. It can't have happened, let's say, or it could never happen again. Which of these three are we in?

Obviously, no country in the world wants its tragedies repeated. That doesn't mean they're willing to deal with the victims of their previous tragedies. Those are two different desires. Are they two different desires?

Half-joking and half-serious, I would sometimes give Yoshie a hard time about Japan being one of the few countries to receive Videla. He was also the first South American president to visit China. So it seems the general had Asian inclinations. At the time, we were still in London. I was outraged to see those influential countries legitimizing the dictatorship. They wanted to go on buying meat and wheat from us. And I imagine we bought much more expensive goods from them.

Anyhow, there was a military ambassador in Tokyo who had been a colleague of Massera's, and in charge of ESMA. A real gem. That son of a bitch went around boasting about the ethnic homogeneity of Argentinians. Clearly he had never visited the North and I doubt he mentioned our immigrants and Jews, either. Under Menem, that guy was president of the Argentine Japanese society. Later on he was jailed for crimes against humanity. The point I'm making is that they all went to Tokyo, ministers, businessmen, bankers, priests. They weren't exactly traveling incognito.

The Japanese government declared Videla an honored guest. It put him up in a palace, he had two audiences with the prime minister and even met with former emperors. If you search in *The Japan Times*, you can find a daily record of his visit. There's not a single mention in those articles of his military rank. Nor is there a single word about the disappeared, the prisoners, the exiles. In the photos the general is wearing civilian clothes, something he rarely did over here. I suppose that in Japan military uniforms stirred painful memories and were less suitable for doing business. According to the press, the meetings were about Japanese investment in Argentina.

That same year the Japanese Gardens in Palermo had been renovated. They looked beautiful and whatever, but they were reopened by Videla. *The Japan Times* reproduced a comment from a local Tokyo newspaper in which the dictatorship—this I'll never forget—was described as a "moderate government." In Argentina at the time, there were approximately as many people of Japanese origin as disappeared people.

Yoshie reminded me that, prior to Videla's trip to Japan, Argentina had won a youth football championship in Tokyo with Maradona on the team. Even he had heard about it through the media. He explained that Argentina's popularity had grown in the wake of that triumph, and somehow it had smoothed the way for Videla's visit. Honestly, I had no recollection of that. You see how memory has the ability to skip or to fast-forward?

I was never really sure whether Me had started operating here thanks to the dictatorship. I think its Buenos Aires office opened after the debt was nationalized. What I do know is that Yo landed just before the Malvinas. He would always say that his first experience here was war and that he couldn't believe it, because in the States the same thing had happened to him with Vietnam. But I don't know much about his company. I was falling in love, so I didn't want to ask too many questions.

Talking with Yo, I realized that his country also had its disappeared people. He told me there was even an association of mothers, the Hiroshima Mothers' Group, although they didn't have the impact of the mothers here. As I understand it, there is no precise data about the number of victims. Many disintegrated as if they'd never existed. Others were cremated, and with the city in ruins, it was impossible to carry out a proper body count. So their names were crossed off by simple elimination. If they didn't turn up, they were considered dead.

Yoshie was never able to bury his mother or sisters. His dad, at least he was able to say goodbye to him. He saw. He knew. But in their case, nothing. Even when dead, they were untraceable. They ceased to exist twice over.

The inability to mourn is something we're very familiar with in Argentina. To disappear or to be obliterated belongs to another dimension of death, you might say. It impedes what my therapist (did I mention she was a big shot?) called *psycatrization*. In other words, it prevents mourning. Which means that memory is more endangered than life itself.

As soon as the war was over and they began to uncover the effects of the bomb, the American occupiers banned the broadcast of any testimony. According to them, testimonies could disturb the public peace. Some peace! But I don't think it was just about Japan and the States. The whole world needed to believe that the good guys had fought the good fight.

Before any information became available, Hiroshima and Nagasaki were like a horror with no official images. I think this somehow contrasts with the Holocaust. Beyond all the differences, of course, the Shoah remained visual in everyone's imagination, didn't it? When you hear *concentration camp*, you don't see an empty space. You see people, victims. The piles of bodies in Mauthausen function as a collective memory. The dead in Japan, on the other hand, were vanquished and their silence belonged to the victors, who fortunately were on our side.

If you think about it, the first image that springs to mind when you think of the atomic bomb isn't of the victims. It's the mushroom cloud. You see the explosion, not all the people it killed. Isn't that the height of disappearance? That's why the survivors, whether they realized it or not, were already rebels. They didn't need to behave heroically. Their mere existence was a radical act, because they weren't supposed to have survived. To me, that was Yoshie's political side. He was radical because he was alive.

The number of times my dad used to argue with me: What has anti-Semitism got to do with those bombs! That was a war between countries! When it comes to human rights, these kinds of distinctions amaze me. Is everything fair game during a war between countries? Let's say there'd been a Jewish state at that time and it had fought against an anti-Semitic power, would the concentration camps have seemed any less unforgivable to us?

Take Palestine, for example, which was the issue we most clashed over. Doesn't killing children and civilians in those territories warrant as much condemnation before as it does after the recognition of a Palestinian state? My dad was livid. How dare you compare the concentration camps to . . . ! I'm not comparing, Dad, I'm not comparing, I would say. I'm just trying to understand the way we think.

Regardless of who won the war, in my opinion there's another link to the case of Japan. The productivity of death. The gas chambers and the atom bombs are—what should I call them? Products of killing industries. Pure deadly efficiency. Only an industrial power could've invented them. Other countries can at best try to emulate them. Here, for example, we did a pretty good job of following the Nazi model.

Although they occurred at almost the same time, to me it's as if the two exterminations were from different eras. The gas chambers were supposed to be secret, there was nothing to show the public. But the bombs were dropped for the whole world to see. In the concentration camps, or in the clandestine prisons over here during the dictatorship, the aggressor was sickeningly apparent. In Hiroshima and Nagasaki it was invisible, there was nothing to rise up against or to surrender to. It was something against everyone and for no one. I'm not saying it was worse. I'm saying it was the future.

Afterwards we invent soothing stories to tell ourselves. The Holocaust was inhuman. The bomb was a mistake (Yoshie told me this is what one monument in Hiroshima calls it, a *mistake* that must never be repeated). Or that the disappeared were a bad dream, diabolical, and so on. As if there had never been a logic, even a bureaucracy, behind it, with thousands of employees conscious of their actions, following a plan. We invent all that so that kids can sleep tight. Or rather, so that their parents can.

I never quite understood why among my friends Yoshie had the reputation of being serious. My sisters (Sara more than Monica) found him too formal. Once again, I think this was a problem of translation and interpretation. We didn't laugh in the same language as him. His sense of humor didn't attract strangers, which is how we warm to people over here. His was inward, so to speak. You had to get close to him to learn to laugh at the things he laughed at.

He loved jokes about death. In his case, this was deeply ironic. The more I knew about Yoshie's life, the funnier they seemed to me. His sense of the tragic was so strong that any joke could make him feel relieved. He knew lots of poems and fables by heart. They were very important to him, because his father had taught them to him. He would recite them in Japanese and then translate them for me. I think I found them more fascinating before I understood what they meant. This often happens to me with languages I don't know. The translation disappoints me slightly, as if the original goes from meaning potentially everything to saying something very limited.

So, for example, I learned that Zen monks wrote poems about their own death. Yoshie explained that they would write them while they were still in good health, and then pretend later on that they had thought them up on their deathbed. I was surprised that many of them were humorous. There was one he used to repeat a lot that went something like this:

> *I thought I would live*
> *for about two hundred years,*
> *being pessimistic.*
> *But death has come suddenly,*
> *when I'm a mere boy*
> *of eighty-five.*

There was also a fable with a similar theme. A man fears he will die without leaving a worthy goodbye poem, and so he starts to practice from an early age. Each time he finishes one, he sends it to his master. Until on his eightieth birthday he sends him this:

> *Eighty years I lived*
> *by the deeds and the grace of our sovereign*
> *and my beloved family.*

My heart is now at peace
amid moons and flowers.

Then his master (who must have been immortal or something) replies, When you are ninety, alter the first line.

It seems some of the monks would say goodbye with a few satirical verses. Yoshie told the story of a poet who, at death's door, copies out another poet's farewell. And he adds a heading:

This poem is the work of someone else.
I promise I shall plagiarize no more.

Whenever we had a barbecue, I would ask him to recite this other one:

When I die, bury me
in some old tavern
beneath a barrel of wine.
With a little luck,
the drops will reach me.

But the one I remember most, at least whenever I go into a hospital, is the one about the doctor attending to a dying man:

The doctor praises
his ode to death
then pushes off.

I once asked Yoshie whether he had thought of writing one. He became very solemn. When I'm dying, he said, I won't say a word. If anything, I will listen.

When he'd had too much to drink, he liked to tell Zen riddles. He would relate them in the form of a dialogue and even do the different voices. Those were the only occasions when my friends laughed with him.

I can still hear Yo changing his tone. In a reedy voice, the young disciple asks, When you die, O master, where will you go? In a deep voice, the old master says, I have to go to the bathroom. He considered this the

greatest Zen riddle of all time. He said that the disciple is expecting a transcendental answer, but his master understands how dubious those kinds of
answers are. So instead, he moves on. Or maybe he is saying that the only
thing we truly know about ourselves is our body and its needs.

Sometimes he had difficulty condensing these stories for me. Or he
couldn't find the right word, and so he would try in English or French.
We would repeat each sentence until we were satisfied. He explained to
me that in Japanese there are some essential words, like *death*, that don't
have an exact equivalent. If I understood correctly, they prefer to name
the specific way in which someone dies. Of old age, in battle, of a broken
heart, in an accident. That way, they evoke the sort of life a person had.
Rather than one universal death, you could say that there are many individual deaths. It seems to me a good way of respecting each and every
one of them.

But wasn't that destroyed in Hiroshima and Nagasaki? The concept and
the language describing the concept were shattered because there, it was
the Death. With a capital *D*, the sort that doesn't exist for them. A noun
en masse. In English, on the other hand, it's incredibly easy to kill or die
with words. *To die for. I'm dying to. It's killing me. To death.* In Spanish too.
Who knows what dying must be like in all those languages I'm going to die
without ever learning.

A colleague told me that in Albania they have two different verbs for
dying. One is generally for animals. The other is reserved exclusively for
humans and bees. I wonder what sort of worldview lies behind that. The
sting, what gives the bee its identity, is its most mortal part and can be used
only once. In other words, it finds itself through self-extinction. Doesn't
death contain something of that Albanian sting? When you learn to speak
it, you are left in silence.

Once, Ari, who was addicted to sci-fi, lent Yo his *El Eternauta* collection.
Comics are a great way of starting to read in another language, I used them
with my students in London. Yoshie promised Ari he'd read it. Every night
before he went to bed he would devote some time to it. Only when he gave
it back did I realize that at one point in the story an atom bomb falls on
Buenos Aires. Yoshie didn't comment on this. He returned it to Ari, ruffled

his hair, and said, I liked it. I think I'm right in remembering that the junta disappeared the author the same year my son was born.

As soon as Yoshie was able to understand them, I recommended he read Argentinian short stories. He had very little spare time, and I thought the shorter texts might appeal to him. Finally, I got him interested in a few by Silvina Ocampo and Hebe Uhart. I felt proud, as if those two women and I had won a battle. When he started to nose around in my book collection, I hid the volume by Lamborghini, just in case. The one with a story that poked fun at Japanese honor, and featured a tasteless joke about Hiroshima. I don't know, maybe he might have found it amusing, had I explained it in my own way as a satire on the errors of translation.

It was thanks to him that I read Tamiki Hara. His suicide had a profound effect on him. After the war, all books in Japan had to pass a kind of inquisitorial filter. That New York chick he'd dated told him this was an outrage, how was it possible that his own country had set, blah, blah, whatever. I remember my friend Silvia. She had a bookshop in Barrio Norte and they carted her off, pregnant. The three of us fled a few months later. Pregnant, she was. They'd forced their way in as she was closing up shop, because she sold dangerous books.

Maybe the most brutal thing is not that you were bombed. Most brutal of all is that they don't even allow you to tell people you've been bombed. During the dictatorship here, they would kill one of your children and you couldn't tell anyone. Except that over there, in Japan, they were trying to implant what we in the West call democracy, weren't they? This never even occurred to me before Yoshie. It's totally nuts. Thousands of deaths don't bother you, until you meet just one survivor and then they start to matter.

Mind you, once books about the bombs started appearing, there was a whole avalanche, a sort of belated catharsis. People had started to forget, when all of a sudden they were swamped by a whole library. As with the Holocaust, many of the testimonies were anonymous, or by people who stopped being anonymous when they told their stories. A whole community that had lived in silence now lived in order to speak.

Speaking of victims, it always struck me that in Chile, which after all had its own massacre, the military organization in charge of maritime alerts is called SHOA. Not long ago, after the Concepción earthquake, I read that acronym again. I guess that's randomness for you.

There is the direct pain of those killed or tortured, and there is the almost spectral pain of their relatives. It happened and didn't happen to them. Whenever we touched on the subject, Yoshie didn't say much in the first person. He talked mostly about his sisters and father, who hadn't been able to tell their stories, as though to him, speaking was about making the dead talk.

Then, of course, there's the rest of us. Those who survived relatively unscathed, and were seemingly able to get on with our lives. That can also be painful. I've never been fully able to assess what it means *not* to have died, *not* to have been tortured. The effects of the trauma of what might have happened to us. I believe that there are secondary effects. They're not a smashed body, radioactive vital organs, a scarred back, but they're in everything we do, or everything we don't say.

When he got back from his trip to Tokyo after his aunt's death, Yoshie told me about the Delta Group activists. They had started off in Hiroshima, and were making a name for themselves. I knew from my English friends about another women's group, which had protested for years at Greenham Common air base. They would have parties and hold debates next to the barbed wire fences. They camped out there during the Malvinas war, and the British police had arrested a few of them. I had been following their activities ever since. Shortly before I returned to Argentina, thousands of women gathered to link arms all around the base. My friends and I planned to go and show them our support, but in the end we never went.

Yoshie had mixed feelings about the Delta women. I couldn't make him see that, in the long run, the aim of these women-only groups was true integration. I tried to explain the need for women to learn to fight our own battles, to get angry together. Otherwise, we end up playing second fiddle yet again.

But look what's happened now. Since Fukushima, women have organized the biggest protests. Women who are more concerned with the well-being of their family than the company's future. I don't see this as the thinking of a housewife, this is politics that begins in the home. The Plaza de Mayo mothers and grandmothers started off that way too.

Sadly, if you do an internet search for the Delta Group these days, what comes up is a multinational technology company.

———

Yoshie used to make business trips to Brazil and Chile and occasionally to Colombia or Mexico. If it was Ari's turn to stay with his dad, we would travel together. Yoshie barely left the hotel, he slept, ate, and had meetings there. Half the time I don't think he was quite sure which city we were in. But he never seemed fazed. He simply arrived, spread out his papers, and got to work. If he needed to go out, he called a cab.

I would sleep in and linger over breakfast, a rare luxury for a mother. I would read the local press, translate for a while in the bedroom, and then take the opportunity to walk around and get to know the place a bit. That was the agreement we reached. I didn't have to go anywhere with him, or attend any of his business lunches looking like an idiot. Each of us was free to do what we wanted until evening. Then we would have a drink together, and all the rest. We slept on our sides, me hugging his back. The opposite of how I slept with other men. In winter it was perfect. He gave off an uncommon amount of heat.

Yoshie wasn't too interested in museums and that kind of thing. He claimed to have seen them all in Paris as a young man. Now he preferred to watch people. According to him, a conversation with a stranger was worth more than any monument. On the other hand, he was a master when it came to hotels. He found in them nuances and mysteries most of us didn't see. He would register them instantly, while I was still unpacking. The soap brand, the newness of hair dryer, the towel absorbency. Number and condition of hangers. Location of electrical sockets. Lamp angles. Size and thickness of the pillows. The type of DO NOT DISTURB sign. The contents of the minibar. And, of course, the make of television (ah, those days when remote controls were a source of wonderment!). He hated to go to bed in front of an inferior model.

He never allowed himself many consecutive days off. A week and a half seemed excessive to him. I managed to persuade him on only one occasion. It was Yoshie's fiftieth birthday, I think, and we decided to mark it with a special trip. He suggested New York, as I'd never been there. I raised every objection I could think of, except for the main one, of course. No way was I prepared to run the risk of him suddenly deciding to call Laura or Laurie, and ruin our holiday. I always suspected he was still a bit in love with her. I could deal with that. We all have to negotiate with somebody's past. But to stir up the unconscious, that is going too far.

In the end I won, and we went to London, where he had never been. The thought of showing him my haunts, my friends from there, made me happy. Emilio went out of his way to arrange everything so that Ari could stay with him. I'm not sure whether this was because he had started to warm toward Yoshie or because he didn't want our son to go to London with someone else, or what. But he did it. At my age you don't believe in intentions, you believe in what you get.

I had no money, and Yoshie was keen to pay my expenses. With a very male mind-set, he seemed excited to be the one footing all the bills. In the end we agreed that I would at least cover the cost of the hotel. I longed to go back to the first apartment the three of us had lived in when we arrived, in Bloomsbury, near Tavistock Square. I found a decent enough hotel in the square itself. We were lucky, in fact.

Yoshie made a daily list of places to visit and ticked them off one by one. The amazing thing was that he never seemed in a hurry. It was interesting to see the mixture of relief and surprise he showed while interacting in English once more, in an English that was different from his. As if he were carrying around a second foreigner inside himself.

Every morning after breakfast we would sit by the tree in the square dedicated to the victims of Hiroshima. He said it wasn't because of the tree, but because the benches were nicer on that side, and the morning sun at that time, and so on. So we would sit there for a while, without speaking, and I would think of Virginia Woolf. I gazed around the square in search of number 52. The first time I went to London, I couldn't believe a hotel had replaced her house. I know it was bombed, but my point is, why didn't they rebuild it afterwards? The woman died for a room of her own and they demolished her house.

It was impossible during that trip not to talk about the Malvinas, which was still very recent. I told him how the Americans had participated on both sides. How they had propped up the regime in Argentina, especially before Carter, and in the war they had sided with the British. Yoshie didn't really understand our connection to the islands. And it wasn't that easy to explain. In the end everyone, supporters as well as opponents of the dictatorship, was programmed to insist that the Malvinas were Argentinian, although most of the time they'd been a Spanish colony, and then, above all, British. The islands weren't so much something that had been taken away from us as something we'd hardly ever had. Obviously, I didn't put it to him quite like that, because I wanted him to take our side.

That same year, or the following year, I'm not sure, we beat England. Thanks to the hand of God, Maradona's feet, and who knows what else. Ari was beside himself with joy. He always says it was the first World Cup he remembers properly, and the last he would wish to have ever witnessed. See how poor Messi gets us to every final and then we lose? I always tell Ari that to me this seems in a way more Argentinian. To promise a lot and to end up losing.

When the team went to La Casa Rosada to celebrate, President Alfonsín didn't come out onto the balcony. We all watched it together on TV. I was moved by such a gesture. Rather than making the most of the opportunity, he stood back. The trial of the military juntas had just ended. There, too, you could say we had reached the final. And while we were celebrating that, we scored an own goal.

Yoshie considered the Argentinian state courageous for acknowledging its crimes, and apart from Germany, he couldn't think of any other country that had the guts to do that. My sisters and I tried to explain to him that this was all well and good, but the trials had been very limited and in the end they had legislated to forget. It took us twenty years to begin repairing the damage of that oblivion.

In my view, Alfonsín's greatest achievement was to stop the constant alternating between democratic and military governments. Before that could happen, they had to deal with the armed forces in a way that caused the minimum amount of distress (for them, of course). As I see it, from the very start, they intended to try only the generals. No lower ranks, no torturers, none of the other murderers were to be brought to justice.

Soon after we won that blessed World Cup, it was impossible to continue investigating those crimes. We lost with the Full Stop Law. The military achieved the rest with the Easter revolt. I can still remember Ari sitting on Emilio's shoulders in the Plaza de Mayo singing to Alfonsín. After that it was "Happy Easter, everyone," and they changed the head of the army, and if you'd been given the order to violate human rights, then you got off scot-free—that's what we call reconciliation.

A few days before the Easter revolt, a terrible storm struck Buenos Aires, and the Nichia Gakuin School was flooded. Yoshie arranged for a group of Japanese companies, including Me, to help pay for repairs. The next day, I went with him to inspect the damage. The basement looked like a river. The kitchen, classrooms, and refectory were full of families bailing out the water.

After a couple of relatively good years, I began to have money worries again. I reduced my budget, cut costs, and renegotiated my debts. I speculated from Monday to Sunday. I had become a maternal calculating machine. Ari took part in the crisis by saving little folded notes. I took my cues from the state, and my son took his from me. His earliest savings were in pesos ley. By the time he started school we had the peso argentino. And now his pockets were stuffed with australes. It pained me to see him plunged into this monetary chaos, the changing colors, national heroes, and numbers. He collected all the different notes obsessively, like stickers.

Yoshie was struck by the way we Argentinians were so well informed about the exchange rates of the dollar, the French franc, and even the yen. The way we did mental conversions and followed the changes in interest rates. The way everyone talked incessantly about money. Even young kids, who still save in dollars, because they keep an eye on devaluations. This general awareness of the economy fascinated him. His surprise was short-lived. After the first crisis hit, he understood it as well as anybody. We talk about money here because we don't have any, and when we do, it's instantly stolen from us.

One day, he described to me in a wealth of detail, which I couldn't begin to replicate, how all our creditors claimed to support democracy, and yet none of them was willing to improve the terms of payment of the massive debt the dictatorship had run up. All at once, I understood the way our country works. It was about making money out of every coup d'état, and selling out the next government in order to control democracy. Just then, interest rates shot up again. Making the country pay its debts was far less important than ensuring they were impossible to pay.

When everything started to get fucked-up again, Yoshie grew nervous about the future of his branch. He said that a new business structure like his couldn't withstand this kind of collapse. He found it hard to believe that a currency could devalue so fast. Apparently the opposite was happening to the yen, and that made it less competitive now. Yoshie agreed with me that the States might be pulling the strings (You see, you see! I told him). Its industries were on red alert because Toyota was now bigger than General Motors, he always used that example. We couldn't talk about it without quarreling. Everyone here knows that the States is behind all of this, Yo. *Mah-riera*, please, don't oversimplifying! he replied (he rarely managed to use the imperative). They're the ones who oversimplify us, those sons of bitches! Sorry, if you don't live there you can't understand them. To hell with understanding, d'you hear me?

He used to complain about how weak our ties with Japan were, despite all the Japanese immigration into Argentina. He claimed that one of his tasks was to strengthen them through the business sector. To me this reeked of hypocrisy. Really, I said, since when were multinationals so culturally aware? Without cultural awareness business not last, he replied, offended. You silly goose, I said, sighing, no business can last over here.

When the era of hyperinflation began, and the price of goods would increase while you were waiting in line to pay for them, Yoshie started to have problems sleeping. That was when we nationalized him. He was staggered by the situation, and spent days trying to figure it out. I told him not to waste his energy, that it was simply a coup d'état by another means. For you everything is a coup, he said. Precisely, I replied. Now you've understood my country.

Apparently, in Japan they were having their own crisis, which I couldn't help imagining almost as paradise. It was their first major tremor in a while. No matter how many earthquakes they'd suffered, they weren't accustomed to feeling the ground shake beneath them. Yoshie was in a bad mood, and had little time for us. I was feeling more vulnerable than usual. I missed the courteousness I'd started to take for granted. I hated to ask him for money but Emilio had several mouths to feed, and my sisters were as hard up as me.

It was around that time that we started to fight a lot. Yoshie's angry side appeared, something I'd never seen before. During one of our quarrels he threatened to leave me. Although we patched things up, I'm not sure I got over it. Emilio always said that when a player talks about leaving the team, he has already left. I think the same applies to couples.

It was the year of the first pardons. The ones Menem imposed without consulting Congress. What did we expect our most unpunished president to do, other than legalize impunity once and for all? Emilio voted for him, although he doesn't like to remember that now. That's the way it goes, we live in a country of secrets and conspiracies. The people responsible for the Malvinas were released from prison, together with hundreds of torturers and coup-mongers. Judging their crimes as equal to those of the state, they freed a few terrorists into the bargain. In the second wave, the other dictators, Videla, and even his minister of economy were released. Yoshie couldn't understand what was going on. Why imprison them if afterwards they let them out? he asked.

Seeing them walk free, I thought of leaving again. But neither Ari, who had only just started high school at the Nacional Buenos Aires, nor, if I'm honest, I myself felt capable of uprooting ourselves again. That precipitated a crisis in my relationship. Exciting as it was at first, the idea of being with someone who could leave at any time destabilized me. There was talk at his company about closing the Buenos Aires branch, or relocating him. That hurt me. Then I was the one on the verge of ending things, but I was afraid to add another separation to my CV.

As if this weren't enough, politically speaking we were increasingly at odds. He favored privatizing public companies. He insisted that what mattered wasn't to preserve them in their disastrous state, but to modernize them, and so on. I think at that moment, in the nineties, I started to have that same weird sensation I'm experiencing now, you know, when you feel that history is running backwards? That the world is set on rewind.

While Yo and I were separating, rumors started up again about the nuclear waste dump in Gastre, province of Chubut. After a quiet period, there were reports of dubious comings and goings in that part of Patagonia. It seems they sent twenty guys to a uranium mine that had been closed for years. Later on, some mysterious deaths were uncovered in the vicinity and bodies turned up showing signs of uranium poisoning. This indicated that the dump that had supposedly been shut down was being secretly rebuilt at another location. Just a fortnight after they declared that the project had been abandoned, the state purchased tons of a substance used, what a co-incidence, to help seal nuclear waste facilities.

As always, it all began long before that. Jorge has done a lot of research on the subject. He explained to me that during the dictatorship there were plans to build six nuclear power plants, as well as a waste dump near Gastre. Under Alfonsín it was announced that the chosen location was that town, which would become the first of its kind on the planet. The Chubut Antinuclear Movement sprang up and, in the end, it was put on hold. This was only a few months after Chernobyl.

So that was the plan that Menem resuscitated until thousands of people marched through the snow like an apparition. They came from all over, from Trelew, El Bolsón, Bariloche. They say that no one had ever seen so many people in Gastre. Once again the planned waste dump was buried. The nuclear phantom, less so.

You don't even have to travel far. Just over a hundred kilometers from Buenos Aires, the Atucha power station is still operational. It's already more than forty years old, but I doubt they're in a hurry to shut it down. The new one, which they called Néstor Kirchner, quickly reached full capacity. And yet we have more wind power in the south of Argentina than any other country.

The other day I saw that they were commemorating those protests in Patagonia. When I went to pick him up at the newspaper in Avenida Belgrano, Jorge showed me the Greenpeace report. It said that a French company had offered to finance the construction of the dump, in return for several thousand hectares of land in the same area. If we'd accepted that offer (did we?) Argentina would have simply become the nuclear dump for France. Who the hell wants waste that lasts thousands of years? And even if some countries do find a place to store it, how can they guarantee it won't end up polluting them?

Sometimes, when my pessimism gains the upper hand, I imagine that the history of the world was written by an Argentinian economist.

As for our breakup, well, we are what we are. I need to feel a certain amount of pain. Not because I like it, but because it measures my willpower. Losing someone is a test of your limits, isn't it? Neither Yo nor I was quite sure where ours were, and things gradually worsened. We accused one another. We would speak on the phone, hang up, and then call back. We tried to leave each other several times. We hurt each other enough to be sure that we needed to split up.

When Yoshie stopped coming home, Ari kept asking about him. Even Walsh seemed ill at ease. Seeing how my son missed him was what upset me the most. I started making up stupid excuses and I ended up talking to him about the complexities of love, the fragility of human relationships, and God knows what else. I wished I hadn't. Excuses were probably better.

Ari took it badly, and I could feel he was blaming me again. I resolved to swallow my pride for my son's sake, or for my own, or both. I contacted Yoshie and asked if he could at least call Ari from time to time. He promised he would. Much to Ari's delight, he called once or twice. Then he vanished again.

I felt bitter about it. There are some types of rejection you can't subject teenagers to. I find it hard to accept when someone I trust breaks a promise. I'm quite rigid about things like that. The only promises I don't keep are the ones I make to myself.

I couldn't say exactly when I discovered that he was leaving the country. Our accounts of that part of the story never coincided. Yoshie swears he told me. And that he even suggested meeting up, but that I said no because I was upset with him. That's not how I remember it.

I assumed that was the end of it. Wouldn't that have been the most natural thing? To my surprise, a few years later he wrote to me on my birthday. A brief, friendly message, without any rhetoric. I liked it and wrote back. I was polite, nothing over-the-top. He replied at once, asking me about Ari, about my life. It was quite a long message. I told him stuff, he told me stuff. We kept at it. We bantered. And before I knew it, we were in touch again.

We called each other on the phone again. At first with those calling cards that sold you minutes, and later over the internet. The first call lasted two hours. We grew nervous. I teased him about his use of typically Iberian expressions. I asked him if he wanted Ari's number and he said no, that he felt ashamed but that he would send him a present the next day.

Every now and then we'd exchange photographs, book recommendations, or a few words of the sort that need no explanation. We saw each other once in Madrid. He introduced me to his *madrileña*, who seemed neither here nor there. He looked both the same and older, I don't quite know how to put it. He said I was prettier than ever. Which means he thought I had aged. It was late when we said goodbye, with an embrace.

As I said to Jorge the other day, there are people whom you're always close to but who don't change your life at all, and others who change you in a short space of time, just like him. That's why I wish Yoshie the very best. In life as well as in love, I mean that sincerely. More or less.

7

THE FLOWER
IN THE
RUBBLE

THE SUITCASE GLIDES ALONG beside him like a red pet animal. As he walks to the taxi stand, Mr. Watanabe observes the undulating roof of Sendai airport. The rhythm of its curves and the reflections on the glass bring back the images of this same building engulfed by the tsunami. The airport floating amid a sudden sea, transformed into an absurd ocean liner.

The earthquake's epicenter, he recalls, was located a little over a hundred kilometers from here. He repeats silently the formula, part arithmetic, part nightmare, that hundreds of millions of people all over the planet have had to learn. If a tremor of more than seven on the scale has its epicenter in the sea, there will be a tsunami; the time it takes for the waves to reach the shore is the time you have to run for your life.

He is only a few minutes from the city of Natori. There he can get a car from any of the rental companies. Operating like this, without booking ahead, will allow him to carry out an initial reconnaissance of the area. With the dearth of visitors, he is sure he'll have no difficulty finding somewhere to stay. As the taxi starts up, so do his doubts. Watanabe wonders whether it was a good idea to improvise this trip to such an extent. Everything that seemed simple before he left home suddenly strikes him as complicated.

On the far side of the desk, the young receptionist eyes him with a look of amazement verging on alarm. His face gives the impression of having just woken up. His left nostril is pierced with some symbol that Mr. Watanabe can't recognize.

Sorry, he says. I wasn't expecting any customers this early, or at all, to be honest. The town hasn't had many visitors recently. My name is Tatsuo, at your service. Are you a journalist?

When he says no, Tatsuo seems even more astonished.

We only see foreigners, says the young man. Journalists and photographers. A photographer, then? (Watanabe shakes his head.) Oh, how strange. The only Japanese people who come here are either soldiers or politicians, you know? Or nuclear technicians. You aren't a politician, are you? (Watanabe smiles and makes a gesture of denial.) Well, that's obvious. You're alone. Politicians go around with bodyguards and all that. They're unable to take care of themselves. From your appearance, I don't think you're an army man, either. And, with all due respect, the nuclear technicians that come here are usually younger.

As they're alone, the two men continue to chat while they complete the paperwork. For a while now, Tatsuo has been alone in the office. His employers, he explains, insist they maintain a minimum service even if there are no customers. So he and his colleagues do shifts, mostly serving no one. Seemingly desperate to talk, Tatsuo tells Mr. Watanabe that his family are all in Sendai, the largest city in the prefecture, he declares, with a mixture of pride and sorrow, and the place where, for that very reason, most of the tsunami victims are to be found.

Tatsuo asks him if he saw Emperor Akihito's televised speech. Although Watanabe didn't pay the slightest attention to the event, he implies that he did. From what he glimpsed in the press, the emperor emphasized the need for national solidarity, the collective spirit, the *aikokushin* and all that stuff. In other words, epic anesthesia.

All of a sudden, he is assailed by vague fragments of the speech made by the current emperor's father, Emperor Hirohito, days after the bomb at Nagasaki. If his memory serves him correctly, no such broadcast has ever been made again until this year.

Hasn't he had this thought before? Mr. Watanabe wonders. Is he turning into one of those old people who repeat themselves without realizing?

When his focus returns to the conversation, Tatsuo is making fun of the dark suits the emperor wears on important occasions. Oddly, he praises the empress's traditional kimono. Young people nowadays think it's cool to be conservative.

At least this emperor didn't fall from the sky like some of the others, says Watanabe, and he has tried to promote peace with our neighbors since he took over.

I don't know, replies Tatsuo. Possibly. I was born the year after.

According to the young man, some social networks are saying that a passage from the emperor's televised address might have been censored. Watanabe asks if he knows what the passage referred to. Tatsuo says he doesn't, but other comments suggest it could be related to the radiation in the worst-affected areas, like the neighboring prefecture. Watanabe thinks that, except for nuclear waste, nothing can remain hidden for long. Lies have changed pace.

He prefers a small car, one he can park anywhere, and which doesn't stand out. When he fills in the form, he realizes he isn't sure how many days he wants it for. Odd though it seems, he hasn't yet decided. In fact, at this moment, he doesn't feel too sure about anything: why he has flown here, why he wants a car, and where exactly he will go. Before he can arouse suspicion, he rents it for a week.

As a special service, Tatsuo insists on offering him the intermediate model for the same price as the economy one. Given the way things are going, he remarks, he doesn't think his employers will object to the discount. Watanabe accepts with a slight nod. It's a Toyota Verso, the youth announces.

At full speed, Tatsuo explains that the Verso has enough space to accommodate four pieces of luggage (but I only have a small red suitcase, Watanabe thinks). A direct fuel injection system (and what might an *indirect* injection system be like?). An in-line four-cylinder engine (no idea what happens when the cylinders aren't in line). One hundred and twelve horsepower maximum (why would I want more horses? he wonders, remembering the Olympic rider Hiroshi). And a panoramic sunroof (ah, Watanabe says to himself with a smile, that I like).

After consulting the map Tatsuo gives him, and making a couple of quick searches online, he aims to visit Iwate, Miyagi, and Fukushima, the three most devastated prefectures.

Then he goes and purchases a radiation meter.

Before setting off, Watanabe maps a route and its possible alternatives. He tries to find his bearings by comparing the foldout map with the online ones, which give very different perspectives.

Instinctively, he tends to trust everything he sees in print as if the mere investment in paper, ink, binding, and distribution guaranteed an effort that wouldn't allow for negligence. What floats on the surface of a screen, by contrast, has the transience of a puddle of water. And yet, on his analog map, Mr. Watanabe keeps coming across slight variances, omissions, and inaccuracies, which the GPS resolves with an ease that makes him feel as astonished as he is grateful.

Almost all the major roads appear to be reopened, although they are not always in a very good state. However, the local roads remain an unknown, a scribble of cracks. Often, the information says one thing and the comments on forums something different. To complicate matters, those comments often contradict one another.

Since there's no consensus about the precarious portions of his journey, Watanabe relies on his intuition. He will start by heading north on National Route 4. Terrain permitting, he will attempt to turn off onto the secondary roads toward the coastal towns. At that point, he'll make his way south.

He fires up the Verso, and leaves in a car that isn't his to a place he doesn't know.

THE SKY PIERCES the transparent roof: an endless blue tile. Mr. Watanabe has to make an effort not to be distracted by that other landscape circulating above his head. In the end, he thinks, we never look where we should. Although he has just had breakfast in Natori, he feels hungry. Given his small appetite, he knows this is a sign of anxiety.

The road looks unnervingly clear. He passes scarcely any other vehicles. Some parts are still full of cracks from the floods and the shifting of the tectonic plates. From time to time there is a brief rumble beneath the wheels, like bags full of air popping.

At intervals, Watanabe drives past small police checkpoints. The officers cast him strange looks. A few order him to stop the car, give information about the state of the roads, and ask him questions before allowing him to go on his way.

To amuse himself, or perhaps because he's afraid the truth won't sound plausible, he tells one officer he's writing an article for a Tokyo newspaper. He tells the next one he's making a documentary about the tsunami. He explains to the following one that he works in television (well, he thinks, that isn't so far from the truth). The next one seems more mulish, and he tells him that he has relatives who have been affected. Every good lie, reflects Watanabe, is based on different layers of truth.

He can't find any music he likes, and keeps the car radio tuned to the news. According to the latest estimates, the total number of people wounded, killed, or missing has risen to almost thirty thousand. It's a number that, because of the years he spent in Argentina, gives him a particular feeling of revulsion.

In different locations across the region, the radio informs him, radioactivity twenty-five times above the maximum safety level has been detected. Despite appeals for caution, the hypothesis has begun to spread that people residing in those areas won't be able to return to their homes for a long time. If at all.

A river of cracks down the asphalt. Bags of air beneath the wheels.

In the prefecture of Iwate, as the sunroof frames midday, Mr. Watanabe turns toward the coast on Route 343. The GPS informs him he is approaching Rikuzentakata, a place that remains associated in his mind with an unfortunate headline: WAVE WIPES QUIET COASTAL VILLAGE OFF THE MAP.

To be expelled from the map, wiped off the planet. To cease being real. "The town no longer exists," he'd read in March. And yet its name is still there, flickering on the radar. He imagines a silhouette traced around a hole, like the chalk drawing around a corpse. He wonders what difference there is between disappearing beneath a ring of fire and a blow from the ocean.

At the next fork in the road, Watanabe turns toward the sea and takes the 340. He reads a sign that seems like an elegy: TAKEKOMA KINDERGARTEN. A moment later, another that says: MURAKAMI DENTAL CLINIC.

His car moves forward, he enters the town, and he both wants and doesn't want to get out. He is surrounded by a landscape in pieces, but he looks only straight ahead. He looks only at the ocean.

A couple of kilometers farther, the beach comes into view. He steers along mud paths hardened by the sun. He gets as close as he can and leans his head out of the window. The murmur of waves fuses with the noise of cranes.

He stops the car, climbs out, and runs toward the beach.

He is running fast in his mind, slowly in his body.

In the distance, one of the workmen watches him with dismay, fearing perhaps that he means to plunge in fully clothed and be carried away by the current.

But Mr. Watanabe stops running, drained from his exertions, startled all of a sudden by a tree on the shore. A tree that is no longer really visible.

Only the base and roots remain. The water's ax has lopped off almost the entire trunk and has sliced a meter into the earth where the tree once grew. With its roots exposed to the elements, the stump now looks like a hesitant spider or a paralyzed crab.

As he walks back to his car, he contemplates the reconstruction work. Its painful slowness. Its patience from another era. Its conviction.

Then he notices that a man is waiting for him next to the car. He is wearing a hi-vis jacket and a safety helmet that doesn't seem to offer much protection. They both bow at the same time, as if they had seen the same object on the floor.

A journalist? asks the man.

Just curious, replies Watanabe.

What's the difference? the man says with a grin.

During their exchange, he learns that Toshiki lost his wife on the day of the tsunami. The wave took her and she hasn't turned up yet. Toshiki knows she won't come back, but he'd like to recover her body. To have somewhere he can visit her. He is now working as a volunteer, he explains, so that he doesn't go crazy. He helps the fire department, which has lost most of its men, and the local health services, which still can't cope.

Before leaving, Watanabe asks if he has thought of moving away, of starting a new life. Toshiki removes his helmet. He is completely bald and yet smooths his head. He gazes at the sea and replies: I like this town. I want to live here. This place exists. It's ours.

Mr. Watanabe returns the way he came. He leaves behind the gap that was once the town hall, turns onto Route 45, and heads northeast.

After an unexpected roundabout, which he enters slightly too quickly, and a nerve-racking series of bends that seem to twirl through the compass points, he is almost at the coast's edge. Now he drives parallel to the narrow bay of Ōfunato, which acted as a funnel for the tsunami.

He slows down. Reaches for his phone. He enters the place name in Wikipedia and, scrolling with his thumb, three facts catch his eye. One. On March 11, following the earthquake, the sea here swept three kilometers inland, while in Tokyo he walked a similar distance to his house. Two. The city of Ōfunato is a sister city to Palos de la Frontera, the port from which Columbus's caravels set sail for the Americas. And three. Fifty years ago to the day, it gained notoriety after being hit by a tsunami caused by an earthquake in Valdivia, Chile, the biggest in the history of the world.

As he drives on in his car, Watanabe observes the intricate destruction all around him, as though a flotilla of ships had smashed to smithereens on the shore. Yet, despite everything, the destruction is matched by a sense of order. Every vestige has been classified, gathered, and organized with an almost unreal efficiency that inspires as much horror as the preceding chaos. The pine trees are piled up alongside one another. Remnants of houses are also heaped up, outlines of the homes they once were. Cars are pressed together like an exaggerated sculpture made of millions of beer cans.

All this apocalyptic symmetry, Watanabe imagines, is a part of some industry whose aim is to dismantle and undo. To de-produce.

Clouds cross the sunroof as he drives through the outskirts of Ōfunato. He lowers the window. He breathes in what he is seeing. The mountains and the sea seem to be arguing: cool air descending from one, a wave of humidity rising from the other.

He zigzags through streets that have lost their edges. Their steel girders torn out, the buildings also reveal their roots. Others preserve a precise memory of the water, thermometers unable to forget the sickness that assailed them: the first floor ruptured completely, the second badly damaged, the third with a few blemishes, the fourth filthy, the fifth intact.

By the road, a drinks vending machine flashes. He pulls up across from it and stares at the lengthy cable trailing behind a wall. The machine is still lit up, colorful, inexplicably upright, like a drunken sentry who hasn't realized that the enemy has already attacked. All at once, every object appears to have some other meaning. Maybe because destruction is illegible, a language no one can speak.

Only then does he become aware of the hollow sensation in his stomach, the throbbing at his temples, the dryness in his mouth. He feels in his trouser pocket for some change. He steps out of the car. He inserts the coins into the luminous slot.

Nothing happens, except for the noise of the wind.

In the center of Ōfunato, a tilted house welcomes him. The tide washed it here and deposited it in that strange lozenge-like position. Anyone trying to inhabit it would live a sideways existence.

In his rearview mirror half a white vehicle quivers. When their two gazes meet, the floating head of the other driver nods a greeting. For a second, before passing the tilted house, he sees an optical illusion: a head on top of a house on top of a mound of earth.

He stops outside a half-demolished building. A cross on one of the walls, made with a spray can, attests that it has been searched by the rescue services. Mr. Watanabe approaches the building and, changing his glasses, pokes his head inside. Among the rubble he sees several pieces of porcelain (three teacups, two bowls, a blue dish) set out on the floor, without a scratch, misinformed. A postwar picnic.

Meanwhile, across the road, a family is tending their flowers. They're working on their knees in the improvised garden they have made on the foundations of what was once their home. Some neighbors are watching them from their surviving window.

Watanabe strolls through the holes in the city, ashamed to look around him and unable to avoid it. These ruins aren't like others he remembers. Everything here has become floppy, unraveled, deboned. The workers are cleaning up an ambiguous substance, something between solid and deluge. The cranes lift up all kinds of objects, now crumpled, that had seemed immovable. Bent like a metal rag over a railing, a car awaits its turn. Over on the far side of the bay, he spies the cement factory's ironic chimney. The ground is strewn with shards of what was once indivisible. But what's really astonished him since childhood is that things keep their wholeness.

Farther on, away from the port, he stands motionless before a sight that ought to be a mirage: an enormous boat grounded in midavenue, navigating the afternoon. Around it, abnormal fruits, bits of clothing hang from the branches of cherry trees.

The Verso turns south. Watanabe munches on the one and only piece of *hosomaki* he found left in a denuded grocery store. After his brief excursion around the prefecture of Iwate, he is ready to explore the prefecture of Miyagi. Spring cushions Route 45 like a parenthesis. The asphalt is one dark sentence; the digression of flowers does its best to change the subject.

In this year of cold fronts, rain, and fear, the plum trees have blossomed late. Now that they have finally done so, he thinks, they give the impression of not wanting to stop. The blossoms slow him down, cajole him, and almost without realizing it, he lifts his foot off the accelerator.

Some cherry trees have kept their petals, refusing to accept that the *sakura* season ended at least a couple of weeks earlier. These late flowers look like flames. Mr. Watanabe remembers that the samurai considered cherry flowers their companions, as much for their brief lives as for their color, which resembled the blood that bloomed in combat. Nowadays they are supposed to denote innocence and rebirth. This shift leads him to reflect on the moral omissions of today. He has always thought that the awareness of death is the basis for any appreciation of beauty.

He recalls the poisonous splendor of the oleander, the official flower of Hiroshima, the first to appear after the atomic bomb. Oleanders are capable of enduring far more pain than the gardeners who grow them. He has seen them divide highways in the States, Spain, Argentina. Far from home, surrounded by this empty landscape, Watanabe feels like he is traveling backward. Each kilometer repays a debt.

Suddenly, a car overtakes him, and he grips the steering wheel, startled. He can't remember when he last encountered another driver. During the days of *sakura* season, families, couples, and friends gather beneath the trees, but now there is no one here to celebrate the endurance of these cherry blossoms. They survive without an audience. The only ceremony is spring itself, the silent miracle of its insistence.

For some years now, Mr. Watanabe has preferred plum trees. The worldwide interest in cherry trees has reached such an extreme that they sell apps to follow in real time the appearance of the first buds, the progress of their blossoming, the effect of the atmospheric pressure on their petals. Pocket pastures.

This year, however, all the weather indexes are busy measuring the direction of the wind and radiation levels. He himself intends to use his brand-new dosimeter when, tomorrow or the day after, he reaches the prefecture of Fukushima.

During the past few springs, he's noticed that young people take selfies next to the cherry trees. What really blossoms there are the observers. Unlike photography in his day, it isn't so much the events that are immortalized as the photographers themselves. From that point of view, the trees here are lonelier than ever. No people smiling in front of them, no lovers kissing beneath their shade, nor youngsters pulling funny faces.

Watanabe feels the urge to take a picture of himself with one of those that dot the horizon.

He stops by the roadside. Gets out of the car. Walks over to a tall, gleaming plum tree. He takes his phone out of his pocket and points it at himself. He feels embarrassed and puts it away again.

Outside the railway station at Kesennuma, the rubble browns and dries out. Mr. Watanabe skirts it slowly, walking with his eyes on the ground, measuring each portion with his feet. The railway tracks resemble scattered matchsticks. A sign on a post welcomes past visitors.

As he walks along the tracks, an oddly rapid movement amid the stillness, he tries to imagine the daily routine of this city before the earthquake. Perhaps the eloquence of wreckage is based on that, on the need to complete what is not there.

Watanabe raises his eyes toward the harbor, which is blocked by a wave of debris. In the distance, the lone silhouette of a cherry tree stands out, like a crane striving to raise the fallen landscape. Stripped of all context, its isolated blossoms contradict (or highlight?) the surrounding destruction.

May I be of some assistance? He is surprised by a voice behind him, carried on the wind.

He turns and a mouth smiles at him, puckered as if to whistle. It's a young firefighter with a very wrinkled brow. A firefighter with two faces, two ages, he thinks.

Are you looking for someone? the young guy asks, spinning the helmet in his gloved hands.

More candidly than anticipated, Mr. Watanabe murmurs: No. I don't know. Possibly.

Did you have relatives here?

Not here. In Nagasaki.

The lad's smile is swallowed by the wrinkles on his face.

Aha. I see, I see.

Watanabe peers down at his shoes. The fireman's boots are enormous.

Forgive me, says the lad, do you know what today's date is, and where we are?

Mr. Watanabe raises his head.

Of course, he replies, indignantly. Do you, young man?

The fireman puts his helmet back on and his wrinkles disappear.

I have to get back to work. There's no end to the wreckage from the burned-out boats. We still have a lot of clearing up to do. Good afternoon.

Yes, we still have a lot, Watanabe says, sighing, and turns around.

THE AFTERNOON LOSES HEIGHT and reddens. It's that time of day when everything suffers an attack of shyness. The road trembles, wavers, turns hazy. Mr. Watanabe changes glasses again.

Although this stretch of National Route 6 is in passable condition, there are few cars. Especially going south where he is headed. He finally makes his way into the prefecture of Fukushima, closer and closer to the nuclear power plant. The circles are narrowing and seeking their center. Watanabe imagines the ripples in a pond, contracting in reverse.

As the kilometers go by, he drives through communities that still show signs of damage and the fear of radiation, but are outside the areas forced to evacuate. At least for now, he thinks. He notes that these communities are partially populated and are struggling to return to normalcy. The inhabitants move about with a certain emphasis, as though determined to fill the gaps left by their absent neighbors.

Tired and hungry, he decides to have dinner and spend the night in the first town he comes by. The Verso's GPS tells him it is called Sōma. The name makes him think of the drug they take in *Brave New World*.

Before he arrives, he stops at a gas station. He buys two bottles of water and uses his radiation meter for the first time, with no significant results. While he fills up the Verso, he chats with another driver, who informs him that he lives to the west of the city. Sitting in the back seat are a boy and an enormous dalmatian. When the man says a name that Watanabe can't quite hear, he's left wondering whether he was referring to his son or the dog.

The driver tells him that though Sōma is almost fifty kilometers from the power station, and therefore safe from harm, half the inhabitants have chosen to leave. While he is talking, he keeps looking over at the back seat. Watanabe wonders if the man's wife has stayed home, or if he is a single dad, or if he might even be fleeing himself. The tsunami, explains the driver, flooded the eastern side of the city, engulfing the coast, the harbor, and their famous strawberry farms. Our strawberry farms, he repeats, in an overly loud voice.

At that moment, Mr. Watanabe remembers that one of Me's competitors is increasing its investments in agriculture. More precisely, in strawberry farming. Japanese manufacturers are making strange investments and selling video games to balance their books, he laments, meanwhile their Korean rivals are inventing organic diode screens. It's even rumored that they are working on a television that will emit smells to reinforce its images. All that effort, to reproduce something as old as synesthesia. Technology, like acid trips, comes from within.

When the driver pulls away, the dalmatian sticks its head and front legs out of the half-open window. The boy pulls it back and the dog resists. The boy thrusts his arms through the window to get a better grip. The dalmatian's head remains trapped in the rectangle, like a hunting trophy barking freely.

The father slams on his brakes. Gets out of the car. Tethers the dog. Shouts at the boy. Then climbs back into his seat, raises an arm to wave goodbye, and speeds away from the city.

Watanabe goes over to the cashier. Despite the promises he's made himself, he can't help thinking about what's happening in his industry. His will has retired, but not his subconscious. In order to offset the crisis in local markets, and the fall in productivity, the companies have started to buy up foreign businesses. Among the latest rumors he has heard, the one that most strikes him is the offer Canon is planning to make for a Swedish manufacturer of surveillance cameras. Billions are involved. Money, safety, and surveillance: that seems to be the new formula.

Cash or card? repeats the checkout girl.

What? Watanabe comes to his senses. Oh, sorry. Card.

As he pays, he is surprised by the amount. In fact, he can't even recall the last time he filled a gas tank. Could it have been in Madrid? Or during a trip somewhere with Carmen? The checkout girl informs him that prices have risen again due to the emergency. And also, he suspects, because people are questioning nuclear energy.

Oil always wins, says the checkout girl, adjusting her little cap.

You're absolutely right, says Watanabe.

His polite response seems to make the girl extraordinarily happy, as if she isn't used to customers telling her she is right—or any of her other fellow human beings, for that matter. All at once, she livens up and becomes talkative.

You should have seen it, she exclaims, the lines that formed during the night. Back in March, I mean. Where your Toyota is parked, it was impossible to walk. People came from all over to get a few liters. The limit was twenty per person, not a drop more. They had to wait so long that some of them left their cars and went home to sleep, then came back in the morning. I'm not exaggerating, sir.

To the west of the city there are open windows. Next to one of the open windows is a garden. In the garden is a little girl. In that little girl is fear. That would be the summary of his first scouting mission in Sōma.

He has just leaned over the fence, said hello to her, noticed her distrust. Watched her play in the late afternoon. Observed with relief, and secret surprise, that a little girl is still able to have fun with a Hula-Hoop. He has marveled at the speed of her waist. Reflected on how this small body is the center of all concentric circles, the reason the future will go on spinning despite everything. He remained silent as long as necessary, waiting for her to come over to him.

My name is Midori, the little girl says, still making the hoop spin.

I imagined so, Mr. Watanabe whispers, smiling.

What did you imagine?

That your name was Midori. I could tell.

She stops spinning, grasping the hoop as she looks askance at him. Her disbelief gradually melts before the seriousness of his gaze.

What's your daughter's name? Midori asks.

I don't have any children, replies Watanabe.

Really? she says, astonished.

If we all had children, he says, there would be too many people.

Here, there aren't too many people. There aren't enough children. My best friend isn't here.

And where has she gone?

I don't know. She went away with her parents. At school they say she's coming back soon.

And what do your parents say? Why did they stay?

I don't know. Dad and Mom say there's nothing dangerous here. And if Dad and Mom say that, it's because there's no danger.

Mr. Watanabe contemplates her in silence.

That's right, isn't it? Midori insists. Isn't it?

He smiles. Her doubts dispelled, the hoop starts to spin more energetically than before.

At the far end of the garden, a curtain is quickly drawn.

A few streets down, he sees a line of people waiting to be examined by a team of technicians in white overalls. The technicians seem to move with disoriented slowness, like astronauts outside their spacecraft. They guide each person inside a mobile unit, then close the door.

As he has no better ideas, Watanabe decides to join the line. This way he can observe things more calmly and pass unnoticed. He stands behind a young boy who is propping up a racing bike.

You aren't from here, says the cyclist, turning toward him. Which town are you from?

Watanabe replies that he has come from the neighboring prefecture. Then he adds that due to the lack of personnel, they are allowing citizens from the south of Miyagi to get tested in the north of Fukushima. That he likes Sōma a lot. And that he has a niece here called Midori.

The young man gives his full name, although Mr. Watanabe retains only the last name: Hoketsu. The line advances slowly, amid protests from those complaining that at this rate, they'll miss their dinner. The cyclist Hoketsu tells him that the examination schedules are getting later and later, perhaps because the areas being checked are steadily growing, and there aren't enough personnel to deal with them. The technicians assure them that thanks to these mobile test centers, the town isn't in any danger. But then why are they wearing those suits? the young boy argues. Why don't they take them off when they get here?

Just as they are nearing the end of the line, when they are practically the only two left, the cyclist Hoketsu draws close and says something in his ear.

You know what? he whispers. There's something worse in the air than radiation leaks from the nuclear plant. Spirits. Nobody talks about that.

The spirits of the dead are traveling through the air, and the radiation could be affecting them too.

As soon as the young man enters the mobile unit, Watanabe starts to dread the examination. He wonders whether a particularly sensitive instrument could detect residual traces of atomic radiation in his body. The mere thought of testing positive, arousing the concern of the experts, and being subjected to an emergency procedure is intolerable to him.

It's a mistake, he tells the technician at the door, sorry. Actually, I live in Tokyo. Here are my papers. I just came here to see my niece Midori.

It's a mistake, he repeats.

And takes flight.

He walks at a brisk pace. It's already getting dark. He needs a hotel and a restaurant. Or possibly a hotel with a good restaurant; he is more hungry than sleepy.

Suddenly, he hears a voice and comes to a halt. A voice that resembles a song and a prayer. He follows the plangent trail. Beneath a dissenting cherry tree still in bloom, he makes out an old man. Shabbily dressed, eyes closed, and a half smile on his lips, the old man is singing in a childish tone: *Sakura sakura yayoi no sora wa* . . .

Watanabe stops to listen, partly because the voice intrigues him and partly because he is waiting for the old man to open his eyes. He wants to see what they look like. For them to look at each other.

Good evening, sir, good evening, a passing couple greets him.

They walk arm in arm, obviously out of step. The man struggles with a stiff left leg. She pauses at each step, bringing her shoes together before taking the next one.

Watanabe returns their greeting, and when he bows, he discovers with embarrassment the muddy marks on his own shoes.

They introduce themselves briefly. They motion toward their house somewhere in the distance. He tells them the near truth. It becomes immediately obvious that the Arakakis are one of those couples who disagree with each other by default.

This is the best time of day for a stroll, wouldn't you say, declares Mr. Arakaki. There's the breeze, and it's cooler out.

Yes, says Mrs. Arakaki, but it's a bit late.

All the better. That way we work up an appetite.

But then you eat practically nothing.

Watanabe tries to agree with both of them, even as he glances sidelong at the cherry tree.

Do you know him? asks Mr. Arakaki.

Sorry, who? replies Watanabe, distracted.

Old Kobayashi. He's a little touched, if you get my meaning. He lives off handouts. He's been here who knows how many years.

He does handicrafts, too, adds Mrs. Arakaki. And he isn't all that crazy. He's a very nice man.

I never said he wasn't nice, her husband retorts.

I know. He's simply a free man.

There's no such thing as a free man.

But some are freer than others.

When old Kobayashi has finished singing, he pulls open a plastic bag, extracts a chamber pot, and exclaims contentedly: Chirp, chirp!

As they bump along together, they tell him about the city's precarious recovery. Mr. Arakaki praises the groups of volunteers that are helping with the relief efforts. His wife declares that life returned to normal when the government started to collect the garbage again. Garbage, thinks Watanabe, the height of normalcy. Together the couple laments (and their agreement on this one point creates an almost disturbing effect) that the delivery companies still won't service their region, as they have a fragile parcel they wish to send to their daughter in Tokyo. They explain that it's a glass dinner set for her wedding anniversary.

Do you know what I read the other day? asks Mrs. Arakaki. That when water is served in beautifully colored glasses, the taste of it changes. It's scientifically proven.

Scientifically? says her husband. Are you joking?

Yabai! she replies, losing her patience. The power of suggestion has a scientific basis too. Psychology proves it.

Everything's scientific nowadays!

You may know a great deal about taxes and invoices, but you know nothing about colors.

The discussion continues for a while. Until, turning toward Watanabe, the couple ask his opinion. They seem prepared to accept his verdict, whatever it is. To avoid offending either of them, he offers to deliver the parcel to their daughter in person as soon as he gets back to Tokyo.

Moved by the proposal, the Arakakis shower him with thanks and insist he dine with them. He tries to refuse. He explains he has been driving all day, that he is looking for a hotel, and that, given the hour, he would be most grateful if they could recommend one. The Arakakis shake their heads in unison. They make all kinds of exclamations. They entreat him not only to dine with them, but also to stay the night at their house.

It's the least we can do, Mr. Arakaki concludes.

You can't imagine how happy this will make my daughter, Mrs. Arakaki adds, tugging at his arm.

He settles himself in the guest room. Which is in fact their daughter's old room, untouched since her departure. Photographs showing the speedy development of the absent girl, posters narrating her evolution from princess to goth, school certificates, picture books, necklaces and bracelets, gadgets that were once technological novelties and the cause of an ephemeral enthusiasm. Everything is immobile, as if time's batteries had run out before the astonished gaze of a thousand toy animals.

Once we reach a certain age, Mr. Watanabe reflects as he connects his phone to the charger, our houses stop moving. It happens little by little, without us noticing. The windows start to shut. The present ceases to run through the corridors. It's not until a stranger—or a much younger person—enters that everything becomes terrifyingly clear. Then, every detail betrays us. Every object loudly professes just how much its owner has aged.

After opening his little red suitcase, taking a shower with unutterable relief, and changing his clothes, he checks his phone. He decides not to look at his texts and emails. He reads in the foreign press about vast quantities of tritium and cesium that are leaking into the Pacific Ocean: waves of radioactivity dispersing into the sea. Environmental agencies calculate that at this rate, in a couple of years it will amount to a hundred years' worth of the power station's output during normal operation. According to those same studies, it will be only a matter of time before the contaminated waters reach the coast of California.

He can't find any mentions of this in the national media. The same kind of cover-up happened with American foreign policy when he lived in the States, he thinks.

He browses the websites of *Fukushima Minpo, Fukushima Minyu,* and other regional media outlets. He reads that in the bay closest to the plant, a fish has been discovered with levels of radiation astronomically higher than the maximum permitted for human consumption. He tries to imagine the insides of that fish; its gills, its internal organs, its nervous system flooded with cesium. Thousands and thousands of becquerels per kilo in just one specimen. If all seas are one and the same, thinks Watanabe, that fish would be all fish.

Someone knocks several times on the door, causing a tiny gorilla on the adjacent shelf to wobble. Mrs. Arakaki announces that dinner is ready.

The table is laid with far more food than three people can eat. Watanabe attributes this excess to his hosts' hospitality, and possibly also to a longing for family feasts. The three of them clink glasses.

This sake, says Mr. Arakaki as he raises the drink to his lips, is wonderful. We buy it from a brewery in the Aizu valley, in the west of the prefecture. They don't filter or pasteurize it after the fermentation process. And it's made exclusively using rice from our region. What a shame they have nothing like this in Tokyo.

Watanabe keeps the wine in his mouth for longer than is polite.

They have lots of other things in Tokyo, argues Mrs. Arakaki.

To think that our honorable guest hasn't yet been to the Sōma Horse Festival, her husband continues, ignoring her comment. You must come back to see it. There's no other spectacle like it in the world.

There won't be any horses this year, my dear. Don't you see that there isn't even enough transportation? We can't live as if nothing's changed.

Mr. Arakaki doesn't answer. He pours himself another glass of sake and turns on the television. It's time for the evening news.

As soon as it catches his eye, Watanabe recognizes the Me TV set. An old model, typical of the beginning of the century, he estimates. Reliable and solid, if a little clunky compared to the current minimalism. Too many buttons, perhaps, for its available functions. A not entirely user-friendly menu, which makes you too reliant on the instruction manual. Still intended for analog leisure, back when a television was only a television, and telephones just telephones. Clear, balanced sound. Definition more than acceptable for its time. And, damn it, admirable resistance. Mr. Watanabe feels a surge of pride from seeing it in perfect working order.

Having finished his appraisal of the device, he transfers his attention to what's on the screen.

They are interviewing the mayor of Ōtsuchi, a small town in the prefecture of Iwate. A few kilometers to the north, Watanabe realizes, of where he was driving earlier that afternoon. He thinks he has heard the name before. Possibly because, as the reporter mentions, there is—or, unfortunately, used to be—a large Tokyo University marine research laboratory there.

Speaking into the microphone with the disconcerting calm of someone who has already seen too much, the mayor gives a few facts about his town's devastation. Ten percent of the inhabitants have lost their lives, one of the highest figures in the entire region. Actually, he points out, he wasn't really the mayor, but felt obliged to take over the post. His predecessor's dead body was found on the shore when the waters subsided.

Now, at the dinner table, not even the exchange of glasses or the clink of plates can be heard.

I've lost five assistants, says the accidental mayor. One of them drowned before my eyes. Another killed himself out of sheer despair. That was before the helicopters arrived. There were corpses floating everywhere. Colliding with one another. I can still see them when I look at the ocean.

Watanabe asks if he can turn up the volume. Mr. Arakaki passes him the remote control, and he sits holding it in his hands like the offspring of an old family pet.

When the helicopter rescued me, the mayor is saying, I saw our town from the air. I thought everything was over. Everything. My assistants were between twenty-five and thirty. The same age as my children. I can't understand why I'm the one who has survived.

Watanabe turns up the volume further. The voice starts to buzz uncomfortably. It sounds like it's coming from inside the room, from someone eating with them. Mrs. Arakaki glances at him out of the corner of her eye.

All the farms have been destroyed, shouts the accidental mayor. We had a fleet of six hundred fishing boats. Now only a handful are seaworthy. So in addition to being destroyed, abandoned, and in mourning, we can't go fishing either.

At these last words, and not before, the mayor bursts into tears.

Mr. Arakaki helps himself to some more seaweed salad.

Watanabe lowers the volume.

The reporter reappears in a different part of the Ōtsuchi coast, interviewing one of the few fishermen who still have their boats.

I'm doing all I can to bring food for my neighbors, says the fisherman. I go out fishing twelve hours a day. I can't do more than that. My arms aren't what they used to be.

The interviewer asks him whether, after all this suffering, he and his family have considered leaving the village. Moving somewhere farther away from the sea.

Our life is the sea, replies the fisherman. The sea is all we have. It's a part of our family. Occasionally it gets furious. But most of the time it protects and teaches us.

And on this occasion, the reporter asks, what has the sea taught you?

That sometimes you have to go out fishing twelve hours a day, replies the fisherman.

Lying back on the guest bed, amid a liquid silence like an effervescent beverage, Watanabe makes one last search on his cell phone.

Something everyone had been fearing for weeks has been officially confirmed: a nuclear meltdown did indeed occur in the three reactors that were operative when the catastrophe struck. A flow of molten energy. Its power dispersed in an uncontainable vapor. The plant has become a pressure bomb.

In spite of this, or perhaps because of it, Mr. Watanabe decides he will continue his journey south.

He falls asleep with a circle of light on his stomach, his fingers wrapped around his phone.

At dawn the next morning he opens his eyes abruptly.

He spruces himself up and prepares to set off early before his hosts get up. Partly because he wants to make the most of the daylight hours, and partly to avoid Mr. and Mrs. Arakaki's bickering. He plans to leave a thank-you note for them in the kitchen, together with his card. He writes out the message carefully. He closes his suitcase and makes his way along the corridor.

No sooner has he stepped into the kitchen than Mrs. Arakaki pops up, as if out of a cupboard, with a cup of freshly brewed tea. Then she hands him his breakfast wrapped in paper napkins.

She accompanies him to the door. Eyes moist, she confesses that he reminds her very much of her older brother.

HE KEEPS HEADING SOUTH, beneath a sky so clear it seems suspect. The sun is a gold medal out of context. The sunroof floods with light and starts to get hot.

As his water bottle empties, his maps begin to contradict each other. According to the paper map, he is somewhere between the districts of Kashima and Haramachi. The GPS places him in Minamisōma. That town is also shown on the paper map, but a few kilometers farther on. Could the place names of this region have switched? Could the ground have moved so much? In the surrounding fields, sunflowers gleam like a cascade of coins.

Wait a minute. Isn't this something he's seen or thought before? Mr. Watanabe wonders. Is he turning into one of those old people who repeat themselves without realizing it?

In any case, he knows he is entering the thirty-kilometer radius. The voluntary evacuation zone. Its inhabitants have been told to leave the area or else to stay indoors. He can't get over the irony: they are placing in the hands of the people a decision relating to a power plant they were never consulted about in the first place. Privatize the profits and collectivize the problems. A mixed economy, he says to himself, averting his gaze from the road.

On the dirt tracks leading off either side of the main road, he sees the NO ENTRY signs. With unnerving indifference, the rice and soybean fields stretch beyond them. The same fields which, until the disaster, were renowned for producing the country's most exquisite rice.

He is thrown by the contrast between the serene appearance of the countryside and the grave warning signs. The landscape offers him one vision, and the signs force him to reinterpret it to the opposite effect. When you can no longer believe your eyes, he thinks, the whole world verges on mirage.

His car penetrates the morning and the sky fills with clouds, like a wall being stacked with bricks.

Minamisōma turns out to be more extensive than he'd thought. According to official charts, the northernmost part of the town falls just outside the evacuation zone, while the south is wedged between the thirty- and the twenty-kilometer radii. The city is therefore divided by two sets of safety rules and two states of mind. An amphibious municipality.

After a few minutes, he comes to a crossroads by an Eneos gas station, one of the designer-brand oil companies with which Me does business. Watanabe remembers that the earthquake had caused a fire at one of its refineries in Sendai, right where his journey began.

The traffic lights blink. The sporadic pedestrians hasten across the street. As he awaits his turn, an enormous hospital catches Mr. Watanabe's eye. He turns in the opposite direction.

He drives in a straight line toward the east. He has no plan. He doesn't concentrate on what he's doing. When he improvises like this, he lets himself drift along in a sort of hypnotic trance, until something grabs his attention. He drives through the half-deserted streets with dreamy satisfaction: all he has to do is follow the arrows and lights. Only three other cars, all the same color as his, cross the tracks where trains no longer pass.

A pharmacy brings him out of his reverie. Its red-and-yellow signs, its ideograms designed for the nearsighted. Is it possible it has stayed open, despite the lack of customers? He parks and walks over to it. A tiny sign of apology answers his query.

Opposite, he notices a bank. What exactly happens to people's loans, mortgages, fixed-term deposits in a state of emergency? The savers have gone, and yet their accounts remain. The creditors leave, but the debts still exist.

He permits himself the luxury of crossing the road at random, without looking right and left.

Although it's a peak hour for business, the bank is also closed. Nevertheless, the cash machine works perfectly and even gives him small denominations. He takes his money and returns to the Verso. Money has a life of its own, Watanabe says to himself.

He drives toward the town center down an avenue free of traffic jams. Whenever he's stopped at a light, the few local drivers observe him with concern as if they suspect he may have lost his way, or possibly his mind.

Before reaching city hall—not exactly what he's interested in seeing—he turns left toward the south, where the traffic becomes even more infrequent. Has he made it within the thirty-kilometer zone? He tries to tune in to a local radio station but all he hears are brief noises, crackles, an electric silence.

Presently, he sees a sign that makes him slow down and adjust his glasses.

YO-NO-MORI. I didn't die.

In a moment of confusion, Watanabe had whispered the words in Spanish.

It's the name of a park, the ideal place to stretch one's legs.

He soon locates a parking area near the entrance, opposite a sports ground. White lines separate space after empty space.

There are only a couple of cars in sight. Mr. Watanabe leaves his perfectly aligned with the others. No one wants to take the place of people who won't be coming.

Positioned behind a pile of cardboard boxes, a young yakitori vendor eyes him hopefully. Watanabe smiles at him and walks on by.

He heads for the park's entrance. The ground turns to earth.

In Yo-no-mori Park everything seems to arrive late. Light arrives late from the ragged clouds. Shade, to the stone benches. His gaze, to the branches stripped of blossoms. Watanabe counts no more than half a dozen people walking around. The center is deserted. So, too, is the iron horse on the playground: an animal with more holes than substance.

He makes out two figures in the distance. Two figures stooping among the sunflowers. One bigger than the other. He draws closer, cupping his glasses with the side of one hand. He has left his sunglasses in the car.

A man, roughly his age or slightly younger, is sowing seeds with the help of a little girl. A little girl with faint shadows under her eyes. For some reason, she reminds him of his little sister Nagae. The man is making furrows in the ground with his hoe. The girl opens her fingers to let some seeds fall.

The men greet each other, without seeming surprised at the other's presence.

Here we are, says the man, standing up straight, bowing, and wiping the palms of his hands on his thighs. Sunflowers absorb the toxins from the earth and lower the levels of cesium.

Plants make the best company, Watanabe replies. They ask so little and give so much.

That's right, says the man. There are people who think gardening is just a distraction. On the contrary, there's no better way to pay attention to life.

Hello, darling, says Watanabe as he crouches, his lower back stiff from hours of driving.

Say hello to the gentleman, sweetheart, the man says.

The little girl hides behind his legs.

They introduce themselves. Mr. Sasaki: teacher, resident, and activist. His granddaughter, Ai: shy to start with, but once she gets to know you, well, you wouldn't believe it. And Yoshie Watanabe: journalist, recently arrived from the capital to visit his sister in Sōma and to do research for an article about the situation in the region.

When he hears he is a journalist, Mr. Sasaki stands up straighter and becomes loquacious, assuming this to be some sort of interview. He complains that the Tokyo media is not properly reporting the realities of the situation. That the only thing TV channels want is shattered families and decontamination suits. That they aren't interested in showing the people who are struggling to carry on with their lives at home. Watanabe is glad of the misunderstanding, which will allow him to speak little and listen all he wants.

The teacher talks at breakneck speed, and gesticulates slowly. His body is arriving late to his own thoughts.

It turns out that they have a few things in common, which makes their exchange easier. Watanabe learns that Sasaki studied in Tokyo. That he spent some time in Hiroshima with the Jesuits until he left the order and became a Spanish teacher. Now he devotes all his time to his family, to books, and to flowers. Just like Watanabe, he appears to have lived several lives.

Watanabe admits that he, too, is retired (although he still writes the occasional article, he adds, remembering his own lie). That he spent his childhood in Nagasaki. And that he lived in Spain for more than ten years. Mr. Sasaki is delighted to learn this.

They speak about how Madrid has changed. How expensive Barcelona has become. Sasaki acknowledges his soft spot for Córdoba. Watanabe prefers Granada and the Almería coast. The teacher reminds him that that's where an American plane accidentally dropped the thermonuclear bombs, and to this day no one knows how much they polluted the sea.

Bored by the conversation, Ai starts to gambol about the park. Her grandfather watches her out of the corner of his eye while they talk. He invites Watanabe to sit down on one of the stone benches.

On a more personal note, Mr. Sasaki confides that moving would present a risk for his wife. Settling in a strange place and changing her habits might worsen her current state.

When a loved one's health fails, Sasaki says, sighing toward the trees, how can I put this? Your center of gravity changes. Mine is much lower. Do you know what I mean?

Mr. Watanabe responds with an affirmative silence.

According to the teacher, four out of every five inhabitants in this part of town decided to leave. He preferred his family to stay put. He knows of some neighbors who left in a hurry and are now living with distant relatives, in cheap hostels or shelters. Over time, he claims, this has become so awkward that some of them are returning and are even bringing their children back with them. Which is a relief for his granddaughter.

As if the wind had carried his words to her, Ai turns around in the distance, waves, and laughs.

Fortunately, his house was relatively undamaged by the earthquake. And his water and electricity were not cut off. So, where would they be better off? They avoid opening the windows for longer than a few minutes a day, and they have blocked the vents. In theory, he explains, they should go outside as little as possible. But lately, tired of being shut away inside and always eating the same things, he has started to go for walks. He takes his car to go shopping on the far side of the city, outside the evacuation zone. He strolls in the park or to the edge of the Niida River. Naturally, each morning he checks his dosimeter, and if the radiation levels are high, he stays at home. If they are average, he goes out on his own. If they are low, like today, he takes his granddaughter with him. And they plant sunflower seeds.

In any event, says the teacher, brushing off his dusty trousers, it's a crazy situation. I write a blog, you know, about everything that's happening here.

I'm amazed to see it's getting more and more visitors. They keep sending me comments.

Watanabe takes his phone out of his pocket.

With the enthusiasm of youth, and the false modesty of adulthood, Sasaki adds, It's nothing special. But it might interest you.

Watanabe types. He locates the blog.

It's obvious you're a seasoned journalist, says the teacher. Instead of plying me with questions, you let me talk.

That's the key, he replies, putting away his phone. That's the key.

I'm going to tell you something, says Mr. Sasaki. I've spent weeks looking into the big nuclear *jiko*. And I can assure you that there are some suspicious coincidences.

Breaking the rule he himself has just subscribed to, Watanabe asks what they are.

The teacher starts to list them: Secrecy by the authorities. Contradictory news, data wars. A gradual widening of compromised zones, unfinished evacuations. Suppression of health reports and omissions in subsequent studies.

The Americans, he says, did it in Pennsylvania. The Soviets did it in Chernobyl. Now they're doing it to us in Fukushima. Governments believe, or pretend to believe, that in an emergency situation we are incapable of facing the truth. Although they have no proof of this, because they've never even tried to tell us the truth, they continue to pull the wool over our eyes. It's the perfect strategy! If they succeed, they manipulate the information to their own advantage. If the deception is uncovered, they swear they were lying to us for our own good.

Yet, Watanabe interjects, information is far more difficult to control nowadays.

That depends, replies Mr. Sasaki. If you take the trouble to delve into the revision history of every article on Wikipedia, for example, you will see the struggle to control the ones about nuclear accidents and their effect on public health. I'm not talking about specialized literature, of course, but that's where people go for information. As for more scientific sources, well. As you know, multinationals finance the investigations of their own activities.

In the distance, the little girl is scaling the iron horse. Her grandfather rises to his feet. He calls out her name in warning. She freezes, hesitates for an instant, then keeps climbing.

Let's take Namie, he goes on, which is in the forced evacuation zone. They say there are only wild boar left there. The residents fled north en masse, believing they'd be safer. The government had signs that the fallout might spread in that direction but they didn't dare tell anyone. Now they're distributing medical guides, not too different from the ones they gave out at Hiroshima and Nagasaki. The displaced families prefer not to say where they are from. In Tsukuba, apparently, they've been asked to provide radiation certificates. Several colleagues have written telling me that their female students fear being unable to marry or get pregnant. Just like after the war, if you follow me?

Perfectly, murmurs Mr. Watanabe.

All of a sudden, his breath feels restricted. The breeze has stopped, or else the pollen is affecting his lungs.

He inhales deeply. Coughs. He feels his wrist. He searches for his vein with two fingers.

Sasaki asks if he is feeling all right. He indicates that he is with a flick of his hand, as though repelling an insect.

The teacher tells him about the contaminated rubble on the southeast coast, in the prohibited zone. Every day, more and more residents from the neighboring towns are organizing protests. No one wants these remains in their backyard. Fears that the wind could spread the toxic dust are mounting. In the meantime, the task of clearing up continues. The aim is to bury everything as quickly as possible.

Overcoming another brief coughing fit, Watanabe asks what the authorities have to say about this matter.

Mr. Sasaki applauds his granddaughter, who is waving to them from the summit of the hollow animal. Afterward he replies that the politicians say one thing and then the exact opposite. They don't want people to panic, only to be reasonably fearful. That's impossible.

As impossible as fearful reason, Watanabe remarks.

Sasaki suggests that whenever a power plant opens, senior managers from the electricity company should move nearby with their families. Many of the prefecture's mayors now spend their entire time kicking up a fuss about the company responsible for Fukushima. Generally speaking, they are the same people who vaunted the supposed advantages of building the power plant in the first place. Anyone who spoke out against it was accused of being old-fashioned.

Squinting, Mr. Watanabe tries to guess what the teacher's opinion of it was at the time. He doesn't dare ask.

What the authorities fail to see, says the teacher, is that catastrophes spark revolutions that no one would otherwise attempt. We all want to return to normal, but I wonder if we can or if we should.

I think I'll write those words down, says Watanabe.

If I end up dying because of these politicians, Sasaki adds with unexpected glee, I swear on my granddaughter's life that I intend to keep haunting them. It must be exhausting to be a ghost, don't you think?

That's what I've been telling myself for centuries, he replies.

The teacher lets out a hearty guffaw, and his gaze floats, as if his laughter were a bubble about to burst. Then he grows serious.

He asks Watanabe about the situation in Sōma. He wants to know if his sister is having any difficulties. Watanabe describes the domestic routines of the Arakakis, referring to them as his own relatives. Almost inadvertently, he makes up a few details to complete the picture.

Sasaki maintains that the alarmists are complicating matters. He compares the term used by the media at the beginning of the crisis, *evacuation*, with the one they started to impose later, *exclusion*. Where his house is situated has officially gone from being a *voluntary* area to one *preparing for emergency*. What was first called an *evacuation zone* is now *on alert*. The state, the teacher complains, uses toxic language. Those who have chosen to remain, saving the government a lot of money and resources by doing so, receive scarcely any aid. Many of his friends have left because their basic needs weren't being covered. According to what he has heard, they have to put up with a great deal of discomfort in the shelters, when they still have perfectly good homes.

Ai comes running back to her grandfather's side. Laboriously, he picks her up in his arms. He releases his grip as soon as her little shoes touch the ground. Rubbing his back, he looks at Watanabe with an amused wince.

Listen, he says. I have neighbors older than me, who have agreed to live in dreadful conditions simply to be slightly beyond the thirty-kilometer radius. As if radioactivity can be neatly divided into districts! Don't tell me that isn't crazy. When I think about them it makes me want to cry. At our age, death isn't so scary. What's scary is suffering. Some of them have died in offices. Gyms. Libraries. Well, that last one wouldn't be so bad. I'll tell you something. Even if they had died here due to lack of medical attention, at least they would have had an honorable death. In their own home. With their loved ones. What more can you ask?

Mr. Watanabe tries to swallow. His throat resists. He moves his hand toward Ai's little head, lets it hover above her. It's your new hat, he says. The little girl remains stock-still, awaiting contact. Like an elevator that resumes working, his throat gives.

The teacher asks about the hospitals in Sōma. How well equipped they are. Watanabe extemporizes as best he can until the other man starts speaking again.

Until recently, says Sasaki, delivery vehicles refused to come here. We received no mail either. There were shortages of essential items, like in the old days. While only a short distance away, people wanted almost for nothing. They thought that a stupid invisible circle would really protect them. Such was the confusion that even rice packed prior to the accident was being rejected by supermarkets that were still up and running. Until a truck came from I don't know where, deposited a load of vegetables here, and then sped away. Like a robbery in reverse, my friend! Luckily some stores are starting to open their doors again. The other day, I was overjoyed to see the Café Eisendō open. My granddaughter loves their cakes. And Yamada's fishmonger, where I buy fish for my wife.

Cakes! shouts Ai, who had appeared to be absorbed in her game.

Tomorrow, sweetie, tomorrow, replies her grandfather.

The little girl protests. He gives her a stern look and she calms down again. Then for the first time, they fall silent.

You know what infuriates me the most, the teacher says finally, looking up. What the hell is the use of decentralizing political power if we continue to delegate our most basic responsibilities as citizens?

We've always trusted the inside enemies more than the outside friends, says Watanabe, unsure how to respond.

In order to prevent the collapse of farming industries in the region, Sasaki explains, the authorities have raised the exposure levels approved for human consumption. As no one wanted these products, the government acquired the surplus of locally produced rice and vegetables and dispensed them to schools. This apparently legal measure at last mobilized families to do something about it, and now all food destined for consumption by schoolchildren is tested for radiation.

Watanabe, who has come to recognize when Mr. Sasaki requires prompting, asks him about the results of those tests.

With an almost mocking laugh, the teacher declares that this is where the problem lies. These test results usually indicate that the food is safe. Yet many of the tests are incomplete, because the proper instruments aren't available.

What we call safety, he says, is little more than a series of rules designed so that violations go undetected.

Checking the time on his phone, Mr. Watanabe thinks that he should get back to his car before it gets too late.

To top it all off, says Sasaki, growing increasingly indignant, some children who refuse to drink school milk are being labeled traitors. Remember the war, my friend?

Mr. Watanabe sighs in agreement.

The truth is I don't remember it at all, the teacher adds. I hadn't even started school. How old are you?

A little older than you, I fear, replies Watanabe.

You don't look it.

Tell that to my back.

And you're still working!

Only occasionally. Some things you never retire from.

That's true. I teach my grandchildren, and I learn more from them than they do from me.

They stand up. Sasaki takes his granddaughter by the hand. They walk slowly toward the exit, at Ai's pace.

As they cross the park, they discuss the latest about the power plant. In spite of everything, the teacher isn't opposed to atomic experiments. Nuclear fusion is a scientific development, he argues. The power plants are an economic decision. And nuclear weapons, a military misuse. There has to be some distinction.

Think of this, Sasaki says. If the first ever use of gasoline had been napalm, you wouldn't want to touch that car today.

They come to a halt beside the Verso. The yakitori vendor has vanished. Sasaki asks about his plans. When he mentions his intention to drive south, the teacher advises him not to cross the Odaka district, which is right in the middle of the exclusion zone. Waving in various directions with his free hand, he suggests making a detour on the 399, or possibly the 349, which is farther away and therefore safer.

As they say goodbye, Ai leans in to look at the inside of the car. Her grandfather scolds her, apologizes, and adds with a smile that curiosity runs in the family. He wishes Watanabe the best of luck with his research. He remarks that today the air quality is perfect, lifting his finger above his head, like a bony arrow pointing at the clouds.

I confess I'm a little worried about leaving you here, says Mr. Watanabe.

You're very kind, Mr. Sasaki replies, but don't worry. Be a pessimist, like me, and you'll see what a relief it is.

As Watanabe drives off, the teacher and his granddaughter dwindle in his rearview mirror until they become one radiant dot.

LEAVING MINAMISŌMA, he stops off to buy water and to snack on some cookies. He checks his dosimeter again. He has just read some information about the threshold of microsieverts at which there is no immediate health risk. Mr. Watanabe considers that subtle, insidious adjective qualifying the risk, and everything it says by omission.

He evaluates the numbers on the screen of the dosimeter. It seems to him that his entire life has been spent calculating fears and calibrating warnings. Leukocytes in the blood. Financial risks. Hematocrit levels. Balance sheets. Seismic magnitudes. Radiation levels.

Watanabe wonders how much of statistics is intimidation, and how to weigh that factor in what is being measured.

Everyone now consults these dosimeters obsessively, like a tribe seeking its atomic oracle; as well as the wind direction, which now brings nightmares. The enigma is in the air, it *is* the air.

To avoid the prohibited area and the inaccessible roads, Watanabe follows Mr. Sasaki's advice. He makes a detour west and takes the 399. By midday, he reaches the Katsurao checkpoint.

As he is slowing down, he sees a police van drive off. It is full of officers clad from head to foot in white overalls. One of them stares at him through the window, until the van moves away.

The officer on duty asks him the routine questions, plus a couple that are new to him. Mr. Watanabe tells him that some of his relatives live a bit farther south, and that he has come to help them clear out their houses. He mentions his brother who is a Spanish teacher and has just retired. And his granddaughter, Ai, who is all grown up and about to start university. She wants to study French, he explains, although he would prefer if she studied economics. First and foremost, young women today need to be practical.

The officer interrupts Watanabe's story with his gloved hand. He repeats some safety warnings, wishes him luck on his mission, and waves him through.

A quarter of an hour later, he glances at the GPS and sees that he is parallel to the nuclear power plant. Fukushima Daiichi and his car, separated only by the last circle. He rolls up the windows, cuts the air circulation, clenches his stomach.

Driving along the empty road, Watanabe notices once again, or he thinks he does, a difficulty when breathing, as if the oxygen were filled with tiny needles.

He accelerates. He comes across side roads blocked off by barriers bearing DANGER signs, bindweed spreading indifferently beneath them.

A few kilometers later, he comes to the Kawauchi checkpoint. The easternmost tip of the town is closest to the power plant and part of the exclusion zone. Here in the west, a handful of residents are holding out, together with a few police officers. The police, one resident explains, had no choice but to move their checkpoint to this side of town, so as not to break the restrictions they are meant to uphold. The latest rumor is that any minute now, the government will order a complete evacuation. In any case, adds the resident, stepping away from Watanabe's car window, our harvest has already been lost.

Leaning back in their folding chairs next to their patrol cars, noses and mouths covered, the officers look at him as if he were an alien. He, on the other hand, has never felt so close to his native land. Each time, he has more difficulty persuading them to let him pass, so he invents increasingly dramatic reasons: elderly folk who can't walk, grave illnesses, imminent funerals. He is aware that, only a few weeks ago, the state announced it was implementing the Emergencies Act, giving the police the right to arrest and fine anyone illegally crossing the barriers into evacuated zones.

As he wrangles with an officer reluctant to let him through, Watanabe, perhaps inspired by his time in Argentina, weighs the possibility of bribing him. He lets slip an ambiguous comment about the flexibility of fines. The officer's expression hardens. His body is set for a reprisal. Watanabe realizes that, accustomed to driving on Hispanic roads, he has just committed a serious cultural blunder.

He masks his anxiety. Smiles innocently. Gazes at the officer with evident admiration, and he repeats his last sentence, with a slight variation that removes all doubt and restores honor. Once more, he invokes his sister: alone, ill, incurably so, waiting for him to help her evacuate.

He divides his attention among the damaged asphalt, the map on the GPS, and the see-through roof. He makes up for the loneliness of his journey by imagining, as he did when he was a child, that he's competing with the clouds. He still isn't sure who is chasing whom.

For an instant, he has the impression that a piece of cloud is falling onto the road.

There are an increasing number of potholes, cracks, abandoned objects. After driving for so many hours, he is no longer alarmed by the jolts to the wheel, the steering going off course, or the unforeseen obstacles.

But whatever has just struck the front of the vehicle doesn't resemble any of that. The force of it was something else. The sound different.

Watanabe grinds to a halt, climbs out of the Verso, walks back.

And he sees a dog writhing.

The first thing he does, in vain, is to look all around in search of some kind of help, which he knows won't be forthcoming. He is unable to muster another reaction. All he can do is spin in circles. The landscape, the light, the objects, everything shrinks before his eyes.

He sees only his most recent gestures, the last few seconds, as if he were still in the act of slamming on the brakes.

He was distracted, and he didn't see it. He didn't see it, and it was there.

In this area, he surmises, there must be legions of pets roaming the countryside, abandoned by owners who'd left their homes, believing they would be returning shortly.

This dog, for instance, what's left of its breathing presence, is wearing some sort of collar.

There must also be a fair number of cattle wandering aimlessly, hoping for an unlikely survival. He remembers reading, back when the subject scarcely mattered to him, something about these animals being slaughtered, and compensation being paid to their owners.

Health, money, slaughter.

Watanabe realizes he has killed, is about to kill for the first time in his life. Something is instantly activated in his body, something that originates deep in his gut.

There's no other way out for this mound of blood, fur, and helplessness, which he is incapable of looking in the eye.

Yet, at the very least, he owes it that: a look. To take in its existence. To acknowledge what he is killing.

He stares fixedly into the animal's eyes. Then he gets into the car, shifts into reverse, and rolls over it again.

The GPS spews out places, roads, distances. He drives on and on toward the south. The forbidden east seems so close on the map, so far beyond his capabilities. Watanabe again feels an intermittent tightness in his chest. Why does this sensation come and go?

What's choking me, he thinks, is this detour.

He takes a deep breath. He looks at the wheel purring in his hands. And, at the first opportunity, turns abruptly to the left.

Leaving the main road behind, he slows down as he enters a bumpy back path that no one has bothered to guard or block off. It's a steep, winding track, surrounded by mountains filled with moist green, patches of shadow, and fragments of sunlight. His breathing deepens. His body softens.

Mr. Watanabe proceeds slowly east toward the coast he was avoiding and desires. Gradually he is penetrating the periphery of the prohibited zone, the realm of the last circle.

Halfway along the path, he makes out the columns of a Shinto shrine. He doesn't stop.

Once he has climbed the mountain, he exits onto a wide highway. Having all that space to himself once more seems daunting; in a sense, he thinks, the narrowness of the dirt track protected him. The glare forces him to change into his sunglasses again.

He picks up his speed and his journey south. He sees fields left fallow. He drives past a sewage treatment plant. He wonders if it is still working, what effluents it is extracting.

For a few minutes, he follows Route 35. He drives through the first set of traffic lights he has come across in a long time. Squinting, he thinks he sees the moving blur of another car.

His plan is to turn left at some point, to get as close as he can to the coastal towns. But where?

He keeps going. As is his custom when in doubt, he allows himself to be carried by his own momentum, waiting for some kind of trigger; he lets the random signs decide for him.

Before long, he sees a particularly sharp bend. Very much like a turning point, he thinks. He takes a left at last onto Route 246 and heads straight for the coast.

Soon afterward, amid the cracks in the asphalt, he comes to a fork in the road. Its choices diverge like a pair of trousers about to tear. He slams on the brakes.

Ovine clouds drift over the sunroof.

As he contemplates the fork in the road, the engine running, he recalls the verse by Gesshū Sōko that he used to recite as a youth:

> *The launched arrows*
> *against each other*
> *meet and divide*
> *the air in flight.*
> *Thus I return to the source.*

Mr. Watanabe consults the screen. The profusion of data doesn't help him decide, so he unfolds his old printed map. There he sees that one of the branches leads to the tiny village of Hirodai.

He tries to search on his phone. The signal is very weak and the page takes too long to load. In fact, he doesn't really need any additional information: he feels the urge to go to Hirodai. He intuits that he should acquaint himself with it; that, in some sense, he is choosing between two directions in his memory.

He remembers that platform in Madrid, at Atocha Station, seven years earlier. He had just left Carmen's house. She had told him that she definitely wouldn't be going to Tokyo. They were fine as they were and there was no need to go such a long way away.

He had just stepped off the train. He was standing, motionless, between platforms one and two. He focused on that detail because it seemed to present the starkest choice. On one track the trains arrived at the station. On the other they departed.

Watanabe is well aware that, in that moment, he'd had the impulse to go back. The adjacent track was waiting for him. There was still time to get on a train and return to the point of departure. He'd looked at his phone, squeezed it hard, and was about to call her. Then he put it away again and left the platform, walking slowly through the station where, since March 11, everything was only semi-operational. Toward the fractured city, which didn't know what to do with its fragments.

It had been a covert process for him, like digging a tunnel. The bombs in Madrid that year had brought him to the end. Since horror seemed to be pursuing him, perhaps it was best to go in search of his own.

Mr. Watanabe drives on, steering between the cracks.

8

CARMEN
AND THE
LESIONS

I KNOW MYSELF. WHEN MY FINGERS ACHE, it's because I'm on edge, and I've clenched my fists in my sleep. When my knees crack, it means the weather's going to change. When my children argue about politics, I get a stiff neck. I know these bones. Now my fingers have seized up. This means I've been thinking too much about him.

All week that Argentinian guy has been writing to me. He refused to take no for an answer, so I had to tell him something. He kept plying me with questions. He even wanted to know about my relatives across the pond. Look, I said in the end, if you're so interested, come to Madrid and we'll talk. He said he found me through that Mariola woman.

I remember her. She came over here for a conference once. Yoshie introduced us and we behaved like ladies, which neither of us was. She was, well, pretentious. Affected. Wanting to take up the whole space. Argentinian, need I say more? She seemed keen to show how clever she was. I let her do all the talking. I laughed a few times. Then I left them to it, because they hadn't seen each other for centuries.

But hey, no hard feelings. If she shows up here again, I'll even invite her out for a coffee. That whole jealousy thing seems stupid to me. Other people's pasts can't hurt us, can they? We've got more than enough trouble with our own. It's the same with back pain. You can find the stiffness in someone else's back. You know how to treat it. But when it comes to your own, what can you do?

We met by a fluke, through an architect friend. It was early summer and Yoshie had just arrived in Madrid. Instead of renting, he decided to buy something here as an investment. He'd found a flat in the neighborhood of Los Austrias. The guy wasn't short on pesetas, he was the director of the Spanish branch of Me—the ones who make the TVs. And my friend was doing the plans for the renovations. She was on a family vacation (just before she and her husband split up, by the way). While the work was being completed, she kindly offered Yoshie the use of her house, on the sole condition that he water her plants. Her entire roof terrace was covered in them. The express jungle, we used to call it.

My friend lived in a loft apartment in the Hispanoamérica neighborhood, right next to the Colombia station. She had asked me to do her two small favors. To pop in and check on the construction and put her mind at rest, and to check to see whether her Japanese client needed anything. Not only had he paid part of her fee up front, he was new to the city. I didn't mind the first favor. The second was a bore. But one day I called him on the phone and introduced myself. I offered him my help and so on. In the weirdest accent, he suggested we meet at the new apartment to see how the renovations were going. It seemed like a splendid idea to me. That way I could kill two birds with one stone. I never imagined there'd be three.

I took the metro to our first meeting and got off at Ópera. I know this because as I walked out into the square and saw the Teatro Real, which was being renovated, I remembered that the architect had dropped dead while showing some journalists around the theater. What a spectacle! The entire country was upside-down. Spain was busy reconstructing, or rather, dismantling itself. We had the Barcelona Olympics, the Expo '92 in Seville, the whole shebang. I set off in search of the address I'd been given. Strangely enough, it was a few minutes' walk from where I used to live as a child. I'm not saying I saw that as a sign or something, but yes, it was amusing.

In that hot weather, it turns out that said gentleman had stuck Post-its on each plant pot, listing their needs in that surgically precise handwriting of his. Frequency of watering. Composting. Flowerings. Leaf removals. Growth. When I entered my friend's loft and saw what looked like a plant laboratory, I wasn't sure what to make of him. Without asking me, Yoshie came in with a tray. I take tea, he said, smiling, and you coffee, correct? I looked at him and thought, He's either the ideal man or a lunatic. But I'm a curious person.

Yoshie enveloped you gradually. In small ways, he anticipated your desires. At first, how can I explain, I found this both flattering and disturbing. Maybe that's why I wasn't swept off my feet. He made out like he didn't notice people liking him. But I think it suited him not to understand a word, that was his trick.

After each attentive gesture, he would withdraw immediately, as if he expected nothing in return. That wasn't true, of course, but it left me intrigued. So, I thought, this guy doesn't want anything from me? Aren't I good enough? And before I knew it, I was the one who was flirting. I like things to be clear.

I still remember the look of horror on his face the first evening I invited him over to my place, a modest apartment in Leganés, and he saw my Grundig. A bulletproof German piece of junk. In less than twenty-four hours he had sent me a Me TV. I was really grateful, but what can I say, I was attached to my old set. It had fewer knobs. So I watched that one every day and, whenever he came around, I would switch them out.

He was still settling in and he seemed a little lost. He would get flashbacks to his own country. We'd be walking down Gran Vía, and he would start to tell me about the trips he'd made to Nagasaki. He was fascinated by some volcano there that had erupted for the first time in two hundred years. One day he asked me a very strange question. What use is a volcano that doesn't explode? Volcanoes have no use at all! I replied. It seemed to me the most sensible answer. Yoshie stopped dead in his tracks and clutched my arm. Exactly, he said, sighing, exactly what my father said.

When we met, that volcano had just become active again. It took the Japanese completely by surprise. Looking straight at me, he said it was unbelievable that this force, buried for so long, could reawaken. I thought he was referring to, I don't know, his youthful ardor. But no. He carried on talking about that blessed volcano. Nobody's perfect.

The truth is, I learned next to nothing in Japanese. I remember that *España* is *Supein*. Easy. Like Spain. I also know that *Madrid* is *Madorīdo*, which sounds like *m'a dolido*—"it's hurt me"—pronounced by a Japanese person. Madrid has hurt me. It makes complete sense.

Yoshie's spoken Spanish was quite decent. He even read a few of my books. Occasionally he would get in a muddle and start to speak in French, or stick a few Americanisms into a sentence. Since he knew the language, he assumed he would quickly adapt. The poor man was in for a shock.

You can't imagine what he sounded like. With that Argentinian drawl of his, and all those *y* sounds instead of double *l*'s. *Kahs-tee-sho.* That was roughly how he pronounced my last name. He had a habit of addressing people as *vos*, he used it with everyone at first. Which is fine if you're Argentinian, charming even—but for a Japanese! To top it all, when he tried to correct himself, he ended up using the formal *usted* with children or dogs. The result was hilarious. I told him to keep it simple, that everyone got what he was saying. No, no, he dug his heels in. I have to adapt, have to learn. He won first prize for stubbornness.

He made me laugh a lot, sometimes without meaning to. On one of the first nights he spent at my place, I warned him to be careful because of some problem with the *retrete*—our most common word for toilet. He stood there, stark naked, gazing at me solemnly, as if I'd touched a nerve. Well, I suppose a toilet could be considered a sensitive topic, but in a different way, am I right?

To cut a long story short, he starts to get all philosophical on me, talks about the passage of time, age, Japanese attitudes towards work, and goodness knows what else. So I interrupted him, and said, Yoshie, sweetheart, this is all very interesting. But what has it got to do with the cistern in my bathroom? It was hysterical, because he asked me the same, Wait a minute, *Kah-men.* What has bathroom to do with professional life? I was flummoxed. We might as well have been speaking Japanese!

It took us a while to figure out what was going on. Only when I said *váter, váter closet*, did he get it. It turns out he was confusing *retrete* with the French *retraite*, which means "retirement." I didn't even remember that word, I studied French at the convent school a thousand years ago.

They don't use *retrete* in Argentina, he argued. But they do go to the toilet, don't they? I was pulling his leg. Shit, I hope so. How can I not know this word? he went on. I was taught to say *inodoro*! Ooh, I said, drying my eyes, that must be in South America. Over here *inodoro* is an adjective, and it means "odorless." Adjective, he repeated, even more bewildered. I don't understand idea. And since we're on the subject, I said, mischievously, it's not a very good adjective for a toilet. I was in stitches. Then he started to tell me a tale about two monks who find the meaning of life while going to the bathroom.

I am one of the few people in Madrid who was born in Madrid. My parents were from Andalusia. My father was from Priego, in Córdoba, and my mother from Beas de Guadix. As soon as they married, the two of them moved here together to try their luck. Just then the civil war broke out. It must have been tough for them starting from scratch in those circumstances, with almost no work available, and with half the family on either side of the conflict. I discovered that later on. They never really liked to talk about it.

We lived in cramped conditions on Calle Segovia, which ended at the river. But they didn't let me stray that far when I was little. Our house was in the city center, back when that meant almost the opposite of being filthy rich. Apart from Atocha and one or two other streets, it was a pretty poor area. Lavapiés was a slum with no bathrooms. It had communal toilets (oh, *retretes!*) and a sink in the yard, and even then, you considered yourself lucky. House prices there have only recently started to go up with the property boom and rezoning. Real wealth has always been in the Salamanca neighborhood.

Although we went through hard times, I have a few happy memories. Don Vital's grocery store with its shiny cans of tomatoes, chickpeas, herring, and dried cod that made me retch. He kept a jar of candies beside the till. If you smiled at him nicely, he would give you one. Or the cobbler's shack. He was as skinny as the shoelaces he sold. I don't know why, but I always loved the smell of leather and glue. Or our Sunday visits to the churros stall. They would skewer them on reed husks. Or the bakery that smelled of ovens and hills. I think there's a Mexican restaurant there these days.

Goodness, and the coal merchant's! With that noisy shovel and the darkness in the back. They sold us ice in summer. My brothers and sisters and I hated being sent to fill the coal bucket, because on the way back it weighed a ton. It was the worst chore you could be given, that and watching the milk boil. You had to get up earlier than the others, and stare at the pan without getting distracted. We used to draw straws to decide whose turn it was. One day I discovered that my older brother was cheating. Instead of snitching on him, he and I came to an agreement.

It was the opposite with the waste paper. We would fight over who took it to the depot. They paid by the kilo, and whoever went earned a few coins. The owners were called Don Justo and Doña Pili, and they went everywhere together. They were both blind as bats, which was a blessing, as they would occasionally overpay.

Most of all I remember the mattress stripper, a hefty man with a bald, pointy head. He came in without saying hello. Took our mattresses outside. Tossed them on the sidewalk. Sliced them open. Ripped out the wool just like entrails. Pulled it apart by the handful. Put it into piles and then beat it with a club. Hard. Again and again. Then he stuffed it back into the mattresses. Sewed them up. And on top of all that butchered wool was where we slept.

As the postwar period faded, I saw shantytowns spring up on the outskirts. People arrived from the countryside and farmers became laborers. I remember San Blas, Fuenlabrada, Móstoles, Getafe, those places that are still producing footballers. And of course my current neighborhood, Leganés, which also started life as a suburb, and now is a city within a city. Nowadays, the trains will take you to those places in no time. The subway never stops expanding either. Like a fist opening. The friend of the Generalissimo, the one who built the Valley of the Fallen, invented whole neighborhoods, with no transport network, nothing. In the end, we are governed by bricks and mortar.

When I was a child, Madrid was full of holes. This terrified and delighted me. Night was night. There were men with long poles who lit the gas lamps and night watchmen who went around with big bunches of keys. In my imagination, they opened all the doors to the city. At dawn, the farmers started to come in from the nearby villages. They would spread out their tarpaulins and sell their produce right there. Melons in the summer, turkeys at Christmas. We bought a lot of melons. As for turkeys, that depended on what sort of year we'd had.

People no longer remember and Yoshie found it hard to believe, but five minutes ago Madrid was a rural capital. The whole country was rural, in fact. I saw with my own eyes the way every strip of land was filled in with city. Beyond La Castellana there was nothing, only Chamartín Stadium. In those days, it wasn't even called the Bernabéu and it didn't have any towers, either. They were built later on, for the World Cup, during the era of shopping malls. Plots of land were infected as if by the measles. Madrid was different then, Spain was different. Or not, it depends.

———

My brothers went to school at the Santísimo Corazón del Espino, which had a good reputation. My sisters and I were taught by the Siervas de la Extrema Caridad at a convent school called Nuestra Señora del Continuo Amparo. It was on the other side of La Latina, at the bottom of Carrera de San Francisco. We were surrounded. On one side we had the city's largest seminary. On the other, the Capilla de los Dolores. And on a third, the basilica where Franco attended official ceremonies. The holy trinity.

My one nearby relief from all this was Las Vistillas. I learned to roller-skate in those gardens. Roller-skating was the closest thing to running away, you could outpace the people who were chasing you. On weekends, if we got good grades, my father would take us for a picnic in Parque del Retiro, which was like a real country retreat. Cars would drive right into the park. We went to mass at an Opus Dei church that later belonged to the diplomatic corps. In fact, my eldest sister ended up joining them. Opus, I mean, not the Foreign Office. Pupils who couldn't afford the monthly fees had a different study regime. They dressed them all in black, and they came in through the back door, where no one saw them.

I grew up very fast because of the nuns. If you got a question wrong, they would make you wear donkey's ears, and if they caught you talking in class, they stuck a cardboard tongue in your mouth. With rebellious girls like me, they used a carrot-and-stick approach. Until you'd do anything just to keep receiving a pat on the head. I must admit the nuns taught me well. They turned me away from all religious temptation.

I'm not sure how badly behaved I was. All I know is that they made my life impossible. My sisters' less so, at least that's what they tell me now. I went to bed and woke up feeling guilty. Guilty for playing games, for laughing too much, for raising my voice, for listening to the radio, for failing to do my homework, for doing it badly. For painting my nails, which was a sin. For lying to Sister Gloria. Everything at school made me feel guilty. That's why I never repent for anything now.

Sister Gloria! She spoke to us about the devil, because she was diabolical. My friends and I would pray for her to catch a cold so she wouldn't come to class. One of those really bad colds that went on for ages. One day our prayers were answered, she caught a vicious pneumonia and was carted off to the hospital. That's when we began to believe in the Virgin Mary. At my school, Yoshie once told me, the devils were Chinese.

When I was fifteen, my parents enrolled me at a typing academy at the Glorieta de Bilbao in case I wanted to be a secretary, or rather, so that I would become one. I had great difficulty persuading them to let me stay on at school. I was determined to go to university. For the same reason that I loved my mother so much, I didn't want to end up like her.

In the end I studied nursing, the only subject my parents deemed respectable. I discovered that unlike the students of other subjects, our lectures took place in a separate building, away from the male students. What a test! It felt like being back at the convent school, except that we were champing at the bit.

Although I'd planned to become a nurse, as soon as I heard about physiotherapy I was hooked and there was no stopping me. I felt a mixture of fascination, fear, and liberation. Treating the whole body. All by myself. Muscles, skin, joints. Moving, pulling, touching, and seeing what happens.

The French were years ahead of us. Over here, the field of physiotherapy was still in diapers. First you did basic nurses' training. Then you were supposed to specialize. But what you actually did was start work at a hospital as an auxiliary on a nurse's wage. I cut my teeth at a few clinics, until I switched to my actual specialty. We physiotherapists weren't organized. No one understood our job, including us, really. The whole country was injured, and we didn't even realize it.

In the first hospital I trained at, I was finally able to work alongside men. I thought I might burst with fear, dizziness, overexcitement, everything. I got used to it more quickly than I'd imagined. Before going out with Enrique, I went crazy for a year or two. Let's say I did a crash course in urology. I never told Yoshie about that.

From that moment on, the city seemed like a different place. I started going to places I didn't even know existed, where it was considered bad taste to be sober, and it was the done thing to kiss anyone you wanted. I would leave our family apartment with my hair scraped back, in a knee-length skirt, my blouse buttoned to the neck, and wearing a bra from my grandmother's day. Sixty seconds later, I would step outside with my hair loose, my skirt rolled up, two buttons undone on my blouse, and without a bra.

Not long afterwards, at my second hospital, I fell in love with my dearly departed, a very handsome orthopedic surgeon. The family photographs don't do him justice. We met at the same hospital where we said goodbye. That's what I call loyalty to the public health sector.

Enrique and I fell madly in love. We could never see enough of each other. On our days off we went to Casa de Campo with a couple of sandwiches and our wandering hands, or to Café Comercial. Whenever we could borrow a friend's car, we'd take off. That was our dream. To run away somewhere. Any place that wasn't here.

We ended up getting married quickly. I wasn't getting any younger and my mother was constantly in a state of nerves, because I was the only member of the family who wasn't leading a respectable life. We wanted a civil wedding but our parents kicked up such a fuss that we agreed to a brief ceremony at the Iglesia de San Sebastián Atravesado.

We tied the knot the day before Working Women's Day, not that it meant much to us then. Minister Fraga celebrated our first anniversary by taking a dip on the beach of Palomares with the U.S. ambassador, to dispel rumors about those nuclear thingamajigs that they'd lost there.

Soon after Nacho was born, the first physiotherapy convention was held in Barcelona. I look back on it with regret, because I wanted to attend but couldn't. By the time Sonia was born—no, Rocío—we'd already been incorporated into the public health sector. After that things became more regulated. Sometimes I envy the training young people get here nowadays. It's so specialized and advanced. Well, at least I worked in a country where things were improving.

As I see it, you fall in love twice. With the same person, that is. Once when you meet them and a second time when you lose them. That happened to me with Enrique. We weren't getting along so well during those last years, why lie about it? He had his ways, like everyone, but time led me to forget them. After he died, I started to appreciate him again, like I did on our first day. It felt like I was losing him again. Not just my husband, but somebody who'd already left long before he did.

I didn't break down while he was ill, there was too much to do. Nor did I want him to see me depressed, as he had enough on his plate. Whenever I take care of someone I get a strange feeling of euphoria. I want to control everything, and I feel stronger than I am. The worst part came afterwards, once his suffering had ended. Then I saw my own pain, and that he had been caring for me too.

I went through a very bad patch but I got over it as best I could. I didn't lie around on the sofa. People suggested I see a psychologist or something. No way, not me. Once you start, you never stop. You become a junkie of your own problems. Seriously, that happened to a couple of my friends. Moving forward was more important to me than looking back.

I went back to work the week after Enrique died. People said that it was too soon, that I shouldn't ask too much of myself, and all that other nonsense. Burying myself in my work was the best thing for me. What I found hard was going home. The house closed in on me, it felt alien. Thankfully, the children were grown up, so I could invent excuses to stay out late.

In the beginning I was fearful of everything. Going to the bank, taking the car out. Cinemas, Christmas. Traveling on my own. But when the routine of doing those small things became normal again, I felt doubly contented. Isn't getting something back more fulfilling than having it? I enjoy being by myself now, I quite like my own company. I had to work for that.

My physical energy gradually came back and I started to have fun again, but differently now. Life was sad but at the same time more real, if that makes sense. I met Yoshie when I was going through that phase, though in some ways I was still reluctant. Afraid of making another commitment to something and losing it again. I preferred not to face love head-on, as it were.

It seemed unthinkable. I thought it was all over, and in any case, what was the point? Then suddenly, *whoosh*, he appeared from so far away. I've never believed in Prince Charming. Princes make me laugh, we've had more than enough of them here. This was different. Here was a person who had lost more than I had. Someone who knew how to say goodbye. And, oddly enough, learning how to do that teaches you how to love.

We kept some of our stuff at each other's places. But we didn't move in together. We were too old for that, and we were happy that way. With time to breathe in between so that we were pleased to see each other again. Sharing some things and not others. Together yet apart. When you're alone by choice, you find a different kind of serenity. As much as you may enjoy sharing it, you feel the space is yours. Pretty or ugly, it belongs to you. Just like your own backside.

We loved going away together almost as much as we liked returning to our homes. A weekend, a few days, just enough. It was like marriage with a return ticket—I recommend it to everyone. Not that we had that many opportunities. He worked like a maniac, way too much for someone his age. Interestingly, Yoshie swore he'd never had so much time off. Not because we work any less in Spain (I'm fed up with all those clichés), but because here, according to him, we know how to enjoy our holidays.

He was surprised at how I tended to accumulate my days off, to use them all at once. He needed a bit of reeducating. That was one of the things he admired about Europe, our awareness of leisure. He called it a philosophy, because it had to do with notions of emptiness, and goodness knows what else. One day, he informed me that in Spain and France, people take ninety percent of the time off they are allowed by law. This statistic puzzled me. What the hell did we do with the other ten percent?

The fact is that with Yoshie I was rejuvenated. Or perhaps better yet, I felt excited about things in a way that I hadn't when I was young. I was filled with a new energy that was more mental than physical. I'd grown a kind of tiny antenna. My children told me they hadn't seen me laugh like that in years, loud and hearty, the way laughter should be. Those things aren't part of your character, they come with practice. That's what I used to tell my patients. The more you do something, the better you are at it, and the more you need it. This applies as much to a kneecap as it does to a heart.

According to my friends, I started to dress better. Were they implying that before meeting Yoshie I went around looking like something the cat dragged in? The only difference was that I wore brighter colors and the occasional plunging neckline. When you're young you look good without doing anything, but now I had to work for it. And that's what I saw when I looked in the mirror. My desire to see something pleasant looking back at me.

My children insisted they were delighted for me, especially Nacho and Sonia. She adores everything Japanese. Yoshie won them over in no time and Nacho's partner, too—husband, sorry, I can't get used to it. Rocío took longer to come around. At first she was resentful. As the youngest, she was closer to her dad, I guess. As for my grandchildren, who came along a few years later, they loved this strange-looking gentleman who played with them. We would take them to the park, and give them presents I could never have afforded on my own. No children, but grandchildren! he would joke. What a bargain!

Looking back, were we happy? To be honest I never asked myself that question, so I suppose the answer is yes.

It wasn't that Yoshie liked order. What terrified him was disorder. They seem like the same thing, but they aren't. More than once I opened my eyes in the middle of the night and found he wasn't in bed. I could hear him filing away papers or tuning his banjos. To me, it was lack of medication.

His obsession with those banjos! Scarcely a day went by without him checking up on them. He explained something to me about the change in humidity between Buenos Aires and Madrid. He would sit on the sofa with several of those instruments and disappear. He spoke to them in a separate language, composed of clicks and vibrations. He reminded me of myself when I'm examining my patients' joints.

When you impose too much order on things, something strange happens. Instead of owning them, they stop being yours. They could belong to anyone. They lose some of their character. They go back to the store. Why have them if you're not going to shake them, squeeze them, let them wander about the house? A bit of mess is healthy. The same applies to having children. It teaches you to accept that nothing stays still. When you're the mother of several toddlers, you never expect to find things where you put them. And you know something? In the end you're grateful for that.

I was surprised by Yoshie's lack of punctuality. He was forever arranging books and straightening paintings, and then he'd arrive late to everything. Aren't the Japanese supposed to have the most reliable trains in the world, and all that other nonsense? He tried to blame it on Latin America, but he couldn't fool me. He liked making people wait, and he had found my weak spot. Thanks to a couple of asshole boyfriends, I've dreaded being stood up ever since I was a teenager. So when he did finally show up, instead of getting angry, I all but thanked him.

The closer we got, the more he talked to me about Japan. Sometimes, depending on the kind of day I was having, I would feel a little hurt. I sensed he wasn't altogether happy here with me. If he missed his country so much, why had he never gone back to live there? Yoshie maintained it wasn't so simple. That place he remembered didn't exist anymore. I have no place, he said. No matter where I am, I'm far away.

He would spend hours listing the differences between our two cultures. At first, I thought he was hoping I might change my habits. In fact, he just needed me to realize that we seemed as alien to him as he did to us. When you were least expecting it, he'd come out with one of his cryptic sayings. Frog who lives in well, he'd say, doesn't know size of ocean. Bottom of lighthouse is always dark. And so on. All right, I countered, if you get me started on Spanish proverbs, you'll be in that chair all night.

Once he got used to it, Yoshie realized he could learn a lot about himself by doing business over here. Argentina was like a mirror in which he could see his own back. According to him, our two empires had responded to modernity in opposite ways. He asked if I could dig up some history books for him. He'd read them when he couldn't sleep and the following morning would regale me over breakfast. I'd told him I liked to wake up slowly, but he was raring to go. There he went again with feudal traditions and honor or siguiriyas and haiku. He made my head spin and he was only on green tea.

Yoshie believed that, in some ways, we Spaniards resemble the Japanese more closely than we do the Argentinians. This sounded far-fetched to someone like me who had relatives in Córdoba and Rosario. It was much harder for him to be invited into someone's house in Spain than in Latin America. People here like you only in bars, he complained.

Sometimes our gestures made him uncomfortable. Too much arm waving for his lordship. Men must keep a balance between what they express and who they are, he used to say. You must be kidding! All that self-control will give you constipation. And yet at the same time I think we fascinated him. You only had to hear the words his colleagues used to describe us. Passion, fire, Spanish madness. Mainline baroque. Although I recognized none of those things in myself, I shouted *¡Sí!* and *¡Olé!* and they were enchanted. It was all part of the guided tour. Afterwards, on my way home, I would think, Could they be right?

Let's be straight. It took time for me to get to know my body, to know what it likes, I mean. Young people having endless orgasms might happen in porn films, but at least for me, it was a struggle. I'm not saying never—well, hardly ever. That's not the point. It's about feeling like you can do whatever you want with another person, even if you don't in the end. Because you're free inside. Not in there, I mean your head.

When I was twenty I had a nice pair of boobs and a mass of preconceptions, mostly about myself. Those are the worst kind. Let's just say that I had to stop caring so much about my body before I could take care of it. I was worried that everything would end with menopause. Then I realized this wasn't true, that with it, other things began. Because desire is something you're always learning. It's true that as you get older you become invisible, but with those who do see you, you make magic.

Strangely enough, in the end you find good company more satisfying than the act itself. Pleasure tends towards friendship. That doesn't rule out the physical by any means. On the contrary, as you get older your body becomes everything, from when you get up in the morning to when you go to bed at night. Not everything about it has to be erotic anymore. Of course the erotic is still there, and sometimes in an even better way. Ask Yoshie, who was constantly begging for massages.

The first time I gave him a back massage, he got slightly emotional. He confessed he'd never been touched by a left-handed woman before, and he told me a few things about his school in Nagasaki. I told him that the nuns had put me through hell to make me right-handed but it was no use, and they'd finally given up. Who'd have thought I would end up using my hands for a living.

We made love very slowly, almost without moving. Sometimes we seemed to be falling asleep. You feel more pleasure that way, and at that rhythm, even what's ugly looks beautiful. In my profession, you stop making those distinctions. You see all kinds of things and all of them are interesting, especially to the touch. When the hand knows what it's doing, no body is unworthy of attention.

It exasperates me when men see old photographs of me and tell me how cute I was. It turns me off. What do they mean, *was*? If children can be cute (my grandkids, for starters), why can't there be cute old people? People who think that beauty just evaporates, who can't see that it's transformed the way energy is, those people don't deserve to be touched. Yoshie knew how to appreciate every season, so to speak. Perhaps he got that from reading haiku.

I don't mind going into details, really. He let me lead and I was grateful to him for that. Other men are so busy giving you instructions they leave you no room to maneuver. Occasionally he would go limp, or I would have an attack of sciatica. We'd have hysterics over these things and laughing got us excited all over again.

Yoshie used his tongue and his nose—it's not what it sounds like, but if only it were! What I mean is he talked to me, and he smelled me. He said I gave off the aroma of a guitar. Not of the wood but of the strings when they've been played. I'm not sure it was a compliment, but if I was a guitar, then I felt like playing him a concert.

Another of Yoshie's quirks was his lack of concern about bedding. We were at odds over that. He could sleep just as well with two blankets as with none. He considered it an advantage that he didn't feel the cold. I felt sorry for him, as being warmed by your loved ones is a pleasure from the gods. I think the poor man was actually cold, and he didn't even realize it.

He could certainly move his body. We took up ballroom dancing. Yoshie wanted to lose a few pounds, and claimed that pasta in Argentina had been his downfall. Some evenings we would go out to dance tango. He knew the essentials: starting off, the tango walk, the short basic step, but not much else. I could see that he especially enjoyed it. A lot of men our age have a fondness for tango. I don't think it's because it reminds them of their youth or anything, but it's the only way they have of smelling young skin and clasping slender waists. The women allow themselves to be led, because it's part of the ritual. As soon as I cottoned on to that, I started to leave the club before him. I'd let him walk me to the cab. Then I'd suggest he stay awhile, and he raised no objections.

Whenever Yoshie spoke to me about those memories, it gave me the shivers. I would listen, of course, but if he wallowed too much in all that horror, I would cut him short or distract him. I was worried that poking at his wound would only hurt him more. In my experience there are things you get over and leave behind. If you don't want something to be repeated, you don't go around talking about it all the time. It's pure common sense.

The day of the fiftieth anniversary of Hiroshima, I remember it clearly, Yoshie didn't say a single word on the phone. In the media they talked of nothing else and yet he remained silent. He was immersed in his work. I thought he might need some company, so I went to spend the night at his place. As soon as I opened the door, I found his television lying on the living room floor, smashed to pieces. He claimed he had an accident while cleaning. I didn't ask any questions, and we watched a comedy movie on the small set in the bedroom.

But the next morning he *did* talk, as soon as we'd got up.

He told me he had a splitting headache, that he had spent all night dreaming strange things and thinking about everything he had heard. He was furious that the bomb had been turned into a kind of symbol, for politicians, the peace movement, or whatever. It was no longer something real. Nowadays everyone denounced the bombs, but no one wanted to think about the burns, the pus, the scars, the tumors. Yoshie was shouting as he said this to me. I had to agree with him. People never think enough about the body. Eventually he calmed down, accepted the pill I gave him, and went off to work.

As you grow older, you're as likely to forget one thing as you are to remember another. Yoshie started to go back. As time went on, he became increasingly concerned about things he couldn't change. I tried to help him turn the page, but he saw only what he was leaving behind, like someone running backwards.

Reliving past ordeals is something I don't understand, honestly. Imagine that you suffered an injury in the past. Do you put a strain on it? Make it work harder? If you pull a muscle, you put a cold compress on it and rest. You gradually resume normal activity. That's the way we work, what can you do? The same applies here. No one denies atrocities were committed, but you can't become obsessed by the suffering, the pain, the bitterness. There's been enough division in this country.

Some people are on a mission, the people my children admire so much these days. They speak as if they are the owners of the past. They didn't even live through it, and yet they think they can tell you what it was like. They try to convince you that you're a victim of war, poverty, the elites, the nuns, there's always something. And you must continue to be that all your life. If you so much as step out of your role, heaven forbid! I won't go on because I'm starting to rant.

Politics aren't really my thing. I have my opinions like everyone else, but they belong to me, not the entire neighborhood. There's a reason the ballot is secret. There are some who value controversy above friendship. Yoshie and I had similar ideas about that. He knew how to avoid arguments, change the subject, and go on. He told me he'd learned this while living with the Yankees.

Around that time I was having difficulty making ends meet. I already knew what that felt like. My children didn't. Nacho had left home and was sharing the bills with his friend, or boyfriend, I wasn't really sure at the time, but Rocío and Sonia were still living with me. They were studying for their degrees, and they realized they might not end up getting a job in their field. This left them disillusioned. I had to tighten the screws when exam time came round. Of course, we could never have imagined today's circumstances, which have grown direr. When I look at my grandchildren and think they might be forced to go abroad, I feel like I can't breathe.

Yoshie's company had its ups and downs, too, even though by then Me was the fifth-largest TV manufacturer in the world, as he reminded me every five minutes. At first, things went full steam ahead. It arrived in style and opened its headquarters in Madrid. It was based in Castilla, past the towers, just before you get to the old Real Madrid stadium. The branch made tons of money, which it then reinvested. For every million pesetas it made, it spent a million and a half, according to Yoshie. Then it started to invest in cable TV, and bought up channels all over the country. I imagine that was a blunder.

Yoshie once told me that he didn't really understand how the Socialist Party in power here worked. He had always thought socialism was something else. He used to say there were lots of opportunities for business in Spain. As soon as he got here, Yoshie became one of the sponsors of the Japanese pavilion at the Expo '92 in Seville. He went to see the work and came back terribly excited. He told me that the whole building was made of wood from his country's forests, held up without a single screw or nail, and exposed to the weather. He was proud that their pavilion was like no other, and built by people from all over.

He went on so much about his blessed building that we went to Seville that summer to see it, not long after we got together. We traveled on the high-speed train for the first time. No one knew how ruinous it would be. Seville, hot? An inferno! As soon as we arrived, we went straight to the pavilion. When I saw it in front of me, I forgot everything. I even stopped feeling thirsty, I swear. I remember embracing him on the walkway, and it was like crossing a frontier.

The Japanese pavilion ended up being the most popular exhibit, yet it lasted no time at all. As soon as the expo was over, they dismantled it, strip by strip, as if it had been built only so that we would remember it. It turned out that the building was made not of wood but of memory. I thought it was a pity. He saw it differently, he thought this made it invincible.

I suppose that by spending lots of money, Yoshie increased the promotion of Me's products during the Barcelona Olympics. I can still remember one of its commercials. A huge guy, dressed like a samurai, his face in shadow, approaches, dribbling a ball. He pauses in front of the camera, yells something in Japanese, then tears off his samurai outfit to reveal a gypsy costume. He gives a flamenco wail. Tears off the gypsy costume and underneath he is wearing the colors of the American basketball team. All of a sudden the lights come on. And you see that the guy is the spitting image of Magic Johnson. He says with a smile: *It's me.* He shoots, he scores. Applause, then the slogan appears: *Me. You. Us.* My children explained the play on words to me.

Despite my children's current objections, the early years of that administration were good. Afterwards, the whole thing about Felipe González got darker and darker. My children criticize the way I vote. They try to convince me that everyone from the past is useless. Does that include me? How should I know if joining NATO was the right thing to do, or if the constitution needed revising? All I know is that I was able to save when he was first elected, and that by the end I could scarcely get by. I'll leave the rest to the experts, who are everywhere, apparently.

Even Yoshie had begun complaining about how the economy was being managed. I can't remember what problems his company ran into. He had to attend some meetings in Japan. They were recovering from a terrible earthquake. This affected him deeply, because when he was a child, his aunt and uncle had told him about an earthquake that was impossible to beat, and this one had come close.

I was shocked when Aznar won the election. I had voted for him, but not so that he would win. It was more of a wake-up call, wasn't it? Lots of people nowadays omit the fact that they celebrated his victory.

Thanks to liquid crystal screens, Me hit the jackpot again. Half the country bought a new television. Meanwhile, I clung to my old German gadget, of course. Yoshie was determined not to fall behind his rivals. It was Samsung here, Hitachi there. His main concern was how the image shifted as you moved around the screen. Wait a minute, I'd say, isn't that normal? Don't images change when you look at them from a different angle?

The markets were buoyant, business was thriving, things were fucking great, but I don't know who for. The hospital was hiring fewer and fewer staff. Suddenly they were talking about the public healthcare system as a drain on the economy. Energy was privatized. But they also lowered taxes, which we are always grateful for. The housing bubble has burst, they announced, and the only thing I could think about was my grandchildren blowing soap bubbles.

Then came that whole thing with the weapons of mass destruction. That's when I changed my mind about the government of the day, and Yoshie did, too, I think. We even went on a protest march. I couldn't remember the last one I'd attended. Causing havoc in the streets isn't my thing—my thing is treating lesions. The Iraq War made him angry, I'd only ever seen him like that when the Twin Towers were blown up. That day he called the company to say he wouldn't be going in. Yoshie, missing work.

After several years of studying the Spanish economy, he began to explain to my family and me what was going on. I don't know if he actually knew what was going on, but he sounded as if he did. That's what our family meals were like, him talking about interest rates and me about broken joints. They weren't all that different.

According to him, our economy grew thanks to the euro. Just imagine that now! Besides—and this was what really caught his attention—thanks to a surge in immigration, consumption had gone through the roof. Yoshie always insisted that immigration was the most important aspect of our economy, and that anyone who didn't understand that would ruin everything. Nacho and Sonia, who are all for lost causes, loved that idea.

He also claimed that when the next crisis hit, Asia's influence would become clear. Our idea of Eastern countries had to change, because we still believed that they needed to learn from us. He tried to explain to us how the system (for heaven's sake, what system?) had been founded on Western values, and now that Asia was superseding us, it was only natural to adopt a few of its principles.

I remember when they opened that tiny cultural center near Chamartín that offered courses in Japanese arts and crafts, calligraphy, ikebana, that kind of thing. We became friends with the director, Rikako. What a nice woman she was! She'd been educated at the oldest school in her country, in Kyoto or somewhere like that, and she was so pretty. Yoshie didn't admit it, which proved I was right.

That reminds me, Rikako died recently, poor thing. I went to visit her at La Paz hospital, and I did what I could to help her, through the few contacts I still had. The last time I went, we talked solely about flowers. At one point, we fell silent. She looked at the arrangements her students had sent to her. She asked me to change the *frower water*. Then she asked me, in that frail voice she had by then: Did you know that my name means "scientist"? I'm not sure why she told me that. I never saw her again.

One day I found him rearranging his banjos. He took them down off the wall, dusted them, and replaced each one on a different hook. I stood watching him for a while, without saying a word. I went to make a green tea and a coffee. I came back with a cup in each hand, and, playing dumb, I asked him what was going on.

Yoshie told me he would be retiring the following year. He said this as though informing me it was going to rain the next day. He was gazing at the wall as he spoke. It was like he was reading the subtitles of his own words projected there. I said that at last we would be able to eat supper whenever we liked, and enjoy proper weekends. I asked him to take note of what it was like, because it would soon be my turn.

As well as his age, I think what made him unhappy was how the times were changing. It's the first thing those bastards mention when they give you the sack. Sales were in free fall because of the rise of home internet, and the company wasn't sure how to reinvent itself in order to survive.

Me broke with a tradition of goodness knows how long: it closed branches and reduced personnel. Yoshie was so upset that I became an expert at the problems his company was facing. The owners warned that unless measures were taken, they'd be forced to sell the company to Panasonic. But don't you have a say in any of this? I asked. I get to decide only how to do what the directors decide to do, he said.

All of a sudden, the most senior executives were seen as a burden rather than a fount of knowledge. This was new for Yoshie as well. He would speak nostalgically about an old model that was dying out. He complained that everything was changing too fast. Sales strategies, client relations, meeting formats, everything. He was being asked to perform an increasing number of tasks, just when he had less energy for all that.

The younger employees respected his seniority, but didn't understand his way of thinking. Moreover, he declared in astonishment, he'd never had so many female colleagues. Is that maybe what's bugging you, darling? I said. *Kah-men*, please! he protested.

When Yoshie first arrived here, he didn't have a clue about work-life balance. To him, a work problem was a life problem. To stop working was, in a sense, like dying. He couldn't understand that for me it meant the opposite, having more time and starting a new life. Of course, he had no grandchildren. And for that, I feel sorry for him.

During his last year of work, he thought constantly about leisure time. That summer, he tried taking his annual leave all at once, to see what it felt like. He discovered that he had a fear of emptiness. This made him feel terribly disappointed, because his parents had taught him that emptiness is the true meaning of existence. What kind of parents teach their children that? Yoshie concluded that all the years he'd spent working had made him stupid. I'd take him out to get some air, we'd eat some ice cream, and he would calm down a bit.

If what health experts say is true, overtime ends up making you sick. In Japan they even have a special word for people who drop dead from overwork. I can't remember what it is right now, but I swear they have one. Apparently, their government is worried, and they are considering passing a law obliging people to rest. If I'm to believe Yoshie, measures like that are always aimed at saving money, because sick leave and medical bills are costlier than just giving a few days off, and because people spend more money when they're on vacation, which is good for the economy.

I used to find this kind of argument outrageous. My surprise surprised him. Everything is economics, Yoshie would say, good and bad. Pleasure, family. Violence, war. Economics is life. Well, for me the body is everything—you either break your back working, or your accounts don't add up.

For reasons best known to her, my daughter Rocío is seeing a shrink. Sometimes she even insists that pain can be psychosomatic. In my day, we didn't have the time or the money for that sort of thing. When you raise several children, I can assure you there are more pressing things to think about. Besides, I don't believe in such superstitions. For your information, sweetheart, our bodies are far more complex than all your self-help manuals put together.

He changed a little, or a lot, it depends on how you look at it. On the one hand I thought he seemed, I don't know, more lighthearted. Liberated, having done his duty. On the other, he had a haunted look, as if amazed that he'd made it that far. To old age, to retirement. That he was still alive.

Some mornings he woke in a state of euphoria. He raised the bedroom blinds, yawned, and seemed to devour the sun. Other mornings his alarm would go off (he still used one, but set it an hour later—how daring of him!). He would reach an arm out to switch it off and duck beneath the covers, intimidated by all that free time before him. Yoshie reckoned he had been living like a European, but when he stopped working, his reaction was completely Japanese.

Now that he had the entire afternoon to have lunch, he found it difficult to spend more than an hour at the table. He never understood why we Spaniards took so long over meals. According to him, we confused eating with socializing. I tried to explain to him that eating is a communal activity and that socializing is also a form of nourishment.

He became more concerned about his health. Before, he used to avoid doctors like the plague. In the old days, he would rather endure pain than have them run tests. Setting foot in a hospital makes you feel ill, so he thought. It used to drive me nuts. Finally, when I persuaded him to get a checkup, we caught a few things. If I hadn't thought of keeping the test results at my place, I'm sure he would have thrown them in the garbage.

Yoshie became convinced that he would be struck down at any minute by something connected with the radiation. He would attribute the slightest twinge or feeling of malaise to the contamination inside him. He believed that working so much had distracted his cells, that he had been able to fool them by moving around. Now the moment had arrived, and to stay still was to awaken the monster.

I suspect that the death of his old classmate played a big part in that. The guy he went to school with in Nagasaki. Yumi or Yuri, I don't know, his name escapes me. He found out through an American colleague. Terminal cancer. He seemed fine and then all of a sudden, goodbye. Yoshie was quite down when he heard the news. Clearly they had been close as children. He got hold of his photograph and placed it on the shrine in a corner, away from the others. He would even go over to it sometimes and whisper. I've no idea what he was saying.

Maybe that's why he stopped smoking overnight. Like someone cutting off their arm. Speaking of limbs, he started to practice aikido. He gave up ballroom dancing and enrolled in a class at Rikako's cultural center. He explained that aikido had been developed when he was a teenager (I thought it was much older, or that we were much younger) after the war, when there was a ban on martial arts. It all shocked me a bit. That martial arts could be banned, that he should start practicing them here, and that we were both postwar children.

He explained that aikido was all the rage while he was living in France, and so it was something he'd always wanted to try. Yoshie became fascinated by the idea that each movement could be perceived in terms of circles and spirals. He would even do drawings to show me. He loved the idea of proportionate self-defense. He said that you learned to put yourself both in the position of the assailant and the assaulted, which led, actually, to peace. I nodded, just to be on the safe side.

I must admit that aikido had a few things in common with my work. Joints and how to immobilize them. The importance of inertia, balance, and displacement. Turning, twisting, and stretching. Yoshie explained that the word roughly meant "way of energy." That's what it was all about, knowing how to use your energy properly.

Given that his own energy was all over the place, as soon as I took early retirement, we decided to go out on walks together as a serious form of exercise, an hour every day. Yoshie didn't know how to stroll. He would speed ahead. As this was great for my cardiovascular issues, I tried to keep up with him.

Whenever we stayed in Leganés, after breakfast we would leave my apartment, walk down Calle Getafe, and take a few turns around the Casa del Reloj gardens. He would check his watch while he walked, as if he had a meeting to get to or something. And he couldn't help pausing to look at the bullring, which still seemed really exotic to him. What we enjoyed most about those walks was observing the changes in things that seemingly stayed the same. When you are rushing from one side of the city to the other, you don't notice anything—the city is so big you don't even see it. That's another good thing about retirement. Although you're getting old, you learn to look at things anew. You have more *and* less time, if you see what I mean. You fall in love with little things and you pay attention to them, like those children who are forever asking questions.

We never got bored of our daily excursions. On the contrary, they gave us things to talk about. We would invariably discover something we'd missed the last time round. You see, Yoshie would say to me, we're not going in circles. We're moving in a spiral.

With all that walking around the same places, he took to repeating stories he had already told me. He would talk about his house, his mother's hands, his sisters' toys, his father's body beneath a fallen tree. I didn't have the heart to interrupt him, and yet I felt that spinning around in circles like that couldn't be good for him. We started to have our differences—or to realize that we had them. Sometimes we would argue during our walks, and you know where that leads. A couple that can't go for a walk in peace is going nowhere.

I still take that same walk through those gardens. Or rather I did, before I became like this. Up until recently, I would always go if the weather wasn't too chilly. A half-hour stroll at my own pace, a little more slowly, of course. And I would remember him.

As I said before, he changed very little, or a lot, it depends. He had never looked forward to retirement. Yes, he was keen to work less but not to stop altogether. On the other hand, I couldn't wait, because I was tired, because of the atmosphere at the hospital, the chaos in the public health sector, my grandchildren, because of everything. When the time came, I could feel my age catching up with me even as a weight lifted from my shoulders. I filled out the paperwork, my colleagues brought me a cake. My children arranged a surprise party with a few of my friends. The next month, my life was completely different.

Yoshie found it harder to accept. Like a lot of men, he valued himself through his work. Sometimes, I could see that he was feeling a bit down and I'd try to cheer him up. Now you can spend all the time you want in the *retrete*! Then we'd laugh. But as soon as his guard dropped, he would let out a sigh for his company. If it wasn't the yen that was making it uncompetitive, it was the euro, or it was Toshiba, which had started subcontracting, or this, that, or the other thing.

With the banjos it was different, don't ask me why. He still looked at them, but he tuned them less frequently. He no longer cared if they sounded so-so. Sometimes he would even say it amused him. That now, instead of a choir, they sounded like neighbors trying to get along. He hadn't lost his fondness for music. I was getting a bit fed up with jazz, so one Christmas, I gave him something different. One of those bizarre fusions of traditional Japanese music in the form of Spanish madrigals. Yoshie went through a phase of playing it on a loop. He told me he wished he could live right there, always between two places.

To be frank, I find Christmas a bore. I love it when we get together as a family. But not in December. All the shopping and engagements make my head spin. Isn't the end of the year supposed to be a time for reflection? Yet the whole thing seems designed to prevent you from having a moment to think. Without being aware that you're going to die, you don't enjoy celebration as much. And people walk all over you. *Mamá*, says Nacho, you're talking politics! That may be, Son, but I can't find anything about it in the newspapers.

Fear of death is a funny thing. I was talking about it to my brothers and sisters at dinner the other day. The closer you get to dying, the less you like it and the more you understand it. You don't want it to happen to your loved ones ever. And yet you begin to see that it makes sense. Imagine how awful it would be, I don't know, making doctors' appointments, paying your taxes, or shopping for sales—for all eternity. I'm not exactly looking forward to dying but it will no longer catch me unawares.

Aging is different, of course. You never get used to that. You wake up one age in your head and, as the day wears on, you realize what age you really are. I fought against it until I became a grandmother. It was as if I were shouting, I'm not what it looks like, I'm not old! Things are different now. You can't kid your grandchildren. And they've made reaching this age worthwhile.

Yoshie was horrified by old age. After all his narrow escapes, he wasn't expecting it, he thought it would never happen. I guess that's what Madrid meant for him: the place where he confirmed he had grown old. That's why I'm not surprised it was his last stop before returning home. If indeed he had a home.

The best thing about our retirement was that we could finally travel together. We spent a couple of years visiting all sorts of places. When I was young, I couldn't believe how many elderly foreign tourists there were. But once I became one of them, I immediately understood. What a pleasure it is to mix leisure and experience. I've gone to more places since I got old than at any other time in my life.

Every cloud has a silver lining, as the saying goes. But every silver lining also has its complications. Now that we were spending all our time together, Yoshie started to seem a bit less special to me. I had always thought of him as mysterious. Now I sensed that some of his silences stemmed from a lack of desire or initiative. Sometimes the mystery is simply absence. I used to say it to my daughter Sonia, who has just separated from her husband. Don't get married, my girl, it just makes things worse.

Of course it was lovely. We gorged ourselves on traditional food, walked around a lot of museums, took thousands of photos, laughed a lot. Yet, at some point, it became a kind of padding, a pleasant way of filling the time we weren't quite sure what to do with. It's very important for me to spend part of the day staring off into space, and I started to miss being at home, doing nothing.

When we'd arrive at our hotel, our backs stiff from the flight, I wondered if Yoshie wasn't weary of all that. He claimed to dislike traveling. What he really liked was to have traveled. A week before a trip, the idea of leaving would start to make him uneasy. On the eve of our departure, it appalled him. With only hours to go, he would invent excuses to miss the flight. Then a week after, he'd think it was the best place he could possibly have visited. That was the traveler's task, he said. To prepare that future moment.

The same would happen to me, actually. What I most enjoyed about our trips was remembering them together. Like when you're back after some time away, and you wonder whether you couldn't experience the same joy simply by staying at home. Well, no, smarty-pants, you can't.

Now that I had my first cell phone (the rogue had conspired with my children to get me one), we invented a game. Every day, we sent each other a brief text message about one of our trips. It could be a memory, an anecdote, an image, anything. Messages such as:

The belvedere in Toledo, when we realized one of our suitcases was missing.

Driving in the Pyrenees, with the Chet Baker CD that skipped.

The steaming soup on the Stockholm ferry.

The ice-skating dogs in Hamburg.

The angler in the Highlands who told us his brother was learning Japanese.

That unique wine in Cagliari that cost an arm and a leg, and which we then found in the store opposite your place.

The little boy in Avignon dressed as a bullfighter.

The Loch Ness Monster doll that appeared upside down every morning. And so on.

When you're old, every place you see becomes important. You feel that you're saying goodbye. It's one layer of joy and another of sorrow. One on top of the other.

My fondest memory, and I don't mind sounding corny, is the time we spent in Venice. I'd never been there. He insisted we avoid the crowds in San Marcos by staying on the Lido. That way, he said, we could see Venice from a distance. What a snob. I didn't let him wriggle out of the gondola ride, of course, with a glass of champagne and all the rest. The gondoliers were so handsome. I would have given them a free lumbar massage any day.

The only tense moment was at the abandoned hospital on the Lido. Imagine how horrified I was, after working in hospitals for more than thirty years, to see that ruined building. Yoshie seemed to find it fascinating. For heaven's sake, he wanted us to sit there all afternoon, like consumptives or something.

When I persuaded him that it was time to leave, I noticed a beautiful antique typewriter lying on the ground. I suggested we take it back as a present for Nacho. He loves old junk. I bent down to pick it up. It weighed a ton. Instead of helping me, Yoshie grabbed my arm and he wouldn't let me move it. He was stronger than I'd imagined. It was brusque and unpleasant. That evening, I felt like I didn't even know him.

Not working filled him with the past, as if his memory had suddenly expanded. Yet he didn't seem at ease with what he remembered. He started to have panic attacks and problems breathing.

Occasionally, he would fantasize about us going to Japan. Not for a visit, but forever. Although I never said yes, he behaved as if it were an option. We visited Tokyo. It was great and took my breath away. We brought back a few of the latest gadgets for my grandchildren, lots of clothes for my daughters. And I thought to myself, No way would I ever live there.

The food was good, although everything tasted of fish, even dishes that didn't contain any. If such a thing even exists in Japan. They eat fish for breakfast, seriously. They have tea with everything. Green tea that's so bitter you feel you're chewing a plant. And they slurp their soup so noisily that you have to look away so as not to stare.

The bathrooms are impeccable, I'll give them that—and talkative. Yes, they have talking toilets, I'm not joking. Robots instead of *retretes*. I got nervous when I heard them pipe up. Despite all the tea, nothing came out. I suppose I need peace and quiet to pee.

Seeing Yoshie in his own country unnerved me a little. He wasn't the person I knew in Madrid. Not better or worse. Just different. I was afraid that if we ever moved there, I wouldn't only have to get used to another culture, but to another man.

Interestingly, that worried him too. He told me he no longer knew his own language. You mean you don't understand it? I asked. Of course I understand, *Kah-men*. They don't understand *me*. Every time I say something, they look at me like I am a foreigner!

In my view, Yoshie ended up going back first and foremost because of his retirement. Second, I don't know. Homesickness, roots, call it what you will. I asked him to stay and he asked me to go. Learn Japanese at my age? No way. It was easier for him to stay, he had already adjusted, we only had to carry on as before. The final straw was the Atocha bombing. I think that changed both of us.

After the attack, I lost all desire to do anything, including to travel, make plans for the future, anything that involved leaving my loved ones. When we ate as a family, we talked less. When we did talk, we would occasionally quarrel. We couldn't even agree about who was responsible. We had the impression, I don't know, that we would never feel good about anything again for the rest of our lives.

Perhaps we hadn't changed, perhaps the city had. The air was heavy. We walked differently, it felt like the ground was moving. We looked over our shoulders. We loved everyone more, and everything scared us. We ended up asking everyone we met what they'd been doing on March 11 at twenty to eight. We couldn't move on from that morning. Or rather, the opposite—we still didn't believe it, we kept having to ask the question because it seemed so unreal. I thought about the mothers. About the mothers without children.

And Yoshie? What did he think? He had always told me that he dreamed of retiring to some Mediterranean beach. A little house on the Costa del Sol. All that ended after March 11. He never mentioned it again. That's when I began to sense what was going to happen.

Our last trip together was to Barcelona. It was a couple of months after the bombings and I didn't want to go, but Yoshie kept insisting.

He'd been invited to a symposium of international businessmen. I almost dozed off once he began his speech. He made a touching gesture at the start, though. He paid tribute to his old schoolmate from Nagasaki, the one who had died not long before. He talked about how they had met up again in the States. He said he'd been an admirable colleague, an example to them all, and that he would never forget him. He got a standing ovation.

Everyone and their mothers turned up at that circus. Kings, presidents, Nobel Prize winners. Felipe was there, he never misses a trick. Zapatero. Lula. Gorbachev. Even the Spanish astronaut who had been to the moon. And Angelina Jolie, though I've never understood what exactly she does at these things.

There was also some controversy—this is Spain, after all. There were rumors about the cost of the venue, as well as urban speculation. Here? Never.

I couldn't say when it was, towards the end of that year or the beginning of the next. We had a few serious talks, and finally he put it to me. He was leaving with or without me. Yoshie had given this a lot of thought and he was absolutely clear. Tokyo or nothing. It wasn't easy for me, and I struggled to reach a decision. I liked the idea of us going away together and I didn't want to lose him, but my family, my life was here. What was I to do? Run after a man, like my mother had?

Besides, after all those years, I had just finished paying the mortgage on the apartment. It meant something to me. When I married Enrique it was our dream to have a place of our own, and I had achieved that. It was nothing special, but it was mine. The apartment in Leganés where we'd always lived. Three bedrooms, big balconies, overlooking Plaza de la Fuente Honda, next to the ancient psychiatric hospital. We couldn't have afforded anything remotely as big anywhere else. Funnily enough, it's shot up a lot in value since then.

Neither of us left the other. We simply disagreed about how to go on with our lives. He blamed me for being frightened of change, and I criticized him for being incapable of staying put, even in the places he felt happy.

After a few dramatic scenes, his departure was relatively calm. We're too old to start creating fresh resentments. We've got quite enough with the past ones. I even helped him pack his boxes. That dreadful rug was full of holes by then, but he stubbornly refused to throw it away.

In the end, he didn't take all that much with him. He shipped the essential things back to Tokyo. He tried to leave me a lot of stuff, which I didn't want. I don't like to inherit things when someone dies, so you can imagine how I feel when they're still alive. The only thing I did accept, because Yoshie dug his heels in about it, was that banjo, the one that had belonged to Charlie so-and-so. What on earth did I want it for?

I didn't go to the airport, I couldn't bring myself to. My clearest memory is of his last day over at my place. The guy wouldn't admit defeat so easily. He arrived with a flower bouquet designed to impress and a bottle of my favorite wine. He put on an innocent expression and after we clinked glasses he asked me again, in case I'd had a change of heart. He already knew the answer, but romantic movies have destroyed people's common sense.

After the door closed, I stared at it in a daze, as if it were a painting. Yoshie had left to catch a train at Atocha Station. Now that he had more time, he was in the habit of walking. From here it takes no more than fifteen minutes. I poured myself another glass and stepped out onto the balcony. I turned toward the Casa del Reloj, even though you can't actually see it from my place.

At that very instant, I'll never forget it, I had the mad idea of running to the station. I, who never run. I simply had to catch up with him, speak to him, tell him what I was feeling then and there.

But I know what I'm like when I drink. So I came in from the balcony, put down the glass, and turned on the TV.

Yes, we've kept in touch. As far as I know, neither of us has got together with anyone else, which helps, I suppose. We all have our pride. As soon as I found out about the earthquake and Fukushima, I called him. I asked if he needed help or anything. That was before I had this.

The last real message I remember sending him (the kind you plan, write, and edit before sending, like a letter) was to tell him about something I had seen that made me think of him.

I was spending the weekend in Cuenca with my family. We were driving somewhere and we came across a protest march against the nuclear waste dump they want to build next to the area. Some of the protesters were from here. There were a few politicians and even some foreign activists, carrying placards in English mentioning Fukushima.

One woman was holding a banner that caught my attention. It showed the radiation hazard symbol and the words: I DON'T WANT TO DIE AT 60 FROM CANCER, I WANT TO DIE AT 90 FROM AN ORGASM. I'm not sure how fighting against nuclear waste will help you have extreme orgasms at such an age. Perhaps she likened the orgasm to recyclable energy? I wish I could have asked her, but the children wanted to get going. So I wrote to Yoshie about it.

From that day on, more and more stories about the dump appeared on the news. As soon as the new administration took office, it chose that location next to Cuenca to bury nuclear waste. It will cost a cool billion euros, others say even more, the zeros make my head spin. The person most in favor of the dump was the president of Castilla–La Mancha. They say she's on the way to becoming a minister.

In fact, the project was the idea of the previous administration, but they'd shelved it because of the technical studies. I mentioned some of this to the Argentinian journalist when he brought up the subject. Then the other party won the elections and all of a sudden, Villar de Cañas was once again the ideal place for all our garbage. Now the minister of industry is warning that our electricity bills will go up unless we build the waste dump. Higher still? How on earth is it that we, who live in the country with the most sun in Europe, can't start seriously developing solar energy?

The topic interests me because in the end, it's science. The other day I read that the Germans aren't sure how to bury their waste and the Finns are consulting anthropologists and theologians. Bearing in mind how long radioactivity lasts, they say they'll need to invent warning markers that can still be understood a hundred thousand years from now. That's some faith for you! At this rate we won't last another hundred years. But thanks for the optimism, Helsinki.

As for power stations, well, it doesn't matter that the one in Garoña is the smallest. If they give the go-ahead for it to be reopened, the expiration date of all the others will be extended and they'll remain operational until they're sixty years old. Just wait and see, nuclear power stations will stop working when they're older than us!

So the fight over energy here is the mother of all fights. I don't know why that surprises me. This country needs an osteopath to get its structure moving properly, or some hydrotherapy to get things flowing at last.

As I say, we still speak once in a blue moon. He sends me a birthday present every year. I'm less attentive about that kind of thing, but the Christmas after the earthquake I bought him a CD that had just come out—Gregorian chants of Japanese music, which I thought might interest him. The strange thing is that Yoshie never acknowledged receiving it.

Considering what we had together, it would have saddened me to lose touch with him completely. No one's made of steel. Which is precisely why I broke my hip. I'm a lot better now. I'll pull through, I'm resilient. I know how to mend myself.

On a couple of occasions, he even invited me to Tokyo again. I made polite excuses. Such visits seem a little dangerous to me. I prefer to be at peace, each in our own little home, where the past is the past.

9

PINEDO
AND THE
ANTIPODES

JORGE PINEDO PULLS THE TAB on his beer can. The froth rises, swells like a wave, and spills over the sides, flooding the top of his desk and drenching printouts with handwritten notes in the margins. Pinedo stutters a curse. Jumping up from his chair, he asks a colleague for some paper tissues. She opens her leather bag once more, smiling to herself as she considers the possibility of starting to sell them around the newspaper office. For an embarrassing moment, he is torn between staring at his colleague's lips and blotting his desk before the liquid spreads to the keyboard.

Once he has sat down again in front of the screen, he rereads a news article about the projectile dug up at Sendai airport, in northeast Japan. The missile, Pinedo copies down, is undetonated, weighs a quarter of a ton, and resembles the bombs used in World War II. It was discovered while the airport was being reconstructed, after it was damaged by the earthquake and the tsunami.

Next Pinedo checks the article against other sources, and changes his summary. Official statistics estimate that each year around two thousand defective bombs are found in Japan. In fact, not long ago they discovered yet another in the center of Tokyo, close to a busy subway station. The area has been cordoned off, and they still have to decide whether to remove the projectile or carry out a controlled explosion. Experts, he finishes typing, estimate it will take several decades to unearth the remaining bombs.

Pinedo takes another sip of his beer. He closes the windows and prints a copy of the document. Then, with a sigh, he quickly reads over the piece he was supposed to be working on for the next day's newspaper.

Avenida Belgrano has the air of a smoker's lung: as the traffic strains its capacity, it fills with gray fumes. The falling rain is mixed with lead.

Pinedo looks at the night sky, the X-ray of Buenos Aires. He pulls up his lapels and walks away from the building that both feeds and devours him.

They have been saying for a while now that the offices will move after the newspaper is bought out, but so far this hasn't been finalized. He fears that moment as much as he desires it. As soon as it becomes a reality, he will take advantage of the personnel purge and negotiate his own departure. He needs to write in a different way, at a different pace, from another perspective. With an objective that isn't the electric amnesia of current affairs.

But what about money? Pinedo wonders for the umpteenth time. How long could he make it last? Nothing lasts very long, he tries to answer himself, we here know that full well, and maybe knowing this is an advantage.

He presses on, dodging umbrellas. Every bus that passes is overflowing, its passengers hanging from handles like acrobats. The lines at the stops discourage him. He could try the subway but he calculates that, having to change lines, he would miss the last train. He gloomily scans the mass of windshields: downtown on a night like this, a cab would be a miracle. His phone announces a minimum half-hour wait. He keeps to the smaller roads of San Telmo, avoiding Avenida Independencia, in the hope he might find a recently vacated cab. Finally he gives up, accepts that the rain is his, and walks down Calle México toward the river.

He crosses the main artery of Paseo Colón, the hidden Calle Azopardo, and turns into Avenida Ingeniero Huergo, the back of the neighborhood, the city's border. Here grows an alien, wealthy area, where, in the end, he might find it easier to catch a cab. Or, if all else fails, a film at the Dársena Sur movie theater. He makes the final stretch of Calle Chile, which naturally extends from a police station to the Catholic University. He walks along Avenida Alicia Moreau de Justo, and so, by way of this patriotic cross between socialist feminism and patriarchal neoliberalism, his face dripping wet, he reaches Puerto Madero.

Pinedo vividly recalls the years before the real estate boom in the port. His not so terribly athletic youth on the playing field. His erratic jogging sessions past the customhouse, the unchanging brick of the warehouses. This is why he finds it impossible now to avoid a sense of unreality every time he walks through the landscape of serial restaurants and pretentious towers. These streets, he reflects as he reaches a bridge, are still part of a design, a life-size model.

Not that during that time of acne and literary aspirations the area possessed any great charm; on the contrary, it was an eyesore. Yet with urban development, Pinedo muses, its hideousness hasn't diminished, it merely raised its price.

On the far side of the bridge, a dog is chewing on an empty plastic bottle. Seeing Pinedo approach at a brisk pace, it lifts its muzzle and looks at him defiantly as though warning: Don't even think about stealing my void.

With some degree of frustration, which he regrets he is growing accustomed to, Pinedo wonders if he will ever finish this investigation into nuclear disasters, which should culminate in a series of articles. At least, that's what the newspaper had approved. The problem is that his focus is expanding at the same speed as his research, and the horizon is broadening more quickly than he is able to take notes. The more he writes, the more he has left to write.

First he read about the atom bombs. Then he moved on to Fukushima and its suspicious circumstances. Soon he began to connect them to the anniversary of Chernobyl. At that point, it was impossible not to continue with Three Mile Island and other past cases, which he'd investigated until he forgot why he was investigating them.

In comparing these histories he has become obsessed with the collective memory of disasters; the way that countries forget the pain they have suffered or caused, the way that all genocides end up resembling one another, plagiarizing each other, both here and in their antipode. He is amazed that what's ours can be found so far away.

Pinedo notices that the rain is helping him, the drops are threading his ideas, his mind is clearing.

On the other hand, he tells himself, for a long time he has wanted to devote his energies to a project with no deadline, a book that is an end date in and of itself, the vanishing point of everything. The one that appears to survive in a larval state, a sort of fetal vampire that feeds off his current discoveries.

Journalism would be its mouth, the first voraciousness. What would literature be? Probably the stomach, the absorption of all that material. He no longer believes that one medium works with more reality than the other. He rejects this notion, which he'd once subscribed to, and suspects that both deal with exactly the same thing at different stages. That's why he questions the boundary between real events and fictions, between witnesses and characters.

Pinedo recalls José Martí's pioneering account of the Charleston earthquake, so powerful they said it'd caused a crack in the Florida peninsula. In Martí's account, published in an Argentinian newspaper, you see the destruction, you hear it and touch it. And many universities, including Pinedo's own, continue to study it as a classic in disaster journalism. Except for one small detail: The author wasn't actually there. He wrote the article from New York, more than a thousand kilometers away. Does that make it any less valid as a recollection of the facts?

He wonders what makes a reliable witness, how much of what they think they see is actually invisible. And what portion of those invisible facts is revealed thanks to conjecture, interpretation, imagination. Truth, Pinedo reasons, is important. Except that truth depends less on data than on underlying metaphors.

He wanders past the lit doorways of the docks, unsure whether to go in and have a drink. Inside the bars, floating heads watch him as they might a fish who has strayed to the wrong side of the tank. When faced with options he can never make up his mind, overwhelmed by the responsibility of weighing them before he acts. Similarly, he always hesitates before all the possible constructions of each sentence he utters, tormented by the prospect of stumbling.

Treading on his own reflection, Pinedo wonders how much of his need to write is related to the stutter that causes him so much embarrassment. Could writing be his way of ceasing, if only for a moment, to stutter over everything? Or maybe it's a way of using that stutter to actually say something.

As a child, when he had difficulty pronouncing a word, he would shut himself away and spell it on paper. He drew the letters, and plop! He marveled at its perfection, its roundness when written. Roundness when written, Pinedo repeats, noticing the tiny ridges on the roof of his mouth. He recalls when he first learned the word *cacophony* and to his surprise, discovered that, in addition to illustrating its own definition, this tongue twister summed up his problem with words. Tongue twister, the story of his life.

He has found out recently that the adjective *catastrophic* was first documented in 1911, exactly a hundred years before Fukushima, but it was an earthquake in Lisbon that gave the word its current meaning. Prior to that, *catastrophic* referred only to the denouement of a story. The last great earthquake in Chile, Pinedo remembers, happened just when the official congress on the Spanish language was about to take place. The various academicians were going to present a new dictionary. Then the congress was canceled, and all those words had to wait.

After several retreats and vacillations, he stops outside the Dársena Sur movie theater. Fiction has always helped him focus on his own life. He checks the movie times and confirms that tonight is not his lucky night: he has missed the last showing by a few minutes. The door is barred (barred with a lock, locked by a bar, a tongue twister bar), and there's no one at the ticket booth. Pressing his nose to the glass, he tries to catch the attention of an employee he sees, who does his utmost to ignore him as he examines his cell phone.

Pinedo walks back the way he came, and, as if his path were a sentence rephrasing itself, he thinks once more of Yoshie Watanabe. It's not easy to tell an obsession from intuition, stubbornness from a hunch.

He has to admit that as the emails, calls, and rejections pile up, his interest in Watanabe has become rather personal. He's still trying to understand his hidden affinity to him, what the old man stirs in himself. In fact, the main reason he persists in pursuing him is to find an answer to that question.

Like an exasperated percussionist, the rain increases its rhythm. The water lashes. Shoulders hunched, Pinedo makes a dash for the nearest shelter and takes cover in a doorway with gold buzzers. He resists the temptation to flatten his hand against them, less out of respect than to avoid being chased off.

He thinks of those four women about whom, as things stand, he knows quite a bit less than he would like to. For every little detail he discovers, he has to make up the rest. Could this be the formula for fiction? Real things multiplied by the workings of the imagination?

Mariela's case is different. Since she offered to collaborate with him, Pinedo has exhausted her with his questions. When something absorbs him, he finds it difficult to change the subject: his enthusiasm is mono-thematic. Is he imagining it, or is she returning his calls more slowly? He can't blame her.

Apart from being understandably weary, could it be that Mariela is a little disappointed? Did she perhaps offer her help to provoke some sort of intimacy? When they met at his mother's birthday party, they'd hit it off right away and she'd behaved like someone much younger. They'd spent the whole party engaged in banter. His mother, he recalls, was uncomfortable with this.

They'd exchanged numbers. They started to meet and stayed out late talking in cafés, went to the theater, shared books. He suggested she translate an article for his newspaper, which she did with admirable speed and elegance. Then he dared to reveal his ambitions, his deferred projects. Mariela encouraged him to persist. No one had ever listened to him before with such understanding.

Until, one evening, she mentioned Yoshie Watanabe. He was captivated by her story. He immediately felt that it involved the stories of many others, that it fanned out in all directions.

From then on, their relationship changed. Mariela drew closer and closer to him, stimulated by the reversal of their roles, which now made him her confidant. At the same time, almost unconsciously, he started to distance himself from her, so that he could break into her past. Like someone burgling a house little by little with the owner's consent.

The rainstorm shows no sign of abating, so, famished and dripping wet, he finally decides to take refuge in a bar. He runs in sodden sneakers. As he splish-splashes toward the illuminated shapes flickering in the distance, Pinedo senses that he is being followed, observed from behind, or from above. That someone, somehow, is monitoring his movements. He blames this on his empty stomach. Or, more likely, on his tendency toward paranoia—a national tradition. But just to be on the safe side, he lowers his head and sprints.

After all his hemming and hawing, Pinedo enters the first bar he comes across. This inevitably happens whenever he thinks too much before he acts: reality imposes its common sense on him, like a slap in the face.

He crosses the threshold, shakes himself a few times, and chooses a table by the window, facing the door. Best to be vigilant.

Upside-down umbrellas jostle in the stand, forming a ragged bouquet. On the television at the far end of the bar, people are talking soundlessly. For an instant, he has the impression that the missing noise from the screen has tipped over, as from a fish tank, into the venue.

His intention is to have a snack, dry off a bit, and once the storm has subsided, to call a cab. Someone comes to serve him. He orders tea and a toasted sandwich. He tries to guess what they're arguing about on the television. He thinks he understands. Then he becomes transfixed by the surface of the windowpane, the streaks of water, their ephemeral Morse code.

When the plate and cup appear before him, Pinedo comes back to his senses. He raises his head, says thank you, and as he takes a sip of tea, spills half of it down his trousers.

No big deal, the waiter says as he walks away. You were already soaked, so it's hardly going to show.

Pinedo notices someone staring at him from the adjacent table. The moment he stares back, the eyes move away. He is absurdly upset by this, as the illusion of his one-way mirror shatters.

He tries to recover from the trivial, radical effect of someone else's attention. He fixes his gaze on the same spot as before, but is distracted by the knowledge that he isn't the only one observing; that to look is an action that can never be solitary.

As his eyelids open and close, he feels he is taking on the other person's point of view, absorbing it into his own consciousness, and that he can see inside as well as he can see outside.

Then he cranes his neck, and he finds that the customer at the adjacent table has disappeared.

Feeling a sudden urge to go outside and smoke, Pinedo rummages in his pockets as though missing items might respond to insistence. He can clearly visualize his lighter on his desk at work, mocking him.

One of his pockets starts to throb. This isn't an epiphany. It's his phone, which has survived the rain and his clumsiness. Its tickle on his leg intimidates him. Except when work requires it, Pinedo tries to avoid phone conversations. Not just because of his stammer, but also because of the loss that phone calls highlight: you're listening to an absence, feeling accompanied by someone who isn't there.

When he finally answers, the caller has hung up. He knows the number very well.

He smiles and stares through the windowpane covered with hieroglyphs, at the distorted outline of the city.

Like those trompe l'oeils he had difficulty focusing on when he was a child, the image escapes him, and Pinedo is once again looking in.

He can see the bar's floating interior, the furniture, the customers, their translucent bodies, his own tired face. He finds himself ugly, but he recognizes himself. He draws his mouth closer to give himself a taunting kiss. The glass mists up and his reflection is lost.

The rain intensifies, punishes. He hasn't seen such a downpour in years. As if all that research into foreign disasters had brought the apocalypse to his door.

Sooner or later, Buenos Aires is flooded. And it always floats to the surface.

10

LAST CIRCLE

THE ENGINE STILL RUNNING, Mr. Watanabe stares at a fork in the road. Its choices diverge like a pair of trousers about to split.

He feels the urge to go to Hirodai. He intuits that he should acquaint himself with it; that, in some sense, he is choosing between two directions in his memory.

Ovine clouds drift over the car roof.

He drives on, steering between the cracks. Soon the road begins to climb. The surface remains exactly as it was after the earthquake, when the ground ceased to be a ground and the present broke apart. The car advances with the rhythm of a horse, avoiding the fissures so the wheels won't get stuck. It is more like a jigsaw puzzle of a path. Watanabe imagines that each piece contains the hint of a movement, a possible detour to somewhere else.

He comes to a halt at the entrance of the village, which is located at the top of a slight hill. According to the GPS, at this very moment he is twenty kilometers from the nuclear power station, on the exact edge of the critical zone. Neither inside nor outside.

He steps out of the car. This time he decides not to look at the dosimeter.

He begins to walk around Hirodai. The fact that this is the closest he has ever set foot to the Fukushima plant makes him feel he's floating, and his shoes sink less into the ground.

His first impression of the village isn't the accumulation of things and spaces that comprise it, but the overwhelming sum of its silence. A very specific silence that Watanabe recalls having heard only once before in his life. There are peaceful silences that are a cure for noise, and others that emphasize absence.

And farther away, in the distant background, the sea. The echo of the waves, which his experienced ear instantly associates with the swish of a cassette tape or the crackle of vinyl, just before the music starts.

Since his arrival, Mr. Watanabe's sense of smell has been sending him disconcerting signals. He has the impression that this place somehow smells like yesterday. As if smells reach his nose with a delay, like when sound and image are out of sync. The only aroma that remains independent of time is that of damp salt.

It's also hot and getting hotter. The lack of movement in this place seems to have fixed the strips of sunlight. Watanabe undoes another shirt button.

He wonders whether Hirodai is like this at all hours of the day, or if the remaining inhabitants are finishing their lunch. He heads toward the town center. Everything looks as unscathed as it does deserted. Streets without cars. Houses without inhabitants. Shops without customers. Schools without students. This is the without town, he thinks. There's no destruction: just subtraction. A pure subtraction. A number minus itself.

Everything has the look of a house that's for sale. Lowered blinds, parched flowerpots. Dried mud on the benches, fountains no longer running. Squares visited only by the cats and dogs that run over to lick his shoes. Buses with seats draped in white fabric, transporting ghosts. Closed temples. Idle offices, bureaucracies that have finally achieved perfection.

Watanabe finally comes across a few people, all of them elderly, moving slowly along and propping themselves against walls. Gazing into infinity, their faces covered with surgical masks.

All children and young people appear to have been evacuated. Only grandparents, great-grandparents, elderly widows and widowers chose to remain. This place, he reflects, has turned into a kind of demographic prophecy. The rehearsal of a future where only the past exists. Chained to a post, a bicycle leans.

All of a sudden, on a street corner, he sees an old man kicking the air. He seems to be carefully following the movements of something Watanabe can't see, possibly an insect or something stuck to his trouser leg.

Mr. Watanabe approaches gingerly. When they are almost on top of each other, the old man raises his head and asks his name.

Ah, says the old man. I met a Yoshie many years ago. His family was from Toyama. Good people. They loved the sea. He studied things. Strange things. I once saw his photograph in the newspaper because he had died. My name is Sumiteru, a pleasure.

Unable to curb his curiosity, Watanabe asks what the old man had been doing before he walked up to him.

When? replies Sumiteru. Just now? Ah, playing soccer. I always wanted to. When I was young, when our country won the bronze medal, I dreamed of going to the Olympics. Back then no one around here had the slightest interest in soccer. But it's never too late to play.

ON HIS WAY BACK TO THE CAR, he walks past the entrance to a small guesthouse. In carefully painted lettering, a sign announces: HINODESO MODERN MINSHUKU. Although the guesthouse gives every impression of being closed, the sound of a radio reaches him from inside. With nothing to lose, and assuming there won't be many choices of places to stay, he calls out a couple of times.

The radio falls silent. After a long pause, footsteps grow louder as they approach the door.

A stocky man in a stained apron appears, a pair of rubber gloves dangling from the pocket. The stains don't look as though they were made by food, but something thicker and shinier.

Bowing, Mr. Watanabe explains he is searching for somewhere to stay the night. The man bows in return and ushers him inside.

The Hinodeso guesthouse looks modest but pleasant. Apparently Mr. Satō, its owner, is the sole occupant.

Forgive me for taking so long to open the door, says Mr. Satō. I was out in the back, repairing some ceramics. Do you like kintsugi?

More and more, replies Watanabe.

Do you practice it?

You could say that.

I used to when I was young. Then, what with the family, I let it slide. Until I said to myself recently: Why not? Naturally, I only use cheap objects. What's important is repairing them. Do you have a moment?

Mr. Satō hurries off, disappearing into the back of the building. He returns holding a cracked bowl in both hands. Gold radiates from the base, as if it were supporting a sun tree.

Look, says the owner, what lovely cracks.

———

When Watanabe confirms that he wishes to stay at the hostel, Mr. Satō glances toward the entrance, and—with the expression of someone contemplating an endless line of people waiting—announces that the house will offer him the biggest room at the standard price. He thanks the man with a sardonic grimace and goes outside to fetch his luggage.

On his return, the owner is no longer wearing his apron and has adopted an air of enthusiastic efficiency. He asks Watanabe if he is hungry. He admits he is. The owner instantly brings him soup with tempura left over from his lunch. He downs the remains with a voracity he himself finds surprising. His host sits down across from him.

There were thousands of us here in Hirodaimachi, says Mr. Satō. Now only twenty or thirty are left. At first, I thought of leaving, like everyone else. How could I not be worried about Fukushima? But I felt I didn't have the strength to move, and the town, as you've seen, is intact. As we're on a hill, the tsunami didn't affect us. Besides, where would I go at my age? I prefer to stay in my own home. My memories are here and memories need their own space, don't you think? What I miss most are my grandchildren. My daughter Suzu decided to take them away with her until the situation improves. I agree it's for the best. I hope they'll be able to come back soon. Life without grandchildren is too long. That's what my deceased wife used to say. Do you remember Kurosawa's seven?

Watanabe nods, finishing the soup with a slight sucking sound.

That's how I want to go, Mr. Satō continues. Listening to the sails of a windmill. Or in the mountains, like my grandfather. My grandfather loved the mountains. Whenever he had a problem, he would leave the village and climb to the top of Mount Otakine to meditate. Do you know what he did when he realized he no longer had the strength to carry on climbing? He decided to go up one last time and there he stayed, waiting for the end.

And how long did your grandfather have to wait up there? asks Watanabe, wiping the corners of his mouth.

To be honest, I don't know, replies Mr. Satō. It was before I was born. My father told me about it.

After appointing him as guest of honor, with a hint of ceremony Mr. Satō hands him a key ring with a metal ball attached. Heavy, grubby, a thing of beauty. That's the key to our exotic room, he explains: Western style. No sliding panels. A large double bed instead of a tatami. And a raised dining table.

When American tourists came, the owner says, they often used to ask for that room. That, and forks. It was quite amusing.

Mr. Watanabe walks along the corridor, rolling the metal ball in his fingers. He'd almost forgotten the way an old-fashioned fob smells, of damp metal and multiple hands. He's never been against technological progress, not to mention that he'd made a living from it, and yet he regrets that it has caused the loss of such smells. Most modern doors work with a disposable key card or a digital code. Weightless. *Inodoro*. This is what he is thinking now as he clasps the keys.

He enters the bedroom, slips off his shoes, and, following his usual custom, puts out his few belongings. His clothes in the wardrobe next to the door. His toiletries in the bathroom. His devices charging in an outlet. Ōe's book on the bedside table. Then he slides his little red suitcase under the bed, like a pet that has just digested a meal.

He has always felt comfortable living in hotels: bursting in, spreading out, and quickly running away. He enjoys the combination of a strange place and a portable home. The possibility of a private space where one leaves no traces, or rather, where one's traces merge with those left by a continuous throng. We also take our past with us to hotels, Watanabe believes, but that past becomes present, it is nomadic.

In his experience, the art of packing isn't what to include but what to leave out. The more selective we are, the more our luggage resembles us. Not a bundle of possessions: an assortment of sacrifices.

Once he's settled in, while he is relieving himself in the bathroom, Mr. Watanabe goes online for a few minutes. He checks his inboxes. He sends a message to the Arakakis, thanking them for their hospitality. He visits Mr. Sasaki's blog. He reads the latest entry, smiles, and leaves a comment.

Afterward, he comes out of the bathroom and searches for one of his webcams. He needs to make sure that the world is still out there, enjoying life regardless.

He has a quick shower. He changes his clothes, buffs his shoes. He puts a couple of things in his leather bag and slings it over his shoulder.

THE AFTERNOON BURNS his forehead. He has left his phone charging in his room but doesn't care. He has just set a goal for himself that enthuses him: to meet every remaining inhabitant of this abandoned village. Given that he has already seen at least a dozen of them, he thinks this is achievable.

He wants to see, greet, approach those people. Mr. Watanabe feels they all belong to the same family, a small gathering of the last ones.

As he walks through the emptiness of Hirodai, he feels he is fulfilling an ancient fantasy. To contemplate what life looks like when there should be no one left. A posthumous perspective.

For a few minutes, he follows an elderly man with a green plastic watering can who is inspecting the houses in the town center, window by window. He pauses at every flowerpot, raises his arm, and sprinkles slowly. He goes from the houses to a garage, where he refills the container time and again. His movements convey a recognizable type of effort: when one's will prevails over physical limitation.

During one of his breaks, Watanabe walks over to the garage and says hello. Surprised and pleased to see a visitor, the old man invites him inside. He offers him a cup of tea, which Watanabe gladly accepts. If his taste buds aren't deceiving him, it is the same green tea that he normally drinks in Tokyo.

The old man's name is Ariichi. When he was young, he explains, he put his savings into the garage, the first in the town. Later on, his sons took it over. Now it belongs to no one. Every day, he does his rounds in the different parts of the village, to look after the outdoor plants of the neighbors who have left. Unlike Mr. Satō, he is convinced they'll be returning shortly or at least that if he does the watering, they'll come back sooner. The few who have stayed behind seldom leave their houses. He thinks this is foolish. Watanabe asks him about the radiation.

The radiation doesn't scare me in the slightest, says Ariichi. Before the cancer gets me, I'll die of old age. The others think they're scared of the nuclear plant but believe me, it's not that. What frightens them is death and they won't avoid it by shutting themselves away in their bedrooms.

Over his second cup of tea, Watanabe discovers that Ariichi's apparent calm belies a different anxiety. His main concern is for the graves of his ancestors that lie in a burial ground a little farther north, two or three kilometers inside the prohibited zone. He has visited them there all his life and envisaged his grave next to theirs. Although he has had no trouble gaining access to the cemetery, what if all of a sudden they refuse to let him in? Recent rumors have made him fear this possibility. That's why he thinks that, when the next Obon comes, all the neighbors should gather on the shore to light bonfires in honor of their dead.

I don't feel ready yet, he says, to cross the frontier. I need them to wait, do you see? To wait for me a little longer.

Wandering away from the town center, Yoshie makes out in the distance a tiny old woman in a doorway, wrapped prematurely in a shawl, as if the chill to come at nightfall could make her catch a cold beforehand.

As he draws nearer and his tired eyes start to focus on the old lady, Mr. Watanabe realizes she is positioned differently than he'd first thought. Or rather, even if he had perceived her correctly, his mind modified the image to make sense of it. She isn't facing the street leaning against the door, but rather the exact opposite. She has her back to him and her face is pressed up against the door, like a salamander.

He is able to discern her movements only once he is a few meters closer: the old lady is trying to force the lock using some sort of implement, pushing the door with an aggression incongruous with someone her age. (And gender, thinks Watanabe; then he recalls his arguments with Lorrie and feels ashamed in midthought.)

Hearing his footsteps, she stops pummeling the door and turns toward him, giving him her sweetest smile. She asks if he's connected with the police. He introduces himself, explains that he is passing through and that he is staying at the Hinodeso guesthouse. She welcomes him to Hirodai. Declares that she is pleased to meet him, but doesn't mention her name.

I've run out of rice, the old lady explains, concealing the implement beneath her shawl. No rice and no preserves. I know that my neighbors have some. They left weeks ago, or was it months, I don't remember. They have some, I'm sure. It's difficult to cook here. What would you do without rice?

I'd order sushi over the phone, replies Watanabe, failing in his attempt to crack a joke.

She fixes him with her stern gaze.

They don't need the rice, she says, or the preserves. Don't you think it's a waste? All that food in there. I've seen it from the yard, on the shelves. If they come back one day, I'll apologize and thank them. There are several jars, all full.

He nods, preoccupied by the blotches on her hands, her raised knuckles: an archipelago with five stony islands.

Now, sir, the old lady adds with a bow, if you'll excuse me . . .

And she brusquely resumes her hammering, paying him no more attention, as if Watanabe had vanished into thin air.

What about the trains? he wonders sometime later, what's become of the trains that no longer depart, the cars no one enters, the platforms waiting for someone to wait on them? What fraction of the world's journeys is lost each time a train remains in place?

All the lines that used to run through the region, a couple of incalculable age informs him in wispy voices, have been suspended. It is suspected that the tracks linking the town to Hirono, Hisanohama, and other places might contain high levels of radiation due to the transport of waste from the nuclear power plant.

Mr. Watanabe asks for directions and heads for the station.

No sooner has he entered the building than a rumble of metal startles him. A screech in motion, rotating, growing.

A moment later, he sees the man in a wheelchair.

The man coming toward him, screeching as he smiles.

His name is Mr. Nakasone, a former ticket collector at the station. He worked here all his life, he says, until he had the accident. He has never lived anywhere else. In his present condition, moving out of his home would create more problems than it would solve. He now depends on the few families who have stayed behind. While there's at least one neighbor willing to help, he prefers to remain. He has two homes, counting the station. The trains are his family, he explains.

Those trains that he has seen depart and arrive so often he has lost count, he recalls, motioning into the distance. He means this literally: for many years he kept a precise tally of the number of train services he supervised. Not out of vanity, he adds, but just to be aware of the passage of time.

Afterward he names the few living relatives he has left, including a cousin in Futaba. The other day, two soldiers came to her house and took her away. They had an evacuation order. At first, his cousin slammed the door in their faces. The soldiers read out a decree. His cousin argued that by staying in her house she was harming no one but herself. They told her that wasn't the issue. Of course it is! she protested.

They move together toward the platforms. Watanabe offers to push the wheelchair, Mr. Nakasone refuses with an abrupt gesture. He immediately changes his mind, and rubs his forearms.

It's not because of my arms, he clarifies, but because it's comforting.

They advance in silence along the station walkway. The only noise is the screech of wheels, like a stream of rodents.

Watanabe notices the old clock presiding over the entrance to the platforms. It is speckled with shadows.

Isn't it a bit behind? he comments.

That clock hasn't worked for years, replies Mr. Nakasone.

Lifting some caution tape out of the way, they emerge into the open air. The heat is starting to subside. The light divides, rectifies the tracks.

It's very strange, says the former ticket collector. The platforms seem smaller when they are deserted like this.

They approach the tracks. Look down at them.

Are there only these two platforms? Watanabe asks.

Only these two, Mr. Nakasone nods. One to arrive and the other to leave. No need for more.

HE REACHES THE TOWN'S VANTAGE POINT and, wrinkling his brow behind his sunglasses, he turns in a slow circle.

He looks south, toward the invisible city of Tokyo. He looks west, where the mountains are shining. North, where weeds have overrun the fallow fields and the high-voltage cables dwindle toward the nuclear power plant at Fukushima. Watanabe tries to imagine that energy moving back and forth, its fiery course. Then, finally looking east, he searches for the sea.

He descends the steps leading from the hilltop to the beach. He does so with great care, taking pains not to trip on the stones. No doubt it would have been a lot easier to drive down, but he knows full well that when he has a steering wheel between his hands, his natural impulse is to leave. And right now, he still has a mission to complete. If his math is correct, there should be at least two or three inhabitants left to see.

He pauses at the foot of the steps to enjoy the ocean, seeping in between the rocks with the sound of rolling dice. His nostrils fill with its scent, a scent that seems like the very first to have existed on earth.

As he walks toward the water's edge, for once he is unconcerned about his shoes. The sun spreads a sail over the waves. Mr. Watanabe half closes his eyes and extends his arms. What exactly he is trying to embrace, he isn't quite sure.

Then he recalls the divers of Mie, in the Kansai region, who would plunge underwater bare-chested in search of mollusks and algae. He would like nothing more than to see one of those legendary figures emerge in this instant.

By chance, a silhouette glitters at the water's edge. He runs toward it.

It is neither a young diver nor a mysterious mermaid. It is a small elderly man with a slight paunch, who declares how pleased he is to meet a stranger at last. He says he is Dr. Nagai, a retired radiologist, at his service. A pen and a thermometer protrude from his shirt pocket.

They converse without looking at each other, facing the lightened sea, as though reading subtitles on its watery screen.

Watanabe isn't surprised to hear that Dr. Nagai is the only remaining medic in town. For that reason he cannot leave. If he went, he argues, who would look after the locals? His grandchildren live far away and he has convinced his wife to visit them. He is spending some time alone, as alone as one can be beside the sea, he adds. Even the authorities, after advising people to evacuate the village, have left. The council offices have relocated to the southwest, away from the danger zones.

So we are now a zombie community, he says.

The two men exchange lighthearted comments about the eccentricities of some of the locals. Dr. Nagai relates various anecdotes. When he mentions Yuma and her compulsive housebreaking, Watanabe interrupts him. He asks if he is referring to the old lady who was forcing open the door to her neighbor's house. The doctor says he doesn't know which door it was this time, but that she does the same to all of them. She's been behaving like this ever since the evacuation. Watanabe suggests she may simply be hungry.

Yuma, hungry? says the doctor. I doubt it. At first, my wife and I used to invite her over for lunch. As soon as the meal was finished, she would rise from the table and thank us very politely. Shortly after, we'd see her breaking into other houses.

They continue to chat as they stroll along the beach. Mr. Watanabe notices that his shoes are sodden. He takes them off and walks with them hooked on his fingers. The bag on his other shoulder is starting to feel heavy and he switches the items around. Observing his gesture, Dr. Nagai inquires about the state of his scapulae and its customary stiffness. Watanabe describes his aches and pains. The doctor nods with the vehemence of one who is a sufferer as well as an expert.

After a certain age, he says, we don't know whether to complain more about engine failure or the holes in the bodywork.

Watanabe asks him if he has noticed any changes in the health of his neighbors since March. The doctor observes that, in strictly physical terms, no one appears worse than they were. In fact, he admits, some patients seem healthier than before, or at least a little more active.

It's not easy to tell one thing from the other, he says. My patients have to struggle now to meet their daily needs. Perhaps that effort keeps them alert. Maybe they feel they are surviving danger. In short, they've had no choice but to start again from scratch.

You can't imagine how much I sympathize with them, replies Mr. Watanabe.

They walk back up the beach and stop next to a black car. The doctor tells him that his previous cars had all been white, the color of ambulances. And that he thought a change would do him good.

Exhausted from the walk, his shoes still soaking and his shoulder throbbing, Watanabe accepts the doctor's offer to return together.

On the way back, Dr. Nagai proposes to examine him. A routine checkup, he explains, just to be on the safe side. Watanabe replies that there's no need, that he feels fine. Accelerating slightly, the doctor asks—implores, almost—if he's sure.

Just an examination with the stethoscope, he insists as he parks in the town center. A blood pressure check. An eye scan, at least.

Watanabe thanks the doctor, tells him perhaps tomorrow, and escapes from the car.

Close to the hostel, in an alleyway he has not walked down before, he passes the entrance to a kindergarten. He turns around and walks back. He rereads the sign: NAGAE'S GARDEN.

He knocks on the door. Tries unsuccessfully to push it open. He peers in through the windows. He can just make out some toys lined up along the edge of a table, nearly leaping into the void.

He goes to ask for help from Mr. Satō, who doesn't understand why he is so interested in the nursery school. Apart from the obvious coincidence with his little sister's name, Watanabe finds it hard to explain even to himself. All he knows is that he wants to go inside.

Always ready to please his customers, or in this case his only customer, the guesthouse owner ends up calling Mrs. Takahoshi, an old friend who worked for many years as a teacher at Nagae's Garden.

From what Watanabe can glean from his tone, Mr. Satō and she seem to enjoy something more than friendship. The final, melodious whispers appear to confirm his theory.

Mr. Satō informs him that his friend still possesses a set of keys and that the kindergarten principal, who has left town, had asked that she pop in from time to time to look after the plants in the playground.

You're in luck, says Mr. Satō.

That depends, he replies.

With a speed almost verging on the impossible (which makes Watanabe suspect she was already in the guesthouse), Mrs. Takahoshi appears in reception.

Without asking any questions or waiting for any explanation, she leads him to Nagae's Garden. She walks ahead of him, as if she were on her own. The swiftness and detachment of her gait make her seem taller than she is. Mr. Watanabe thinks to himself that under different circumstances, he would have liked to ask her out to dinner. That he would even have liked to hear her refusal.

The door creaks as it opens, like wood that has lost the habit. She opens the shutters and switches on several lights.

Nothing is out of place and yet somehow this orderliness merely underlines the desolation: everything is there, but no one is there.

There's a distinctive sound, he thinks, a kind of hum where people ought to be but aren't. In places meant for children it is even more deafening. An empty cot can be more terrifying than an occupied coffin.

They walk through classrooms papered with drawings. They weave around desks covered in a fine skin of dust. They brush past colorful, alien objects.

Mrs. Takahoshi steps out into the playground to examine the state of the plants. With a disapproving look, she goes off to fetch a trowel and some scissors. Then she bends down, tugging the hem of her dress, partly so as not to crease it and possibly because she feels observed.

Mr. Watanabe follows her movements carefully, and then decides to speak.

Who is Nagae? he asks.

She turns around, looks at him in surprise, and immediately recovers her air of aloofness.

The name was the former principal's idea, says Mrs. Takahoshi. We worked here together until she retired. It was her first granddaughter's name.

Watanabe stoops and passes her the scissors.

And how is Nagae? he asks, smiling. What is she doing now?

She takes the scissors and cuts off a leaf.

The girl was never born, Mrs. Takahoshi replies. That's why she named the kindergarten after her. She said that this way her granddaughter, wherever she might be, would be able to play.

They finish seeing to the plants and wash their hands.

Watanabe hasn't spoken again. Mrs. Takahoshi appears to sense the effect her last reply has had on him and, in an attempt at conversation so forced it seems like ventriloquism, she begins to tell him stories about the school.

He is moved by his guide's sudden exertions and friendliness. He is tempted to misinterpret them.

In my day, she says, we taught forty children or more. By the time I retired there were twenty at most. More recently I think this dwindled to fifteen. After Fukushima, only five were left. They didn't go onto the playground and they brought their own water. The authorities told us that it wasn't a problem for the children to go outside, but that it was better they didn't. That it was all right for the children to drink running water. But better that they didn't.

Recovering his voice, and with it his attention to Mrs. Takahoshi's ankles, he asks whether they still drink the water at her house.

I do, she replies. I'm a widow.

Like Mr. Satō, he says, unable to repress his impertinence.

Like half the town, she corrects him.

Watanabe nods, lowers his head, and retreats into silence.

Mrs. Takahoshi perches on a desk. The posture takes years off her: it's easy to imagine her among children. She asks if he is from Tokyo. He falters in his reply. He says yes, then no, and then partly. At last he finds an answer that satisfies him.

I'm partly from many parts, he replies.

Mrs. Takahoshi slaps her thighs, perhaps a common gesture in her days as a teacher.

They install the power plants here, she says, sighing, and the electricity and the money go to Tokyo. As soon as there's a disaster, the problem is ours, of course. I used to think that at least it would create jobs, but look at this place.

I'm not much of a Tokyoite either, he says, perusing the shelves.

Did you know that in this area they charge us less for electricity? she goes on. That discount is an insult. It's as if they're admitting there are reasons for them to compensate us.

Suddenly, on one of the shelves, forgotten among the toys, Watanabe discovers a lithium battery shining like a coin. He slides it out with one finger and lets it drop into his other hand. Without quite knowing why, he slips it into his leather bag.

Mrs. Takahoshi starts to close the shutters. He asks her permission to use the bathroom.

When he comes out, he notices she has switched off all the lights except for the one at the entrance. He gives a deep bow (which strains his back slightly) and thanks her for the tour. She replies that it has been a pleasure talking to him. Then, as her hand grasps the handle of the front door (a broad, firm hand that seems to belong to someone else), she asks him his opinion of salvation.

Caught off guard, Mr. Watanabe clumsily articulates a couple of ideas. He has always thought there are certain kinds of deeply held convictions that are impossible to express. To allay her disappointment, he adds a phrase that sounds sincere as he improvises it.

As we get older, we lose opinions about things. That is to say, we gain ideas.

Mrs. Takahoshi relaxes her grip, lets go of the door handle, and looks at him.

I hadn't thought of it that way, she says. I still change my opinions. Regarding salvation, for example. It's been a long time since I lost hope in any external power. And lately, I'm not even sure about our inner powers. I'd be happy now with a tiny light inside my head.

He can't help but look up at the old lantern spreading a halo around her hair.

I think people are too keen to control their departure, she continues. To decide how, where, who with. To me, all that seems pointless. I'd go so far as to say it's counterproductive. The circumstances are random. The only thing that we can control is what goes on inside our heads, before the moment comes.

Watanabe can feel his eyes growing moist. He feels an urge to ask Mrs.

Takahoshi to fly to Tokyo with him. He contemplates her worn face, the wrinkles on her brow, her dry lips.

We should go, she says, yanking the door open.

The dusk weaves among the alleyways.

Mrs. Takahoshi smiles at him, blinks a few times, and vanishes amid an echo of footsteps.

It takes a while for Watanabe to move. Something besides his legs is weighing him down.

Instead of returning to the guesthouse, he heads in the opposite direction. He notices a slight burning sensation in his throat. He rummages in his bag for a piece of spearmint chewing gum, and instead feels the battery. Without thinking, he raises it to his mouth and licks it. He doesn't stop when he realizes what he's doing. He licks the lithium battery as if it were a frozen caramel, rolls the tip of his tongue around its smooth curves, imagines its energy awakening in the warmth of his mouth, connecting the dormant voltage with all the words yet to be said.

Then he slowly spits it out into the palm of his hand.

HE CROSSES A SMALL PARK, where, he assumes, kids used to play with their parents after kindergarten. There's a bare patch of lawn and children's paintings on a yellow wall. He observes the still swings. The frames where only shadows climb. The merry-go-rounds that don't go around. The slides growing old.

Mr. Watanabe sits on a swing to rest. A few last rays of the sun doodle on his face in color. He lets his bag drop to the ground. Staring straight ahead, he pushes off, tentatively at first, then harder.

Slowly he rises into the air, at once trapped and liberated by the swinging motion, these movements forward and back that increase in speed.

Out of nowhere, a cool breeze rises. Watanabe is astonished to feel cold.

He hears the sound of something moving through the leaves. He puts one foot on the ground and looks up. His sole leaves a groove.

Then he thinks he sees Walsh, the cat.

By the time he returns to the guesthouse, it's pitch-black outside. He finds Mr. Satō hunched over the table, working on a sudoku puzzle. He stands up to greet his guest.

Sudoku puzzles calm me, he says, because they make time stop. The exact opposite of kintsugi, don't you think?

In that outpouring of affection that has less to do with the recipient than one's own emotions, Watanabe embraces him. His host remains as stiff as a board. Then he announces that he is steaming some vegetables. He mentions dinnertime.

Watanabe tells him later perhaps. Now he needs to rest.

In his room, lying on his back, shoes off, he becomes engrossed in deciphering the stains on the ceiling. His vision dims. He closes his eyes and breathes out. A *jisei* verse comes to his mind. He can't recall who wrote it:

One final wish:
to be able to seize
the air.

He remembers Chekhov instead. He opens his eyes, alarmed. He notices once more his difficulty breathing and calls reception. Asks if there is any champagne.

With great regret, the owner informs him that his stock of alcohol ran out weeks ago, except for canned beer.

Mr. Watanabe thinks that for certain rituals, a can of beer would be in very poor taste. Nothing would vex him more than to pull the tab and see the froth rise, swell like a wave, and spill over.

And so he sits up energetically. He splashes water on his face. Puts on his shoes and goes out to take another stroll through the quiet town. At his age, he reflects, eating dinner is the least of his concerns. Spring evenings are so pleasurable.

Outside once more, he walks toward the night and feels, for the first time in a long while, that he has time.

Far off, among the mountains, clouds gather.

11

AND THE
WATER

THE WATER RIPS THE SACK OF CLOUDS, slits it with its blade, runs through the thunder's drumrolls and the lightning's circuits, sews its stitches across the night sky, and dives headfirst into the sea like an acrobat from his trampoline.

The water punctures the ocean, probes it, turning small into big and narrow into boundless, flows among underwater tensions, Patagonian extremes, fractured channels, echoes around voiceless islands and bays, navigates the remotest capes, quenches the frozen fire scaling the heights, explores the Strait of Magellan, melts the borders uniting the Pacific and the Atlantic.

The water bursts against the surface, widening every circle of the River Plate, perforates its cloudy skin, churns the mud, disperses the residues and the toxic soup, merges with the current, splits into forces fighting one another, tests whirlpools, black weeds, and injurious fish, stirs up sediments, slime, clay, sand, with sewage waste and blood, the liquid from the sky doesn't clean the river away, it simply rouses its memory.

The water lives, unfolding its wrinkles like an old sheet, swims toward the coast, slips between reeds, reaches the shore, makes land, impregnates the plain, advances toward the lights, those lights that ripple with an aquatic pulse, connects to the tips of fishing rods, trickles down anglers' hoods, contributes to the sweat of a runner oblivious to the storm, to the fluid of lovers driving along the Costanera, to the plow of the tire, the sowing of brakes.

The water works the city, eroding its profile, slowly catches the sickness of Buenos Aires, drips its insomnia, is diluted in its glitter and its grime, resounds at the wrong moment above Luna Park stadium, sends a message from the former Central Post Office, marches around the Plaza de Armas, lays siege to the Casa Rosada, spins around the Plaza de Mayo, is deposited in the Banco de la Nación, bounces off terraces that never stop broadcasting rehashed news and laundered linen, floods the drainpipes, slides down walls, scrapes off the mold, filters through windows, invades homes and the lung of the bedroom, laps at every doorway, sits on the thresholds stained by footsteps, leaflets that sell nothing, and penultimate cigarettes.

The water lands, crashes into the pavement, spreads in countless directions, shatters like a succession of microscopic vases, gropes the ground, becomes elastic, picks up speed, circulates around the disorderly asphalt, bathes the network of streets, pumps its torrent, alters the beat of traffic, occupies avenues at widemouthed traffic lights, swamps the corners with their kiosks, their cats, and their mythologies, accumulates at the edge of curbs, and finally finds its course.

The water flows urgently along the gutters, pushes the column of fury, the decisive wave, reproduces both shipwreck and rescue, drags along garbage, broken shapes, scattered particles, traces of energy, takes with it the remains of the night, sweeps them to the mouth of the drains, those drains where all things end up, in the depths, the farthest depths, where the fragments reunite.

ACKNOWLEDGMENTS AND FOREIGNERS

Most of the poems quoted throughout the novel are my own translations, which have now been translated into English by my translators. In other words, they are small fits of collective admiration toward their respective authors. My foreign compatriot the writer Juan Rodolfo Wilcock used to view our homeland as an immense ongoing translation. I wonder if this could be applied to all countries, including the imaginary ones.

I would like to thank Matías Chiappe, Vanina Colagiovanni, Sergio Drucaroff, Garth Greenwell, Paz Posse, José Ángel Rodrigo, Víctor Ugarte, David Unger, and Silvia Valls for their generous contributions. As well as Alexandra Carrasco, Fernando Iwasaki, Julieta Obedman, Ana Pellicer, Carolina Reoyo, Pilar Reyes, Eloy Tizón, the editorial teams at FSG and Granta, my translators Nick and Lorenza, my father, and my brother for their thorough readings. I'm thankful to my grandmother Dorita, for remembering the lost music of the word *shammes*. To the *hibakusha* double Tsutomu Yamaguchi, a stranger whom I would've been thrilled to meet. And to the painter Hans Thoma, for writing this variation of an ancient epitaph attributed to Martinus von Biberach:

> *I come from who knows where,*
> *I don't know who I am,*
> *I'll live who knows how long,*
> *I'll die I don't know when,*
> *I'm going who knows where,*
> *I wonder why I'm happy.*

—*A.N.*

A NOTE ABOUT THE AUTHOR

Andrés Neuman was born in Buenos Aires, Argentina, in 1977 and grew up in Spain. He was selected as one of *Granta*'s Best of Young Spanish-Language Novelists and was elected to the Bogotá39 list. *Traveler of the Century* (FSG, 2012) was the winner of the Alfaguara Prize and the National Critics' Prize, Spain's two most prestigious literary awards, and *Talking to Ourselves* (FSG, 2014) was long-listed for the Best Translated Book Award and short-listed for the Oxford-Weidenfeld Translation Prize. Neuman has taught Latin American literature at the University of Granada.

A NOTE ABOUT THE TRANSLATORS

Nick Caistor is a British translator of works in Spanish, French, and Portuguese. He lived in Argentina for a number of years, and was the BBC Latin America analyst. He has translated more than seventy works of fiction, including those of authors such as Isabel Allende, Roberto Arlt, Mario Benedetti, Julio Cortázar, María Dueñas, Fogwill, Juan Marsé, Eduardo Mendoza, Juan Carlos Onetti, and José Saramago.

Lorenza Garcia was born and brought up in England. She spent her early twenties living and working in Iceland and Spain. In 1998 she graduated from Goldsmiths with a first-class honors degree in Spanish and Latin American studies. She moved to France in 2001, where she lived for seven years. Since 2006 she has translated and cotranslated more than thirty novels and works of nonfiction from the French, the Spanish, and the Icelandic.